T0278598

heart-
shaped
lies

heart-
shaped
lies

elizabeth
agyemang

DELACORTE PRESS

Text copyright © 2024 by Elizabeth Agyemang
Jacket images: necklace used under license from Shutterstock.com;
shattered glass copyright © 2024 by LoveTheWind/Getty Images

Visit us on the Web! GetUnderlined.com

Educators and librarians, for a variety of teaching tools,
visit us at RHTeachersLibrarians.com

Library of Congress Cataloging-in-Publication Data is available upon request.
ISBN 978-0-593-48449-4 (hardcover) — ISBN 978-0-593-48452-4 (trade pbk.) —
ISBN 978-0-593-48445-0 (lib. bdg.) — ISBN 978-0-593-48451-7 (ebook)

The text of this book is set in 11-point Bembo MT Pro.
Interior design by Michelle Crowe

Printed in the United States of America
10 9 8 7 6 5 4 3 2 1
First Edition

Random House Children's Books supports the First Amendment
and celebrates the right to read.

To anyone who has ever lost sight of who they are

179, 304 likes

theshadebooth: What ever happened to social media prank star #TommyHarding? Once the darling of internet personalities, Tommy was known for his funny prank videos and viral posts like "Why you should check your privilege at the door" and "Watch me learn how to braid my girlfriend's hair." But after a series of controversies and botched apologies, the now-infamous prank star is finishing up his senior year of high school while undergoing an account rebrand. Tommy was last seen posting teasers of "the greatest prank of the century" to his three million followers during his senior trip to Florida's Sunny World Resorts and Parks. Tommy's account has since been deactivated.

[**Edit: this post has been updated.** As of earlier this morning, Tommy Harding has officially been declared dead. Ongoing questioning of his classmates and those closest to Tommy is currently being conducted by police at Sunny World Resorts and Parks. Follow the hashtag and subscribe for updates on the developing situation.]

View all 11,313 comments

heatherbc:
Oh my gosh. I cant believe this is real :_(

HardenatorsHeartTommy281:

I'm heartbroken.

OfficialFansofHarding&Frimpong:

Rest in peace Tommy. You will be missed. Priscilla's account also posted a touching goodbye to her cohost. Like and share her post to celebrate Tommy's memory.

JusticeforKiara:

Play ignant games win ignant prizes. #it's_what_he_ deserves

Seagurlheartsharding:

Of course a Kiara stan account would post that. Have some class. A boy is dead.

how it started

chapter one

ONE WEEK EARLIER . . .

Kiara

THE GOSSIP ACCOUNTS were wrong. Despite what they all seemed to claim, Kiara Stephens was *not* breaking up with Tommy Harding.

She didn't know how the rumors had started. In the vlogs Tommy posted for his online followers, he and Kiara were always cuddling on sofas or feeding each other food in the school cafeteria. Fan-made video compilations ordained their interracial relationship as "hashtag couple goals." And just last week, Tommy had surprised her with matching outfits from their dream university. He'd even booked Kiara a meeting with his alumni connect during their senior trip. This way, Tommy had said, she wouldn't have to stress so much about the fact that only one of them had gotten in so far.

What Tommy and she had was love. Real love. Like the kind that people *killed* for.

So why was it so hard for Kiara to deny the negative claims about their relationship in front of a camera?

"Smile," Tommy whispered as he reached for Kiara from the bus seat next to her.

His words were drowned out by a blare of honking cars. Kiara strained to keep from jolting forward and spilling the iced coffee she was holding. But, like the bus driver steering their senior class dangerously through airport traffic, Tommy's hold on her was indisputable.

"Can we film later?" Kiara asked. "I just want to go through some notes I wrote for the wait-list process."

Tommy's lips quirked. "Don't tell me you're nervous, babe."

"I'm not," Kiara lied.

But like always, Tommy saw right through her. He was like his camera in that way: focused, attentive to detail, no matter how insignificant. Through its lens, Tommy documented everything, from the sun-kissed gleam of Kiara's dark brown skin to her russet eyes and prickles of sweat that lined her forehead as she fought to stay neutral on camera.

They were heading to Sunny World, Florida—literally the most radiant place on Earth. This was where dreams came true and miracles happened. Tommy had probably planned a romantic stay for them to combat the trolls' breakup rumors. They should be making out and basking in their relationship. And yet, in a few hours, Kiara would be having an admissions interview that could change the trajectory of her future. She'd made everything about herself. Again.

"It's just really rare for a college to change their mind about admitting a student, so I don't want to botch this interview," Kiara acknowledged.

Again he drew her closer, this time brushing his lips against the edge of her ear. Warmth flooded through her cheeks. But the swell of butterflies she'd once felt for him was quelled by the sting of Tommy's nails digging into her skin.

"Relax. All you have to do is show up and be your cute little self. I promise they'll take you off the wait list."

"It's not that simple."

"Yes. It is."

"No. It's not. The interview's just, like, the first part. I sent in my additional documentation, plus the extra essay. But it could still all not be good enough."

From the corner of her gaze, Kiara caught the glow of a tiny red dot blinking from his phone screen. She frowned.

"Wait, are you livestreaming this?"

"Yes, so behave in front of my fans, will you?" Tommy teased. "This doesn't have to be a whole argument."

"You know that's not what I mean."

But he wasn't listening. Tommy was reading a flurry of comment bubbles that had begun to flood his phone screen. He was in film mode, which meant that right now, they were in a performance. And Kiara would have to be his supporting actress.

"Hey, guys, it's your boy Tommy here. Me and my girl, Kiara, are about to cut it up on our senior trip to Sunny World. We just landed not too long ago and now we're on the bus to the hotel. The traffic is killing us, but you know I put my queen first. How you liking that coffee I got you, K?"

Off-screen, Tommy pinched Kiara's lower thigh. He didn't say it, but the chastising was clear enough. In the last video of the two of them, Tommy's followers had said Kiara looked like a hostage. He probably wanted her to laugh or something in case his sponsors tuned in for this broadcast.

The count of viewers watching the livestream doubled. Fifteen, thirty, sixty, and then one hundred fifteen. It was a low number considering what Tommy was used to. Not that Tommy ever blamed Kiara for the dip in his viewership. But she couldn't help feeling like somehow it was her fault. Of all people in the world, of Tommy's three point three million followers, *he* had chosen *her*. If the general public perceived Kiara badly, then it would reflect negatively on him. Sponsorships would be lost. Brand deals would be rescinded. It wasn't fair of her to be the reason Tommy got canceled again.

So Kiara forced herself to smile at the camera and raise the iced coffee he'd purchased for her earlier that day. It really had been a sweet gesture.

"Loving it," she said. "Thanks, babe."

Tommy grinned. She'd done well. Hopefully his fans would be satisfied.

That was the thing about dating a viral prank star. If they were pissed at you, then so were their fans. For Tommy, that meant an army of preteens and edgelords could flood Kiara's social media accounts at any moment, with or without Tommy's request.

So when Tommy kissed Kiara, she didn't flinch or think about the fact that the flurry of hearts showering his screen belonged to Tommy's fans watching the livestream and not Kiara herself.

She counted to three before she pulled away. But the show wasn't over. Tommy patted his shoulder, gesturing for Kiara to rest her head there.

It was soaked with sweat. The bus had no AC and Tommy refused to open the window for some reason. Half of their grade was packed together like sardines and cooking in the heat, but Tommy's solution was to plaster sunscreen onto his pale skin and slap a baseball cap over his head, despite the sweat coating his forehead and dripping from his straight brown hair onto said shoulder.

After a moment of hesitation, Kiara acquiesced. At least she'd had the foresight to tie her Senegalese twists up in a bun so the strands of her hair wouldn't stick to her cheeks as she rested her head against Tommy's shoulder. She took a sip of her iced coffee and let herself zone out as Tommy spoke to his followers.

"Tonight I'm gonna have some special content for you all on my channel. Stay tuned. It's gonna be the prank of the century. Right, Alex?"

At the mention of his name, Tommy's right-hand man and best friend, Alex Heart, loomed over their seats holding a mini mic and digital camera like he was some sort of paparazzo.

Sunlight glistened off of Alex's dark brown skin as he filmed, and his shoulder-length locs gleamed softly, framing his sharp features.

The two of them never wasted a chance to use their good looks to entice Tommy's audience. For Alex, that meant hiding behind his ridiculous camera and using his rich, midnight voice to orchestrate things from behind the scenes. As Alex filmed Tommy and Kiara for his B-roll, he flicked through his phone and started reading comments viewers were posting from the livestream.

"Seagurlheartsharding asks, 'What are you most excited about for this Sunny World trip?'" Alex said. "This is your first time in Florida, right, Tommy?"

"Yeah, kind of. But it definitely won't be the last," Tommy said, grinning. "I'm really excited to see the park and film some pranks because I know my fans have been missing those lately. We had some lawsuits we were fighting from haters, but it's nothing we couldn't handle. Things are gonna be bigger and better than ever. It's a new me, but you already know there's nothing more important to me than my viewers."

Kiara almost choked on her iced coffee. What in the word soup had he even just said? Alex seemed amused too, though more at Kiara's reaction than Tommy's act.

"We know. We know," Alex said. "You're obsessed with your fans."

Kiara's cheeks burned. "That's not what I was thinking."

"No?" Alex said, fighting back laughter. "Please, tell us exactly what's on your mind, K."

"She's just jealous," Tommy teased, still speaking directly to the camera. "Kiara thinks I love you guys more than I love her."

"Don't you?" Alex asked.

Tommy frowned. "Why the hell would you say that?"

"He's just joking," Kiara said.

"Well, I'm not laughing. You already get hate enough as it is, K," Tommy said. "He doesn't have to make things worse."

Alex snorted.

"What are you talking about? Your fans are more obsessed with Kiara than you." As if to prove his point, Alex grabbed Tommy's phone, pointing the screen at himself before turning it back to Kiara and Tommy.

"Viewers, what do you think?" Alex said. "Who loves Kiara more: you guys, or Tommy?"

Somehow, the question seemed to ruffle Tommy more than the first one had.

"Of course they love me more," he snapped. "And of course they mean the world to me, just like Kiara does."

One of the fans watching the livestream added a link to a poll so viewers could vote. Tension filled the air, and Kiara swore that one of their classmates in the seat next to Alex had stiffened in anticipation. But Tommy grabbed his phone from Alex and deleted the comment with the poll before the results could be posted.

"Sorry, but polls like that go against the harassment policies on the app. I appreciate the love, though. You guys are the best."

Guilt ate at Kiara. The fan whose comment Tommy had deleted would probably create a troll account now that he'd chastised them. Tommy would lose more followers and hate posts would start popping up. All because of her.

"Someone on the livestream is asking if you're doing any fan meetings while you're in Sunny World," Alex said, pivoting, it seemed, to a more positive direction.

"It's a secret," Tommy said, winking at the camera. "Though, I may have something special planned on the Lovers' Gondola." But he squeezed Kiara's hand beneath the gaze of the camera. In that moment, she knew that the date he was speaking of was really for her.

"You hear that, ladies? Tommy's got a ticket for an empty seat next to him in the Lovers' Gondola," Alex said. "Any takers? No? Comment below, and one lucky girl could win the chance of a lifetime. I might even throw in a date with me on one of the rides," he added, winking for the camera.

Once again, the girl next to Alex bristled in her seat. Kiara realized she hadn't imagined it. Actually, after taking another look at Alex's seatmate, it was obvious that the livestream was drawing the girl's attention too. When they'd all climbed onto the bus after they'd left the airport, Kiara hadn't registered that Priscilla Frimpong was sitting next to Alex. She shouldn't have been surprised that the other girl would want a front-row seat to Alex's messy games.

Like Tommy, Priscilla was an influencer herself, and though her makeup content had only recently started taking off, Priscilla and Tommy had been filming together with Alex at their heels for almost as long as Kiara had been dating Tommy—i.e., since freshman year. Yet, despite their common connection, Priscilla and Kiara themselves had never gotten close. In fact, the only thing Kiara knew about Priscilla was that she was loud, high-strung, and had family money from the continent. Oh, and Priscilla was one aunt removed from African royalty. Kiara knew that, because Priscilla made sure *everyone* knew that.

"Desperate much?" Priscilla said. "None of Tommy's viewers want to date you, Alex."

"And none of yours believe the Wakandan accent is real, Princess," Alex answered.

"It's realer than your bot subscriber count."

"A number that, may I remind you, is still higher than your GPA."

The pair launched into a bickering match that made Kiara want to throw herself out of the bus, or, better yet, in front of it, if she thought the driver actually could steer in a straight line. Tommy and his friends never stopped when they got like this. If Kiara had been smart, she would have brought earplugs and some sleep-inducing supplement. But the only thing she had on her was her book bag filled with textbooks (yes, she would be studying during her senior trip) and the sunglasses she'd gotten at the airport. So instead, she took a loud, overdrawn sip of her drink, hoping the sound of her obnoxious slurping would somehow shut them up.

If only Kingstown University knew what they were putting Kiara through.

"Would you guys shut up? I'm on live," Tommy snapped.

"How about we end the video?" Kiara whispered.

"How about a longer kiss?" Tommy answered back.

If Kiara had to fake any more smiles for the camera, her muscles would lose their memory of what a real one was. Again, there was that pressure on her thigh, the sharp jab of pain as Tommy pinched her. It felt like being trapped and pinned down all at once.

Kiara bit back a cry. She knew how stressed her boyfriend was. Just like her, this week was going to make or break his career. But the pain radiating through her was palpable. Kiara didn't realize that she'd been squeezing the coffee in her hands until the bus took a sharp left turn and everyone jolted forward.

All at once, Kiara's and Tommy's bodies crashed into each other. The iced coffee spilled all over them, drenching Tommy's shirt and soaking his pants.

She pulled herself away from Tommy just as Priscilla and Alex stopped their fighting to turn to the sound of Tommy's irritated shout.

"You all right, Kiara?" Alex asked.

At the front of the bus, the driver gave an apology over the speaker. Kiara blinked back a wave of dizziness that had overtaken her. She couldn't focus on the driver's words. Warm, metallic blood filled the inside of her mouth. She'd bitten her lip when their bodies collided.

Yet even before Kiara could orient herself, Tommy sprang from his seat. The attention turned to him once again.

Sometime during the turn, he'd dropped his phone. Kiara eyed it, lying forgotten on the ground as Tommy wiped off the remaining flood of iced coffee from his clothes.

"What the hell? Did you break my phone?"

"I don't think so. It fell before the coffee spilled," Kiara said.

"I'm not talking about that one," Tommy said. He reached into his soaked pocket and pulled out a phone that was dripping with iced coffee. The screen was on the home page, but no matter how many times Tommy swiped to open the messenger app, it remained frozen.

Kiara hadn't even known he'd had a second phone.

But then again, she shouldn't be surprised. Tommy was always messaging his fans. Or, more accurately, his fans were always messaging him. Their communications were constant, even if the volume had begun to dwindle in the wake of his notoriety. It had gotten to the point that Alex and Tommy had purchased a set of smartwatches to keep up with the constant string of DMs and emails Tommy received. The fact that Tommy had added a burner phone to this roster of devices showed just how demanding his fans really were. And Kiara hated that. His fans put so much pressure on him. But no one seemed to be able to admit that the reason why Tommy kept lashing out at others and acting out was that he couldn't carry the weight of being the perfect prank star his fans wanted.

Maybe this trip could be different, though. Maybe Kiara could help him break out of the social media hamster wheel Tommy had found himself trapped on. "You don't have to be so accessible to your fans, you know. You're allowed to not film or message them for a week and enjoy our senior trip," she said.

But if this phone really was for keeping in touch with his fans, Tommy didn't admit it outright.

"You don't understand," he said. "I'm screwed. I'm so freakin' screwed."

Kiara moved to inspect the condition of the burner phone, but he pushed her hand away.

"Forget it. You're just making things worse." He kicked the seat in front of them, and Kiara flinched at the intensity of his rage.

Tentatively, she reached for him again.

"It's not that bad," Kiara said. "Just turn it off and on again and see if it works."

"What the hell do you know?" Tommy snapped. "Seriously. Do you have any freakin' brain cells, Kiara? Is there even one useful thought floating around in that head of yours, future Miss Valedictorian?"

Kiara clenched her fists, swallowing back against the knot of hurt forming in her chest.

"I'm just trying to help."

"Yeah," Tommy spat. He wiped the drenched phone against the few dry patches on his soaked shirt. "And look how great that's been."

"Tommy," Alex whispered, "you're still on live."

Suddenly, the color drained from Tommy's face and, for the first time ever, Kiara felt thankful that they had an audience.

At least this way, they couldn't blame the fallout on her.

Slowly, tentatively, Tommy picked up the phone and turned the camera back at himself. It was still filming the livestream.

"I'm sorry, guys, I lost my temper. The coffee is, like, one hundred degrees," Tommy lied. "I don't think I'll have any second-degree burns or anything, but I'll probably need to go to a clinic or something when we get to the hotel. Better safe than sorry, right?"

If Kiara was one of his fans watching the livestream, maybe she would have believed him. That's how convincing his lie was. But

15

she'd literally been drenched with the iced coffee too—keyword, *iced*. It was cold, lukewarm at best, not second-degree-burn coffee. Yet on video, no one would be able to tell. Not with the generic cup the iced coffee had come in.

Tommy's comments section filled with sympathetic dirges. Kiara stared back at the words, dumbfounded.

"I'm sorry," Kiara whispered. "I'll pay for your other phone if it's damaged."

He closed his eyes, took a breath, and smiled.

"Don't apologize," he said. "It's okay, babe. I'll admit, you got me. It was a pretty funny prank." On the phone screen, Tommy's reflection flashed a grin to his audience. More hearts filled the screen. "Told you guys this trip is gonna be epic. The prank wars have just begun. Wait until I get her back."

Kiara supposed she should be relieved that he was taking the whole thing as a joke. But she couldn't help the nervous buzz of anxiety that began to hum through her. If he was using this moment to declare a prank war, then one way or another, he'd follow through on the promise. He always did when it came to his fans.

"Thanks for watching, everyone. Tune in later tonight," Tommy said.

He ended the live just as their bus pulled up to the hotel's curb.

Kiara placed her hand against Tommy's shoulder. "Babe, I really am sorry. I'll pay to get you a new phone. Just let me know how much it costs." She'd have to work extra hours at her grocery store job. But if that meant Tommy wouldn't be upset with her, then Kiara would eat the cost.

But he wouldn't look at her. Tommy didn't even acknowledge the fact that she'd spoken.

At the front of the bus, one of the chaperones began giving the senior class instructions on how they were supposed to conduct themselves for the weekend stay at Sunny World Resorts and Parks.

"We should go to our rooms," Priscilla said.

Giving up, Kiara agreed and joined the line of their classmates exiting the bus.

Outside, a curtain of heat engulfed Kiara. The warmth and glittering glow of Florida sun was a welcome reprieve from the stifling tension of the last few moments. Kiara breathed it in, along with the Sunny World scenery.

The resort was breathtaking. Magical, really. From the hotel structure in front of them to the buildings in the distance, everything had been constructed to fit Sunny World's theme. Kiara had been reading up on it in their brochure. There was the Moonlight Hotel, a towering castlelike structure painted a deep black with beaming lights draping from the windows like starlight. It looked even more magnificent in the distance. The Planet and Asteroid hotels stood farther off. Both hotels were dome structures, the first with ringlike sculptures orbiting the hotel, the second with craterlike indentations encircling the building.

And then there was the hotel where their senior class would be staying: the Sunshine Hotel. Like the Planet and Asteroid hotels, theirs was shaped like a dome. But it was massive, towering over all the other hotels like a version of the sun itself. The hotel had been painted a bright yellow and was covered with ivy that had been sprayed a gleaming red, and beds of sunflowers lined walkways leading to the building.

"Should we look around?" Kiara said. "Maybe there's a repair shop or something on the park property that I can take your phone to?"

Tommy shook his head.

"That's sweet of you, but I'm not sure if I can trust you with it."

"Is it at least turning on?" she asked.

He frowned, angling the phone away from her. "Why? So you can go through it? Clingy much?"

"Please," Kiara said. "As if I'd want to read the corny thirst traps your fans send you." She'd meant to sound lighthearted and teasing, but she couldn't stop the accusation that bled through her words. She hadn't missed that despite how defensive he was acting, he hadn't really confirmed or denied what the burner phone was for.

A flicker of amusement flashed in Tommy's eyes. It was almost as if he could see the thoughts swirling in Kiara's head.

He brushed a finger against her waist. "Relax. I'm *your* boyfriend, not the internet's. It's mainly just where I store backup footage for my channel. The messages on it are the same stuff you see me and Alex getting from my fans. No thirst traps. Though, if you want somewhere to send me yours—"

Kiara laughed and pushed him away. "In your dreams," she said, relieved, if only a little bit.

The moment was interrupted when Priscilla appeared behind them. "Is it broken for real or just dead? Maybe the battery just needs to be charged and it'll work again."

"Maybe," Tommy said, releasing his hold on Kiara and glancing back down at the phone. Kiara tried not to be too annoyed that Tommy and she had finally stopped fighting with each other when Priscilla decided to butt in.

"Let's just go to our hotel and figure things out there, okay?" Priscilla said, seemingly oblivious to her unwanted presence.

She grabbed her suitcase from where the chaperones had lined them up for students to take, and Kiara and Tommy joined her.

Most of their classmates were already making their way up to the block of rooms the school had assigned them. While Tommy went to grab Kiara's things, Priscilla struggled with a second suitcase. Why she could possibly need two suitcases and a carry-on for a weeklong trip, Kiara didn't know. But she offered to help, and together they pulled it out from the pile.

"Are you excited?" Priscilla asked.

"Yeah," Kiara said. "I've never been to Sunny World before."

Priscilla laughed. "Really? How cute. But actually I was talking about us. We're sharing a room. Guess we'll finally get to know each other better." Her plastered-on smile screamed otherwise.

"Yeah. Exciting," Kiara repeated. Though, of course that was a blatant lie on Kiara's part.

Outside of the fact that she didn't really know Priscilla well and had only agreed to room with the girl because Tommy had suggested it would make filming his videos easier, Kiara wasn't exactly a fan of their school's princess. First, there was the whole fact that Priscilla frequently showed up in Tommy's videos as a guest star. Kiara knew it was because the other girl was building her own vlog channel, but still. Having strangers on the internet ship your boyfriend with one of your classmates wasn't exactly reassuring. Even though they both always claimed to just be costars, their friendship was another piece of Tommy's world that Kiara had never felt secure about. On top of that, Priscilla herself wasn't exactly a joyride. She wasn't mean or anything. She just had this glossy, IRL filterlike personality that made it hard to figure out what was real about her and what was a performance for her burgeoning channel.

Kind of like Tommy. Or at least the version of him that he showed to his fans.

"Did I get everything?" Tommy said when he returned with both his and Kiara's suitcases in tow. Alex trailed behind him, rolling his own suitcase and filming equipment. He caught a look at the mass of suitcases Priscilla had brought with her and did a double take.

"Did you pack your whole closet in those?"

"Only the stuff that would fit," Priscilla said, ignoring Alex entirely and directing her words to Tommy instead. "Think you could help?"

Had she been all pouty and flirty when she'd made the request? Yes. But Tommy seemed completely oblivious.

"Sorry," he said. He gestured to his and Kiara's suitcases. "Kind of swamped here."

Kiara smiled.

It wasn't like she was the clingy sort of girlfriend or anything. But she couldn't help the flutter of warmth in her chest at Tommy's words. Being Tommy's second choice compared to his fans didn't hurt quite so much knowing that, when it came to his attention for other girls, Kiara was always first.

"I guess only girlfriends are granted suitcase-carrying privileges," Alex said, laughing.

"Shut up," Priscilla said. "That's not what I meant."

"How about Tommy takes our things, and you and I can carry your stuff up to the room?" Kiara offered.

Again, Priscilla flashed that plasticky smile of hers.

"It's fine. I'll handle it myself."

"Oh, stop being such a princess," Alex said. He reached over Priscilla and grabbed one of her heavier suitcases.

"Would you stop?" Priscilla snapped. "I said I'm fine. And Kiara wouldn't have even minded if Tommy did help me," she continued, swatting at Alex. "Would you?"

The question hung heavy in the air for a moment. But then Kiara shook her head, reassuring the girl with a smile.

"Not at all."

And then, rather dramatically, Kiara brushed her hand along the length of Tommy's shirt, where the iced coffee stain still remained.

"How about I wash this when we get to our rooms?" she whispered.

"I like the sound of that," Tommy said, grinning now too.

Priscilla looked away. Alex shot her a glance.

Something seemed to pass between them, something Kiara couldn't quite read. Not for the first time, Kiara wondered if their constant bickering was actually a pretense for something else. Yet just as quickly as the moment had come between Alex and Priscilla, Alex ushered Priscilla to gather the rest of her things and they were back to being frenemies again.

"We'll meet you upstairs," he said.

Grabbing a trolley, they carted their suitcases and equipment toward the hotel and left Kiara and Tommy behind.

Tommy seemed to realize that they should head up too. He slipped the burner phone into his pocket and grabbed Kiara's suitcase along with his. "It's no big deal about my burner, by the way. I'll get it fixed."

"Are you sure? I really can help out if you want."

"But you have an interview to get ready for, right?"

"I—" Kiara swallowed. "Yeah. I mean, is it okay if I still go?"

Tommy seemed to consider that for a moment. After all, he'd been the person to connect Kiara with the contact at Kingstown University. If the iced coffee debacle had truly angered him, she doubted Tommy would still let her use his connections.

"It's fine," he said, and Kiara's breath caught at the softness in his voice. "A promise is a promise. You're going to be amazing."

And as they climbed up the alabaster stairs to the hotel entrance with their suitcases in tow, her smile wavered only once, when a tall figure in the distance waved at her from the crowd of seniors still waiting to grab their suitcases.

A flood of surprise caught Kiara. She grinned and waved back, almost before she could stop herself. In an instant, though, Kiara realized her mistake and looked away. But Tommy had already caught the exchange between her and his stepbrother.

Kiara tried to play it off, nudging Tommy playfully.

"You didn't tell me Jason was coming on the trip."

"Why do you care?"

"Because we're friends," she said. "Just like you and Priscilla are."

"And is that supposed to be reassuring?" he said.

"If we trust each other, then yes. It should be."

Tommy wrapped his arms around her waist, tightening his grip on Kiara just like he had in the bus.

"I trust you," Tommy said. "It's just everyone else I don't trust. Why do you think I got a burner phone in the first place? I love my fans. I do. But this way, I can keep things separate instead of having them calling and messaging me on my actual phone."

Guilt gnawed at Kiara. She began to speak, the admission on the tip of her tongue. But then, she stopped herself. This whole day had been as much of an emotional roller coaster for him as it had for her. And Kiara's interview was getting closer and closer.

She didn't need another reason to make Tommy or his fans mad at her.

A quick glance at her own phone told her, at least, that the view counts on the now-posted livestream were ticking up. The iced coffee prank-war moment was going mini viral. Kiara couldn't tell if things were looking up or worse for them. She held her breath in anticipation.

Tommy's mouth curled in a frown. But then he loosened his grip around Kiara before he pressed a soft kiss on her cheek.

His fans were happy, so he was happy. So, Kiara decided, she was happy too.

THE ROOMS INSIDE the Sunshine suite were themed as well. Kiara and Priscilla entered the room they'd be sharing to find two queen-sized beds, a TV, couches sporting sun-shaped pillows, a coffee table, and a mini fridge that was packed with sodas.

The walls were painted a pale yellow and the sheets and decor inside the room sported sunshine ornamentation, from the hand-stitched embroidery of the pillows and blankets to the stenciled patterning across the walls. There was a bathroom that was equally as warm and yellow, with a lounge area that was connected to it.

Kiara expected Tommy and Alex to head down the hall to their rooms after the two had wheeled in Kiara's and Priscilla's suitcases. Instead, they put down their things too. Tommy immediately began assessing the damage that his second phone had incurred in the iced coffee spill while Alex unloaded a laptop and some filming equipment.

Why the second boy was preparing to film in their room, Kiara didn't know, but she guessed it had something to do with the fact that he would be making videos for both Tommy and Priscilla's separate channels during the duration of the trip. As their producer, Alex took a cut of the earnings both received from sponsorships and ads. It was the perfect arrangement, especially for an aspiring filmmaker like himself.

Deciding it may be best to avoid the whole situation as much as she could, Kiara began looking through her suitcase for clothes she could wear to the interview. She grabbed a blouse, a blazer, and a pencil skirt, then ventured into the bathroom to change.

By the time Kiara returned, Alex had nearly finished his setup, Tommy's mood worsened by several degrees, and Priscilla was, well, being Priscilla.

"No makeup?" Priscilla said. "Bold."

Kiara squinted at her. "Not wearing makeup isn't a statement. It's literally just letting your face breathe and be its natural self."

"Again, there's a whole movement on that," Priscilla said. "Like, Alicia Keys does it and so do some other influencers. I'm actually planning on making it the theme for my next era."

"I think you look great," Tommy said.

Kiara smiled.

"Thank you."

In between fussing with his broken burner phone, Tommy had shifted to scrolling through his feed on his main phone. He hadn't bothered to take off the coffee-stained shirt he was wearing and instead was replaying the livestream.

Kiara cringed as the sound of his voice shouting at her filled the room.

"The bathroom is yours if you want to clean up too," Kiara said.

"It's fine," Tommy answered. "I'm just trying to see how much damage control I need to do now."

"Why? What are people saying?"

"Nothing," he said. His voice was somber, aching. "Just that I need anger management. Thanks for that, Kiara."

"It was, you know, a really strong reaction for an accident," she hedged.

Maybe anger management could help? Or, did influencers have therapists? Kiara had only experienced a semblance of what a person's life was like when thousands of people had an opinion on their choices and mistakes. Maybe talking to someone would help Tommy deal with the pressures of being famous?

"You keep saying that," Tommy said. "But was it really an accident? The whole thing was seriously kind of embarrassing."

Kiara laughed. "Tommy, you did a prank where you wore an adult diaper. I think this is probably the least embarrassing video you've posted," she teased.

"I looked like an asshole, Kiara. And people are already saying things are off between us. The fact that you managed to keep from spilling the coffee all the way from the airport until I went live feels like a pretty messed-up coincidence."

"Well, it was one," Kiara said. "I don't know why you're making this such a big deal. I thought we were past this."

"I don't know," Tommy said. "Maybe because I've been sabotaged before, I'm fighting three lawsuits and you just so happened to ruin the phone I've been using since I revamped my channel?"

"You seriously think I'm purposely ruining your videos?"

Tommy ran his hand through his hair. But he wouldn't meet her gaze.

"I don't know. I mean, what's keeping you from it? You're still friends with Jason even though I told you what my fans say about you and him."

"Dude, can you give it a rest?" Alex said. "Kiara clearly didn't plan what happened. And Jason literally goes to our school. How the hell is she supposed to avoid him when he's your stepbrother?"

Kiara and Tommy both turned to the other boy in surprise.

It was rare for Alex to speak out against Tommy. Usually Alex treated Tommy's outbursts like he was watching a spectator sport; he never voiced his opinions unless it meant cheering Tommy on, and Alex seemed to have a complete lack of personal investment in the outcome of Tommy's exploits. The sudden departure from his usual modus operandi must have meant that Tommy had been going off about the incident while Kiara had been changing. Clearly, Alex's patience was waning.

"The view count for your livestream were some of your highest to date," he continued. "Your fans love Kiara. So what if your burner phone got messed up. Your messages history should be saved through the cloud anyway. Just pull them up on your smartwatch if you need them that bad."

"I'm not just worried about some texts, Alexander. I had a lot of important content on that phone. I don't even know if it all managed to get backed up on the cloud. And don't give me that stepbrother-loyalty crap with Jason. Who do you think leaks all the stuff about me to the blogs if it isn't him?"

"Jason doesn't even have any social media accounts," Kiara

said. "Trolls and your fans literally track everything you do, babe. Obviously they'd impersonate him to get under your skin."

Tommy laughed. "They shouldn't bother, then, since you do that well enough."

Kiara glared at him.

"No one asked you to put your whole life on the internet, or mine. If it's making you so paranoid, why don't you just stop?"

"Funny how you'll defend him but never me or anything I care about," Tommy said.

"Look," Alex said, interrupting the fight that was clearly brewing. "I just searched and there's a phone repair store near the hotel. Just get it fixed there."

Alex was trying to be helpful, but already Kiara could see his words backfiring against whatever narrative Tommy had painted in his head about the incident.

"Then you and Kiara take it," Tommy snapped. "Maybe even hit up Jason to go with you since you guys are just best friends now, right?" He threw the phone at Alex, who managed to catch it before it almost struck him in the face. Alex hissed as the hard plastic hit his fingers.

"Dude!" he snapped. "You're such a prick sometimes." But despite his words, Alex grabbed his wallet and headed to the door. "Coming, Kiara?"

Kiara bit the bottom of her lip. "Actually, I have this important thing. . . ."

Tommy laughed. "Of course she won't go. Of course."

Kiara whirled toward him, her annoyance flaring. "You literally just said I should still go to the interview. There's no way I could get your phone fixed without being late to it or missing it entirely."

But Tommy wasn't listening to her. He grabbed his suit-case, which he still hadn't taken to his room, and started digging through it until he found a paper bag. Inside it was a flask. Tommy stormed into the bathroom and slammed the door behind him with the drink in tow.

"Ignore him," Alex said. "And it's no big deal. Good luck on your interview, Kiara."

Without another word, Alex left.

It was just Kiara and Priscilla now in the room. In the bath-room, the shower sputtered to life. Priscilla started unpacking and humming to herself, as if this whole trip wasn't off to a terrible start. Kiara noticed *she* hadn't chimed in to defend her.

"So what's this interview for?" Priscilla asked innocently.

"Nothing, really." As if Kiara was going to just confess her darkest secrets to a girl who kept her phone on her like an IV tube.

Priscilla rolled her eyes. "Sure. Did you, like, win another award? Get a bajillion scholarships to every Ivy League?"

"Something like that," Kiara said, not looking at Priscilla as she answered. Instead, she grabbed a towel from Tommy's suitcase. "He didn't go in with one," Kiara explained at the questioning look Priscilla gave her.

Priscilla shrugged and started taking small boxes out of her suitcase. All of them had brand names Kiara had never heard of and seemed to be makeup palettes and accessories.

"The brand deals I have to promote," Priscilla said by way of explanation.

"Do you even, like, use any of them?" Kiara asked.

Priscilla glared at Kiara. "Why would I promote products to my fans if I don't use them?"

Yet even as Priscilla said the words, Kiara followed her gaze back to the boxes, all of which clearly had never been opened before. Kiara decided against pointing out the obvious. Still carrying the towel, she walked to the bathroom door and knocked three times.

When Tommy was in one of his moods, it was like talking to a wild animal that might lash out at any time. Kiara had to be patient and coax him back to his regular self.

"Tommy," she called, her voice low, gentle. "You left your towel."

Why he was showering in Kiara and Priscilla's room, she didn't know. But it probably wouldn't be a great situation if the chaperones walked in on them while he was searching for a towel.

Again, Kiara knocked on the bathroom door. Still, Tommy didn't answer.

"Are you really that mad at me?" she asked. "I don't think the coffee could have messed the phone up that badly. Hopefully the repair people will be able to fix whatever's wrong with it." She knocked a fourth time.

Again, no answer.

Kiara twisted the knob but it was locked. On her phone, she checked the time. She had less than a half hour until the interview began.

Part of her just wanted to leave things as they were. Tommy probably just needed space. In a few hours, he'd get some messages of validation from his fans and feel better again. But another part of Kiara felt guilty for ruining whatever plans Tommy had made for the day.

"I'll make it up to you," she said before draping the towel on the doorknob for Tommy to take when he finished showering. But as she did, Kiara's gaze fell to the ground, where a puddle of hot water had begun to collect at her feet.

More and more, the puddle grew until the hot water was flooding beneath her and soaking the carpeted floor.

"Tommy," she said again, raising her voice now above the rush of the shower. "Tommy!"

Why wasn't he answering? Why would he just let the shower run so wildly?

Kiara turned to Priscilla, hoping the other girl was as panicked about the situation as she was. Instead, Priscilla was busy finalizing the equipment setup Alex had abandoned when he'd gone to have Tommy's burner fixed.

"Is the water leaking?" Priscilla asked, squinting at Kiara in disbelief.

"He's not answering. I think we should call a chaperone."

"He literally took a whole flask in there, Kiara. I think we shouldn't. Not unless we want the chaperones to catch him wasted."

"Are you sure that was the only thing he took with him?" Kiara asked. "Nothing else?" The meaning of Kiara's words hung between them for a moment.

Sneaking alcohol on a senior trip would have been a stretch for Tommy at one time. But ever since his online persona had begun to rise, Tommy had started expanding his circle of influencer friends. He'd also picked up their partying habits, from sneaking drinks during school events to taking hits at parties and experimenting with more and more substances. Kiara had tried to broach the subject with Tommy once before. It hadn't gone well.

So Kiara had gotten Alex to promise to watch over Tommy

and keep him ashore from as much of those things as he could. But even his producer couldn't be around him all the time. Who knew what Tommy had snuck in his suitcase for this trip?

Understanding settled in Priscilla's expression. "I'll call Alex to come back here."

But Kiara wasn't listening anymore. She grabbed the doorknob, twisting despite the lock, and ramming her shoulder against the door. It was probably a futile effort, but Kiara had to do something.

"Tommy!" she shouted. "Tommy!"

Suddenly, the door swung back. Kiara stumbled into the steaming bathroom just as liquid drenched her from above. Kiara screamed, falling to the ground.

Something plastic landed on the floor, and Tommy's laughter filled the bathroom.

When Kiara looked up, Tommy was standing at the foot of the bathtub. He held the phone he'd been using to stream the livestream earlier, and from the soft pings coming from the device, Kiara could tell he was on live again.

"Gotcha!" Tommy shouted. "Now we're even."

Behind her, Priscilla approached the door. But Kiara couldn't process the fact that he was laughing to himself on camera while shower water filled the bathroom of the hotel and millions of people watched her be humiliated. She couldn't think of any of those things, not with the scorching-hot bathwater on the floor soaking her skirt and the fumes of urine radiating from the liquid that had fallen on her when she'd entered the bathroom. She looked across the room to where the empty container had rolled.

It was the same cup that Kiara's iced coffee had come in.

Kiara felt sick. Worse than sick. She wanted to disappear.

"Kiara, are you all right?" Priscilla asked.

"Oh, relax. It's just a joke," Tommy said. "Kiara and I are pranking each other this whole trip, remember?"

There was silence as Tommy, Priscilla, and however many hundreds of people on the internet watched the interaction with bated breath.

One weekend. That's all she had to survive. One weekend of fake smiles and playing pretend for his fans. But in that moment, as she sat on the bathroom floor drenched with Tommy's piss while hundreds of his followers watched, Kiara realized something: despite her perfect GPA, despite her accolades and all her efforts to make a mark for herself, somehow she'd still ended up here, trapped. But it wasn't in her small hometown or the apartment that her parents could barely afford for Kiara and her siblings. No, Kiara was trapped in a relationship, and dating Tommy Harding had forever made her "the girlfriend."

She couldn't break up with him like the rumors claimed. Not just because so much of Kiara was tied to Tommy. But because she *needed* him. And somehow, that was worse than any cage Kiara could ever have imagined being stuck in.

"Kiara?" Tommy said. "My fans want to know if you're okay."

She closed her eyes.

"Tell them, Kiara. Go on," he said.

I hate this. I want to break up. I never want to be on your livestreams ever again.

The beginning of tears pricked Kiara's lashes. Her interview was in less than an hour, but now Kiara would need to change and figure out something else to wear. Of all people, Tommy should have understood how important today was for her. But Kiara couldn't even be upset with him. Not when all his fans were watching. So she smiled and buried her thoughts deep in the recesses of her heart. And then Kiara turned her attention directly to Tommy's audience.

"He got me. Good one, babe. Prank of the year."

If Tommy was relieved that she'd gone along with his bit again, he didn't show any signs of it.

"See, guys? You can relax. We're just joking around."

To finish off the act, Tommy pulled Kiara into a hug so his viewers could get a close-up of the two of them embracing.

Someone in the comments sent heart emojis and wrote, "they're too perfect to be real."

And for once, Kiara thought Tommy's fans just might be on to something.

chapter two

Priscilla

AT FIRST, PRISCILLA thought she'd imagined the tension in the room. But the moment the livestream ended, Tommy and Kiara recoiled from each other's grips. Kiara wrapped her arms around herself. Tommy deflated under the burn of her glare.

"It was just a joke," he said. "Come on, Kiara."

But she didn't answer him. Instead, Kiara stomped to the corner of the room where Tommy's things were still gathered. She grabbed his key card, snatched a fistful of clothes from her own suitcase, and stormed from the room.

Behind her, the door slammed with a resounding *thump,* leaving Priscilla and Tommy to stare at each other in silence after her departure.

"What just happened?" Priscilla said.

"It's nothing."

"Is she, like, switching rooms?"

"She's probably just borrowing our shower—she has a meeting to get to soon."

"And you decided to just . . . pull your little prank on her *now*?" Priscilla squinted at Tommy. As if that would explain why he'd just dumped a whole container of who-knows-what on his girlfriend on a livestream.

He shrugged. "She tried to prank me first."

Priscilla couldn't tell if Tommy was joking. Like, he had to be. Right? Clearly, Miss Valedictorian and their school's "first ever" fifth Black class president hadn't spilled her iced coffee all over Tommy on purpose.

"Besides," he said, "the crappy iced coffees she drinks always smell like piss anyway."

Priscilla couldn't believe him.

"Tommy, that is so freakin' gross. Like, why would you—" Priscilla shook her head. "Do you know how much bad publicity you'll get if she decides to do a tell-all about this? You've barely been uncanceled for, like, a month now."

Just this year, Tommy had nearly set his neighbor's house on fire while filming a prank involving fireworks, a birthday cake, and his neighbor's plant as target practice. Then there was the "handing out plastic sandwiches to homeless people" debacle, which had only been two weeks before the time Tommy pranked a grieving family into thinking their grandparent was alive by playing audio recordings from the old man's headstone. Priscilla had even started writing apologies for him after Tommy had botched the first two he'd written himself in a plagiarism scandal.

"I thought it was hilarious," Tommy said with a shrug. As if Tommy's definitions of *funny* and *cruel* didn't often overlap.

Did he even care about getting canceled again? More importantly, did he realize it wasn't just his image on the line?

Priscilla was sure that someone in the live had spotted her. Her makeup and beauty channel was just starting to take off, and Priscilla really couldn't do with more Tommy-related bad press.

Not when Priscilla's parents had cut the cord on her credit cards and allowances after she'd professed to them that she wanted to "do makeup" instead of study for med school.

Goodbye, American Express unlimited card. Thoughts and prayers to Priscilla's wardrobe. At this point, ad dollars and revenue from sponsorships were the only things keeping Priscilla afloat. If she could just keep her sponsorships now that things were finally looking up, maybe, just maybe, she'd be able to prove to her parents that this career path—or lack of one, as they called it—was feasible.

"You have to call her back here," Priscilla insisted. "Let's film an apology—no, actually, how about I do a makeover for Kiara so she looks amazing for her interview."

Priscilla started pacing and typing furiously on her phone, but Tommy grabbed her hand and tossed her cell phone onto the bed.

"Relax, Priscilla. I thought you'd enjoy it."

"Why would I enjoy that?"

He stared at her, his knowing gaze burning a pit of shame into Priscilla's stomach.

"It's not like I said you should humiliate her in front of thousands of your followers."

"And making a petition for the two of us to break up under some fake screen name isn't the same thing?" Tommy said. He laughed. "Just think of it as me planting a seed, all right? My views are higher when Kiara and I are fighting. I don't want my fans to blame you when we break up."

Priscilla swallowed, twisting herself away from Tommy's hold. "I don't know what you're talking about," she lied, unable to meet his gaze. All those times Priscilla had sent tips to the gossip accounts, she'd tried to be discreet. But clearly, Tommy had made the connection between the bad press he and Kiara were constantly getting and the fan ships of Priscilla and him as a couple. "I know I said crossing boundaries is what we have to do sometimes to keep our fans hooked, but this is a little too much." But even as she protested, Priscilla couldn't help the thrilling rush she felt at his words. He'd said "when" they'd break up. Not "if." *When.*

It was finally happening. He was really keeping his promise.

"Whatever's going on with your relationship with her, that has nothing to do with me," Priscilla said. "But if you're going to cut the cord, don't draw it out. Just do it already."

Tommy laughed. "That's what I love about you, Priscilla. You're not above getting your hands dirty for what you want. I meant what I said before. She's with me now, but you should be mine."

Priscilla froze. A small piece of her yearned for him to say the words again, even more plainly. But the other part of Priscilla couldn't quite erase the pit that had burrowed in her chest since he'd done that bathroom prank on Kiara.

"I just don't think it's a good look for your brand," Priscilla whispered. "Or mine."

She hoped that changing the direction of the conversation from their non-relationship to the one they did have with their sponsors would be enough to knock some sense into Tommy.

Instead, Tommy seemed determined to prove that he didn't care about his reputation and that, yes, the sparks between them weren't just from teasing their fans online. He pulled Priscilla to the bed next to him, his thigh brushing up against hers as he rested his hand on Priscilla's. Heat burned at her cheeks. Tommy traced circles along the lines of her palms. Priscilla swallowed. Tentatively, she shot a nervous glance at the door.

"Tommy," she whispered. "What if someone walks in?"

"The door automatically locks. We're fine."

With one hand still massaging her palm, Tommy pulled Priscilla toward him so her head was resting on his chest while his other hand was wrapped around her waist. This wasn't the first time Tommy had made a move on her. In the beginning, she would bat his hand away playfully. But Tommy's advances had grown more and more persistent. At the end of sophomore year, she found herself flirting back. By junior year, their playful on-and-off-again flirting on camera and in real life had grown into a full-blown crush that Priscilla had begun to harbor for him. Priscilla had found herself sinking into his desires, and making excuses for the fact that Tommy already had a girlfriend.

As Tommy held her, all of the questions and doubts that had been racing through Priscilla melted. It was only her and Tommy, and the intoxicating scent of his skin. His hands trailed lower and lower against Priscilla's thighs, which should have felt nice but didn't quite because he was still hot and sticky from the day. It also wasn't great that Tommy's breath reeked of liquor.

Just how much had he managed to drink in the time that he'd locked himself in the bathroom?

Suddenly, the door beeped with the sound of a key card, then burst open. Priscilla jumped from the bed, pushing Tommy away in the process.

"It's just Alex," Tommy said.

Sure enough, the person standing in the doorway was none other than Tommy's right-hand man. Priscilla didn't know how long Alex had been standing there listening at the door before he'd decided to barge in. But if he had been there longer, his bored expression gave no hint of how much he'd overheard or, even worse, seen.

"You know we still have to film in the park today, right?" Alex said. "If we're really sneaking in after it closes for the kegger party tonight, you're gonna actually want to, you know, get your costumes ready."

Priscilla smoothed out invisible wrinkles on the summer dress she was wearing, not quite managing to meet Alex's gaze. It was still morning and most of their class planned to spend the full day in the park. While there, Priscilla would have to find a place to stash her costume and hide so when Sunny World closed that night, she'd be able to slip into it after coming out of their hiding spot.

"We were just getting ready," Priscilla said. "Tommy was helping me film a vlog to figure out what to wear."

"Yeah, clearly," Alex said. "Should I leave you two? Or do you want someone who actually knows what they're doing?"

Priscilla threw a pillow at him, which he unfortunately managed to dodge.

"You disgust me."

"What? I thought you two were just filming?" he said innocently.

Mischief gleamed in his dark brown eyes and a dimple formed on his cheek, which was annoying because Priscilla had made it a point to ignore how attractive he was.

Alex was tall and toned from playing tennis, but he also had an alt style to him. He wore his locs swept back in a ponytail and was constantly wearing rings and bracelets that glowed like cool embers against his dark, rich brown skin. There was a time when

Priscilla almost had, like, a thing for him. But she learned quickly that Alex was an asshole. Even more so than Tommy, which was sort of hard to believe. The fact that Priscilla had a thing for both boys just proved that everyone had a hamartia, even internet princesses like Priscilla.

Tommy pulled Priscilla back onto his lap.

"Alex doesn't care. We don't have to pretend in front of him."

Priscilla pouted. "It's not about pretending. You're still taken. I'm not a home-wrecker."

"What difference does it make? I'm going to break up with her eventually."

"But when? I'm being serious, Tommy."

Tommy sighed. This time, he was the one to pull away.

"Look, Kiara and I have history. It's not that easy when millions of people are watching your every move."

For once, he was actually being real about their situation. As Tommy's very public, and very popular, girlfriend since freshmen year, Kiara Stephens had cemented herself in Tommy's IRL and online circles when he had asked her to dance at Homecoming four years ago instead of Priscilla.

Not that Priscilla was still salty about that or anything.

Kiara had wormed her way into Tommy's life after they all started high school, when Priscilla had been forced to study abroad in London for a semester after her grades had taken a hit, which was less than ideal in a household of a tech genius (Priscilla's father) and Yale med school graduates (her mother and two older siblings). But Priscilla had known Tommy first. She loved him. She *deserved* him. She even shared an IMDB page with Tommy as his vlogging costar.

Everyone who had watched their flirty videos shipped them.

There was even a Change.org campaign for Priscilla and Tommy to get together, which, in Priscilla's defense, she had started only as a joke. But if nearly ten thousand people thought you and your boyfriend should break up, who the hell was Kiara Stephens to get in the way of democracy?

"I know it's complicated for you. And yeah, that's why I wrote into a couple accounts about you two breaking up," Priscilla said, finally admitting to her role in the gossip posts. "But these pranks and antics aren't what I want."

"I know. You deserve so much more. And I'm trying. I really am. But I'll end things with her when the time is right."

Priscilla rolled her eyes.

The problem, she thought but didn't say because, ew, no way was she that desperate, was that Tommy had been promising to break up with Kiara for months. Even before the senior trip, he'd filled Priscilla's head with wondrous ideas of all the places they'd go and things they'd do once they were internet-official. Yet so far, Tommy's words had amounted to little more than pining and flirtatious banter on camera. Which is why she'd been forced to take things into her own hands.

Tommy loved her. Hadn't he just said so himself? Okay. He hadn't said it *exactly,* but his admission today was close enough. Kiara was the only thing standing between them and their happily-ever-after. Well, her and that little voice in the back of Priscilla's head that always seemed to remind her that her crush on Tommy had been unrequited until just last year, when Priscilla's subscriber count and views had started to rise with her platform. The other part of her questioned if the feelings she thought she had for Tommy were for him or the persona she, like so many others, had fallen for in his videos.

As doubt swarmed in Priscilla's head, she was yanked from her reprieve when Alex slammed his bottle of water on the table. Priscilla hadn't even noticed him grab one.

"So are we figuring out this kegger situation in the park or not?" he asked.

To Priscilla's annoyance, Tommy seemed relieved to change the subject.

"You fixed my burner phone?" he asked.

"Yeah," Alex said, holding it out. "The guy says it should be working again."

"It better be."

Tommy grabbed the phone from Alex and began testing it.

Normally, this would be the point when Priscilla stopped paying attention. She'd never been very involved in Tommy's pranks except for cleaning up the fallout from them. But this year, Tommy would be filming during the senior prank. It was an annual tradition, one that had started three senior trips ago. Someone had managed to sneak into Sunny World Park after it had closed for the night. They'd opened the gates for the rest of the senior class and thrown a rager without the park or their school knowing. The tradition had continued, and this year, Tommy had taken the reins of organizing it.

But he claimed that things would be different with him in charge. It wasn't just going to be a rager after midnight, but a full-blown night of debauchery, with costumes and everything. Tommy had even managed to convince a few Sunny World workers to operate some rides while the seniors were inside for the night.

Alex and Tommy had been plotting it all for months, with Tommy certain that the party would be the perfect opportunity to film content for his channel and skyrocket him back to fame after his slew of cancellations. But knowing Tommy, he was probably planning his own special prank in the midst of everything happening.

"You realize this phone is my lifeblood, right?" Tommy continued.

"Are you sure it's not just where you stash other girls' numbers?" Priscilla said.

She'd said the words in jest, but Tommy's nervous smile made her stomach drop.

"Is it?"

"You're delusional," Tommy said, laughing. "It's for work. It has all my raw prank footage. And I don't have to use my real number when I hit up my contacts—including my connect at Sunny World for the prank tonight."

"Isn't the point of senior prank night to not get caught?" Priscilla said. "I don't think our school or our chaperones will just be okay with you livestreaming a rager in the park after it's closed."

"What do you think the costumes are for?" Tommy said. "No one will recognize our faces. Plenty of seniors are having their spring break here. I'll just say I got the footage from one of my fans at another school in the park tonight."

"Well, keep me out of it," Priscilla said, frowning. "And don't ask me for my help if another lawsuit comes up."

For one thing, she didn't have her parents' lawyers to turn to this time around. But Tommy and Alex didn't need to know that.

Priscilla stalked over to her laptop so she could at least start planning her next video. The current brand deal she'd secured was from an up-and-coming lipstick company. They'd sent Priscilla a collection of their products for her to promote. But she'd been avoiding filming because, well, the lipsticks weren't something she actually would use if she had a choice. They had this weird chemical smell to them, and the pigments weren't organic. Priscilla had combed through the ingredients list to make sure. The first video Priscilla had filmed had run through all of these factors to her audience. But when she'd sent the draft to the brand, they'd threatened to cancel the sponsorship if she came off negative in any way. So Priscilla had been forced to go back to the drawing board. Instead of testing out the makeup herself in a video, she decided to showcase the colors in a different way.

She grabbed a Sharpie and a pad of sticky notes from her book bag, then tweaked the film setup.

"Help me come up with names for these lipsticks," Priscilla said, turning her attention to Tommy and Alex.

Just as Tommy needed Kiara's appearances to stimulate his audiences, Priscilla's newest fans loved seeing her and Tommy flirt on camera. So that's what she was going to do. Shamelessly flirt and somehow pretend that he hadn't just admitted that she was his second choice.

"Are you still working with those sweatshop-labor brands?" Alex asked.

"Can you not?" Priscilla snapped. "I'm going to have to edit this out."

"You should just post the review you made. Screw what the brand thinks," Alex said, ignoring the fact that, yet again, his backseat commentary was ruining her video.

"I can't. They're the ones paying for the video, so they approve what goes out," she explained. "Besides, I inform all of my viewers to do their research for products or brands that I promote."

Alex laughed. "I thought the fact that you were promoting it was the research part."

"Well, it's not," Priscilla snapped. "Now shut up so I can film."

It was nothing short of infuriating how Alex was constantly holding Priscilla to some invisible standard that he didn't seem to have for Tommy or the videos they filmed.

"Aww, you made Princess mad," Tommy said. "Let me make it better."

Tommy stalked over to where Priscilla sat, his lips brushing Priscilla's cheek for a fraction of a second as he leaned over her shoulder and plucked one of the lipsticks she was testing from her hand.

Priscilla swallowed, forcing herself not to be distracted by the closeness of his presence.

Lipstick. Right. She needed to think about lipstick.

"That's Berry Burst," she said.

The color was a grimy, grungy purple-red that reminded Priscilla of the tinge that sometimes developed on metal when it got sunburnt. "Or how about Sweet Revenge?" Priscilla said, laughing as she wrote down the idea for the name using the lipstick itself. Against the yellow sticky note, the tinges of red in the lipstick color looked bolder and more effervescent.

"Hmm," Tommy murmured. "I wonder how it'll taste on you. Should we make that part of the video?"

"Right," Alex said, "because poison control busting into this room over a lipstick-tasting video is definitely worth the views." He laughed. "Is being deranged a requirement to be an influencer? Or is that just you two?"

Annoyed, Priscilla pushed Tommy away and spun to face Alex.

"What about being an asshole?" she said. "Is that required for film school rejects, or does it just come naturally to you?"

Alex's lip quirked. "Hey, I got into my second choice. I can handle a little rejection. Maybe that's something you should work on, though. Side chick doesn't really suit you."

Embarrassment flooded through Priscilla's cheeks. She tried to come up with her usual nasty retort but no words seemed to find her. So instead, she pushed past Alex and stalked to the lounge in the other room. Sunlight streamed from the bay windows that lined the walls, and the soft evening breeze whispered gently in the quiet room. Priscilla sat on a bench near the window, pressing her eyes shut to try to calm herself down. Behind her, the door opened.

She clenched her fists.

"Leave me alone, Alex."

But when she looked up, Tommy was standing there.

"Priscilla."

She turned away.

"I'm fine. I actually have to give Alex props for that one. Talk about hitting where it hurts."

Tommy sat beside Priscilla. Against the sunlight, a soft glow fell across his pale skin and Tommy's deep brown eyes glittered softly.

"Alex is wrong," he said. "You're not anyone's second choice. I'm breaking up with her. At the end of this trip. I promise, Kiara."

Priscilla glanced at him, her brow furrowing in confusion. "Kiara?" she repeated.

He cursed under his breath.

"Priscilla. Sorry. I got a little tongue-tied there."

Hurt gnawed at her chest. He'd mixed up their names. Again. But so what? It was a tiny mistake. Priscilla didn't know why it bothered her when obviously Tommy hadn't meant it. Like he'd said, Kiara and he had history. Of course it wouldn't be easy to escape her hold.

"It has to be tonight, Tommy. You have to end things or it's over between us."

"I will. And when I do, I'll take you out. We'll go on the gondola ride, make it official like new couples in Sunny World always do."

And in that moment, the embarrassment and hurt that had been churning and suffocating Priscilla faded.

"Will you post us too?"

Being online-official would do wonders for her channel.

When Tommy answered, his voice was strained.

"Of course," he said.

And then he leaned over, brushing his hand along Priscilla's cheek before pulling her into a kiss.

Priscilla pressed her eyes shut. But it was hard to sink into Tommy's kiss. Tommy's tongue kept poking her lips incessantly, and his hands burrowed into her waist as if the pressure of him against her would make up for the fact that he was, honestly, not that great a kisser. But for the first time in the months since they'd been flirting with each other, Tommy was showing that he was serious about choosing Priscilla. She wasn't going to mess things up just because she thought Tommy was a terrible kisser and he smelled like alcohol. So instead of pulling away, Priscilla let Tommy's tongue worm and squirm to its content. She wasn't going to be shallow and complain over one or two, or three, bad kisses. Because faking it, Priscilla decided, was a sign above all else that her feelings for Tommy must be real.

chapter three

Nevaeh

"YOU SHOULD TEXT him."

"Yes, girl! Tell him you're here and want to meet up with him."

"That would be so romantic. Wouldn't that be romantic?"

Nevaeh couldn't stop smiling. She'd never been the center of attention before. Even before she'd started attending the church fundraisers for the ministry that her family was a part of, she'd always been at the fringe of social circles, watching from a distance as her parents were embraced by the church community while Nevaeh struggled to even put two sentences together for an introduction. The morning of their weekend conference had flown by. But here she was now, still dressed in her Sailor Moon pajamas and wearing her hand-stitched wax-print bonnet, while a dozen other girls from the ministry's retreat stared back at her as they got ready for the rest of the day's events. First, there would be the seminar and then, later that night, the speech from Nevaeh's father, and the banquet and dance.

Christina, Nevaeh's best friend and the only other girl in the room probably aware of her impending moral dilemma, elbowed Nevaeh in the shoulder.

"Relax, it's no big deal," Christina said. "You don't have to call Thomas or even meet him if you don't want to. You have your dad's sermon to get to, and Thomas doesn't even know you're here. I'm sure it won't matter if you miss him just this once."

"But this is Sunny World," one of the girls said. "And she just said they haven't even met before." She dabbed her pale freckled cheeks with blush and styled her hair in a tight ponytail. The girl's name was Heather, Nevaeh thought, though this was their first time actually talking to each other, so Nevaeh couldn't be quite sure. "What's more romantic than crashing his senior trip and making out on the gondola ride?"

The thought of being held in Thomas's arms as they floated along Sunny World's most famous gondola ride sent a flutter of butterflies through Nevaeh's chest. Everyone knew the gondola ride was where new couples cemented their relationships. It was said that once they were swept through the romantic arches at the end of the ride during a first official date, their relationship would last for an eternity. Sure, it was corny, but for someone who was used to virtual dates, a ride on the gondola would be a dream come true. But Nevaeh knew better than to hope for such a possibility.

As much as she was enjoying being the center of attention, sneaking off for the day to meet her secret long-distance boyfriend was a whole different story. Faith and Soul Ministry was holding its annual conference, which meant that the ministry's churches all around the state were gathered for a week of seminars, worship, and missionary work. Nevaeh's father was one of the visiting pastors, and he would be speaking that night. Her mother was a board member of the ministry, and, like Christina had said, they'd expect Nevaeh in the front seat of the lecture with her brother, Laurence.

"Christina's right. I can't go. Besides, I don't want to mess up his senior trip. He's probably here with all of his friends. It's not the sort of thing you surprise someone with."

So-called Heather plucked a tube of purple lipstick out of her makeup bag.

"It won't be a surprise if it's a coincidence," she said. As she spoke, she painted her lips. The color was a toxic-looking purple from a brand that Nevaeh had never heard of. Not that Nevaeh frequently wore makeup anyway, but this lipstick reminded her of a chemical spill and, honestly, with its scent and coloring, it might as well have been named "Deepwater Horizon."

"Just go to the park, bump into him, and pretend your senior class is there for a trip too. And if your family starts wondering where you were, just say you stayed in the hotel because you got food poisoning. I do it all the time for these sorts of conferences and no one ever notices."

Heather shimmied into a bodysuit and skirt, which Nevaeh thought was the kind of feat deserving of an Olympic medal or whatever awards there were for accomplishing impossibly difficult tasks. Besides Christina, Heather was the only other white girl in the group and also seemed unbothered by the idea of ignoring all the rules the ministry had outlined for the trip. Instead of attending the seminar, they were going to head to Sunny World Park and a party that would be taking place later that night. Since they wouldn't be able to go back to their hotel to change, they'd decided to dress in their outfits early and spend the remainder of the day in the park.

"Leave Nevaeh alone," Christina said. "You're never going to convince her."

"Thank you." Nevaeh could always count on Christina to

come to her defense. Tired of watching Christina struggle with her own outfit, Nevaeh joined her side to help.

The look was a cross between a ballerina costume and a pirate. She wore a tutu over impossibly tiny, tight shorts, and a poet shirt.

Nevaeh's parents would have fainted if Nevaeh ever wore such a thing.

"What? It's a themed party," Christina said.

"I didn't say anything."

"But you were giving me that look."

"What look? No, I'm just thinking I could never wear something revealing like that."

"Maybe you should," Heather said. "Fort Grover High School's senior nights are known for having the best hookups and break-ups. Your little long-distance boyfriend may be yours today, but after tonight, who knows what other girl will have her claws on him, especially before graduation. Plus, you're a junior. The odds really aren't in your favor."

For someone Nevaeh had literally just met, Heather had a lot of opinions of Nevaeh's dating life. None of which were helping Nevaeh feel any less anxious about the fact that the boy she loved was just a few hotel rooms away. What if Heather was right? What if he was sneaking into another girl's room right this moment? Or maybe another girl was hitting on him?

"You're gonna give her a panic attack," Christina said. She turned to Nevaeh. "Don't listen to her. From what you've told me about him, Thomas will probably just be reading scripture or something in his room while the rager goes on in the park tonight."

"Yeah, totally," Nevaeh said.

Heather didn't know Thomas like Nevaeh did. He was sweet and kind, and always put her first. And even when he couldn't, Thomas was doing acts of service. Like the time he'd had to miss one of their video chats to give sandwiches to the homeless, or like how he volunteered at funeral homes after school. The Thomas she knew would never break into Sunny World Park or join in on the debauchery of senior prank night with his classmates.

Yet even with Nevaeh's trust in Thomas, she couldn't help texting him the question.

Her hands shook as she typed. The moments Nevaeh spent waiting for the three dots to turn into a sentence were like being lost at sea and searching for the first signs of shore. Seconds passed. Then minutes.

When finally he answered, Nevaeh's heart sank.

Thomas: Yeah. I'm going. Our prank night is the biggest part of our senior trip. There's no way I can miss it.

When Nevaeh texted again, the Read notification appeared, but Thomas didn't answer her.

Christina squeezed her hand. "Sorry, Nevaeh."

"Yeah, sorry you're missing out on hooking up with hotties," Heather said, laughing. "I guess even your so-called boyfriend isn't even willing to make that sacrifice."

Chondra, an Indian girl who Nevaeh's parents had introduced her to during service that morning, stood from where she'd been perched at the window. Unlike Nevaeh, Chondra had been at the center of all the group activities earlier that day. Her mother was a prominent member of the congregation and one of its biggest donors. She'd practically sponsored most of the trips. Chondra had a reputation of being, well, not like Christina, which had been the only reason Nevaeh's parents had even allowed Nevaeh to attend the trip.

"That sounds like cheating."

"Relax. If it's out of state, it doesn't count," Heather said, answering Chondra with a shrug.

Some of the other girls laughed along with her. Nevaeh half expected Chondra to work herself into a huff and exit the hotel room like some of the others had when the topic of dating had come up. But to her surprise, Chondra's eyes glittered.

"What happens in Sunny World stays in Sunny World," she said.

Heather snorted. "Exactly."

Suddenly, Nevaeh felt a whole lot less certain she'd made the right decision in joining the group at all.

"It's just one phone call," Heather said. "Tell him you're in Sunny World and you want to stop by while he's in the park. Or just wear a disguise or something and meet him." She nodded toward Nevaeh's sleepwear dismissively. "Didn't you say you've been talking for a year now? That's pretty long to still be on, what, first base?"

Hot irritation licked at Nevaeh's stomach. But instead of focusing on the sensation, she pressed Thomas's name on her contacts and hit Call.

Nevaeh regretted the decision immediately.

She never called Thomas. Never. He'd told her before that phone calls could get him in trouble because his stepmom was pretty strict when it came to who he talked to. But the thought of Thomas in the park with other girls made Nevaeh sick to her stomach. What if he didn't pick up? What if the Read receipt on her last message was the beginning and end for them?

Maybe she could end the call now and just text him that she'd accidentally butt-dialed him?

Before she could come to her senses and hang up, the line connected and a voice said "Hello?" on the other side of the call.

The girls shrieked. Some covered their mouths to muffle their laughter, but Nevaeh's whole body froze.

Yes, Nevaeh had wished that she and Thomas could meet tonight, but being virtual had allowed her a sense of control. There was no randomness with them, no spontaneity that could call for stumbling sentences or awkward gaffes. Nevaeh had been able to spend twelve hours in her day obsessing and deciding what she would say, how she would say it, and how she would react to Thomas's responses. She had even practiced in the bathroom mirror how loudly she'd laugh at his jokes. And now she was just expected to be cute with Thomas in a room with six other girls watching her?

Christina grabbed the phone and hit the Speaker button. She held it under Nevaeh's lips, urging her with a little shove to talk.

"Um, hey," Nevaeh said.

"Hey," Thomas answered. "What's up, babe? Why'd you call?"

A muffled giggle came from the bed next to her. Nevaeh tried to ignore the sound.

"Um, just 'cause. Is this a bad time?" In the background of the call, she could hear laughter and music and voices coming from Thomas's side. "Are you having fun on your trip?"

"It's never a bad time when it's you," he said. "And yeah,

things are pretty cool here. We're actually still in our hotel right now, but we're going to be heading to the park soon."

Unease filtered through Nevaeh. "So, like, are you there drinking and hooking up and stuff?"

"Babe, you know I'm not like that. I just went to try to be a good influence on my friends, you know, keep them from going off the deep end."

Nevaeh smiled. This was the boy she knew. This was the one she'd fallen in love with. "That's so sweet of you, Thomas. They're lucky to have you."

"Not as lucky as I am to have you worrying about me," he said.

More giggles filled the room. A flutter of wings filled Nevaeh's chest, the courage she needed to inch closer and closer to the line she always swore she would never cross. Because Thomas's words did that to her. There was something about the sincerity in them, the warmth and steadiness that radiated from him, that made Nevaeh feel safe and free to test the waters in ways she'd never quite felt able to with anyone else.

"Are you in your room?" he asked. "Are you alone? Do you want to get on video?"

"Go on video!" Heather whispered, grinning from ear to ear.

Nevaeh shook her head. Thomas had seen her in her pajamas before—and less—but she wasn't about to let the other girls know that. Or anything else Thomas and she had done since they'd started secretly seeing each other.

"I can't right now."

"Then how about a picture. You looked so hot in the last one you sent—"

Nevaeh spoke loudly over him, hoping none of the other girls had heard. "I wish I was there with you now. I've never been on any of the rides before in the park. Our family only comes with the ministry, like, every few years."

"I'll take you," Thomas said. "I'll rent out the whole park just for us and we can have our wedding in Sunny World's pavilion."

"Oh my gosh, he's already planning their wedding," one of the girls whispered. The others sighed longingly while some girls shot Nevaeh looks tinged with jealousy.

Nevaeh's cheeks burned, a measure of pride and apprehension warming through her. She'd never been the type to make other girls jealous.

At the Christian private school she went to, most of her classmates shot her looks of annoyance or embarrassment. Because Nevaeh was Little Miss Perfect or Miss Bible Thumper. No one wanted what she had. She'd never *had* anyone, for that matter. Not until now.

"Heather's right. You should meet him," Christina whispered. "Surprise him at the park!"

"I can't believe you got a boyfriend before me," another girl said. "You're so lucky!"

Somehow, their whispers of awe were liquid courage through Nevaeh's body.

"How long until your class is going to be in the park?" Nevaeh asked, surprising even herself.

On the other end of the phone, Thomas laughed. "Why, you driving across state lines to see me?"

"Just tell me." She laughed. "Please?"

"We'll probably leave in a half hour or so. Then we'll be in the park overnight until, like, three a.m. Talk tomorrow when I'm free?"

"Yeah, talk later."

They hung up, and within minutes, Thomas had texted a photo from his hotel view with the words *like you, it's even better seeing it in person.*

Staring at the photo and his words against the bright blue glow of her phone made Nevaeh dizzy with yearning.

Maybe there was a way for them to see each other. If his class would be in the park until the early hours of the morning, Nevaeh wouldn't even have to miss any of the ministry's evening lectures to see him. All she had to do was sneak into the park before they all left. Her parents would be sleeping by then. How would they even know she'd gone?

She chewed her lip nervously, then sighed. "Do you think you guys can get me that disguise you were talking about?"

Christina beamed. Chondra squealed. But it was Heather who dug into her suitcase for the outfit Nevaeh would wear: a pleated miniskirt and a too-tight crop top, both of which were white.

The outfit was so thin that Nevaeh managed to shove it perfectly into the clutch she'd be carrying to her father's sermon. The mask, not so much.

"We'll leave it in a hiding spot outside of the conference room. Remember that huge birch plant thing? I don't think anyone will notice it there," Heather said.

And while Heather and Christina finished up the final touches for their outfits, Nevaeh put on her Sunday best to be the perfect daughter her parents wanted, if only for the next few hours. Because at midnight, she'd don a costume and a mask, and then Nevaeh would become someone else entirely.

chapter four

Kiara

KIARA HAD BEEN on the verge of tears when another reason for breaking up with Tommy found her.

They'd arrived at the hotel just before noon. But Kiara had spent the time since her fight with Tommy tucked in a corner of the hotel lobby, away from prying eyes or cameras, trying to pull herself together before her interview. Sometime during this disappearing trick of hers, she spotted Jason and his group of friends on their way to Sunny World Park. Their voices were filled with laughter as they teased one another and ventured from their rooms. Not Jason. He just stood there, watching Kiara from a distance. Worry colored his gaze. Kiara looked away, wiping her tears with the back of her hand. Yet still, she found herself doing what she always did whenever she had an encounter with Tommy's stepbrother: she compared them.

Kiara didn't know why it had become such a habit of hers. Aside from the obvious fact that the stepbrothers came from two completely different sets of parents (Tommy's white, Jason's East Asian), comparing Tommy and Jason was like mixing up Iceland and Greenland. They were both tall and lean from running

58

track, both honors students and popular in their own right, sure. But what seemed cool about Jason was a steady warmth that he showed beneath his somber maturity. Tommy's easy smiles and cheap jokes disguised a coldness and disdain for everyone except for his fans; Jason's, though, were rare and priceless. Tommy's eyes gleamed with mischief. Jason's smoldered, but it was the kind of heat that kept the cold at bay. And when Tommy had driven Kiara to tears, Jason's lips had brushed them away.

Her cheeks warmed at the memory. It had happened only once. During their last winter break, when Tommy and Kiara's relationship had been on the brink of collapsing. To patch things up, he'd promised to take Kiara out on a romantic date for New Year's Eve. But instead, he'd dragged her to a party that one of his influencer friends was hosting. Most of the party, Kiara had stood on the fringes sipping a drink while Tommy was spirited off by Priscilla.

After hours of avoiding awkward advances from random guys asking her if she'd be up for filming content on their accounts, Kiara had searched for Tommy to ask him to take her home. After she found him, a fight had ensued. He wanted to stay, and he didn't like Kiara questioning how he blew off steam. That was when Kiara called Jason to take her home. Sitting in Jason's car outside the house talking made the dam of emotions Kiara had been holding back come crashing through in a flood of tears: the misery she felt being wrapped in the cloud of Tommy's influencer lifestyle; her anxiety about school and keeping her top spot; and, beneath it all, the unresolved feelings she'd always had for Jason that they'd never crossed as best friends. What had started as Jason's attempt to comfort Kiara had melted away as their lips had found each other.

After it happened, Kiara had tried to tell Tommy the truth. She really had. But he'd gotten involved in a scandal when footage of him being faded at that party came out. Kiara couldn't break the news about her and Jason to him then. Not when Tommy was on podcasts sobbing about trying to get his life together. So she'd told Jason the whole thing had been a mistake. They'd both decided to put whatever feelings they had for each other aside and be the people Tommy needed in his life in that moment: the doting girlfriend and the supportive stepbrother.

But here Kiara was again, crying in a corner despite having forced herself to shower and change into new clothes after Tommy's so-called prank. She'd left the remnants of the original outfit she'd planned to wear in a crumpled, smelly heap on Tommy's bathroom floor. Kiara had meant to put it in her own room, but the thought of seeing her boyfriend's face again after that moment had filled her with a paralyzing dread. The fact that her interview was in just a few moments didn't help.

Jason took a seat beside Kiara. When he spoke, his voice was soft, restrained.

"What did he do?" he asked.

Again Kiara looked away, unable to face him.

"Nothing," she said. "I'm fine. I'm just feeling a little carsick from the ride."

"You're a terrible liar," he said.

He yanked down the sleeve of his hoodie and held it out to Kiara like an offering. Kiara took it, tentatively at first. The fabric was soft. It held the familiar traces of lemongrass and rainfall that was distinctly Jason. As she wiped her tears with the sleeve, Jason drew Kiara closer.

"I told him if he made you cry again, I'd kick his ass."

Kiara smiled.

"Funny," she said.

"I'm serious. Where is he?"

"I'm not trying to get between you two," Kiara said. "Just forget it, okay?"

Unlike Tommy, Jason didn't need to be told no twice for him to understand. Kiara could tell he didn't like it, but he backed down, deciding instead to playfully wipe his sleeve against her cheek. She laughed, and for once, everything felt right. Her mind wasn't racing with a million thoughts, her heart wasn't on an emotional roller coaster that would spur a burst of anxiety. Being with Jason had always been like this. For a time, Kiara had mistaken the feelings of calm she'd felt with him as nothing more than a marker of their friendship. But as her relationship with Tommy had spun more and more out of control, Kiara had begun to realize that what she'd been searching for in Tommy when she'd first started dating him, she'd always found in Jason. But whatever they had or could have had was too late. She'd made her choice, and she couldn't bring herself to damage another relationship just because of her own selfishness.

"You know, I'm supposed to be in an interview right now. I changed and prepped for it and everything, and I just—I just can't bring myself to go. I can't get my hopes up again."

"Is it for Kingstown?" Jason asked. She nodded. "Then what the hell are you doing here, Kiara? Go to the interview. At least try."

"Tommy organized it," she said. Kiara couldn't add that at this point, she wasn't quite sure she could trust Tommy. What if the interview itself was a prank? What if Tommy and his friends were hiding somewhere in the restaurant waiting to film Kiara's reaction to their gag?

"Come on," Jason said. He stood and started pulling a sheepish Kiara up along with him. "Let's go together. I'll sit around somewhere close and make sure he's not up to anything."

"Really?" Kiara whispered.

"Of course," Jason said.

They were still holding hands as Kiara stood.

She wished he would never let go.

THEY ALL BUT sprinted to the hotel restaurant. As Jason led the way, they got separated briefly.

Kiara wove through a crowd of Sunny World visitors and hotel guests and almost ran into a group of girls making their way toward a conference room.

Most of the girls were wearing elegant dresses and the kinds of hats that Kiara had only ever seen in church. In contrast, there were two girls at the edge of the group who caught Kiara's attention. Underneath one of their regular outfits, Kiara caught a flash of a costume that looked like a cross between a pirate and a ballerina. The other had managed to squeeze into a tube dress that she was hiding beneath a bulky coat. As the church girls crowded in front of the conference room, the two girls snuck away in the opposite direction, peeling off their outer layers and discarding the remnants of what they'd been wearing over their costumes behind one of the hotel bushes.

In their determination to leave the group unnoticed, they didn't realize that one of their congregation members was entering from the other side of the lobby. From the looks of the suit and tie he wore and the name tag with his designation fixed to it, the man was a pastor.

If they weren't careful, they'd walk right into him.

Kiara's gaze flicked to her phone. Three minutes. The restaurant was just down the corner. She shouldn't be bothering herself with other people's business. She should focus, bolt toward the restaurant, arrive on time, and save herself from making a bad impression. Yet somehow, she found herself hurrying toward the pastor right before he saw the girls in costume.

Just as Kiara approached the man, the two seemed to realize their mistake. As they pivoted away, Kiara tapped the pastor on the shoulder. Truly, what was she even doing?

"Hi, sir?"

The pastor, a tall Black man with a close-cut fade and stubble, glanced down at Kiara.

"Can I help you?"

From the corner of her eye, Kiara watched as the two girls hurried away in the other direction. Meanwhile, another person, this one a Black girl with a silk press styled in a bob, hurried to Kiara and the pastor's side. The girl wore a long white dress with a tiny hat and a veil over her face.

She was breathless as she approached, yet somehow, she managed to pull herself together enough to speak.

"Dad. May I introduce you to—"

"Kiara," Kiara said, quickly filling the blank space with her name.

Relief flooded the girl's expression and she continued talking as if the two girls were old friends rather than strangers grasping for a way to distract the man, who, guessing from the girl's introduction, was her father.

"She's really interested in Faith and Soul Ministry and wanted me to introduce her to you."

"Yes, that's right," Kiara confirmed. "Nice to meet you, sir."

"Nice to meet you too," the girl's father said. "Are you a local here?"

"Actually, I'm from Jersey. I'm on a school trip—which, speaking of, I better get back with my class."

The two girls in costume had managed to successfully sneak away, which meant Kiara no longer had to interfere.

"We're having a ministry dinner and ball tonight," the girl's father said, stopping Kiara from making her ungraceful exit. "It's from eight to midnight. You should see if your school will let you join." He handed Kiara a flyer from a stack he was carrying that had a logo of a dove and feathers with the words *Faith and Soul Ministry: Annual Fundraising Dinner and Ball*. As he did, Kiara could practically see the panic beginning to seep into his daughter's expression.

"It's good that you caught me here, Nevaeh. I was going to make an announcement for volunteers after my speech," her father said, "but I want you to help coordinate the cleanup for tonight. They usually finish around one or two, but with your help I'm sure it'll go by quickly."

As Nevaeh stumbled to find a response to her father, Kiara spotted Jason where she should have been headed.

"Sorry, I really have to go," she said, and she slipped away from the two.

She was definitely going to arrive at the interview late now. But at least she'd have an excuse for what took her so long that didn't involve washing urine from her clothes.

"You're gonna do great," said Jason, who'd been watching her from up ahead with an amused expression. "I'll stay here and wait for you to finish."

She beamed at him.

"Thank you," she said before hurrying through the corridor that led to the double doors of the hotel's restaurant.

Inside, it was terribly packed. Kiara had meant to save a seat for Tommy's Kingstown contact. But instead, it looked like he might have already left. Just as she was about to give up, Kiara spotted the boy in the picture Tommy had sent her when he'd set up the meeting.

He was a tall, lean Black boy with deep brown skin, curly black hair styled in a high top fade, and glittering brown eyes. He wore a gray T-shirt and fitted trousers, and his shoes looked more expensive than anything Kiara could ever think of owning. Seated next to him was a white girl with straight brown hair and piercing green eyes. The girl had her head bent over a notebook, and her brows furrowed as she wrote intently on its worn, sticker-covered pages. She was dressed in a yellow T-shirt with a sunshine logo and wore orange trousers. On the left side of her shirt, right beneath the Sunny World sunshine logo, the name *Chelsea* was printed.

Kiara froze in her tracks. *No, no, no.* The universe had a cruel sense of humor. Of all the people she had to run into now, it just had to be *her.*

For a moment, Kiara contemplated turning around and pretending she'd been unable to make the interview entirely. Unluckily for her, the boy stood up and caught sight of Kiara.

"Kiara Stephens?" he asked.

Kiara swallowed and forced a smile, pretending that she still hadn't noticed Chelsea sitting in the seat that Kiara should have been in.

"Renton Davis?"

The boy held out his hand for Kiara to take. "Just call me Ren," he said.

"I'm sorry I'm late. I got stopped by this, like, annoying missionary group." Kiara held up the flyer as evidence.

"I'm a missionary," Ren said.

Kiara's stomach dropped. "Oh. Oh. I'm sorry. I shouldn't have said that."

Ren laughed. "Just kidding. I'm not. But the look on your face was so worth it. Sit down, sit down. Hope you don't mind. My friend was just keeping me company until you showed. We already ordered, is that chill? The appetizers should be here soon."

With her stomach still knotted in embarrassment, Kiara slipped into the empty seat beside Chelsea.

"You bullet journal?" Kiara asked, trying to make casual conversation.

"Yeah, I manifest things," Chelsea said, still focusing intently on whatever she'd written. When their eyes locked, though, recognition darkened Chelsea's expression.

"Wow. No way. We meet again."

Kiara forced a smile. "Yeah. What a wonderful coincidence," she said meekly.

Ren turned to the girls in question.

"You two know each other?"

"Kind of," Kiara said at the same time Chelsea answered "Of course."

"We've been in academic competitions against each other since middle school," Chelsea explained. "Kiara's school has beaten mine at—what was it again?"

Kiara forced herself not to roll her eyes. As if Chelsea wasn't keeping a scoreboard on their frenemy math leagues, DECA, and Model UN nationwide group chats.

"I led my school to victory in national DECA and Model UN competitions. And the spelling bee, but that was just me. Chelsea's school won a math league national championship a few times."

"Two, to be exact, one more than you," Chelsea said with a smile. "We've sort of become friends in the process. I was just telling Ren about the top schools I got into."

"Oh?"

"Kingstown, Hartshore, Whelton. You?"

The answer spilled from Kiara's lips before she could think. "Same."

Renton perked up in his seat while Chelsea stiffened in hers. "Really?"

"Yeah. Still waiting for some other answers, but pretty much the same." The truth was, Kiara hadn't even applied to Hartshore. She'd only been able to afford the application fees for three schools. She'd gotten into the Jersey state university of her choice, which was amazing and would mean a great education with tuition she could actually afford. Yes, she'd gotten into Whelton too, but it was too expensive. Kingstown was her first choice. But the whole situation was starting to feel more and more out of her grasp every second she spent in front of Ren, who clearly knew she was lying through her teeth.

"I'm just . . . glad I got a spot. I know a lot of people on the wait list for Kingstown." A half-truth, but all of the best lies were.

"Well, I, for one, am not surprised to hear you got in," Chelsea said. "You know, with affirmative action and everything."

The words were slicing, intentionally vicious.

Ren grimaced.

"Chels," he warned.

Flames of rage burned in Kiara's throat.

"If affirmative action was still a thing, I'm sure it'd be how you'd get into your schools. You know, since—statistically speaking—white women benefited the most from it."

At his seat, Ren snorted loudly. He recovered quickly.

"Well, I know Kiara here through Tommy," he said, directing the conversation to smoother waters. "It was nice of him to connect us even after the two of you broke up."

Kiara frowned.

"What are you talking about? Tommy and I are still together."

Ren blinked, clearly surprised by Kiara's answer. "My mistake," he said. "I must have just seen some fake news online."

Panic began to set through Kiara. Had she missed the news herself? Had Tommy actually broken up with her on his vlogs? Quickly, she pulled out her phone to check the alerts she'd set for her and Tommy, but outside of the rumors floating around, none of the posts referenced a real breakup post from Tommy. Instead, a text message buzzed on her screen.

Tommy: I'm sorry about earlier. I have something for you to make up for it.

Kiara dragged her finger down to pull the message fully open. Attached to the words was an image of a small velvet box wrapped in a bow.

Chelsea was looking at the text over Kiara's shoulder. When she realized Kiara had noticed her reading the message, Chelsea stood abruptly.

"I better get back to my shift at Sunny World," she said, gesturing to her uniform.

"Don't sweat it," Ren said. "I'll just tell my dad you were helping me out." At the questioning look Kiara shot him, Ren added, "My dad owns Sunny World."

He said the words as if it were a boring piece of evening news, the kind that was so unremarkable that it only appeared at the bottom of a news ticker. That explained the expensive clothing and shoes and why Tommy had been so adamant that Ren was a contact who could help Kiara in her time of need, despite him being not much older than Kiara and Tommy himself. She'd memorized the list of all of the notable Black Kingstown graduates. The owner of Sunny World was among them, and his story of perseverance had been a moving, emotional roller coaster that Kingstown had plastered all over their alumni pages. And Ren, well, clearly he was a legacy student, a freshman by the looks of things. Kiara felt a knot unclench in her chest. This meeting would be just the thing to help get her application off the wait list.

"No, it's okay," Chelsea said. "I should go." She grabbed her bag from the foot of her chair, her manner suddenly hurried. "See you, Ren. Kiara, congrats on getting into all your dream schools." With a forced smile, Chelsea hurried from the restaurant without another word.

Lines of worry crossed Ren's forehead, but when he turned back to Kiara, a smirk had worked its way onto his lips.

"Well, since you don't need my dad's help to get your application looked at again, should we cut this meeting short?"

"I'm sorry," Kiara said. "I know I shouldn't have lied. I just blurted it out because the stuff she said—"

"Was messed up. Yeah, I get it," Ren said. "I'm just not sure how much help I can be. Tommy said you already submitted additional materials."

"Yes, I did," Kiara said. "It was just my initial application essay that screwed me over. I thought if I could explain the situation to an alumnus or an admissions administrator, they'd understand why I sent that draft in. I'm pretty sure it's why I ended up on the wait list instead of just being admitted."

"And what exactly did you send?"

Heat warmed Kiara's cheeks. "It's really embarrassing."

"I can't get my dad to help if I don't understand."

Kiara sighed. She guessed she didn't have any other choice.

"I was working on my essays and Tommy was over. As a prank for one of his videos, he submitted my initial application before I was finished. I'd saved an early draft for the essay portion but it had all of my personal notes in it. It hadn't been cleaned up."

"What did your notes say?"

If Kiara could bury her head in the ground or disappear for the rest of her life, she would.

"I wrote placeholder sentences. Stuff like, 'Write about how smart I am blah blah blah,' and 'Write about why the history of your institution interests me despite the fact that it was built off of slavery and your school only changed the names of the halls dedicated to literal slave owners a few years ago. And your school has consistently not supported the women who have experienced sexual harassment ughhh.' It wasn't ever supposed to go out in my full application. I was going to explain my reasoning and add evidence. But Tommy just sent the whole thing, and the admissions committee or whoever read my unfinished essay was pissed about it. It's a miracle I was wait-listed instead of just being rejected.

Good grades, thank you. I think the admissions board just—well, they weren't exactly excited about the idea of a student dragging them in her application."

"So that's why you didn't want to tell that to Chelsea."

Kiara nodded. For a moment, Ren simply stared at her. And then he burst out laughing.

Again, could Kiara be anywhere else but here? Like, literally.

"Sorry, sorry. I just find this hilarious."

"That makes you and Tommy," Kiara said.

"Spare me the comparison, please," Ren said. "I get it, though. It's a sucky situation. But why do you care so much about making it into Kingstown if you have all those critiques?"

The waiter arrived at their table and placed an order of curly fries and wings in front of them.

"Is it okay if I take some?" Kiara asked. Aside from the coffee on the bus, she hadn't eaten in hours—and now she realized she was starving.

"Of course. On me. Dad owns the parks and resorts, remember."

Kiara smiled sheepishly. "I know Kingstown's history is kind of messed up, but so is, like, most of the world's history. I admire all the alumni like your dad who were able to go there and change things and make a difference in the world. It's what I'd want to do too if given the opportunity. I don't think anything is so ruined that it can't be saved."

"Is that why you're still with Tommy?"

Kiara's lips parted, but even as she searched for words, she failed to find them.

"I get it," Ren said. "I get it. And you seem great and super-smart. I'll talk to my dad, see if he can write something up for the admissions board. Maybe like a recommendation letter to argue your case."

"No way. Are you serious?"

Ren smiled. "Yeah, sure. Happy to help you out." His voice hardened, though, as another thought seemed to cross his mind. "Make sure you tell Tommy we're even now, though. No more favors. No more asks. After tonight, I'm done with his crap."

Unease settled through Kiara. She realized then that in addition to helping her, Ren must also be the park contact Tommy had mentioned. He was likely the person who was getting their senior class into the park after hours and the one who'd have the rides operating past closing time. But clearly the connection between the two boys was sour.

"Are you helping Tommy out tonight?" The idea that the seniors would be able to stay hidden in the park without getting caught had been Tommy's plan for the senior prank night. But he'd never exactly explained how they'd be able to get past security noticing them in the park overnight.

Ren frowned. "I don't think that's your business. Trust me, the less you worry about what he's up to, the better off you'll be."

It was more than enough of an answer for Kiara to decide that being in the park tonight for senior prank night was the last place she'd want to be. Whatever Tommy was planning, Kiara had finally had enough.

Ren stood from his seat, holding a hand out to Kiara.

"I have to go. But it was nice to meet you," he said.

Kiara smiled and shook his hand. "You too," she said. He paid the bill and left, and a waiter boxed up the extra food for Kiara to take. She exited the restaurant to find Jason still waiting for her.

"How'd it go?" he asked.

Kiara smiled and handed him the leftovers.

"He's getting his dad to write me a recommendation letter. I'm going to submit it with the rest of my stuff for the wait list."

"Brilliant," Jason said.

He squeezed her hand as they rode up the elevator back to their hotel rooms. But Kiara didn't want the moment to end. She didn't want to return to feeling trapped in a relationship or constantly being afraid that everything she said or did or didn't do was content for the internet. When they entered Tommy's room, Kiara placed his key card on the side table. She didn't care if Tommy stayed locked out for the rest of the trip.

"Are you going to be in the park for the costume party tonight?" Jason asked.

She should be. Tommy would want her there—Kiara knew it. But she shook her head. "Wanna skip it together?" she asked.

Jason raised an eyebrow. "Why, you have something else planned?" Kiara elbowed him and he laughed.

"Whatever it is," Jason said, "count me in."

Their fingers brushed along the side of the table. Butterflies fluttered through Kiara's chest, and her heart beat so loudly she could swear he could hear it. She froze when she glanced up and saw his eyes locked on her, staring.

"What?" she asked, peering up at him, suddenly shy now.

He leaned toward her, and Kiara craned forward like a moth drawn to light.

"You have an eyelash."

"I have many."

His lips curved into a smile. They looked so soft and gentle, so tantalizing.

"No," he whispered. "Here."

Closer and closer he approached, until their noses were practically brushing and their lips were just a breath apart. Their eyes locked. Kiara wanted him to kiss her. She wondered if he wanted to kiss her too. But instead, he caught the stray lash from her cheek and blew it away. There was a loud cough, and the two turned to the door.

Somehow, they hadn't noticed that it was partly ajar, and standing there, watching the whole interaction take place, were Alex, Priscilla, and Tommy.

chapter five

Priscilla

PRISCILLA WOULD HAVE laughed out loud if she wasn't so afraid of Tommy lashing out. He stood beside her, deadly silent, rage radiating from him at the sight of his girlfriend and his stepbrother one touch away from making out.

Considering that Priscilla and Tommy had just been doing that exact thing minutes ago, this was pretty fast karma, even for him. But Priscilla reminded herself that what Tommy and she had done was completely different from what Kiara was clearly on the precipice of doing here.

First of all, Jason was Tommy's stepbrother. Like, talk about home-wrecker behavior. The two were mostly close, though Tommy had always been terrible about hiding how jealous he was of Jason's naturally kind nature, which made him beloved by literally every human he encountered. As good as Tommy was at charming strangers, he'd never been good at keeping friends. Unlike Jason. Which meant that every time Tommy had a fallout, Jason was there, picking up the pieces. It could have brought the boys closer, but instead it just made Tommy even more resentful of his stepbrother. In fact, if Tommy had caught anyone else with

Kiara just now, Priscilla wasn't sure he would have been half as upset. But Kiara had chosen Jason.

Vindictive, much? Maybe.

Brilliant? Absolutely.

"I'm sorry, did I interrupt you trying to make a move on my girlfriend?" Tommy snapped.

Priscilla had to be honest: hearing Tommy call Kiara his girlfriend did sting. But at least they wouldn't be together much longer.

"Relax, Tommy," Priscilla said. "We heard the whole thing. She had an eyelash on her face." Priscilla stood on the tips of her toes and reached for Tommy. "Just like this," she added.

And to make a point, she pretended to grab an invisible eyelash from his cheek and blew him a kiss.

Kiara glared at Priscilla, which somehow made the whole situation even funnier in Priscilla's eyes. Like, couldn't the girl appreciate Priscilla covering up for her?

"Thanks for the reenactment, Priscilla," Kiara snipped. "But if you don't mind, I'd like to talk to Tommy."

"Forget that," Tommy said.

He stalked past Kiara and plopped onto the bed, grabbing his suitcase and pulling out the stash of liquor he'd smuggled in for the trip. There were tiny Sunny World–themed espresso pods that he'd replaced with booze, and then a bottle he'd somehow managed to sneak in. Alex, who was carrying the empty plastic cups they'd gotten from hotel service, ambled toward Tommy.

There was a knock on the door, and when Priscilla opened it, five kids who looked their age stood with armfuls of sodas and other drinks.

Of course Tommy would have organized a pregame before they left for the park.

Priscilla only recognized two members of the group from their senior class: Daniel Jacobs, who was dressed as a surfer, and his off-and-on-again girlfriend, Leah Moore, who'd donned a bikini. The other three Priscilla had never seen before and guessed must have been hotel guests the group had invited to the rager. There were two white girls, one who was in an outfit that looked like a pirate had gotten jumped by a ballerina, while the other had gone with a sexy rocker in a tight minidress. With them was a tall, pale guy dressed in only boxers.

"Priscilla!" Leah screeched. "Yay, you're here too."

Daniel gave a nod, but didn't move to introduce the other friends they'd brought along. But when the ballerina girl heard mention of Priscilla's name, her eyes widened in shock.

"Oh my gosh, Priscilla Frimpong? Like, Princess Priscilla's Page?" the girl said.

Priscilla frowned.

"Um, yes?"

The two girls screamed.

"We freakin' love your videos," the pirate girl said.

Priscilla blinked back her surprise.

"No way," she said.

"Um, yes way," ballerina girl insisted. "Your tricks for using concealer instead of foundation saved me so much from breakouts."

"Wow, you have fans. Are you going to give them your autograph?" Alex teased.

"Shut up," Priscilla said, but she couldn't hide how pleased she was at the turn of events.

Priscilla had never met any of her fans before. Obviously during a party on her class trip wasn't exactly the optimal time for a meeting, but the fact that these strangers knew her must have meant her page was growing even faster than she'd imagined.

The group entered the room, high-fiving each other and passing around sodas and Solo cups. Daniel immediately pulled out a flask and began making soda-and-whiskey concoctions for everyone.

Tommy didn't bother to water down his drink with any mixers.

He filled his cup without speaking. Then he filled another one and passed it to Priscilla, who pretended to drink like she always did so Tommy wouldn't single her out. It was probably bad that Tommy had already been pregaming an hour before in the shower by himself, though Priscilla wasn't going to mention it.

"Anyone got speakers?" the boxer guy asked.

Alex turned on the smart TV and began walking the guy through how to pair the music app with a phone. The soft strums of guitars, keyboards, and whatever alternative music they'd selected radiated from the TV's speakers. The girl in the rocker-minidress settled on the floor between Tommy and one of the other guys. Then, she immediately started giggling and asking to taste-test all of their drinks. On the other side of the room, the pirate-ballerina girl and the rocker girl were huddled together, giggling and glancing at Priscilla.

Compared to Tommy's other ragers and pregames, this one seemed like it was going to be on the milder spectrum, if anything. But of course, Kiara just had to be the person to make a whole big deal about the situation.

"I don't think getting drunk on our senior trip is a good idea," she said, her hands placed on her hips.

"The senior prank is a literal party in Sunny World, Kiara," Tommy said.

"I don't think that's a good idea either," Jason agreed.

Tommy rolled his eyes.

"Fine, suit yourself," he snapped again, pulling back the drink he'd just poured for Kiara and downing it in one gulp.

The boy dressed in only the boxer shorts and sandals clapped Tommy on the shoulder.

"You got any good stuff?"

Tommy grinned. "What do you think?"

He stalked over to his suitcase, his drink sloshing dangerously in his Solo cup as he dug deep into the crevices of his suitcase and pulled out a small paper bag. Three pure white pills were inside. Kiara looked pissed. Priscilla turned away.

The surfer took one of the pills while the rest of the group declined and instead focused on chugging through their drinks.

"You guys can't be serious?" Kiara said. "So you're a pill popper now?"

"It's a party," Daniel said.

"That could seriously mess you up. What even is it?"

Priscilla had to agree with Kiara and Jason on this one. She too felt uneasy being surrounded by Tommy and some strangers (even if two of them were her fans) who were now clearly under the influence of who-knows-what.

"Am I shoving it down your throat?" Tommy said. "My body, my choice, right?" He laughed at his own terrible joke, and then he crushed the two remaining pills into his drink before downing the whole concoction.

Daniel and the boxer boy snickered and gulped their drinks too.

"Dude, you need some serious freakin' help," Alex said.

"Did I ask for your advice?" Tommy snapped. "Just shut the hell up and get me my burner phone."

"Say that again," Alex said. "I don't think I heard you right."

The warning was clear in Alex's voice, but Tommy seemed oblivious that he was treading on thin ice.

"Did I stutter? Aren't you my logistics man? Get me my burner. I need to call my connect to confirm we're all good for sneaking into the park. The footage we're gonna get tonight is gonna be epic. I want my VIP fans to get all the behind-the-scenes."

Alex clenched his fist, clearly not okay with being ordered around not once, but twice in front of the whole party.

"Don't worry about it, Alex," Kiara said. "I met Tommy's 'connect.' It's all good. He said this is the last favor he's ever doing for you."

"What, the park or your admission?"

Priscilla didn't understand what his words meant, but Kiara seemed to tense up.

"If you paid him for that, you can have your money back. I never asked for your help."

"But you seem pretty happy to get it," Tommy said, laughing. "Chill out. I didn't *pay* him for any of it. Hell, he should be paying me to stay on my good side. But that's just the difference between you and him. One of you pretends to like me to get what they want, the other knows I could make their life a living hell and bury them with the dirt I have on them. Take a guess at which one is you."

"You shouldn't be speaking to your girlfriend like that," Jason said, barely managing to hide his own anger. His stepbrother's interruption seemed to piss Tommy off even more.

Before he could lash out, Priscilla cut in, turning the attention back to Alex.

"Just get his phone. You know you're his errand boy."

Alex glared at her.

"Then what does that make you?"

Before Priscilla could respond, Alex stood and sauntered over to Tommy's suitcase and yanked it open.

A tangle of Tommy's clothes and sponsorship products spilled out. The distraction was enough to turn Tommy's attention away from his stepbrother and girlfriend, toward Alex entirely. But with the alcohol and pills in his system, Tommy's rage seemed to be on the brink of boiling over.

"Is your brain short-circuiting?" Tommy said. Boxers and undershirts and jewelry and bags of unknown substances spilled from the suitcase. Tommy stumbled across the floor, grabbing the items and cradling them in his arms as if they were lost treasure. "Look at this mess. You're lucky I don't kick your ass."

Priscilla knew she'd been the instigator here, but hearing Tommy scream at Alex like he was some jester boy tore through her.

This was going wrong. This whole trip was going wrong. Everyone was too tense. Everyone was pissed at each other. This wasn't supposed to be how their last trip of senior year was supposed to play out.

"Let's film something!" Priscilla shouted abruptly. "Come on, let's do a livestream."

Without waiting for Tommy or Alex or anyone in the room to agree, Priscilla pulled out her phone and hit Live. Then, she invited Tommy's account to join. The request dinged on Tommy's phone and on his and Alex's smartwatches. Alex was the one to accept the livestream invitation for Tommy's account. He'd stopped looking for the burner phone too and requested control over the stream. Priscilla granted it to him. And just like that, Tommy's whole demeanor changed.

Instead of slouching and downing his drink, he fixed his posture, discreetly hiding the booze from the camera as he grinned at the now three hundred followers watching the livestream.

To his side, Kiara looked like she wanted to throw up.

"Imagine if you treated your friends like you did your followers, or even your crappy burner phone," she whispered.

"I treat the people who ride for me perfectly fine," he hissed back, too low for the phone's microphone to pick up. "Didn't I get you into your dream school?"

"You were the reason I got into this mess in the first place," Kiara said.

"Did you find my burner yet?" Tommy answered, ignoring her and speaking instead to Alex.

"I got it, just keep filming." Priscilla switched places with Alex and started digging through Tommy's suitcase.

"Damn, seven thousand already," Daniel said, watching the phonecast of the livestream on the TV.

"Those are Priscilla's fans," Alex said. "And some of our classmates, I guess."

The ballerina girl, who'd also been quick to hide her drink once the cameras turned on, waved as Alex panned from face to face and began reading off the names and comments from the accounts watching the livestream while Priscilla dug deeper into Tommy's suitcase, searching for his phone.

"Seagurlheartsharding says the coffee prank this morning was hilarious and people were overreacting about being pissed off,"

Alex said. Annoyance tinged his voice, but he tried to laugh it off. "Look, Tommy, you at least got one of your fans on the stream. Isn't this person, like, in every livestream you've ever done?"

Tommy grinned. "Love you, Seagurlheartsharding. Love my fans. They're the ones who really ride for me." He shot a glance at Priscilla. "Find it yet?"

"No."

"Well, look harder."

"Or," Alex chimed in, "maybe you should get your so-called fans to finally buy your merch so you can afford a new phone?"

"You joke now, but trust me, if anything in that burner gets out, we're all screwed."

"And what exactly does that mean?" Kiara asked.

"It means some secrets are better left with the dead."

Kiara rolled her eyes. "You're always so dramatic."

Despite Tommy clearly trying to scare them, Priscilla wouldn't exactly bet against him. Tommy and Alex filmed everything. Literally everything. She was sure at one point or another they'd caught moments on film that might be better left in the drafts folder than in one of their classmates' hands. Still searching, Priscilla dug through a handful of Tommy's shirts.

"Are you sure you put it in here?"

"Check the front pockets," Tommy said. "Or did you move it after you gave it back to me?" he called to Alex.

"Why would I?" Alex said. "Did you check the side ones?"

"Yeah, I did," Priscilla snapped, unzipping pockets along the outside of the suitcase before finding more pockets inside the sleeves of the carry-on itself.

"Alex is right, though," Kiara said. "Phones are replaceable. People aren't."

"Wow, is that why you're messing with my stepbrother?" Tommy snapped back.

The tension in the party came to a crescendo. Priscilla was just about to give up on her search for the burner when she felt something solid in the bottom corner of the carry-on.

"Let's not do this here. Or on your live," Jason said.

"I don't know," Tommy replied in a waspish tone. "I feel like this is exactly the kind of thing you should do for everyone to see."

Even without seeing the screen, Priscilla knew that the view count for the live had probably tripled.

"Seagurlheartsharding says you deserve to be with someone who cares about you for you. Not someone who . . ." Alex trailed off abruptly.

"Not someone who what?" Tommy asked.

When Alex didn't answer, Priscilla read it: "Not someone who uses you for clout."

Tommy laughed. "Hell yeah, I do. But you know how it is: there are so many users out there."

Part of Priscilla knew she should break the tension of the moment by revealing she'd found Tommy's burner phone. But the other part of her wanted the moment to last. Priscilla wanted Tommy to pull her to his side, live on camera, and confess to Kiara and the world he had finally found his person, someone who was real and genuine and wanted Tommy for who he was. But Tommy's attention was drawn only to his girlfriend.

"I never used you for clout," Kiara said fiercely. "I never wanted any of this."

In Priscilla's hand, the burner phone buzzed with a text message.

Puppet: This was a pretty big favor this time. I held up my end. Your turn. You owe me.

The name on the caller ID read "Puppet."

Priscilla raised an eyebrow.

Tommy had many names for his fans. The Hardingnators. The Hearts-Harding Club. She just hadn't realized that he'd become one of those people who also saved their IRL contacts as anything other than the person's real name. But considering he'd just called Alex his "errand boy," this new development tracked. It somehow completely encompassed both the parasocial relationship Tommy had with his fans—at least, when it came to his die-hard ones—and the transactional one that had become all his friendships.

"Puppet" was probably the person helping Tommy with the senior prank. Except, unlike how Tommy was able to pull strings to get his fans watching his videos or defending his antics in comment sections online, the people in Tommy's real life had even less sway over what he did. Half the pranks he'd done had been vetoed by Priscilla and Alex. But he'd filmed them anyway. And aside from his obsession with keeping Kiara happy, all of Tommy's antics, from being chronically online to talking with his fans almost 24/7, were to keep the unquestioning adoration of his followers.

That very simple rule when it came to all things Tommy explained why his fans hated Kiara: with her in his life, they had to compete for his attention.

This "Puppet" would learn that soon enough. Whatever debt Tommy owed them, whatever promise he'd made in exchange for helping with the prank in Sunny World, was as likely to get repaid as Priscilla's maxed-out credit cards. If repaying the favor wasn't in the interest of Tommy, his fans, or Kiara, then it wouldn't happen.

The only deviation to this rule was Tommy's promise to break up with Kiara to be with Priscilla. Because Priscilla was the exception.

At least, she would be.

"I'm glad you find this all hilarious," Kiara said, shooting her words at Priscilla this time.

Priscilla hadn't even realized the storm clouds from Tommy and Kiara's fight had somehow blown in her direction. She turned to face the couple, shifting her weight so the burner phone was out of their view.

"Tommy's fans have always loved him for who he is, even when he makes mistakes. Maybe you're the one who's been putting him on a pedestal instead of seeing him for who he is?"

A stream of applause emojis filled the screen of the live. Priscilla smiled, expecting Tommy to be pleased with the fact that at least she had the approval of his audience. But instead, ire oozed in his gaze.

"You don't know anything about our relationship," he said. An unspoken warning lingered in his tone. Tommy had already asked Priscilla to lay off him and Kiara. Priscilla chiming in again and bringing his fans into the fray was another line she shouldn't have crossed.

With one last cool glance at Priscilla, he stumbled over to where Kiara still sat next to Jason, wedging his way between them as if that was where he belonged. Tommy brushed his hand along Kiara's neck.

"I know you're not in it for the fame or clout. That's what

makes you different from everyone else," he said. "You're the one for me, Kiara. You've always been."

Kiara bit her lip. But before she could speak, Tommy pulled her into a kiss.

Alex was still filming, and when their gazes locked, she waited for the condescending remark that was sure to come. But Alex didn't speak. Something in Priscilla's expression must have moved him, at least enough not to rub the situation in.

Somehow, that made the whole thing worse.

Priscilla clutched the burner phone tightly in her palm. Tommy was punishing her for trying to force his hand with a public breakup. She should have just been patient. Priscilla should have just let him end things in his own way. But she was tired of waiting. She was tired of the ache that was watching him with another girl and the bitter, twisted knife she felt in her gut at being Tommy's second choice. So instead of handing the burner phone to Tommy or announcing that she'd found it, Priscilla shoved it under the mattress of the double bed.

It was the tiniest form of revenge. But a part of her felt smug about the fact that at least now, he'd spend the rest of senior prank night in a panicked search for his burner phone instead of enjoying the night with his girlfriend.

"How about we head to the park now?" Alex said. He ended the livestream abruptly and started ushering the visitors out.

"Agreed," Jason said.

To Priscilla's surprise, Jason grabbed one of the half-empty flasks of liquor and gulped it down.

The group made their way out of the hotel. Priscilla couldn't look away from Tommy and Kiara. He kept Kiara tucked tightly to his side. His arms were wrapped around her waist while his other hand brushed her lips.

"I got this for you," Tommy said.

He held up a small velvet box, wrapped in a bow. Instead of letting Kiara open it, he did the honors himself. Inside was a heart-shaped necklace with a diamond core. Tommy clasped it around Kiara's neck and turned the necklace over so he could see her initials engraved on the back.

Priscilla clenched her fists, forcing herself to look away. But the gleam of silver in the corner of her gaze was agonizing.

It had happened again. Priscilla had been the second choice. Surely this necklace was proof of that. Yet when she looked back up, Tommy was staring at Priscilla.

"I'm sorry," he mouthed. And then, something else, words she couldn't quite read but made her heart hammer in her chest.

It was the smallest of gestures, but then again, the starving could never refuse crumbs.

So Priscilla smiled. "It's okay," she mouthed back.

She reminded herself that in a few hours, Tommy would be hers. One way or another, Tommy was going to break up with Kiara. Priscilla was sure of that. For now, that knowledge would be enough to keep her worries at bay.

chapter six

Nevaeh

NEVAEH WAS IN anguish. The sun had set long ago. Nighttime engulfed the teeming walls of the lecture hall with a cool embrace.
And yet still the congregation of uncles and aunties that made up
the conference's attendees seemed defiant in the face of it.

They showed no signs of slowing down or wrapping up the
day's events, even as midnight approached. Which meant Nevaeh
would have to sneak out to Sunny World amid their watchful
gaze. On her phone screen, a message from Christina dinged a
notification.

> **Christina:** Where ARE you? The park's about to close. We
> need to hide while the workers don't know we're still inside!

Quickly, Nevaeh slipped her phone back into her pocket before her mother could read the message. Up front, Nevaeh's father
was preparing to take his turn on the stage. She wished he'd been
scheduled earlier. But the other speakers had droned on and on
for hours. They were already behind schedule. And of course, as
fate would have it, Nevaeh would have to sneak out to meet her

long-distance boyfriend in the middle of a sermon that would probably be the most important one of her father's career.

A part of Nevaeh knew she'd never forgive herself for missing it. She should back out. Christina and Heather would understand.

Yet there was another part of Nevaeh that ached at giving up so easily. That was the other Nevaeh, the hopeless romantic who, despite the purity voice ringing in her head, was dying to see Thomas. So what if she missed out on this sermon, the voice told her. Her father would likely just be doing a repeat of his most famous one: the two paths sermon. And no, it wasn't that Robert Frost poem, but more of a mix of the Cain and Abel story, sprinkled with a taste of the prodigal son. The story followed his two children, one who he'd named "Nevaeh" because she was sweet and virtuous like heaven, and the other, his eldest, who would take the winding path through corruption. While the older child had once been lost, he'd found his way back to their family, while the young daughter, Nevaeh, had never fallen off the straight and narrow road that led to salvation.

Yet there was so much Nevaeh's father didn't know, from the lies she had told to even her closest friends, to the messages she'd sent to Thomas. How would Nevaeh's family feel once they learned that, despite how deeply she wanted to be a good church girl, more and more, Nevaeh had found her gaze wandering from her lines of scripture to the hovering ellipses that lingered in the messages between her and a certain boy.

Buzz.

The notifications on her phone were unrelenting. Nevaeh had to make a choice. Now, before it was too late—or never.

Bile rose to Nevaeh's throat. The current pastor finished his sermon and a flurry of applause shook the room before Nevaeh's father took the stage. The intermission was so silent that Nevaeh was sure even a pin dropping could be heard. Her father stood behind the podium, adjusting his gray tie and the lapels of his three-piece suit before casting a look into the audience. When their eyes met, a small smile emerged on his lips. Nevaeh returned the gesture meekly, but a thousand daggers tore through her chest. He turned the page of scripture to the verse he would be reading from. And then, her father spoke.

He began how he always did, with a charming, breathless round of thanks to his family sitting in the audience. Nevaeh's cheeks warmed against the stares of audience members shifting to watch her, her brother, and their mother. None of the church-goers could see how tight Angelica's fingers wound around Nevaeh's wrist, or how her nails dug into Nevaeh's skin.

"Smile," her mother whispered. "Don't look like you just killed a person."

So Nevaeh smiled. Just like her mother wanted. And even Laurence, the prodigal son, who was seated on the opposite side of their mother, was smiling too.

But every benediction her father gave her, every echo of praise and sweeping glorification, tore through Nevaeh like a blade. She bowed her head, pretending to pray as she snuck a glance at her phone through her fingers. Her hands were shaking, and before she even realized, tears pooled in her lashes.

"Pay attention," her mother snapped.

"I am," Nevaeh whispered. "I'm just not feeling that great."

Laurence leaned to get a look at Nevaeh.

Normally, just the sight of her older brother calmed Nevaeh's nerves. Laurence, like her father's sermon's and lectures claimed, was proof that people could fail and make mistakes and fall into the wrong crowds and still be redeemed. But for some reason, seeing her brother now, when Nevaeh was on a literal precipice of her own, made the panic that was on the cusp of drowning Nevaeh overflow.

Laurence was the literal powder keg in their family. He was the cautionary tale. The one not to be. And despite their parents' attempts, they could never hide the edge that always seemed to be in their voices and the veil of disappointment that never ceased to appear on the occasions when Laurence's former acquaintances surfaced with claims of debts and money owed.

"Mom, would you let her breathe? You're always like this. If Dad's going to get the ministry director job, then it's on him, not us."

"This isn't the time or place, Laurence. Or did you forget that the money you stole from Pastor Richard is why your father was disqualified from the running last year?" their mother said. "But, sure. You're right. Nevaeh's the one we need to be worried about."

Nevaeh was going to throw up. Right here. Right now. She was going to vomit on her mother or the old church lady in front of her.

"Excuse me," Nevaeh whispered, trying to stand.

Before Laurence or her mother could speak, Nevaeh ripped her hand from her mother's hold, jolting up so quickly a wave of dizziness overtook her.

"I'll be right back."

Nevaeh took her bag and made her way out of the conference room, pushing past grandparents and weaving through chairs filled with children and families dressed in their church best. At the stage, her father glanced in her direction. He mouthed something to Nevaeh, his eyes filled with worry. But she shook her head and smiled before stumbling into the hallway.

If Nevaeh stayed in that lecture hall one moment longer, all of the pieces of herself that she was holding together would shatter. So, before she could change her mind, before reason could kick in again, Nevaeh stumbled out through the double doors of the hotel lobby. And then she took the last shuttle on its way to Sunny World Park.

chapter seven

Kiara

THE WORKERS IN Sunny World Park had barely finished bolting the front gates when the seniors began to peel from the shadows to take over the park for the night. All of the streetlights that had been beaming in the dark cooled to soft embers before they completely turned off. The rides shut down; the streets emptied.

Inside their own hiding spot, Kiara brushed her hand against her neck, where the necklace Tommy had given her just hours before hung like a weight against her throat. She'd texted him her thanks again just a few minutes before, overwhelmed by the gesture. When Tommy texted her back, though, Kiara's heart tore.

Thomas: You're my other half, Kiara. I'd do anything for you.
I hope you know that.

It wasn't so much of a gift as it was a reminder: three point three million followers and Tommy had chosen her. He'd kept his promise about the interview, and even after their fights, he'd found a way to make it up to her. Tommy had done so much for her. And yet it was Jason who Kiara's mind kept wandering to:

Jason with his warm smile and gentle touch, Jason who had been there to reassure Kiara when her anxiety about the interview had overtaken her.

Guilt gnawed at Kiara. She needed to try harder. Kiara knew the pressures of school and grades, but Tommy was navigating their relationship with millions of eyes on him. Of course he would make mistakes. Kiara herself had struggled to keep her 4.0 GPA. If she could just hang on to what they had, then maybe she could save them too.

"Ren should be here any minute," Tommy said. "He's gonna get the power working again so we can start."

"You literally said that an hour ago," Priscilla said. She pouted and elbowed Tommy playfully, which was pretty hard to do considering how she, Kiara, Tommy, and another girl from their senior class were currently crammed inside one of the park's porta-potties as their hiding spot.

"Are you sure this isn't just some excuse to role-play some hot-and-heavy scenario you have in your head?"

Tommy laughed, but he tightened his grip around Kiara's waist and pulled her closer.

"If it was," he said, "there'd be less clothes and it wouldn't be the four of us."

Priscilla's pout deepened and Kiara couldn't help the rush of elation she felt at the sight of the other girl being burned by her shameless flirting. Kiara wrapped her arms around Tommy and kissed him.

"I could spend forever in here with you," she said. Which was technically true. They would literally be stuck forever if Ren didn't show up like Tommy anticipated.

Since their lunch in the restaurant, the Sunny World heir

hadn't made an appearance—at least, not one that Kiara knew of. So instead of meeting Ren at the hotel, their group had trekked to the park. They'd gone on rides and traversed Sunny World, all while Tommy and his friends snuck drinks throughout the evening. When the park made the announcement for visitors to leave at the end of the night, they'd all found hiding places so they'd be able to stay in Sunny World Park past its closing time.

Being stuck inside a porta-potty wasn't exactly how Kiara had imagined making memories her senior year. She'd actually enjoyed the evening in Sunny World and would have much rather spent the rest of the night curled in her hotel bedroom, gorging on snacks and watching reruns on TV like Tommy and she used to do on the rare occasions when his parents were away. But Kiara would endure this grimy form of Twister they currently were knotted in if it meant fixing what was broken between her and Tommy.

Tommy returned the kiss, his fingers digging into Kiara's waist, his tongue tracing her bottom lip.

"How about we stay here when everyone leaves?" he whispered. "I know some things we can do on our own."

Priscilla cleared her throat. In the other corner of the porta-potty, the senior from their class pointedly turned the volume on her phone up as she played a video in her gallery.

Kiara hesitated. "How about we talk about that later."

"Now is later."

"I mean later-later."

Tommy groaned. "You always say that."

"Tommy," she begged. "It literally smells like moldy vomit in here."

"Then why did you say you could be stuck in here with me

96

forever?" His brows furrowed in irritation and he pulled out the silver flask he'd been nursing throughout their time in Sunny World. "You constantly just say things and then get mad when I read them wrong."

"I'm sorry," Kiara whispered. "But my definition of romantic isn't having my first time be in a public bathroom."

To her relief, a knock sounded on the other side of the porta-potty.

"The coast is clear," a voice said. Kiara recognized it as Alex's. "Everyone's meeting in the employee lounge."

Sure enough, she came face-to-face with Alex and his ever-present cameras as she stumbled out of the porta-potty, gasping for air. Priscilla and the other girl looked like they were going to be sick too.

"Wow, this was so much . . . fun," Kiara said. "Maybe we should head back while we still have time?"

Tommy took a swig from the flask.

"We're supposed to get in our costumes for when I film. Let's just change in the locker room with the rest of the seniors."

"But I feel like—"

Tommy groaned. "Seriously, K? You're killing my buzz."

In the porta-potty next to their hiding spot, Jason stumbled out along with the surfer guy and ballerina girl who they'd met while pregaming.

"I'd say you're more than just *buzzed* at this point," Jason said, his voice seething with irritation. Clearly, the poorly chosen hiding spot and the hours they'd all spent in the park with a very not-sober Tommy had been grating on everyone's nerves.

The two had been at each other's throats all afternoon, more so than usual. And Kiara knew she was to blame. As penance, she stood between them, playing the role of peacekeeper. Well, more like referee, but close enough.

"It's fine," Kiara said. "This is supposed to be fun, so let's have fun."

Together, the group stalked to the employee lockers where Sunny World workers left their character costumes for the day. The suits ranged everything from sunshine characters to celestial mascots that roamed the Spaceland as part of the theme park. In the back office, there was a room filled with masks and costume party outfits for the fall events that the park hosted.

Totally out of season, but the costumes would do.

Jason grabbed a cowboy costume equipped with a hat, a holster, and even a fake gun. In a box beside it, there was a matching cowgirl look. Kiara laughed, examining the outfits.

"What part of Sunny World do you think they wear these ones in?" she asked.

Jason smiled. "Maybe Mars. Pluto might have ranchers too."

Alex looked through a box next to theirs. "Thinking of doing a couples' costume?"

Kiara shook her head. "Tommy and I do that every year for Halloween."

"Oh, I wasn't talking about you and Tommy."

Jason dropped the costume. Kiara dropped hers too. They were saved from answering when Tommy emerged from the back room. He held armfuls of matching black clothes.

"Let's do goth vampires for tonight. Like the death of our senior year. It'll be hilarious on video."

The idea was simple enough. Kiara grabbed a random costume set from him, then hurried to the other end of the locker room to change.

There was a curtain that had been set up by the employees. Clearly, they'd been using the area as a makeshift changing room in between switching out of Sunny World mascots.

Kiara pulled on the ripped, fake-blood-stained tank top Tommy had passed to her and shimmied into pleather jeans that hugged her curves tightly. The outfit was more "zombie girlfriend" than "vampire," but close enough. When she finished adjusting the fit on the costume, she clipped on shimmering crystal earrings to go with it.

Priscilla was changing into her costume nearby too. She'd brought her own outfit down from the hotel. It was a two-piece bathing suit with cute shorts and a knit pullover. A ring of real, sweet-smelling daises was woven through her hair. Where Priscilla had managed to find fresh daises in a theme park, Kiara could only imagine. It wasn't as if she'd made any effort to talk to Kiara since they'd entered the park.

Actually, it was the exact opposite. In the time that Tommy, Alex, Jason, and Priscilla had spent day drinking in the park, Priscilla had become oddly sullen and hostile. It was almost as if Kiara had done something wrong, even though Priscilla was clearly the one blatantly flirting with another girl's boyfriend.

"I like your costume," Kiara said. "It's very sunshine-themed."

"I know," Priscilla said. "Obviously that's what I was going for."

"That's a pretty long way to say 'thanks,'" Kiara replied dryly.

"Why bother giving a compliment if you get pissed at how the person responds to it?"

"I'm just trying to be nice."

Priscilla laughed. "Oh, really? Why the change of heart? I've been Tommy's costar for years. You never went out of your way to be nice before. But *now* you suddenly want to?"

"I mean, I guess I never realized a change of heart was needed?" Kiara said, thrown by the other girl's sudden hostility. "Like, we've talked to each other maybe four times, and three of them have been on this hellish trip. And most of the times it's after you keep trying to flirt with my boyfriend."

"We're just friends."

Kiara forced a smile. "Didn't realize you knew that."

"And I didn't realize you cared," Priscilla shot back.

"Of course I care about Tommy. Why else would I be dating him?" But the words didn't sound convincing, even to Kiara.

"I was talking about me," Priscilla said, though there was a knowing gleam in her eyes that Kiara couldn't quite read. "I'm always with Tommy. Always. You just choose to ignore me."

Kiara grimaced. *Okay, fine.* As relieved as she was to know that others hadn't quite picked up on the hot-and-cold emotional roller coaster she'd been on when it came to her feelings for Tommy, Priscilla's words stung. Maybe she hadn't made any effort to get to know Tommy's cohost. But it's not like the other girl made any effort either. When Kiara explained this, Priscilla just laughed. The sound oozed of bitterness and alcohol.

"That's because you're the girlfriend."

"What's that supposed to mean?" Kiara said, frowning.

"Everything. Nothing. You decide, right?"

Except Priscilla was totally wrong. It wasn't Kiara who was at the helm of their spiraling relationship. It was Tommy. Or maybe neither of them was in control anymore? Maybe they were just passengers strapped into a speeding car that was barreling toward tragedy.

"You guys done?" Alex questioned from the other side of the curtain. But Tommy pushed it aside without warning.

"You could at least check first to see if we're decent," Kiara said, sighing.

"Oh, relax, gorgeous," Tommy said. "I've already seen you naked."

Kiara laughed, rolling her eyes. "Yeah, in your dreams."

But Tommy had this look in his eyes, the same one as when the livestream kept filming his meltdown on the bus: surprise, like he'd just been caught with his hand in the cookie jar. He wasn't joking. He was being serious.

"Tommy, you literally have never seen me naked."

Behind them, Alex snorted. "For real? That's not what you said junior year."

Tommy's face turned tomato red. Yet still he laughed along with Alex.

"I said we basically slept together. What do you think this whole party is for? Kiara and I wanted to make our first time special."

Kiara just stared at him, her mind a rush of emotions all mixed up and clawing at the surface. Just a moment before, he'd wanted to jump Kiara in a porta-potty, and now he was claiming he had some romantic date night planned all along? Tommy hadn't even listened to what she'd said. *Later* meant "not now," as in "Let's sit down and actually figure out what we both want with this relationship before we cross a line that we don't know if we'll regret." Yes, they'd talked about it. Like, once. And then never again, because Kiara wasn't ready and a part of her didn't know if she wanted her first time to be with Tommy. And shouldn't you be sure, like one hundred thousand percent, that the person you wanted to do something so intimate with was someone you loved and even, well, trusted? But as much as Kiara had convinced herself that she loved Tommy, she'd never been sure about the second part. The trust part.

Interactions like these had built up. And now, here he was, bragging to his friend about sexy escapades that hadn't even happened. And then there was the other piece, the fact that, even as Tommy spoke to her, he wasn't looking at Kiara but past her, to one of the locker doors on the far right corner of the room. The locker's insides had been crowded with costumes and objects and its door had been ajar the whole time Kiara and Priscilla had been changing.

It'd been open when the other girls in their class had been changing too.

Kiara followed Tommy's gaze, to where a white light blinked softly from the locker's top shelf. The light itself was almost obscured by an assortment of objects that surrounded it.

"I'm gonna go," Priscilla said. "Yeah, I—I can't."

She hurried from the changing room before Kiara could stop her. As their shoulders brushed, Kiara caught a glimpse of tears streaking from Priscilla's lashes.

"You're such an asshole," Alex said, glaring at Tommy.

"What?" Tommy said. "I'm just joking."

Instead of answering, Alex raced after Priscilla's retreating figure. And then it was just the two of them.

"I shouldn't have said that. I'm sorry, Kiara. There's just this perception of me at school and online and I—I don't know, I just feel this pressure to be that guy. You know?"

But Kiara couldn't take her gaze away from the locker, where that soft, steady stream of light kept beaming. She approached it, ignoring Tommy, who was now rambling to himself about how annoying the whole situation was. There was a sweater hanging from the locker above, obscuring part of the light source.

"Hey, are you even listening to me? Kiara, I'm being vulnerable here and—wait, what are you doing?"

Kiara didn't answer. Instead, she pulled the sweater away from the glittering light. Behind it, someone had placed a hidden camera.

"You were filming," Kiara whispered. "The locker room, all of the girls who were coming in to change for the night. You were filming them."

Tommy cursed under his breath.

"Kiara, it's not what you think."

"What do I think? This whole trip, you were being so secretive with that burner phone and claiming you had something planned during the senior prank. Was it this? Tell me, because I'm really just—I can't believe this. This is too far, even for you."

"You don't even know what you're talking about."

"You're filming girls changing. What the hell else am I talking about?"

Even he couldn't deny the fact. "It's just a joke."

"A joke?" Kiara repeated. "You can't be serious."

"You take everything way too seriously," Tommy said, groaning as if it were Kiara's fault that she couldn't find the humor in the situation.

"So you're telling me Priscilla and Alex were just okay with this whole thing?" Kiara asked.

Suddenly, a chill seemed to overtake Tommy. He stepped in front of the locker, obscuring it and the camera from Kiara's view. With his brow furrowed, Tommy laughed and ran a hand through the side of his hair.

"You don't think they knew about this? Be serious, Kiara."

"I don't believe you."

Tommy sighed. "Okay, fine. They don't know about it. But Priscilla and Alex aren't some freakin' prudes like you. Priscilla wouldn't even care if I told her. It's just video content."

"So it's okay for you to 'just' film other girls in locker rooms without their consent? That's supposed to be normal?"

"It is if you want money and views. How do you think I got you that necklace you're wearing? How do you think I scored you that interview after you bombed your application? It's not free. And sometimes the people who watch my videos and sponsor my content ask for favors. Just like you did, Kiara."

"This is wrong. What you're doing is gross and disgusting and creepy. If I'd known—"

"Then you'd what? Use me for your college acceptance and then cheat on me behind my back with my stepbrother? I guess it's too late for that."

Kiara's heart caught in her throat.

"I—Tommy—"

He laughed. The sound was bitter, buoyed by the angry tears beginning to form at his lashes.

"You were going to just dump me to the curb and be with him. And that's the thing, Kiara. You know more than anyone how much that would hurt me. After everything that happened with my family, after how long it took me to get over my parents' divorce, you knew he was the last person on earth I'd be okay with you seeing. Use me all you want, Kiara. I don't care. I'd do anything for you. Anything. Everything. But did you really think I'd just sit there letting you smile in my face, letting you gaslight me and pretend I'm just paranoid and crazy, while you went behind my back with him?"

"Is that a threat?"

Tommy smiled. And for a moment, it was like the wide-eyed, charming guy Kiara had first felt butterflies for was back again. But then a shadow crossed over his gaze. He laced his hand through hers, and then pulled Kiara into a hug.

"It doesn't have to be," he whispered.

At first, Kiara didn't understand his change in temper. But then, when she turned to face the door, she saw Jason's figure standing there waiting for them.

"They're starting the rides up," Jason said. "Uh, you guys coming?"

Tommy wiped away the tears from his eyes. And despite everything, a part of Kiara hurt seeing him like this.

"Do you mind giving us some privacy?" Tommy said. "We'll be there in a bit."

Jason nodded awkwardly and retreated back outside. The empty space of where he'd been left an ache inside Kiara's chest. She swallowed back tears.

"It's okay," Tommy said. "It's only some locker room prank videos. Just let me have my fun and I won't have to reconsider using my pull to get you into your dream school."

Tommy brushed his lips against her cheek and ran his hand over the necklace he'd given her. His touch and the necklace itself felt like a hot plate against Kiara's skin, searing and choking her, the final reminder of how transactional their relationship had become over the years.

It all seemed to click then: the reason why Tommy and Kiara

stayed together, even though there were a hundred reasons to end things. The internet had known it, even before Kiara had. Tommy must have come to the same conclusion too. He didn't love or want Kiara. He needed her, just like she had needed him. And through their many twisted transactions, they'd wound themselves tighter and tighter until they were too tangled up to function alone.

"I'll rescind my application," Kiara said.

"What?"

"I'll rescind it. Thank you for your help. I appreciate it. But I'll withdraw my application and apply to other schools."

"It's too late in the year."

"I'll take a hiatus."

"You say that now, Kiara. But I know you. We're the same. Opportunists, like and like. The second you get in, suddenly you'll forget this whole unpleasant situation happened and then you'll ask for more favors. If you're so upset about this prank, I'll delete the video. Okay? You can keep pretending like you have a moral compass if it means that much to you. Just wish you had one when you were screwing my stepbrother."

Kiara pushed Tommy away, and he laughed almost manically as he slammed into the locker. Instinctively, she spun to face him, rage seething from every inch of her.

"You know what," she said, "you're right. I do have feelings for Jason. I kissed him. Once. But that's all we did. We never went any further." She took a step forward, glaring at Tommy. "And I did use you," she admitted. "But so what? You used me too. There. Are you happy?"

Tommy sneered. "She finally admits it. See, this is what I actually wanted to catch on camera."

Kiara laughed. "Save the video. Upload it to the internet. I don't care," she spat. "But the reason people abandon you, Tommy, the reason they use you and can't even manage to stay with you, even though they benefit from it, is because you're so freaking fake it's impossible to have something real in the first place."

"What does that even mean?" Tommy said, rolling his eyes.

"It means we're over," Kiara said. "Tell your fans you went too far again or upload some corny breakup announcement. Just never talk to me again."

"I don't believe a word coming out of your mouth."

"Please." Kiara laughed. "Lying is your brand, not mine. Remember?"

This time, Kiara didn't wait for him to try to explain or fix things. This time she left. Outside the locker room, Jason was waiting with a wreath of flowers around his neck and a flask of Jack Daniel's. Walking up to him, Kiara grabbed the drink, chugging it down without a second thought.

"Whoa, whoa. Slow down," Jason said.

"Is this a party or what?" Kiara said. "Where's the music? Did they even get the rides working yet?"

Jason laughed. "I think they literally just got the okay now. Let's wait for Tommy and we can try that parachute ride they have a few blocks down."

"Actually, let's just go by ourselves. Tommy has some tech issues to fix."

Jason paused. "I'm not sure that'd be a good idea."

"You're right. It'd be a bad idea. I love those. Especially now." Kiara wiped her mouth. "Last one to the parachute ride has to do five shots," she said. And then she was running and drinking and racing away before Jason could yank her back to reality.

Kiara had just destroyed her future at Kingstown. And she'd done it by breaking up with her boyfriend of four years. If she was going off the rails, might as well let everything crash and burn. After all, it was their senior trip.

Tonight, Kiara decided, would be one she'd never forget.

chapter eight

Priscilla

PRISCILLA COULDN'T BELIEVE she was bailing on senior prank night. This whole year had been leading up to this. Yet somehow, the night had run its course with a whimper and a lot of runny mascara.

All around her, music boomed and classmates laughed and danced and ventured through the empty park with drunken abandon. But Priscilla stumbled off on her own, wiping away the bitter tears that refused to stop falling.

How romantic.

The area of the park she was heading toward was eerily quiet. In the dark, the attractions and installations loomed like haunted landmarks, the empty rides hovering like twisted apparitions. Priscilla wrapped her arms around herself. She didn't know why, but she couldn't stop shivering even though the warm Florida weather never wavered.

In the distance, the faint sound of voices filled the air. Priscilla's footsteps chased the echoing sounds of the laughter deeper and deeper in the park, until she found herself in front of a tiny teacup ride with glittering lights.

A group of her classmates was spinning wildly on the ride, while a Sunny World worker and other students monitored the machine like NASA engineers.

A hand grabbed Priscilla's shoulder. She screamed and jumped back, only to find herself face-to-face with Alex.

Her immediate instinct was to curse him out, but Priscilla found that with the alcohol running through her system, she was too sluggish to respond as quickly as she normally would have.

Alex panted, almost as if he'd chased her the whole way there. Sweat glistened against his forehead, and his camera, ever-present as it always was, draped precariously from its strap around his neck. Like Priscilla and the rest of their senior class, Alex had changed into a costume: he wore flower-print surfer trunks and a shirt that looked like spray-painted abs.

"You're pretty fast for someone who downed half a bottle of booze," he groaned.

Priscilla opened her mouth to retort, but again, she found that she kept searching for words that evaded her.

"I'm just very dedicated to making senior prank night epic," she said finally.

"Yeah. You'll have something to remember tomorrow," Alex said, clearly referring to the hangover she was sure to have in the morning.

But he'd be there taking photos all night anyway, and half of their class was filming stories as they spoke. Priscilla herself had even promised her viewers behind-the-scenes footage and a tour through the park's Lovers' Gondola. But in her head, she'd imagined doing all of that with Tommy, not as his production assistant or guest vlogger or side chick, but as his girlfriend.

Meanwhile, Tommy had been planning on how to deflower his actual girlfriend.

The shame Priscilla felt in that moment was suffocating.

Suddenly, light flashed before her eyes. Priscilla realized in the moment after Alex had taken a photo of her that the tangent in her mind had accidentally spilled from her lips.

"Do you even care that he treats you like crap, like, at all?" Alex asked.

"If I don't care then why should you care?" Again, the words were meant as an insult, but somehow, they fell far from baring any grit. And tears were still hot on the back of Priscilla's lashes. The topic of Tommy and his rejection still felt too raw, especially with Alex, who'd likely just make fun of Priscilla for being pathetic enough to chase a guy. Like, seriously, who was she right now?

"Let's get drunk," Priscilla said.

"You're already drunk."

"Let's get drunker. And go on rides. All of the rides. Screw it all. Screw Tommy and my followers and those corny sponsors with their weak-ass, cheap-ass, bootleg snake oil they have me selling. I want to literally party until I black out. Go on rides, throw up. Go on some more rides. Oh my gosh, Alex, you can take photos. You always take photos. Make me look sexy like your French girls, like so sexy I forget all about tonight and how unsexy it's been."

Alex frowned. In the dark, the layers of jewelry he wore shone like starlight, casting a shimmering glow over him.

"Just how drunk are you, Prissy?" he asked.

"Drunk-drunk," she answered. "And you're killing my vibe, so if you don't want to party with me, screw off."

"You need to go back to the hotel and sober up. You can't go on any rides like that. Not when there's literally no one who can help if something happens."

Irritation oozed from Alex's voice, but there was concern there too. Priscilla was sure she heard it. Unless that was her empty stomach about to retch. Priscilla covered her ears. "Blah, blah, blah. Go away, Alex. I command you to disperse."

At the teacup ride, two of the passengers screamed while another group stumbled in Alex and Priscilla's direction. They'd been filming on their phones and carried half-empty bottles of vodka. If it were even possible, they seemed to be in even worse shape than Priscilla was.

It took a moment for Priscilla's memory to catch up, but she recognized them as Sophie and Leah, two girls who were in her English class. Leah had been pregaming in the hotel room with them.

"Why are you lecturing me when they can't even walk straight?"

"Look at those two lovebirds fighting again!" Leah said. She squealed, stumbling toward Priscilla and wrapping her in a hug.

Priscilla smiled weakly. She'd barely spoken a word to Leah in the year they'd been in class together, or back at the hotel. But she guessed it was, like, senior prank night and everything. New beginnings and violent ends, or something like that.

"Just make out already!" Sophie laughed and their group of friends roared along with her, as if she'd told the funniest joke in the world.

Alex scowled. Priscilla would normally be annoyed by comments like this too, but for some reason, she found herself laughing along with the group.

"Or are you still thirsting over Tommy?" Leah teased. "You know he's, like, obsessed with Kiara."

The laughter died on Priscilla's lips. Alex stepped in front of her.

"Don't you have somewhere to be?" he said, annoyance thick and heavy in his voice.

"Um, don't *you* have somewhere to be?" Sophie giggled. "Like the Lovers' Gondola ride."

"Yes, oh my gosh, yes. Totally. You two should go on it," Leah said. "This is our only chance to be in the park at night by ourselves. It would be *so* romantic."

"It'll help you get over your thing with Tommy," Sophie agreed. "Even though I totally understand the hang-up. You know Tommy's the reason we're all here, right? He's got a guy he met a while back. The guy's dad freaking owns the park. Like, isn't that amazing. And now look! We have the rides to ourselves. None of the seniors before have ever had them working during prank night. Tommy is incredible."

"I would be obsessed with him too," Leah said, nodding along.

"I'm not obsessed with Tommy," Priscilla snapped.

"And we're not dating," Alex corrected, but the two girls weren't listening. They dragged Alex and Priscilla down the street, shouting at their passing friends to join them for the next ride.

Before Priscilla knew it, they'd arrived at the Lovers' Gondola ride, where another one of their classmates and a Sunny World employee stood at the controls. As they waited in line to get on the ride, Alex fiddled with the smartwatch on his wrist.

"Did you forget how to use it or something?" Priscilla asked, laughing at his failed attempts at signing on to the watch.

"Ah, no," Alex said, a sheepish smile working its way onto his lips. "I think I accidentally swapped watches with Tommy after we changed into our costumes." He unclasped the watch and slipped it into his pocket. "I'll give it back to him tomorrow. But knowing Tommy—"

"He'll probably have lost yours or pawned it off by then," Priscilla said. They both laughed.

"Yeah," Alex said. "Probably."

Silence weighed between them. With everything that had happened, it was strange to realize that maybe Tommy hadn't been the only magnetic force keeping their trio together. Alex was the only other person besides Tommy who really knew Priscilla. He'd seen her at her brattiest, but also at her most vulnerable. And even though they fought most of the time, their squabbles were always like two sparring partners who enjoyed the art of getting one over the other.

"Why are you smiling?" Alex asked.

"I'm not," Priscilla said, cupping her burning cheeks and looking away from him.

Their group approached the line, and she took the moment to change the direction of the conversation.

"Is this safe?" Priscilla whispered, eyeing her classmate, who looked slightly tipsy as they poked at the control panel. She was *positive* Tommy hadn't arranged training for this.

"Oh, so now you're worried."

Priscilla elbowed Alex. "You're the one who said I'm too drunk to be on these."

"I guess this ride seems all right," Alex finally admitted. "It's slow. Plus, they've been running it all night."

The group walked through the glow-in-the-dark lanes of

Lovers' Road, and then boarded the heart-shaped gondola that would lead them through the moonlight cruise under the park. Priscilla's phone chimed. She had two missed calls. They were both from Tommy. A rush of anger sweeping over her, Priscilla texted him.

Priscilla: Leave. Me. Alone.

Her fingers hovered over the Send arrow, but instead of sending the message, Priscilla deleted it and sent one that simply said *asshole* instead. As she did, Alex watched her so intensely she felt her whole body burn with his gaze.

"What?" she asked.

Instead of answering her, he locked Priscilla's seat belt in place and the ride trembled forward.

Lightning bugs dangling from invisible strings filled the tunnel's sky. There was even audio of crickets chirping and a gentle breeze from a fog machine as they drifted slowly into the tunnel. In the gondolas in front of them, her classmates squealed with glee as the ride moved them forward, past floating hearts and paper lanterns as a gentle, steady harp crooned the melody of a love song throughout the ride.

Priscilla had been to Sunny World plenty of times, but she'd never been here, on this ride. It was, like, completely ridiculous, of course, but a part of her had wanted to savor the moment and follow the gondola ride's tradition of taking your first trip with your crush and exiting the ride as a couple. How could things have gone so wrong? How could she have let Tommy lie and string her along so easily?

The tears burned once again in Priscilla's eyes. But she

swallowed them back, burying whatever bitter and painful feeling that had begun to churn deep in her chest. Still, she could feel the hot burn of Alex's gaze.

Why was he staring at her so much? Why wouldn't he look away?

"I know I'm hot, but really, get a grip," she quipped.

Just as she'd hoped, Alex rolled his eyes. But in the candlelit warmth of the tunnel, the accompanying glare he shot her wasn't as harsh as she was normally used to. In fact, she saw concern in his expression. Lines of worry crossed his forehead and his lips were pursed softly.

Somehow this was worse. Priscilla was on the brink of an emotional breakdown and Alex was doing the exact opposite of what she needed him to do in the moment, which was piss her off so she could ignore the swirl of emotions racing through her. Instead, he was being patient and gentle and attentive and all the things that made Priscilla's heart ache.

A slew of incoherent thoughts swirled through Priscilla's mind. And Alex was still staring at her.

Why wouldn't he look away?

"You should make me fall in love with you," she blurted. "I think if I was in love with you, I could move on."

They were daring words to say to her archnemesis, but she figured, what better words of war were there?

Alex laughed, which was annoying because she was deadly serious. She leaned over in her seat, fighting against the strain of her seat belt, and kissed him. Except the ride swerved in that moment so her lips found his cheek instead of his mouth. Alex steadied her, his hands pressed against her cheeks, a gentle light gleaming in his eyes.

"You're drunk."

"So?"

"So, we both know you're not thinking this through."

Priscilla pouted, yanking herself away from his grip.

"He lied to me," she said. She didn't need to say Tommy's name for Alex to know who she was talking about. In fact, if she could help it, after tonight she would never let herself utter his name again. "He said he was leaving her. He said he loved me. But they got back together again. They never even really broke up. And this whole trip, he said it'd be for us. When really, he was just trying to find a way to sleep with her. Can you believe that? Like, for real?"

"I know," Alex whispered. "I'm sorry."

Priscilla was about to ask how he could possibly know anything. But then she realized that the entire time Tommy and she had been messing around—every "rehearsal kiss" that went too far, every time they lied about needing to film when they were really meeting up—Alex had been in the corner, astutely minding his business while knowing full well that his best friend was cheating on his girlfriend. How many other girls had Alex watched Tommy woo and flirt with, all while knowing his heart belonged to Kiara? Had he covered for Tommy's lies? He must have known this whole time how ridiculous Priscilla's pursuit of Tommy was. Because really, how could she, Priscilla Frimpong, make the infamous Tommy Harding grow a heart when even his best friend couldn't seem to make him care about the people he hurt?

"You should have told me."

"I tried."

"You should have tried harder."

"I'm sorry," Alex said, "I really am. I just—at the end of the day, I thought if you were happy, that's all that mattered."

"Then make me happy," Priscilla said. "Or distract me. You're always good at that." Every time she'd been at her worst and most vulnerable, Alex had always been there to annoy her so much that she often forgot what she'd been upset about in the first place. Instead, she'd find herself shouting, and then laughing, and then shouting to keep from laughing because there would be no way in hell she would let Alex know that she actually enjoyed his obnoxious presence.

"Then I'll distract you," he said. "Just for tonight, I'll make you forget about him. But first, close your eyes."

Annoyed at being told what to do, Priscilla glared at him. Which he must have predicted would happen, because suddenly they were reaching a steep drop, and she was screaming that he was such an asshole, then she was laughing and squeezing her eyes shut as tears pooled in her lashes. Priscilla welcomed the warmth of the tears and the fact that she could scream and cry, and no one would recognize the sounds of her broken sobs from the joyful cries of the other gondola passengers ahead.

His hand found hers. She laced her fingers through his, gripping him tightly, tightly, screaming until her voice cracked, until her cries echoed the fractured pieces of herself. The ride raced through a section where the walls were glass and animated marine life swam all around them. Then, finally, they sloped upward to the ride's end. Alex wrapped his arms around her waist, pulling her toward him.

"I can't kiss you now. I want to, but I can't," he said.

Somehow, the words hurt more than Priscilla ever imagined they would.

"You don't have to make excuses."

"It's not an excuse. I just—don't want you to regret anything."

"Oh, I have a lot of regrets, Alex. Only, like, five percent have to do with you."

He laughed. "Only five."

"Fine. More like fifty. Could have, should have, would have, and all that crap."

"There's still time. To figure this out. To see if, I don't know, there's something here."

But they both already knew the answer. The warmth Priscilla felt, the fluttering in her chest, it had always been there. There had just always been one person between them.

Alex squeezed her hand. Priscilla pulled him closer to her. He brushed his lips against her forehead, and the butterflies in her chest took flight.

"Tomorrow," Alex whispered. "After you've sobered up, after you've really thought this through, if you still want this, if you want to try, then . . ." He took off one of the chains that dangled from his wrist and placed it around Priscilla's. The feeling of his fingers brushing her skin made her whole body tingle with warmth. "Wear this and I'll know."

For as long as Priscilla had known him, Alex had always kept two things on him: his digital camera, and the chain he'd gotten during his first solo trip abroad without his family. Each pendant was an object he'd gotten while traveling: a string of cowrie shells from the beach at Cape Coast, a glass stone from Lagos, and coins from Egypt. Of course, Alex had taken a myriad of photos from those trips, but his charm bracelet had always been the thing that he seemed to cling to the most.

"A-are you sure?"

"This is how you know I'm serious," Alex said. "About you. About us. I want us to do something real and just for us."

Priscilla smiled.

"You better get used to me never taking this off."

"A first for a so-called fashion icon. I'm flattered."

Priscilla flipped him off and, still laughing, Alex laced his hands through hers and pulled her closer.

She didn't want this night to end. She didn't want tomorrow to come. But slowly, the gondola drifted to the ride's exit. The other group was already unbuckling their seat belts and climbing out of the ride.

"We're going to the bathroom before we go on the next ride," Leah said, disembarking from the boat ahead of them. "Want to come?"

Priscilla was still holding Alex's hand. She glanced up at him through her lashes, feeling shy all of a sudden. Alex squeezed her hand, smiling down at her with so much warmth Priscilla's heart pounded in her chest and she was sure she would melt.

How could she not have realized that the burning she'd felt toward him hadn't been angry flames, but the fiery spark of desire? And it wasn't just that desire; it was another flame, something that was soft and warm and tender. She brushed her hand along the pendants of the bracelet. She didn't know if it was just this moment, but she wanted to try to see what was between them.

But then her phone chimed in her pocket and Priscilla knew even before she turned to look at it that the message was from Tommy.

Reality came crashing down.

Thomas: The burner phone. I know you have it. Meet me at the rockin rollercoaster.

"It's from Tommy," she said, even though she was sure Alex had seen the message too. "He wants me to meet him and bring his burner phone."

"And will you?"

"I—I mean. I left it in the hotel. I actually was planning on seeing what was on it when I got the chance."

"Trust me, you don't want to do that."

"Um, why? Don't tell me you know."

"Only because I had to get it repaired earlier today, remember? When they rebooted it, I saw some of the stuff stored on there. Not everything, but even the guy who was fixing it was pretty freaked out. It's what made me make up my mind."

"About me?"

Alex's lips curled. "I'm still making up my mind about that, actually."

Now it was Priscilla's turn to roll her eyes.

"I mean about Tommy," Alex admitted. "About this shtick we have going on with his vlog and everything. Why do you think I'm not filming his so-called epic senior prank right now? I've just being enabling Tommy's messed-up behavior. That stops tonight."

A swell of pride bloomed in Priscilla.

"Good."

"Good?"

Priscilla nodded. "We're both growing up." She chewed on the bottom of her lip as another notification went off on her phone.

Thomas: Please, Priscilla. I need you. Kiara and I broke up.

Instinctively, Priscilla gasped.

If only she could have known how that small, tiny, little gesture, that one moment of inflection, would turn out to be the biggest mistake of her life.

"You're going to go, aren't you?" Alex asked.

Priscilla's silence seemed to be answer enough for Alex. He pulled his hand away from her, but she grabbed him, refusing to let go.

"I'm just going to tell him it's over. I don't want to get with him."

"Then text him, Priscilla. Hell, call him and tell him exactly what you wrote but were too scared to send just a few minutes ago."

"You know that's not the same."

"Isn't it?" Alex said. He smiled, but the light didn't reach his eyes. "When you go, and he asks you to be his girlfriend, you'll say yes."

"No," Priscilla said, but she spoke too fast and they both knew there wasn't conviction in her voice. "What if I told you I want revenge? What if I want to get back at him for using me and dumping me and then just trying to string me along again as his backup plan?"

Alex untangled his hand from hers. "Revenge, or a second chance? Be honest, Priscilla. You've always been at least that with me."

"I want closure."

"Sometimes closure means not giving the people who hurt you and use you and treat you like crap access to you so they can do it again."

"You wouldn't understand."

"You're right. I wouldn't and I don't. I really don't."

Alex didn't wait for Priscilla to explain any further. He turned on his heel, not looking back as she called his name. Every piece of Priscilla ached.

She should go after him. Priscilla knew that if she chased him now that they could fix whatever she'd just broken. But when her feet moved, it was in the direction of the bathroom that Leah and Sophie had disappeared into.

Can we meet somewhere else? she messaged Tommy. *Somewhere closer to the Lovers' Gondola?*

Three dots appeared on the screen as Tommy texted back.

Thomas: And you'll have my burner phone. Right?

Priscilla lied. *Of course.*

Tommy sent two heart emojis to her and then one blowing a kiss.

Thomas: I knew you were the one. You've been the only person who understands me—who believes in me. I love you, Priscilla.

Priscilla supposed she should feel all warm and fuzzy about his words. But in the end, she felt nothing, nothing at all.

Another message appeared. *Let's go to the fun house.*

Priscilla: Cool. See you there.

"Are you and Alex, like, together now?" Leah asked, leaning over Priscilla's shoulder to peer at her phone.

Priscilla shoved it into her pocket and ducked to get some distance from the girl.

"Ew, no. We hate each other," she lied.

Priscilla pointed to Leah's makeup pouch on the counter and asked, "Can I borrow that?"

"Sure," Leah said.

Without waiting for further permission, Priscilla began to freshen herself up. She wiped away her mascara, which had become all splotchy from her tears, and then used her finger to dab red from the lipstick in Leah's bag onto her lips.

Meanwhile, Leah sidled closer, arching a brow. "Then why are you wearing his bracelet?"

Priscilla smiled at Leah. "Because I'm keeping it warm for him. Thanks for letting me borrow this," she said, and she handed the pouch back to the girl.

In the stall, Sophie screamed for Leah to help her zip up her dress. While the other girl went on to take care of the fashion emergency, Priscilla slipped out of the bathroom and snuck past the group waiting for them to come out. Then, she followed the signs to the fun house.

chapter nine

Nevaeh

EVEN THOUGH IT was past midnight, Sunny World Park seemed to be alive in the dark. A few subtle lights gleamed in the distance, but the gates where visitors were supposed to enter were shut, and except for a few cars parked near curbs, the parking lot was entirely barren.

Nevaeh texted Heather and Christina again asking them where they were. But they didn't answer. Even her calls went to voicemail.

Maybe Nevaeh had been wrong. Maybe she should have stayed for her father's sermon and just forgotten about this whole thing. Thomas was on a class trip with his school, for goodness' sake. What right did Nevaeh have to interrupt it just to play out a ridiculous fantasy she'd dreamed up in her head?

Yet just as she was about to turn around and book a rideshare back to her hotel, Nevaeh spotted a figure leaning against the wall by the gate.

It was a girl—a teenager, by the looks of her. Faintly, Nevaeh made out pale skin and straight brown hair peeking out from the black hoodie the girl wore. She was crouched over her phone, her gaze intent on its blue screen and the video playing from it. Even though the volume of the video was low, the tinny sound of a boy's voice was clear. A pang of recognition shot through Nevaeh, but before she could place it, the girl looked up. Cool green eyes locked onto Nevaeh, and from the glow of the girl's cell phone, Nevaeh caught a glimpse of a Sunny World worker name tag pinned above her chest.

"Crap," Nevaeh whispered. She spun, hoping the girl hadn't gotten a good look at Nevaeh's face. But of course, their eyes had locked just moments before. There was no way this Sunny World worker could miss the fact that Nevaeh was trying to sneak into the park after hours. The only thing Nevaeh could do now was run and hope the girl and whatever cameras were observing the park wouldn't be able to trace her back to the church conference.

"Wait, where are you going?" the girl called after her. "Aren't you here for the senior prank night?"

"No, I'm—wait, what?"

"The prank? Sneak into Sunny World, throw a rager. You're one of the Fort Grover High seniors, right? Or are you just here to have a good time?"

A flood of relief washed over Nevaeh. She'd thought the worker would, like, write her up for trespassing, but clearly the girl was in on whatever plans Thomas's senior class had tonight.

"I'm actually not one of the seniors," Nevaeh admitted. She refrained from mentioning that she was a junior and that she didn't even go to Fort Grover High. "My boyfriend is, though," she added, just to stay safe. "His name is Thomas Harding and we've been long-distance for almost a year. I'm going to surprise him."

Speaking it aloud felt surreal. She was here. Nevaeh had really come, and in a few moments she would see Thomas in person and everything would be perfect. She couldn't believe this. Sunny World really was where magic happened.

"Oh, really?" the girl said. "How adorable. Well, you know the first rule of senior prank night, right?"

Nevaeh shook her head.

The girl pulled a flask from her pocket. "Can't get in the park without taking a shot."

Nevaeh's cheeks warmed. "Um, but I don't drink."

"Sorry, I don't make the rules. You could always wait outside until your boyfriend comes out. Or maybe you can call him out here to wait with you?"

But it was already past midnight. Nevaeh wasn't sure how long she'd be able to stay herself. And the thought of dragging Thomas out from prank night just to be with her felt beyond selfish.

"It's just a shot," the girl said, and as if to prove that fact, the girl took a swig of the flask herself before holding it out for Nevaeh to take.

"I mean, it's not something I'm really into. And anyway, I don't think it's a good idea to swap spit with a stranger," Nevaeh said, eyeing the rim of the flask. "No offense." As corny as the excuses sounded, Nevaeh hoped the girl wouldn't make a big deal about it. Except when the Sunny World worker gave Nevaeh the once-over, embarrassment burned through every inch of her.

With a disinterested shrug, the girl turned as if to go back into the park, but Nevaeh stopped her.

"Fine," Nevaeh said. "Just one."

Before she could change her mind, Nevaeh gulped down the drink, making sure the rim of the flask didn't touch her mouth.

She almost choked right there and then.

The substance was tasteless yet it burned like fire down Nevaeh's throat. She shoved the flask back into the girl's hand, coughing and pressing her eyes shut all while trying not to vomit.

The girl smiled. "Welcome to senior prank night," she said.

And then she led Nevaeh through an employee entrance into Sunny World Park.

THE INSIDE OF the park was just like Nevaeh had seen in the commercials. The streets were paved with smooth cobblestones that seemed to glitter in the dark, winding their way through the fictional town that surrounded the park's grand entrance. On the intersections between streets stood rows and rows of lanterns. But unlike in the photos of Sunny World at night, the lights had been switched off. All the workers were gone. There were no actors in Sunny World costumes or vendors weaving through crowds. The massive rides stood like haunted monuments in the park; they were dark, empty, and eerily abandoned in a way that made the hairs on Nevaeh's neck stand. And it wasn't just the empty attractions that unsettled Nevaeh. It was the silence that seemed to linger in the air as the girls walked through the park alone. The world was spinning beneath her feet. Even before she had finished choking down the first drink, the other girl had passed the flask back to Nevaeh over and over until the harsh bite of the vodka was the only thing tethering Nevaeh to her surroundings.

Was drinking supposed to be like this? Like you were submerged underwater and your thoughts were racing past the slow, clumsy sequences of your body trudging to catch up? In the distance, a flicker of light caught Nevaeh's attention. There was music too, a slow, steady pounding bass mixed with the muffled shouts of voices.

The two girls worked their way past a fun house attraction and a comet-themed roller coaster through a maze of restaurants and employee break stations. The voices grew louder and the music blared against Nevaeh's ears. Then, almost as if they'd walked into another dimension, they stumbled upon the square where the gathering was taking place.

Nevaeh had expected to see students in outlandish outfits. What she hadn't expected was so many wearing masks along with them. There was a boy their age dressed as a cowboy with a bandit mask covering the top half of his face. As the two walked past, he tipped his hat in their direction. Seniors wore costumes ranging from bumbling, shirtless sailors to mask-clad girls and boys in swimwear. They laughed and danced and sloshed drinks drunkenly at each other, while others lined up to take turns on the handful of rides that were somehow being operated by Sunny World workers.

They passed a group of seniors screaming at the top of their lungs on a kids' teacup ride. At the control console, a Sunny World worker operated the ride while drinking from a Solo cup themselves.

The whole thing was . . . disorienting. Shocking? Thrilling?

"Aren't you guys afraid of losing your jobs?" Nevaeh asked the girl. She just laughed.

"Keeping the park open one night for this is more than we make in a month."

"Wow," Nevaeh said, except it sounded more like a groan.

Words didn't seem to form right when Nevaeh tried to shape them, even the ones with only a few syllables.

"What about you? Do you see your so-called boyfriend here?"

"So-called?"

"You've never met in person. That doesn't really count, does it? It's like being with a pen pal or leaving comments on a celebrity's page and them responding every so often."

"I didn't say we never met."

"Well, have you?"

Nevaeh looked away. "Look, he loves me. We love each other. And when he graduates this year, he's going to school near where I live. We're going to make it work." Annoyed, Nevaeh took another swig from the flask the worker handed to her, waving away clouds of smoke as they walked through a crowd of smokers. "I wanted to make this night special for him."

"Then call him. Tell him you're here. Go ahead."

The words almost seemed like a dare. Too bad for Sunny World girl, because despite what her name suggested, Nevaeh loved dares. Especially, it seemed, when she was a bumbling drunk.

Nevaeh handed the girl the flask back. Then she pulled out her phone and hit Thomas's number. The phone rang for a few minutes before it went to the dial tone.

"Hey! I can't answer, but if you leave a message, I'll get back to you when I can. *See you later, Hardingnators. It's been real.*"

Nevaeh frowned. "Wait, hold on."

Turning slightly away from the girl, Nevaeh sent a text.

Nevaeh: I have a surprise for you. Answer your phone.

A second later, Thomas answered.

Thomas: Hey. Sorry. Things are pretty hectic.

Nevaeh: Can you just pick up? Please. I promise you'll like it when you see it.

Three dots appeared on the screen. And then Thomas answered back.

Thomas: Send me a photo. I'll call when I'm free.

Heat warmed Nevaeh's cheeks. She knew what that message meant.

Please, Thomas added. *Today sucked. I want to see my angel.*

At his words, an idea slowly took shape in Nevaeh's mind. To her right, she spotted a cracked-open door leading to what looked like locker rooms. Inside, she could see a rack of costumes hanging near the back of the space.

"Hold on," Nevaeh said.

She stumbled inside and the girl followed her.

Most of the outfits were for sizes that would never fit Nevaeh. They were either too small or too big or too tall. At the end, though, there was a box with a few outfits that seemed to be for a person who was closer to Nevaeh's size. A bouquet of daisies was inside it, along with some super-skimpy costumes that made Nevaeh's cheek warm at the sight of them. But then, as Nevaeh dug farther into the box, she found a collection of angel costumes with silver wigs, masks, detachable angel wings, and headbands with devil horns. She smiled. This was too perfect. She could even pair it with the all-white outfit Heather had given Nevaeh.

Yet as Nevaeh was about to change, she hesitated. The outfit Heather had given her showed more cleavage than Nevaeh would normally be comfortable with. But with the mask and the angel wings, at least she would have some allure of mystery.

"Do you mind?" Nevaeh said.

But the girl wasn't looking at her. Instead, she seemed focused on a locker on the other side of the room that was filled with more costumes.

"I should go back to my—my shift," the Sunny World girl said. She handed Nevaeh the flask. "Here. You can have this."

"I think I better not," Nevaeh said.

But the girl was already walking away. Nevaeh's phone buzzed.

Christina: Sorry we missed your messages and calls. Are you here?
Heather: Or did you chicken out and bail?

There was a notification from Thomas too. He was requesting a video call with Nevaeh.

Nevaeh's heart leaped. It was happening. It was really happening. She was going to surprise Thomas and they'd be reunited like lost lovers stealing away in the dark. She needed to find somewhere she could be alone for the reveal, somewhere quiet where they could talk and kiss and hold hands for the first time. Here, the only thing that separated Nevaeh from the outside world was a makeshift curtain.

Just a second, Nevaeh texted him quickly.

Thomas: Nevaeh: You told me to call. What the hell.

I promise it will be worth it, Nevaeh typed back quickly.

Thomas: Prove it.

Nevaeh: Just give me ten minutes!

Quickly, Nevaeh yanked off her own clothes and shimmied into the white miniskirt and top. She pulled on the silver wig and angel wings. And, feeling cheeky, she even put on the devil horns. Nevaeh licked her lips and held out her phone. Somehow, in this costume, being sexy felt different from the awkward attempts Nevaeh had made in the summer to impress Thomas. He wasn't whispering in her ear, begging her to try just a little more for him. This was her choice, and with the distance the video call would allow, she didn't have to do anything she didn't want to this time, she decided.

Thomas's image appeared on her screen five minutes before they were supposed to start the call. Nevaeh hit Answer.

"Listen, babe. I'm kind of busy," Thomas began, but he stopped mid-sentence when he caught a glimpse of Nevaeh. "Damn, you look hot."

Nevaeh smiled. He'd never called her hot before. It'd always been cute, or sweet, or innocent. Hot was new. Exciting. But also, she realized, a little bit scary.

"Sorry, I shouldn't have called looking like this."

"No, no. Show me your outfit. I want to see my naughty little angel."

Nevaeh guessed he was trying to sound sexy. But honestly, if it was anyone else but Thomas calling her that, she would have cringed.

"Actually, can you send me a picture? No, do a video message. I'll watch it later."

"But you don't have to watch me later, Thomas. I'm here. In the park."

Thomas frowned. At first, Nevaeh thought it was because he was processing the thrilling reality that she was here, in Sunny World, and just who knows how many feet away from him. But then he looked over his shoulder.

"Crap. I'll call you back."

And just like that, the call ended.

The excitement that had been building in Nevaeh deflated. She'd come all this way and Thomas hadn't even spared five seconds to listen to her so she could tell him she was in the park.

Tears of disappointment pricked her lashes. She wiped them away just as her phone dinged with another message from Thomas.

Thomas: You looked so hot. I love it. Send me a vid. Please babe. This is the last one I'll ever ask for. I promise.

Sure, the message wasn't exactly what Nevaeh had hoped for. But he said "love." Thomas had said he "loved it." "It" meaning her, Nevaeh. And just as easily as the tears had begun to form, a smile formed on her lips.

It had always been like this with him, a seesaw of emotions, hot and cold, fulfillment and then emptiness. But these moments, these were when Nevaeh knew she loved him. People didn't just use *love* in sentences unless they meant it, right? Especially not guys. Especially not Thomas.

Before she could change her mind, Nevaeh started filming. She pointed the phone down, posed in her costume, and blew Thomas a kiss. Then she hit Send.

Immediately, he responded.

Thomas: More.

Nevaeh chewed hard on her lip.

Nevaeh: I don't know.
Thomas: Plz. Promise I won't ask again.
Nevaeh: I know but . . .

Nevaeh deleted the message.

"Okay," she typed instead.

Because that's what you did when you loved someone. Love was sacrifice. Love was making the person you cared about happy. Of course, that wasn't quite what the scripture passages said. But they also didn't have cell phones back then, so clearly they didn't know the serotonin rush of a text message.

Reluctantly, Nevaeh filmed another video and sent it to Tommy. And then she filmed another from a different perspective of herself and sent that too. Just as she was about to film another video, the sound of voices broke her stupor.

Nevaeh spun, covering her skimpy outfit just as the curtain flew open.

Two Black boys who Nevaeh had never seen before stood at the curtain and, behind them, a crowd was beginning to form. Christina and Heather were among the group.

They pushed past the two boys and through the crowd in a desperate attempt to reach Nevaeh.

"Everyone out," one of the boys said. He had deep, rich brown skin and ear-length locs, while the other boy had a fade and was dressed in a Sunny World uniform.

"Nothing to see here," the second boy said. "Get out."

The crowd murmured. Some snuck photos with their phones while others filmed as the two boys ushered them out of the locker room.

"Nevaeh, what are you doing?" Christina said. "Have you lost your freakin' mind?"

All of the adrenaline and alcohol that had been pumping through Nevaeh's veins had made a toxic concoction of courage and recklessness. In that instant, all of that came crashing down.

"Wh-what's going on?" she asked. Her costume suddenly felt ridiculous under the other girls' eyes, and Nevaeh wished she'd never put it on. She peeled the mask from her face, clutching it in her hands.

But it was Heather who answered Nevaeh, Heather who pulled out her phone and showed Nevaeh a livestream playing from an account with millions of followers, three point three million followers who were currently watching a half-naked Nevaeh whimpering in the locker room with Christina and Heather shielding her from the lens of a camera. Nevaeh wrapped her arms around herself, spinning to look frantically at the locker across from her. That, she realized, was where the camera was hidden. The steady stream of white light flittering out the slats in the locker door sent a chill through her.

"His account got hacked. He's trying to fix it."

"Whose account?" Nevaeh whispered. "Why am I— What's happening?"

"Your boyfriend. Don't you know? The mystery guy. He's a viral prank star," Christina whispered.

Nevaeh grabbed the phone from Heather, and sure enough, the account profile hosting the stream had an image of a boy who looked just like Thomas grinning in his picture. But he wasn't alone. In the photo, his arm was around a pretty Black girl with dark brown skin and Senegalese twists. The name on the account said "Tommy Harding."

Nevaeh dropped the phone. Her hands began to shake as a whirlwind of emotions consumed her. First came the disbelief, as sweet and poisonous as it was. Then, even worse, was the twisted knife of reality.

Nevaeh had trusted Thomas. She'd been vulnerable with him. She'd shared her mind, spirit, and personhood with him and him alone. But now, the whole world was seeing her at her most raw.

Even breathing felt impossible. The ground beneath her felt like it was sinking into oblivion.

"I think I'm going to be sick," she whispered. And then she threw up.

chapter ten

Kiara

KIARA HAD BEEN wandering around aimlessly in the park for what felt like hours, half lost, half afraid of what the trek back to the hotel would look like if the chaperones caught her sneaking back in. She was nearly at the exit of Sunny World Park when Tommy caught up to her.

"Leave me alone," she snapped, but Tommy was standing in her way.

"We need to fix this. You can't just—you can't just do this to me."

"I'm not doing anything for you," Kiara said. "Not anymore. I'm doing this for myself. It's over. I'm done, Tommy. I'm done."

"If you're done, there are hundreds of other girls who want what you and I have."

Kiara laughed. "What about the girl you posted on your account just now? Does she want what we have?"

Tommy's face turned tomato red.

"I got hacked. I swear. I had nothing to do with that livestream— I don't even know that girl!"

Kiara shook her head. She'd had enough. More than enough of his lies.

She spun, moving back in the direction of the park. If he wouldn't let her leave, she'd find another way out.

The crowd of their classmates had begun to thin, but the music was still blaring and the rides were still alive, with Sunny World workers operating them and some seniors enjoying the last few hours of the party.

Kiara pushed past her classmates, ignoring their stares as Tommy called after her.

"She's just a fan," he said. "And I swear, I *was* hacked. That's what I was telling you before you went and messed up everything."

Kiara laughed. "That was live, Tommy. Literally live to, what, two million people?"

"I have three point three million followers," Tommy corrected. Like Kiara didn't know that. Like she hadn't gotten the number wrong on purpose. "Some of them are obsessed with me, Kiara. They'll do anything to get my attention, even embarrassing themselves like a stupid slut on live."

Kiara spun to face him.

"You're utterly disgusting. Do you know that? You're a sick individual. Did she even know you were filming her in that locker room? Did any of the girls who you claim were in on your so-called pranks tonight know what you were doing?"

"You did!" Tommy snapped. "You've always known exactly who I am and the type of influence I have. Isn't that why you begged me to get you that interview?"

"I already messaged Ren not to ask his dad for a recommendation," Kiara lied. She didn't know why she said the words. They

139

just came blurting out in her horror and panic. But she'd make it right. She'd find Ren and tell him she wanted nothing to do with the recommendation.

"Why would you do that?"

"Because I want nothing to do with you. We're just going in circles."

"I don't need him to get you in," Tommy said, ignoring Kiara's words. "Yeah, his dad's recommendation would mean a lot. But I got another connect at Kingstown, someone on the admissions board. I already messaged him after we broke up, because that's just how much I love you. You're gonna get in, Kiara. Trust me."

Kiara ignored Tommy and made a sharp turn down one of the alleyways lining the main street, but Tommy grabbed her arm. Pain rippled through Kiara's shoulder. As he spun her to face him, Kiara realized that their classmates had started to gather, many holding their phones up. Camera lights blinked on like extra eyes, trained on Kiara.

"Look at me when I'm talking to you," Tommy snapped.

"Get your hands off me," Kiara shouted.

But instead, Tommy pulled her toward him, holding Kiara so tightly in his grip that her whole body felt like it was suffocating. He pressed his lips against her ear and whispered:

"What do you think will happen when our classmates and Kingstown find out you blackmailed their admissions board to get your application reconsidered?"

"I never blackmailed anyone."

"Didn't you? Didn't you tell Ren during your meeting with him that you know he rents out his dad's park to seniors after park hours? Didn't you say he let kids in and helped them have a rager

140

with underage drinking and drugs while he makes bank off of it?" Tommy pulled her closer to him, so close that his hot breath teemed against her skin. The scents of booze and smoke clung to him. "And what about those photos you made me send my admissions contact? Wasn't that blackmail?"

Bile rose to Kiara's throat. Her heart hammered in her ears, but this wasn't the butterflies from before. This was fear, blood-curdling fear sending a chill through her.

"What photos?" she whispered.

Tommy's lips curved into a jagged crooked thing. It was so warped, so twisted, that it took a moment for Kiara to realize what it was. A smile.

"If you break up with me now," he said, "you'll be ruining your life and destroying your future."

"Do you really think these threats mean anything to me?" Kiara said.

"What threats? No. I'm just making a prediction. A promise. Call it what you will. I just want to make sure you know what you're doing, and who you're messing with. Do you know, Kiara? Do you really know?"

And for the first time ever, Kiara realized that she didn't know. Who was this Tommy standing before her? Who was this chilling, calculating boy she'd once called her boyfriend?

"You're scaring me, Tommy."

"You know I don't want to. Seriously, you're breaking my heart. I just—I can't let things end like this. I need your help, Kiara, just for a little bit more."

But Kiara shook her head. "You can't use our relationship to fix this locker room video situation, Tommy. Everyone knows how much of a disgusting creep you are."

"For the last time, I was hacked," Tommy hissed. "Someone clearly found my burner phone and logged on to my account through it. It's connected to the cloud and the cameras I set up around the park. They must have started the livestream for their own pervy use. Do you really think I would be streaming the video from the locker room when I was talking to Nevaeh?"

Kiara laughed. This was real. This was really happening. Her boyfriend, now ex, was trying to convince her that he had been perfectly innocent in cheating on her with another girl because he hadn't meant to leak it on live.

"Listen," Tommy said, lowering his voice. "Priscilla was the last person with my phone. I think she lied about not finding it in my room earlier. I think she's had it this whole time."

"Why would she do that?"

"Because she's jealous of you, Kiara. She hates you. She'd kill to switch places with you and have me be hers."

Acutely, Kiara realized that more of their classmates had followed them and were gathering now. Most of them had their phones out and were filming the confrontation. But some were gathered beside each other, whispering all too loudly while looking at something on their phones.

Priscilla herself was among the swarm of bodies. Even from a distance, Kiara could feel the waves of resentment emanating from the other girl. Before she could interrogate this fact further, Kiara felt the angry vibration of a notification against her skin. One after another after another.

Tommy's phone went off in his pocket too.

Kiara pulled out her phone and unlocked it. On her screen, at least fifteen notifications warred for her attention—with more piling up every second. Hurriedly, Kiara scrolled to the bottom, where an alert told her in bold lettering that Tommy Harding's account had made another post.

Tommy took his phone out too. In an instant, his face changed from tomato red with rage to ashen white in horror. It was like he'd come face-to-face with death, like the only thing tethering him between the living and the dead was whatever he'd come across on the screen.

Before she could change her mind, Kiara opened one of the notifications with Tommy's post. But this one wasn't a livestream from the locker rooms. Instead, it was a carousel of photos. Scrolling through them revealed a series of text exchanges between Tommy and the girl from the locker room. Kiara knew this because the name ID on the top of the chat logs said "Saint Nevaeh"— the same name Tommy had let slip earlier.

I have a surprise for you, the first message said. The next image showed a photo of Nevaeh. Though the photo wasn't date-stamped, it was clear from her outfit and pose that these were the photos she'd sent Tommy during their live, photos that no one should see, let alone three point three million strangers on the internet. Swallowing, Kiara clicked to the next slide. This time, instead of photos of text chains, a video began playing. It was taken at the hotel their senior class was staying in. Judging from the angle, the video had clearly been shot from a balcony that had a clear view into one of the rooms across from it. Kiara's heart dropped as she caught a glimpse of the interior decor and recognized it as *her* room—then it plummeted again when the camera zoomed in on the two people inside it.

In the video, Priscilla and Tommy were gazing into each other's eyes. They exchanged a few words, and then Tommy pulled Priscilla into his arms, and they started making out. She wrapped her arms around his neck. She closed her eyes and sank into the warmth of his kiss. Kiara gasped.

It hadn't just been one girl. It had been Priscilla too. Which meant that Tommy's lies had spanned much longer than Kiara could have imagined.

But the account's post wasn't over. The next scene showed more photos, this time of another text chain, but between Tommy and Kiara.

Kiara: I love the necklace. Thank you. It's beautiful.
Tommy: You're my other half, Kiara. I'd do anything for you.
I hope you know that.

How could any part of Kiara have believed that Tommy had been genuine? How could she have been so wrong?

"Kiara," Tommy began.

But Kiara's body moved before her mind caught up. A fiery pain radiated from her palm as it struck the side of his face. She'd slapped him. Kiara had really slapped him. She hadn't meant to, and yet the rage and hurt and fear and disbelief had churned and churned until it'd exploded from her fingertips.

Tommy clutched his cheek, which was red again, this time in the shape of Kiara's palm where it had met his bare cheek. In Kiara's head, an apology began to form, but when she spoke, the words seemed to come from the most sunken depths of her heart.

"We're over," Kiara said. "And don't you ever, ever, ever try me again."

And then she was running. Kiara didn't know where she was going, or how she'd find her way back, but all she knew was she never wanted to see Tommy Harding again.

chapter eleven

Priscilla

THERE HAD BEEN another girl. Priscilla stood there, shivering with cold as the realization came over her. All this time, Tommy had said that he was planning to break up with Kiara for Priscilla, when in reality, he was soliciting sexts from another girl. And his text, that corny message from him that he'd broken up with Kiara and wanted to be with Priscilla, all of it was a lie. Now, less than an hour later, Priscilla was standing in the crowd watching as Tommy and his girlfriend—well, ex now—fought in front of their whole senior class.

Angry wasn't even the closest word to describe the slew of emotions running through Priscilla. She wanted to disappear in the crowd. She wanted to delete every sentimental message or post and flirty back-and-forth she'd ever had with Tommy. It wasn't just that he'd betrayed her. It was that she'd been naive enough to have been swept up by him and his charming lies in the first place.

As her classmates continued to film the fallout from Kiara and Tommy's confrontation, Priscilla turned to leave. She needed to find Alex. She needed to apologize to him and ask for more time to figure out what she wanted and, honestly, what she felt about anything at this point. But a buzzing in her pocket caused her to hesitate.

Her phone was blowing up. Of course it was. Had she really thought she'd escape the public vitriol that was no doubt on the way? Priscilla had worked with Tommy. She'd cosigned his actions and even guest-starred in many of his videos. And, even worse, whoever had hacked the account had not minced words, or footage of Priscilla's relations with Tommy. They'd somehow caught them kissing in private. And more importantly, they could leak more about Priscilla or any of the girls Tommy had been with to his followers. When Priscilla flicked her phone on, though, the slew of hate comments and attacks was a gut punch.

There weren't just comments underneath the video Tommy's hacked account had posted. No. People had made their own videos on their own accounts and had started tagging Priscilla in them.

The headlines ranged from newly formed accounts with one or two followers to bigger ones with thousands.

Why @PriscillainPink is a ho and a homewrecker.

Makeup can't hide @PriscillainPink's lies

How @PriscillainPink wormed her way into Tommy's life, one vlog at a time.

It didn't stop there. Mutuals with larger followings than Priscilla had unfollowed her. Priscilla swallowed back the knots of panic in her stomach. Soon enough, her sponsors might hear about the situation and start demanding explanations for the leaked footage.

"Damn, Priscilla. Were you really messing with Tommy behind Kiara's back?" one of their classmates in the crowd said.

"She's such a thot," another person farther in the crowd whispered.

"Who's the other girl in the locker room video and photos?"

"Tommy's the asshole here."

The last sentiment seemed to be the one that captured the crowd the most. As they filmed on their own accounts, their classmates inched closer to Tommy, some girls yelling at him, others throwing their drinks and calling him a cheating asshole. Meanwhile, some guys were cheering him on.

"Get that body count!" one of the aspiring frat boys in their class whooped.

"I was hacked, guys. This isn't what I wanted," Tommy said. "None of this is true."

"Liar!"

"Jerk."

"Manwhore!"

Despite the onslaught from their classmates, Tommy still maintained his innocence. And Priscilla had to hand it to him. He was standing by his boy-next-door act. At least there was something in the world he was committed to.

"Seriously, you guys," Tommy continued. "If you know me, if you really know me, you'll see that everything my account posted—everything the hacker posted, I mean—it's a lie. A blatant lie. I mean, half of that crap was clearly photoshopped. I'm going to be suing the hell out of whoever hacked my account when I find out who they are."

As he searched through the crowd, his gaze caught hold of Priscilla's. And almost like a sunrise parting the dark, his expression brightened at the sight of her. Tommy pushed through the crowd until they were just a few feet away from each other.

"Tell them, Priscilla. That kiss was just for one of the pranks we were filming. From the angle, it looks like we were kissing, but we totally weren't."

The perfect lie, so easy, so immediate. Priscilla was again impressed by how even she hadn't been able to see through him before.

"You're not even, like, my type," Tommy continued. "No offense."

This time, Priscilla did laugh. Out loud. Hysterically. "And thank God for that. Because you're seriously a terrible kisser, Tommy, and a piece of trash. What a relief to know I'll never have a real chance with you."

Tommy flipped her off and Priscilla returned the gesture with a smile. She truly hoped and wished that every single lie and bit of stolen content Tommy had used to build his wack-ass brand would come crumbling down, just like him.

"Will you at least help me take down the video?"

"Always the audacity, never the tact or game." Priscilla laughed.

"Keep laughing. I'll get Alex to help. Good luck securing another brand deal," Tommy spat. And then he stormed away, pushing past the crowd, disappearing into the dark.

And suddenly, it was like a switch had flipped in Priscilla. Their classmates were still filming, some were chasing after Tommy, and others were returning their attention to Priscilla, demanding that she explain what was happening.

Priscilla had never been a crier. She hated crying and straight-up detested when influencers posted themselves sobbing for their online fans. But these tears were real and bitter and broken. Priscilla was drowning in her own sobs.

She moved through the crowd, hiding her tears and hoping no one had caught a clear sight of her moment of weakness. But then someone grabbed her hand and led her through the last scatterings of their classmates. When Priscilla peeked past her fingers, the person was none other than Kiara.

The moment they were far enough away from their classmates, Priscilla yanked her hand out of Kiara's.

"Let go of me. I don't need your sympathy."

Kiara crossed her arms. "That's not why I helped you."

"Yeah, why would you when you just destroyed any chance of me or Tommy going out in public again after this?"

"There's no way you're still caping for that jerk," Kiara said. "There's no way."

Priscilla glared at her. "Of course I'm not. I'm done with him. He doesn't even exist to me, as far as I'm concerned. But that doesn't change the fact that you hacked his account and put me in the cross fire."

Kiara laughed. "Another lie."

"What are you talking about?"

"Tommy said *you* hacked his account."

Priscilla's jaw dropped. "I'm the hacker? He can't be serious. Excuse me, but I didn't see anyone calling you a home-wrecking whore."

Kiara laughed. "Change *home-wrecking* to *white man's* and you'll have half of the messages in my DMs right now."

Priscilla wiped away the remaining traces of her tears, then crossed her arms. Kiara ran a hand through her braids.

"Tommy and I were already in a fight when the account got hacked. I couldn't have posted it. We were literally around everyone from school."

Which was true. The moment after the locker room video had gone live, Priscilla had watched in the distance as Kiara confronted Tommy for his vicious prank. But if it hadn't been Kiara, than who else would have hacked the account?

The answer suddenly came to her. "What about the other girl?"

"What other girl?" Kiara said, frowning.

"The one in the locker video, the girl who was, like, sexting Tommy in the middle of it. What if she posted it?"

Kiara frowned. "Yes, you make an excellent point about why someone would literally leak a video of themselves in such a vulnerable situation. That's sarcasm, in case you don't get the hint."

But Priscilla wasn't listening. Instead, she was playing back the video Tommy's hacked account had posted and memorizing the number that had appeared below the contact in the chat logs with the second girl. Nevaeh. That was her name.

"You can't be serious."

"We need an answer," Priscilla said, typing the girl's number and hitting Call. "Maybe she has one."

The dial tone rang for one moment. No one answered. Priscilla tried again and then a third time.

And then on the fourth attempt, the soft, shaken voice of a girl answered.

chapter twelve

Nevaeh

NEVAEH KNEW SHE'D made a mistake when she answered the phone from the unknown caller.

The voice on the other line sounded frantic. Angry, even.

"Are you the girl in Tommy's locker room video?"

Immediately, Nevaeh hung up the phone just as Heather and Christina returned to the bench where the three girls had managed to find solace from the crowd.

"We got you water. It's tap. From one of the fountains in the park, but it's the best we could find," Christina said, nursing a shot glass filled with the drink. But even seeing clear liquid now reminded Nevaeh of the fiery vodka she'd downed just hours before.

"Just drink, it'll help you feel better."

Nevaeh sniffled. "I just want everything to go away."

"It will," Christina said. "We'll fix this."

Nevaeh took the shot glass and was relieved to find that it was in fact just water going through her system. She'd made mistake after mistake all night. In a span of a few hours, she'd sent photos to a boy who she'd believed loved her, only to discover that he was a viral social media prank star navigating three different affairs.

How could Nevaeh have given her heart away so easily? And for what? For Thomas to film her at her most vulnerable, for him to lure and tease her into doing something she'd known deep down in her spirit felt wrong to her, and for the whole world to watch.

"How many views did the video get, again?" she asked.

"Don't worry about it," Heather said. She'd taken on the self-proclaimed task of reporting the video from different accounts with the hopes that it would be taken down. But so far, they hadn't had any luck. The video was still up and it was only a matter of time before it got around to the congregation. For once, Nevaeh was glad the service had gone on so late. At least that would mean her family would be sleeping through Nevaeh's un-making.

"Please. Let me see it, Heather. I have to know."

Christina and Heather exchanged looks. Reluctantly, Heather handed her phone to Nevaeh.

On the Tommy Harding account, the livestream had disappeared the moment the live ended, which Nevaeh was beyond grateful for. But the evidence of Thomas's cheating remained pinned to the account page. It had more than fifteen thousand views already and the number was only climbing. Nevaeh clicked it again and watched, mortified all over again as texts and photos between her and Thomas were exposed to the internet while his conversations with two other girls followed. There was the girl who'd been caught kissing Thomas in the hotel room during their trip. That girl was a costar of Tommy's, Nevaeh had learned. She was gorgeous and feisty and charming and was a social media influencer herself with a growing following. And then there was the other girl. The girl who Thomas had sworn his love to. Kiara.

She was in almost every video posted on Thomas's channel.

Watch me braid my girlfriend's hair.

Watch me pretend I have amnesia to my girlfriend.

Watch me bake a cake for my girlfriend's birthday.

Watch me help my girlfriend with her college applications.

On and on the posts went. It dawned on Nevaeh then that she recognized this girl, not just from the videos on Thomas's accounts, but in person. Hadn't they met just hours before, in the hotel lobby? Chelsea and Heather had been trying to sneak out of the conference while Nevaeh had stayed behind. And this girl, Kiara, she'd covered for them when Nevaeh's father had almost spotted the two girls. Nevaeh clicked through each video; somehow, she hoped to find something to dispel her current reality. But the pieces all lined up. This was the girl from earlier, and Thomas, or Tommy, or whatever he went by, had claimed her to the world.

Even though she never seemed to smile in his videos, even though her gaze seemed to travel to another boy who sometimes made appearances in footage filmed at Thomas's home, it was clear that this girl was Thomas's girlfriend, and Nevaeh herself was—she couldn't bear to finish the thought. With her eyes pressed shut, she handed Heather back her phone. It was hard to fight tears at this point. After vomiting when they'd exited the locker room, Nevaeh had been inconsolable. Now the tears fell again.

"It's all right," Christina said. "It's going to be okay."

The words felt so empty. Nevaeh knew Christina meant well, but right now, she just wanted to be alone.

Before she could voice her thoughts, though, Nevaeh's phone buzzed. Again. The text message was from another unsolicited number.

[Unknown]: Skank.

Nevaeh deleted it. She realized then that there was a slew of messages and they were all from different numbers and different people.

[Unknown]: Kiara deserved better.

Clout chaser.

[Unknown]: Unalive yourself.

How the last person had the presence of mind enough to censor their death wish yet still send it anyway, Nevaeh didn't know.

The text messages didn't stop coming. And then her phone rang again, this time from another number. And another. And another.

"Forget this," Heather said. "Block all of those numbers and we'll try to reach the app's customer support to get that post of you taken off."

"But it wasn't me," Nevaeh said. "The girl in the video was wearing a mask—you couldn't even see her face. And the costumes, like, there were so many of them. Maybe someone just wore the same one I did."

Nevaeh didn't even know where the lie came from, yet somehow, there was a desperate fire igniting within her to prove that she wasn't the girl in the post. Because the real Nevaeh would never have done such a thing. The good Nevaeh would be in her hotel, reading through scripture and getting ready for the next day of worship.

"It's okay. We aren't judging you."

Nevaeh laughed. She knew the sound was maniacal. Twisted, even.

"Why would you be judging me? You're the reason I even came here in the first place. If it wasn't for you, I never would have tried to meet him in public. I never would have degraded myself like this."

"I mean, you made your choice," Heather said. "You sent those photos."

"Choice? You call this a choice?" Nevaeh wiped away tears, but still they just kept falling. "I wanted to stay in the hotel. And you kept pressuring me and pressuring me. And he—he promised. He said all these things. But it's my fault? Because I trusted you. Because I trusted him. It's my fault?"

She closed her eyes. Maybe the person who'd sent her the death wish was right. Maybe if she just stayed like this, Nevaeh would sink into the oblivion and never emerge.

"Just leave me alone," she whispered. "Please. I just want to be alone right now."

Christina looked hesitant. But when Heather whispered something in her ear, she nodded.

"We'll get you some more water. When you calm down, we can head back to the hotel."

Nevaeh didn't respond as the two girls left. She was too busy rejecting all of the phone calls from strangers who wanted to bash and tear her apart. She swore as, in her haste, she accidentally accepted a call. It was the number form earlier, the one that had asked Nevaeh to identify herself in the account's videos.

"If you want me to unalive myself, don't worry, I might as well be dead as it is!" she shouted. And then she hung up. But the number contacted her again, this time with a text.

[Unknown]: We're not trying to insult you or pile on. We know what you're going through. We want to help.

Nevaeh frowned. Wiping more tears away, she texted back.

Naveah: Who are you?

Three dots appeared on the message screen. Then the number answered.

[Unknown]: We're the other girls. Tommy lied to us too.

Nevaeh couldn't believe it. There was no way. There was no way. But then the number called again, and this time, instead of hanging up, Nevaeh answered it and waited.

"Nevaeh?" the voice on the other end said. It was different from the first one, softer, almost more understanding.

"Kiara?" Nevaeh guessed, and she could almost imagine the soft smile on the other girl's face, knowing Nevaeh had recognized her.

It must have been all those videos Nevaeh had binged of Tommy playing pranks on his girlfriend, or the kindness in Kiara's voice, a gentle reminder of hours before when she had helped Nevaeh even though she was a stranger. Whatever it was, the last strength holding back the final current of Nevaeh's tears melted away, and suddenly she was sobbing and confessing her heart to two strangers.

"I can't believe he posted that. I can't believe he would do that to me. And there's more. There's more things I had sent, from some months ago—for his birthday. He'd asked me. I thought it would make him happy. It's the only reason why I ever did it. But he was just toying with me and using me, and if they get out—I don't know what I'll do."

"We're in the park right now," Kiara said, "Where are you?"

"Wh-why?"

"We need to make a plan. We need to figure out how to fix this mess."

Nevaeh sniffed. For the first time since she'd snuck into the park that night, she looked around at her surroundings. The bench she was perched on was secluded, but not too far in the distance there was a huge, tunnel-shaped building that advertised itself as "The Lovers' Gondola."

"I'm near the gondola ride," Nevaeh said. "Near one of its entrances."

"We'll come to you. Stay there. We're sorry. You shouldn't be going through this."

"None of us should," another voice said, the same one from the first call. Priscilla, Nevaeh determined.

"All right. I'll wait here."

The call ended. Nevaeh wondered in silence when the two girls would arrive and if anything would possibly get better upon the three of them meeting. When her phone chimed again, Nevaeh thought it was Kiara and Priscilla. Except the message wasn't from the two girls or even the strangers spewing hatred at her. No. It was worse.

It was from Tommy.

Thomas: Are you ok?

Nevaeh couldn't believe it. *Now* he was texting her? Now, after everything, he was messaging, even though she'd called and called when the video had first gone up but he hadn't bothered to answer? She hit the video call icon on her phone, but Tommy rejected it.

Tommy: I can't now. There are too many people watching.

Nevaeh wiped away more tears. Her hands trembled as she typed and deleted and tried again to put her scrambled thoughts, her pain, her hurt, her betrayal into words. Yet all she could manage was one plea.

Nevaeh: Please. Delete all of the photos I ever sent you.
Please Thomas. Please. I'm begging you.
Thomas: I was hacked.
Nevaeh: I don't care. Delete them. Please. If you care about me at all, if you really love me like you say you did, just delete them forever before the hacker can post them.

For a moment, Thomas didn't answer. Panic began to spill through Nevaeh, but then the familiar ding of a notification went off on her phone as his message appeared.

Thomas: When I see you, I'll explain everything.

Nevaeh texted him back with a frantic haste that was all-consuming.

Nevaeh: Thomas please.
Thomas: Just meet me at the fun house in half an hour. You can take my phone and delete the messages directly from there so you know they're really gone. I just want us to talk first. You're my saint. You're the only thing that keeps me away from the dark.

Nevaeh tried to remind herself that these were lies, the same sweet talk that he'd used so often to coerce things from her. She shouldn't want to talk to Thomas. She shouldn't want to be his saint. Nevaeh should want to be the daughter her family and the church could love. But for so long, Thomas had been the embodiment of all of Nevaeh's wishes and secret desires. He'd promised her forever. She'd given him every piece of herself in exchange.

In that moment, something tugged at Nevaeh's heart. She wanted the photos gone. He could give that to her. And Nevaeh would make him give her more.

All the vows he had made, every intimate moment they'd shared, bound them to each other irrevocably. It wouldn't be in vain. Nevaeh wouldn't let it.

chapter thirteen

Kiara

KIARA AND PRISCILLA were nearly at the gondola ride when Nevaeh messaged saying that she was heading back to her hotel. She didn't want closure, her text claimed. She didn't want to meet the other two girls. Nevaeh just wanted things to be over.

But Kiara couldn't help the pang of worry that throbbed in her chest as she read Nevaeh's message.

"Do you think she's okay?" Kiara asked Priscilla. "She sounded so heartbroken on the phone. This feels out of nowhere."

"Yeah," Priscilla said. "Almost like she'd been talking to Tommy."

Kiara wrapped her arms around herself. Without streetlights, Priscilla had taken to using her phone's flashlight. Its bright glow cast an ominous shadow of their figures in the corner of the park where they had wandered to.

"What do you mean?" Kiara asked.

"It's Tommy," Priscilla said. "You don't think he's not already making calls and doing damage control? He probably reached out to her and sweet-talked her. Maybe they're even meeting in the park as we speak."

"She won't actually fall for it, though. Right?"

But the thing was, neither of them knew Nevaeh. Maybe she was the kind of girl who'd take Tommy back, no matter the situation. Priscilla too seemed to weigh the possibility. Yet as they stood in silence, a dark gleam sparked in Priscilla's eyes, and when she spoke, bitterness tinged her words.

"We should get revenge."

Kiara stared at Priscilla, waiting for an explanation.

"He's probably gonna use her to fix his image," Priscilla said. "Tommy played us. Both of us. And people need to know the truth. I'm not a boyfriend stealer and I know you're just as messed up about this situation as I am. Of all of us, he betrayed you the most."

Kiara laughed.

"That's an understatement," she said. Yet when Kiara looked up from her own phone, she saw that Priscilla was filming. For her channel. On live.

"You can't be serious."

But Priscilla wasn't listening.

"You heard it from Kiara Stephens herself. I'm not a boyfriend stealer. Tommy and I were strictly professional," she said, speaking to her audience. "And we're going to get to the bottom of whoever hacked his account and is slandering my name. I promise, guys."

It was almost as if Kiara was the one living in a fictional world, one where people like Priscilla and Tommy could defy the rules of reality as they bent and twisted the truth to suit their needs.

How did they define "strictly professional"? Was it holding hands during their prank videos, their gazes lingering moments past when the filming ended while Kiara watched with nervous knots in her stomach and pretended that the intimacy they displayed on camera didn't bother her? Kiara was over Tommy. She was done with him. But what she was not going to do was to keep gaslighting herself into believing that any of the on- and off-screen flirting she'd witnessed between Tommy and Priscilla was suddenly okay now that it was clear that he was a certified asshole. And Priscilla herself—Kiara could have laughed out loud. Clearly, she wanted to do as much damage control as Tommy did.

Priscilla began her sign-off from the live. Before she could finish, Kiara grabbed Priscilla's phone.

On-screen, thousands of viewers were already tuned in to the live.

"Your beauty princess is fake," Kiara said, "just like the crappy bootlegged brands she sells to you."

Before Kiara could say anything else, Priscilla grabbed her phone back and ended the live.

"Excuse you!" Priscilla snapped. "Do you know what you just did?"

As if Kiara cared. She wasn't going to be a doormat anymore. Kiara wasn't going to let people like Tommy or Priscilla twist and bend her to their own ends or hold her back. Not now, and never again.

"Screw all of you," Kiara said.

And then she left. Without another word, Kiara marched in the opposite direction, away from Priscilla, Tommy, Nevaeh, and whatever twisted mess they'd probably end up with.

Most of the senior class had already trickled out of the park, and there were just a few stragglers remaining to continue partying. She searched the crowd, pushing past bodies and pulling off masks as she scanned the park for the one person she wanted to see now, more than anything.

There, laughing amid a small gathering of their classmates at the drinks table, Kiara found him.

The costume he had changed into was a white button-down that he wore completely unbuttoned, exposing his toned chest, and camo swim trunks. Ebony hair fell softy against his face, partially obscuring his eyes. Kiara's heart hammered in her chest.

"Hi," she said.

"Hi," Jason answered. He clenched his fist and unclenched it, seemingly torn about what to say. "I've been looking for you," he said finally.

"I've been looking for you too," Kiara admitted. But she couldn't meet his gaze. Not yet. So instead, Kiara focused on the bottle of booze in his other hand.

"Can I have some?"

"I think you've had enough." His words were clouded with worry. "You don't even like drinking."

"Yeah, and where has that gotten me?"

Jason laughed. "Uh, senior class president, honor roll, Ivy League contender?"

"Semi-Ivy," Kiara corrected.

He couldn't have said a worse thing in the moment. The video from the hacker had thousands of views. And it was only going more viral by the minute. Forget graduation or college. Forget her crumbling future.

"Just pass it over," Kiara said, holding out a hand.

Tentatively, Jason relented, but he tried to reach for it back when Kiara nearly downed the remainder of the drink.

"Not so much," he said. "Did you even eat today?"

"I'll be fine," Kiara said. But the strength of the liquor hit her then. The back of her throat burned and it was as if a haze was beginning to fall over her. They sat on a bench and Kiara finished the rest of the drink. Time passed. Everything felt like a blurry haze.

Kiara stood, but the ground moved beneath her. She was saved from the likely concussion that would have occurred as Jason caught her in his arms.

"I told you, you're a lightweight."

"And you're sexy." Kiara gasped and covered her mouth. "I didn't mean to say that."

Red colored Jason's skin. The warmth of him made Kiara's chest flutter and her heart hum. Tears pricked her eyes.

"I wish I had chosen you," she whispered.

Jason swallowed. His mouth looked so soft. And his lashes. Why did guys always have to have such long lashes? Then there were his dimples. Kiara wanted to press her lips against them both.

"Only a little bit," Kiara said.

"What?"

Kiara shook her head. "I was talking to myself."

Jason brushed his hand against her cheek and ran his fingers along the round corners of her nose, but his gaze traveled to Kiara's neck, where the necklace Tommy had bought her still hung.

And before she could ramble any further, before reality could set and the repercussions of that night could rear their heads, Kiara leaned forward and closed the distance between them.

Their lips brushed, gently at first, tentative and clumsy, like they were stumbling in the dark, searching and searching until they could find the rhythm where their lips and their tongues and their hands could discover, embrace, consume.

Behind them, someone whistled. The sound was the start of hoots and hollers that began to fill the air.

Jason pulled away. It was like the oxygen had been ripped from Kiara's chest. He smiled.

"Let's find a quieter place."

Kiara nodded in agreement. But before they left, she filled her arms with half-drunk bottles nearby on the ground.

At least this way, Kiara would have something to blame her future regrets on—something besides herself.

how it's going

chapter fourteen

Kiara

EVERYTHING WAS A blur. Pain ripped through Kiara's forehead and fire burned her eyelids as they fluttered apart. She didn't know what it might be like to wake from the dead, but she felt close to it. It was as if her whole body had been yanked from a restful slumber into the electric realm of the living. She tried to pull herself up, and the world below her jolted violently.

"Jason?" she whispered. "Tommy?"

Instinctively, Kiara reached for her neck. But when her fingers searched for the necklace Tommy had given her, they found bare skin. She didn't remember taking it off. But then again, she didn't remember anything. There was the fight with Tommy, the viral post from the hacker, Priscilla and Nevaeh, and then Jason, holding her in his arms, Jason kissing her like he was making up for every second and every minute they had missed pretending that their friendship would ever be enough for the two of them. They'd parted sometime after, and Kiara's heart had ached for him. But other than that, everything else was blank.

"Jason?" she said again.

Kiara made to stand, but something cut into her bare palms.

Blood trickled down her fingertips. Glass. There was glass all over the ground, broken and shattered, small pieces and a huge gaping chunk in the wall. Thirty different versions of Kiara peered back at her in the cracked reflective surfaces. She closed her eyes, wishing these other versions of herself away. But when she opened her eyes again, the other Kiaras were there still. So too were the fractured images in the wall where the glass had shattered. Realization hit Kiara then.

She was in a fun house. Not just any fun house, but the one in Sunny World. The problem was, Kiara couldn't remember how or why she'd gone there in the first place.

Slowly, slowly, she rose to standing. Kiara wrapped her arms around herself, searching for an exit and finding two. One path led deeper into the fun house, and the other seemed to lead out. Kiara took the second one. As she emerged into the still-dark scene of the early hours of the morning, she spotted another figure leaving the fun house from the other exit.

The girl was dressed in a two-piece miniskirt and crop top. On her back, a set of angel wings gleamed against the dim light of the early morning.

"Nevaeh?" Kiara whispered.

The girl froze. The morning was silent enough that Kiara's voice rung clear into the day.

"I know you're there," Kiara said, louder this time. She cringed at the sound of her own voice, which was somehow too loud and quiet all at once for her throbbing head. "You won't just disappear if you don't answer."

When still the girl didn't answer or move, Kiara approached her. But it wasn't until she put a hand on the girl's shoulder that Kiara realized her mistake.

Beneath the half mask and the silver wig the girl wore, it wasn't Nevaeh staring back at Kiara. It was Priscilla.

Instinctively, Kiara pulled her hand back. As she opened her mouth to ask why Priscilla was dressed in the same costume Nevaeh had worn the night before, her gaze caught on a thumbprint-like mark on the other girl's skin, and she fell silent.

Dark, purple bruises lined Priscilla's bare arm. There were scratches on her neck too, thin and haunting, like scorch lines cut into her skin by fingernails. And then there was Priscilla's face. A purple bruise marked her chin on the lower right.

Kiara gasped, covering her mouth in horror.

"Don't look at me like that," Priscilla said with a hiss. "Don't you dare."

She didn't bother to explain any further. She just kept walking and walking and Kiara trailed after her, afraid to be alone, afraid to leave Priscilla in the state she was in. Instead of heading to the Sunny World exit, the other girl led them back to the same employee locker rooms where they'd dressed the night before.

Kiara had half expected the place to be a mess after last night. Yet somehow, every sign that a party had taken place was gone. There were no Solo cups on the ground, no wrappers or missing articles of clothing to be spotted. The makeshift dressing room was back to its original condition. The only sign of last night's events were the costumes shoved back into a box instead of the original packaging they'd come in. Priscilla searched through the lockers and found the outfit she'd worn to the park before they changed. Not knowing what else to do, Kiara did the same. It didn't take long for her to find the slacks and blouse she'd worn to the meeting with Ren. There was a garbage chute that led deep into the crevices of the park. The two girls tossed their costumes down it, with Priscilla pulling off the wig and the mask and break-ing down the set of angel wings before shoving them down the chute, where they landed in the incinerator with a loud thump. Then Priscilla grabbed a hoodie and a pair of sunglasses.

"Why were you dressed as Nevaeh?" Kiara whispered.

Priscilla stiffened. She seemed to consider the question for a moment. But then something hardened in her.

"Why did you spend the night at the fun house?" she asked instead of answering.

"I . . ." Kiara blinked back the memory of the night before. But all she could focus on was the shattered glass at her feet and the missing necklace Tommy had given her.

When Kiara didn't answer, Priscilla gave her a smug, know-ing look.

"We were never here this morning," she said. "Okay?"

It wasn't the response Kiara was looking for. But if she interro-gated Priscilla further, Kiara knew she'd have to explain her own presence in the park this late.

Gritting her teeth, Kiara just nodded along.

When the rideshare they booked arrived a block away from the park, they slipped inside, not speaking as they drove away from the haunting metal skeleton of the theme park.

KIARA AND PRISCILLA snuck into their shared room when they arrived back at the hotel. Luckily, their school chaperones weren't awake yet. The moment the door lock clicked behind them, Kiara passed out on her bed, while Priscilla hurried to the bathroom. The steady rush of water streaming through the shower head lulled Kiara to sleep.

Dreams of fractured light and shattered glass filled Kiara's nightmares. She saw Tommy standing there in the fun house waiting for her, chasing her, calling her name over and over again. Sweat drenched Kiara's forehead and her body lurched with pain.

She woke, gasping and clutching her sweat-stained sheets to the sound of banging on her door. In the bed across the room, Priscilla stirred. She must have tried to get some rest too, after her shower.

"Can you get the door?" Priscilla moaned. "Please?"

"Yeah, okay."

Priscilla pulled the sheets back over her face, but in the process, Kiara caught a glimpse of her again. The bruises that had once covered her body were gone. Except for the slight trace of a bruise along her chin, Priscilla's skin looked all but perfect.

The transformation was to be expected from the princess of makeup. Yet still Kiara couldn't shake the eerie feeling beginning to overtake her.

She shook it off though and composed herself enough to open the door. On the other side of it, their chaperone stood.

Mr. Phillips was a retired almost-pro hockey player with a giant build, a graying mustache, and a usually chill disposition. He was also coach of the track team, which Kiara had been a part of since freshman year, one of her many, many extracurricular activities.

"Everyone line up. Now," he said. "We're conducting mandatory attendance."

He spun on his heel, marching to the next door, repeating the same cryptic instructions without answering any questions. Other chaperones knocked on doors too. Soon, the hallway filled with half-asleep seniors lining up with pajamas and face strips still on.

"What's going on?" Priscilla asked, joining Kiara at the door.

"I don't know."

They joined their classmates out in the hallway and slipped inside the line that had begun to form. As one group of chaperones continued knocking on doors, their science teacher Mrs. Kenzie conducted roll call with a clipboard.

"Emily Mason?"

"Here."

"Sandra Peters?"

"Here."

On and on it went. Kiara and Priscilla both answered when their names were called. The whole thing felt endless. But there were two names that remained unaccounted for.

Kiara turned to Leah, whose room was right next to theirs.

"Do you know where Jason is?" Kiara asked.

"I think he's still with the police."

"The police?" Kiara repeated. Her heart jolted. What were the police doing here?

Leah pointed down the hall to a master suite that their chaperones had been using to oversee operations of the class trip. There, a group of officers was filing in and out of the door.

"I think it's Tommy," Leah said.

"What?"

"They're saying he's missing."

Kiara and Priscilla exchanged looks. But Kiara couldn't hold Priscilla's gaze long, not when the memory of waking up in the fun house loomed like a cloud above her. Fear gnawed at Kiara.

"Missing how?" Priscilla said, speaking the question that Kiara herself was too afraid to ask. "Like, they can't find him in his room?"

"Missing like he never came back from the park last night," Leah answered. "At least, that's what some people are saying. The roll call is to see if anyone else is gone too, I think."

A few students emerged from the room with the officers. Kiara's head still throbbed from the hangover, but faintly she realized Alex was one of them.

A few feet behind Alex, two officers and school chaperones followed. Behind them, Jason appeared.

He looked pale, shaken. Kiara had never seen Jason look so . . . haunted. When their eyes met, she looked away. But Jason was already heading toward her. Two of the officers joined him, and so did Mr. Phillips.

"What's going on?" Priscilla asked for the second time.

"Do you think they found Tommy?" Leah asked.

Jason didn't meet their gaze. But when he spoke, it was as if the words were directed for Kiara and Kiara alone.

"He was near the fun house," Jason said. "They found him this morning."

Relief flooded Kiara. Of course Tommy would complicate things. He wouldn't have just left the park after being humiliated in front of his three point three million fans. Maybe he'd stayed to film content for his channel? Maybe he'd stayed and hooked up with Nevaeh or some other girl after all.

"Did he say what he was doing there so late?" Priscilla asked, giving no hint that either she or Kiara had also been in the park into the early hours of the morning.

But a haunting veil clouded Jason's eyes, and even though his lips parted to answer, the words that came seemed to be yanked out by force.

"He's dead," Jason said. "Tommy's dead."

chapter fifteen

Priscilla

WORDS WERE SUPPOSED to be intangible. They were supposed to exist in a separate realm without matter or strength to inflict pain. And yet, the moment Tommy's stepbrother uttered those two sentences, something inside Priscilla crumpled.

He's dead. Tommy's dead.

Fragmented memories of the night before churned through Priscilla: Tommy's hands around her neck; her fingers clawing for release; her lungs laboring for air, gasping, and aching until even the thought of oxygen seemed fleeting. Then, blackness.

She couldn't bring herself to play back the full turn of events from that night. Not with how things had ended. She'd only wanted to give Tommy a taste of his own medicine. That's why she'd dressed up as Nevaeh to meet him. Priscilla had been so angry about the posts, angry about his lies and the realization that there was another girl. Even after his promise to break up with Kiara for her, Tommy had lied to Priscilla. She wasn't the exception to the rule. Priscilla was just another statistic in the girls-who'd-gotten-played-by-Tommy epidemic. But instead of accepting her fate to be another side chick, Priscilla had gotten payback.

She wanted Tommy to feel even a fraction of the hurt that consumed her. She wanted him to face the truth of what his lies had done. But everything had gone so wrong. Priscilla had seen another side of Tommy that night, a side that was violent and hateful. His reaction to learning that Priscilla had been impersonating Nevaeh was terrifying. She'd fought him off and only just managed to escape into another part of the fun house. Sometime after the fight with Tommy, Priscilla had woken in a dark alcove. When she'd stumbled out of the fun house, she'd run into Kiara.

And now Tommy was dead.

This couldn't be real. This couldn't be happening.

What Priscilla had done was in self-defense. Tommy had been alive after she'd left him. Priscilla was sure she'd heard his footsteps chasing after her. But if the police interrogated her, would they really believe that? Would anyone, if they knew how things had unfolded?

Panicked tears welled in Priscilla's eyes. They fell in steady streams. She needed an alibi. She needed something to remove any connection she had with Tommy from that night.

Behind Jason, one of their school chaperones seemed to soften at Priscilla's sobs.

If only they knew the truth.

"The investigation is still ongoing," Mr. Phillips said. "Right now, the thinking is that it was an accident. But local officers are still trying to rule out foul play."

An accident. Relief flooded through Priscilla at the words.

"So they're still investigating everything?" she asked.

"He just said that," Leah said. She'd been crying too, but Priscilla knew Leah's tears were of mourning.

"It's our understanding that many of you were in Sunny World after the park had closed," Mr. Phillips said, placing a hand on Jason's shoulder as if to be clear that the adults would take things from here. "Mr. Harding had a concoction of drugs and alcohol in his system, substances that were prohibited on this trip and shouldn't have been anywhere near the park. Considering the circumstances and the ongoing investigation, we'll be conducting interviews with you all in groups so the police and the school can have a clear accounting of last night's events. We are also asking that all students submit any videos or photos, or anything from that night to the administration and the police for review."

Priscilla and Kiara exchanged looks.

"There are already quite a few videos online that we've been gathering. Better share it with us now before we find something that might get you all in trouble. Not for the death, of course," he added quickly at the look of concern on everyone's faces. "But for trespassing and underage drinking, as well as drug use." Mr. Phillips sighed and rubbed his head. When he spoke again, anger radiated in his voice. "This senior class is an embarrassment to our school and our district. If it weren't for the current investigation, we'd review whether or not expulsion is in order. All actions are being considered."

"That's not fair!" The words came from a boy who Priscilla hadn't even known was in their senior class until she'd spotted him on the plane to Sunny World just the previous morning. "Not all of us were out last night," he said. "Some of us were watching movies and playing board games."

It was pretty brave of the person to admit to not having an actual social life in front of the whole senior class. Past Priscilla would have never been caught dead making such an embarrassing admission, even if she hadn't been at the party in Sunny World last night. But then again, Past Priscilla's need for outside validation was pretty much what landed her in this mess in the first place.

"He's right," another person said. "Aren't there, like, cameras in Sunny World?"

"Unfortunately, there was a system error and the footage from the park isn't available," Mr. Phillips said. "The park and law enforcement will get to the bottom of what happened last night, both with the investigation and the illegal breaking and entering."

Rumbles filled the hallway as everyone began speculating about all of the things they'd just learned in the last few moments.

"Now," Mr. Phillips continued, "we'll combine you in groups according to your hotel rooms. No one leaves this floor unless escorted by a chaperone. We'll have some groups taken downstairs for the breakfast buffet, which was part of this trip, while others talk to the police. There are a few camera crews and reporters around. It would be to your advantage to avoid talking to them or anyone from the news media at this time."

The officers whispered something to Mr. Phillips and he nodded before reassigning chaperones to groups and instructing the seniors to gather according to their rooms. Some of the friends Priscilla had in her other classes ended up with Mrs. Hall, an art teacher whose classes Priscilla had always enjoyed. Priscilla was sure they were in the clear until Mr. Phillips cornered her and Kiara before they went to their room. He was joined by Jason and the officer who had escorted him out of the interrogation room.

"Kiara Stephens and Priscilla Frimpong?" the officer asked.

The girls nodded.

"We'll need you two to come to the interrogation room."

Kiara's eyes widened. Priscilla felt like she was about to vomit then and there. She needed to think. Fast. Something to give her more time to come up with a story that wouldn't have the police questioning Tommy's accident further or wrapping her up in it.

"Kiara just found out her boyfriend died," Priscilla said. She turned to Mr. Phillips pleadingly. "Can we at least get a minute?"

"Your connection with Tommy is exactly why we want to meet now," the officer said, though Mr. Phillips looked more sympathetic. "Don't think of it as an interrogation. We just want to talk and map out the events of last night."

"Can they at least clean themselves up?" Mr. Phillips asked. "Getting woken up this early in the morning with news like this—it wouldn't be easy for anyone."

"Tommy was Kiara's boyfriend. And he and I were like best friends," Priscilla said. "This whole situation is just—it's devastating. Ten minutes. Just give us ten minutes to put ourselves together."

To Priscilla's surprise, Kiara nodded.

"We just want to shower and call our parents," she whispered, but her voice was on the brink of tears.

The input from Kiara seemed to be just the right one to shift the mood.

"The floors are on lockdown," Mr. Phillips said. "They're not going anywhere. And didn't you say there were some other students who you wanted to talk to soon?"

The officer sighed. "Fine," he said. "Fifteen minutes. After that, we'll be back here, sharp."

As Mr. Phillips and the officers left, Priscilla and Kiara made their way back to their room. Priscilla was about to close the door behind her when Jason slipped inside.

"What are you doing?" she snapped.

But he wasn't here for her. Priscilla figured that piece out quickly. Kiara whispered Jason's name as if she were holding her breath and only the utterance of those syllables would give her oxygen.

"Kiara," he said, whispering in turn.

The other girl's lashes were dotted with tears. Unlike Priscilla's tears, Kiara's must be ones of loss. She'd just lost her boyfriend, after all.

Jason pulled Kiara into a hug, and the two held each other so tightly that Priscilla swore they'd break if they let go.

Priscilla's eyes narrowed, her guilt swiftly replaced by suspicion. Unless Tommy's death had shaken them so much that their grief was what was pulling them together, something must have happened between them last night in the park and that morning to make them okay with so obviously showcasing their feelings for each other. Priscilla tucked that realization in the back of her mind to reexamine in the future.

"I'm sorry," Kiara said. "Jason, I'm so sorry."

Jason brushed her tears away. The gesture was so tender, so intimate, that Priscilla had to look away.

"If you guys don't mind," she said, "I'm going to shower and change." This was a lie. Priscilla had already done both when Kiara had gone to sleep that morning. The hot shower had stung against the wounded skin on Priscilla's body, but she'd scrubbed and scrubbed as if she could wash away remnants of last night in the park from her memory. After finishing, Priscilla had been forced to actually use the makeup samples her sponsors had given her.

She'd used the foundations and blushes to paint away the marks on her skin before sinking into a deep, terrible sleep. Three hours had barely passed before the chaperones had woken them up with the announcement. Priscilla was exhausted. If she could sneak in a nap, maybe she'd be able to clear her thoughts and piece together the fallout between her and Tommy before Mr. Phillips and the officers returned.

Instead of asking Jason to leave, though, Priscilla grabbed her pillow and blanket. If she had to, she'd sleep in the shower.

Just as Priscilla was about to climb in, Jason spoke.

"They found a phone on him."

The words stopped Priscilla in her tracks. She placed her hand on the doorknob, pretending not to listen.

"But it wasn't Tommy's," Jason said. "They're not sure who it belongs to."

"Do you think it's the burner phone?" Kiara asked. "Maybe he finally found it."

"Maybe he was filming a prank on his own with it when he died," Priscilla said. She'd given up the pretense that she wasn't eavesdropping on their conversation.

"He and—" Priscilla paused. Something told Priscilla that including Alex in the conversation might not be the best idea. "Tommy did say he was going to do some epic prank, remember? Maybe that's what happened."

None of them said it, but knowing Tommy, he'd definitely be one of the few people in the world who would put himself in harm's way for social media fame.

But Kiara shook her head. "That locker room livestream was the prank he'd been planning on filming."

"You don't think he'd try to film something new as a PR

stunt after getting canceled for the locker room thing?" Priscilla countered. "Maybe he thought doing something bigger, something that could make him seem like a victim instead, would make everyone forgive him. We used to use that strategy all the time."

She didn't have to remind them of the times Tommy had orchestrated stunt pranks where he'd end up with a broken arm or leg to distract the public from canceling him. Instead of critiquing Tommy for the terrible thing he'd just done or holding him accountable, the conversation would somehow always shift to how Tommy just never seemed to know how far too far was.

"Yeah. That sounds about right," Jason said. His voice sounded detached, emotionless. "Make sure to tell that to the police when they call you in to interview. If Tommy was filming something and things went wrong, then—then I'm sure it'll help them close this whole messed-up situation faster."

"Do you know what kind of questions they'll ask?"

Jason frowned. "What do you mean?"

"Well, didn't they interrogate you already?" Priscilla asked.

"Yeah, since I'm his stepbrother. But it wasn't really like an interrogation. It was more informing me and our parents about what happened and asking if I knew anything," Jason said. "They were really thorough. I'll give them that."

"Yeah, and I'm sure they'll be thorough and really great listeners when it comes to me and Kiara's turns," Priscilla said.

As if the police wouldn't already have a set narrative in their minds once they talked to Tommy's ex-girlfriend and one of his two side chicks. The reality dawned on Priscilla then. From Kiara's wide-eyed reaction to Priscilla's words, she too seemed to realize the severity of their situation.

Both girls had been two of the last to leave the fun house.

Priscilla knew it didn't look good that she and Tommy had fought the night before. But if he had still been alive to chase after her, had he come across anyone else in the fun house that night?

"You were the last person to see Tommy last night," Priscilla lied, turning to face Kiara when she asked the question. "Remember? You two were arguing in the crowd. Did you see him after you broke up with him?"

"No," Kiara said, "I didn't."

But she wouldn't meet Priscilla's gaze. And she kept fidgeting as she answered, her hands grasping at something on her neck that wasn't there.

Suspicion churned through Priscilla. But she didn't interrogate Kiara further. Instead, Priscilla picked up her phone, wondering what the internet was saying now that its most hated prank star was dead. The people posting online were probably having a field day with the news that Tommy Harding had died just hours after being exposed as a cheating, lying, creepy asshole.

Instead, when Priscilla logged on, the trending hashtag for Tommy had made him a martyr.

Images of Tommy's face filled her news feed.

Tommy's only mission in life was spreading laughter.

The prank king who flew too close to the sun.

Justice for Tommy Harding.

Priscilla dropped her phone. She'd never had a nervous breakdown before, but every inch of her was trembling.

"Are you all right?" Kiara asked. "Priscilla, you look like you've just seen a ghost."

But Priscilla had. The ghost of Tommy was there, sneering at her from the digital netherworld, just like he had been the night before.

In the curve of his smile, in the gleam of his eyes, and the repeated image of Tommy from thousands of pages, he seemed to be laughing at Priscilla, like this was just another one of his jokes.

And just as always, Tommy's punch line was the person on the other side of the screen.

chapter sixteen

Nevaeh

THE POLICE WERE everywhere. Nevaeh was afraid to even breathe the wrong way as they escorted her into the hotel lobby, along with the rest of the tourists returning from the theme park.

Amid the crowd, she caught pieces of conversations: *Accident. Prank gone wrong. Body in the park. Tommy Harding.*

The officers divided the flow of traffic. Some tourists were told to take elevators, others waited in the lobby and near the elevator bank, while those who wanted to take the stairs were directed separately.

"If you weren't present in the vicinity of the body, you can go directly to your rooms," one of the officers said. "But if you were a Sunny World tourist or employee in the fun house, or any of the tunnels connecting it to the gondola ride, we're going to need your statement."

Nevaeh tensed. She knew she was being paranoid. She had changed back into the outfit she'd worn into the park last night, but she still had the outfit Heather had given her. She'd worn it under the dress she'd worn into the park. As for the horns and wings, she'd thrown them into a bush somewhere in the hotel entrance. Last night had been a mistake. A nightmare.

Just hours before, Nevaeh had been in Sunny World. She'd been on her way to meet Tommy, yes. But she'd texted Kiara and Priscilla that she'd changed her mind and was going home. And Nevaeh had tried to get home. Really. But she quickly realized that she'd gotten locked in the park. Nevaeh had wandered its premises for hours, looking for an exit. She'd ended up staying the night there until morning came and the shuttles to and from the park to Sunny World's hotels had started running again.

But now, Tommy was dead.

What if word came out that Nevaeh and he were supposed to meet that night? If the police found the discarded bits of the costume she had been wearing, if they began searching through the park . . . Nevaeh shook her head, refusing to let her thoughts wander in the direction it was headed. From the corner of her eye, she watched as officers escorted a group of students on their senior trip to a different elevator bank than the rest of the tourists.

Nevaeh recognized the students as some of Kiara's and Priscilla's classmates. If anything, the police would be questioning them. Tommy's classmates had been the ones with him in the park, after all. Nevaeh had nothing to worry about. She should just relax and act normal.

"I'm going to say this again, one last time. If you were in the vicinity of the body or if you spoke to or saw Mr. Harding before his passing, we're going to need you to go to an officer in one of the locations we set up. But if you were among the park visitors who were just entering for the day when the body was found, you are free to go to your hotel rooms."

Whispers trickled through the crowd, and slowly it began to dissolve as a majority of the people who'd been completely unaware when Tommy's body had been found began to make their way back to their hotel rooms. There were only one or two who remained: a Sunny World worker and an unsuspecting tourist who'd ventured into the fun house attraction minutes before the body had been found.

Part of Nevaeh wanted to stay, just to see if she could overhear what the person's account might be. But the other part of Nevaeh, the part that had screamed at Tommy and raked her nails through his pockets in search of his phone last night, knew that her own life would be at risk if she stayed.

An officer glanced Nevaeh's way, almost as if he could see the thought in her eyes.

"Are you a student at Fort Grover High?" he asked.

Nevaeh shook her head.

"No, sir. I'm here for a church conference." She swallowed and added, "I'm not really sure what's going on."

The officer stared at Nevaeh for a moment, as if measuring her face against a criminal database in his head. When it was clear that he wasn't able to place her, the officer nodded.

"You're good to go. But it'll probably be best to avoid the lobby for a bit. They've got reporters setting up. This place is gonna be a nightmare."

With a quick word of thanks, Nevaeh hurried to the elevator doors with the rest of the tourists. When she finally emerged on her floor, she stumbled through the otherwise empty halls.

There were supposed to be a few events happening that morning for the conference. Hopefully, the others would still be out and Nevaeh could slip back into her room unnoticed.

She tapped her key card against her door and then slipped into her room. But Christina, Heather, Laurence, and Nevaeh's parents were waiting for her.

Her mother stood first, her eyes blazing with worry and rage. "Where have you been?"

Christina, who had been seated in the corner of the room away from Nevaeh's dad and Laurence, rushed to Nevaeh's side.

"I'm sorry," she whispered. "We tried to warn you. Why weren't you picking up your phone?"

"It died," Nevaeh lied. It hadn't been until the early hours of the morning when the battery life of her phone had finally died out.

Heather joined Christina's side. "Did you hear the news? Tommy's dead."

Nevaeh supposed if she was a better actress, she could pretend to be shocked or surprised. But she wasn't any of that. She felt nothing.

"They're saying it's an accident," Heather continued. "Which doesn't make sense if they're going around interviewing everyone who was at the park last night. Did you talk to any officers yet? Me and Christina just finished making our statements."

"Statements?" Nevaeh repeated. "What statements? What did you say?"

"Just that we were all in the park together. You and Tommy—"

"Never saw each other," Nevaeh cut in, straining to keep her panic at bay. "Yes, I went to see him, but we never met last night. Not after he humiliated me on his live. I'm just getting back now because I got stuck in Sunny World."

Christina's eyes widened. The look of doubt in her and Heather's expressions was enough to unravel Nevaeh. But if she couldn't even get her friends to believe her, then how would her family? Or the police?

"You didn't say I was involved, did you?" Nevaeh asked, desperately.

Christina shook her head. "No. We wanted to talk to you first." Heather looked like she was going to say something else, but before she could speak, Nevaeh's mother stepped between them.

"Christina. Heather. Thank you both for waiting up for Nevaeh. Now that she's here, we think it's best that the family speak to her. Alone."

Like anything her mother said, there was a finality to her words that reverberated through the room like thunder. With soft, whispered goodbyes, Christina and Heather left the room until it was just Nevaeh and her family.

"Don't look so scared," Nevaeh's mother said. "You're not the one who just spent the last six hours almost filing a missing person's report to the police. Do you know that when the body was found, we spent hours terrified that it was yours? And while we were waiting for answers, members of our own congregation were sending us clips of our daughter doing things in that park that a parent would never want to see—let alone have the whole world watching? Is this you, Nevaeh? Is this really how we raised you?"

"I'm sorry," Nevaeh whispered. "I'm sorry."

"Do you know what you've done? You didn't just destroy your own life, you've destroyed all of ours. Any chance your father had for getting that new pastor position is gone. And do you think we'll ever be able to show our faces to the congregation again? How could you be so reckless and perverse?"

Nevaeh pressed her eyes shut, fighting back tears as her mother's words tore through her. But the worst part was the fact that every negative word her mother had to say about Nevaeh wasn't half as hateful as the thoughts Nevaeh had for herself.

She never should have let things get to this point. Nevaeh had screwed everything up.

"I'm sorry," Nevaeh said, over and over again. "I'm sorry, Mama. I'm sorry."

But sorry wasn't going to be enough. Sorry wasn't going to change the fact that Nevaeh's family and the whole world had seen the photos.

Thomas was gone and Nevaeh's world had become undone.

Her mother reached for her, and for a moment, Nevaeh felt a flutter of hope. Maybe she would understand. Maybe she could see that beneath the photos and the mistakes Nevaeh had made, there was a sweltering pain that had long felt like a cage. But instead of going in for a hug, her mother unzipped the dress Nevaeh was wearing, revealing the costume from Heather beneath it.

The horror that emerged in her mother's eyes morphed into hurt as tears began to form.

"This wasn't how we raised you," her mother whispered. "Nevaeh, you're breaking our hearts."

Nevaeh recoiled from her mother's grip, fighting back the tears that had started to burn behind her own lashes. Seeing the pain in her mother's eyes, seeing the disappointment in her father's expressions, cemented what Nevaeh knew she had to do.

"It's not what you think. Just let me explain. Everyone has the whole story wrong."

But Nevaeh's mother was already leaving the room, and her father hurried behind her. Before he left, he placed a hand on Nevaeh's shoulder.

"That's enough. You don't have to lie anymore, Nevaeh. You

don't have to pretend. Pack your bags. We're cutting the trip short. We can talk about this when we get back home."

The conversation was over. Nevaeh's mother and father left the room, leaving her with Laurence. Yet even he wouldn't meet Nevaeh's gaze. And somehow that hurt more than anything.

"It was one mistake," Nevaeh whispered. And yet, it was as if all of the good things she'd ever done in her life were being erased. It was like everyone Nevaeh had loved was looking at her like she was a stranger.

"How long have you been talking to him?" Laurence said. "How long have you been lying to us about it?"

Nevaeh didn't answer. For Laurence, she knew that was answer enough.

Nevaeh reached for Laurence, but he pulled away.

"I know you're hurting, and you need us right now," he said, "but it—it's just going to take us some time to take this all in. Just give us some time, Nevaeh. All right?"

Nevaeh nodded, swallowing against the harsh burn in the back of her throat.

"I'm going to fix this," she whispered. "I promise I will."

"Nevaeh," Laurence said, "there's no fixing this. Trust me, I should know. Let's just hope it goes away once everything comes to light."

And then he left too.

Nevaeh stood there, alone in the room with the suitcase her parents had already started packing for her and the echoing silence of their departure. But Laurence was wrong. He didn't know how deep and twisted the whole truth was. He hadn't seen Thomas in the fun house last night or the lengths Nevaeh had gone to to steal his phone. No one did, and they never would. Not if she had her way.

chapter seventeen

Kiara

KIARA WATCHED AS Priscilla picked up her phone, waiting for an explanation. When none came, Kiara demanded it.

"What happened?" she asked. "Has the news about Tommy's death broken online yet?"

Priscilla took a deep breath. "Something like that," she said. "Look for yourself."

So Kiara did. She took Priscilla's phone and scrolled through the posts that appeared on Priscilla's news feed while Jason read over her shoulder. The cinema of expressions that played out on Jason's face was the same as Kiara's: grief and sadness morphed into confusion, followed by a wave of downright disbelief.

"They're saying he was some kind of misunderstood boy next door," Kiara whispered. And it wasn't just that. Comments upon comments speculated if Tommy's account getting hacked had driven him to his death.

"They're saying you, Priscilla, and Nevaeh might have been the last people to talk to him," Jason said.

Kiara nodded. Some were even murderino podcasters in Priscilla's DMs asking to interview the three girls.

"How thoughtful of them to reach out to me instead of Tommy's grieving girlfriend," Priscilla said. "Imagine what they'd think if they knew you were here, moving on with his stepbrother."

The words were biting. Priscilla must have known how much they would hurt. She was smiling, waiting for a reaction. But Kiara refused to give the other girl the satisfaction of one. She tossed the phone back to Priscilla and retreated to the far side of the room. It wasn't far enough.

"I'm calling Nevaeh," Priscilla said.

Kiara spun to face Priscilla.

"What? Why?"

"The police are about to interrogate us. Shouldn't we get our stories straight? We need to get ahead of this thing."

"What story? Why would you need to get ahead of it?" Jason asked.

But Priscilla was already dialing Nevaeh's phone number and putting the other girl on speaker.

"Hello? What do—"

"Are you still in Sunny World?" Priscilla asked before Nevaeh could finish the rest of her sentence. "We need to meet up. The police are asking for our stories. You were there last night. Have you talked to them yet? Did you tell them that Tommy was trying to meet you before he died?"

Nevaeh's voice was a soft squeak on the other end of the line.

"But they said he died near the fun house. I wasn't even near there."

Kiara's eyes widened. "What?" she whispered. "How do you know that?"

"I overheard the police talking about it," Nevaeh said. "They were stopping people in the park and interviewing them this morning. I left my phone in the park last night," Nevaeh explained, as if already anticipating more questioning from Kiara and Priscilla. "When I went to get it back early this morning, I was passing by the fun house and it was sectioned off by police tape. That's when I heard the police questioning people."

Kiara glanced at Priscilla, wondering if the other girl was as much on the brink of a meltdown as Kiara was in this moment. Tommy's accident had happened in the fun house, which meant that both girls had been nearby. Both girls might have been the last to see him alive. And instead of helping Tommy, the last words Kiara spoke to Tommy had been meant to hurt him.

"See. I told you," Priscilla repeated. "We need to work together. We need to get our story straight before this snowballs any further."

"Do you hear yourself?" Jason said. "This was my stepbrother. He's dead and you're sitting here worried about your image."

Priscilla glared at him. "Okay, go grieve. I'm grieving too. In my own way."

"Screw this," Jason said. "I'm out."

"Jason," Kiara said. She didn't have any words to make any of this better, so instead, Kiara took his hand in hers, squeezing it reassuringly. Their gazes locked, and for a moment, the storm of pain and frustration that had been churning within him softened.

The moment was interrupted by the sound of Priscilla's laughter.

"This goes for you too, Kiara. What do you think people will say if a few hours after Tommy's death, his ex-girlfriend and his stepbrother are having an entanglement?"

"We aren't entangled," Kiara said, too loudly even for herself.

"Tell that to the internet. There are already some comments floating around about you two, you know."

Jason's cheeks flushed red. Priscilla, seeing that she clearly had ruffled him, kept going.

"If the internet's already speculating if his death was an accident or not, I'm sure the police might still be wondering the same thing." She returned her attention back to Nevaeh on the phone. "And even if none of us saw Tommy last night, the fact that he conveniently died right after his account embarrassed all of us doesn't sound sus to you? We're all connected to this whether we want to be or not. We all want to know what happened. But we won't be able to find out the truth if the internet runs with some fake story. We have to get ours out first."

From the other end of the phone, Nevaeh finally spoke.

"My parents don't even know I'm involved with Tommy or that he died in the park. I'd rather keep it that way."

Nevaeh's voice was uneven. It wasn't hard to tell that the girl wasn't being totally honest about her situation. Whether it was a straight-up lie or just Nevaeh being in denial was less clear. But in a surprisingly non-hostile move, Priscilla didn't call Nevaeh out on her half-truths.

"You don't think they'll piece two and two together?" Priscilla said instead. "There are literally messages of their saintly little daughter sending dirty pics to said dead boy. All it'll take for them to make the connection is one bad news report."

Nevaeh was silent.

Kiara and Priscilla exchanged looks, confirming what they'd both guessed. "They know already, don't they?" Priscilla said, asking the question point-blank.

There was sniffling on the line. Nevaeh's whimpers were answer enough.

For a fraction of a moment, Kiara thought she saw a glimmer of what actually looked like remorse in Priscilla's expression. If it'd been there, the other girl quickly snuffed it out.

"It's all right, Nevaeh," Kiara said, shooting a dark glare at Priscilla. "We'll figure this out."

Jason looked apprehensive. But even he couldn't deny that when it came to scapegoating, the internet had a propensity to make accusations first in the rush of sensationalism and victim blaming rather than looking for the truth.

"This whole thing is painful enough," Jason said. "I get it. It sucks that you have to worry about how you come off even when it comes to something like a police investigation."

Priscilla was right. The situation was dire. Both online and when it came to how their conversation with the police might go. Kiara couldn't deny that.

Of the three of them, only Priscilla seemed to be making it through the speculations intact. Sure, she was the side chick in the internet's eyes, but a kiss that may or may not have been scripted didn't compare to the photos that Nevaeh had sent Tommy. Kiara knew that because her insecurity about Tommy and his overly friendly cohost had always come to that: they're just acting, a potentially scripted kiss doesn't mean anything.

But then there was her own image to worry about. The jealous, bitter girlfriend whose celebrity boyfriend had stepped out on her. The things people were saying Kiara was capable of just because she happened to have a perpetually pissed-off expression in Tommy's vlogs and a good GPA (not good enough for murder, she hoped) were unthinkable.

"We're flying back home today," Nevaeh whispered. "I don't think I'll ever be able to show my face in public again."

"Won't leaving the state during an investigation make you look like you're hiding something?" Kiara asked.

"Unless the police put a warrant restricting her from traveling, she's technically allowed," Priscilla said. At Kiara's and Jason's looks of disbelief, she shrugged and added, "I used to watch a lot of *Dateline.*"

Suddenly, there was a knock on the door.

"I have to go," Nevaeh said, and she hung up the phone.

Their time was up. The police had come.

Swallowing, Kiara unlocked the door. Just as she'd expected, the same officer from before and Mr. Phillips stood there. Fifteen minutes later. Exactly as they'd said.

Except they weren't alone this time. Standing behind them both were two other figures. One was an older Black man who looked to be in his late forties. He was dressed intricately in a suit and tie, and with a Sunny World logo embroidered on the suit's chest pocket. The boy beside him shared the man's features but looked like a younger version of him. Kiara fought back a gasp at the familiar sight of his face.

Ren.

When their eyes locked, Ren didn't make any hint that the two of them had met before. Instead, he let the man introduce them both.

"I'm Anthony Davis, owner of Sunny World. And this is my son Renton."

"Nice to meet you," Ren said, giving a small wave to the three of them.

"Mr. Davis has requested to sit in on the conversation," Mr. Phillips said in explanation.

"Sunny World Park and our hotel chain are conducting an investigation of our own. We're working closely with the police on both ends," Mr. Davis said.

Jason snorted. "Yeah, because my parents threatened to sue you if Sunny World kept refusing to cooperate."

Mr. Davis pursed his lips into a thin smile. "Mr. Harding broke a slew of park rules by hosting a party in Sunny World after hours. His death is a tragic accident. And again, we at Sunny World give our deepest condolences. But this tragedy could have been avoided if he had followed Sunny World rules, like all visiting guests are expected to."

"And you think he did that all by himself?" Jason said. "Who the hell do you think helped him operate the rides? How do you think he got access to the park after it closed?"

Ren stepped between his father and Jason.

"That's what we're trying to find out," Ren said. "We're still conducting our investigation to find the employees who assisted Tommy in operating the rides that night."

Kiara coughed, loudly. Jason and Priscilla shot her curious glances, but she couldn't meet their gazes. She wouldn't.

Ren clearly hadn't told anyone that he and other Sunny World workers had helped Tommy coordinate the prank in the park. But of course he wouldn't. If Jason's family was suing Sunny World, then the revelation that Tommy had help for the prank would hold them in some way accountable for Tommy accidentally dying in the park. And Ren wouldn't put himself on the line like that. In fact, Kiara was surprised he hadn't ratted out the employees who had helped operate the rides as a cover for his own actions. But if Tommy had trespassed on his own without Ren's involvement, then Ren, the employees, and the park could wipe their hands clean of having any culpability.

Kiara suddenly felt relieved by the turn of events. Unlike what the internet was saying, the only people who had anything to hide when it came to Tommy's death was a corporation trying its best not to get sued for millions.

"Now if you'll follow me," the officer said.

Kiara nodded. And then the officer led the group down the halls to the makeshift interrogation room they'd set up.

THE MASTER SUITE of the hotel room was almost identical to the one Kiara and Priscilla were staying in. Except the police had set up the foyer so there were extra chairs across a coffee table. Kiara took a seat next to Jason and Priscilla, while Ren, his father, the officer, and Mr. Phillips sat across from them. Along with some snacks that had been laid out on the table to clearly give a sense of ease to the conversation, they'd set up phones so that Kiara's and Priscilla's parents could call in to the interview.

Priscilla spoke quickly to her parents in Twi, seemingly calming them down about the situation. Though Kiara couldn't be sure, since the only other language she was fluent in was Spanish. But it was hard to focus on any conversation when Kiara's own parents were on the other side of the line. They barely got time to even ask Kiara if she was all right when Mr. Phillips took over the conversation, silencing both sets of parents.

"We just want to reassure you that the school has everything under control. Your children are safe."

"When are they going to come home? We want them home now," Kiara's mom said.

"We are cooperating with the investigation the police are conducting now and are extending our stay a few days so that all students can give a full account of what happened."

In the background, Kiara could hear her younger sister sniffling on the line. Lena had really liked Tommy. Kiara had done all that she could to let her family only see the side of Tommy that they would love. Right now, they were probably even more heartbroken than Kiara could let herself be.

"I'm okay," Kiara said. "Mr. Phillips and the school are taking good care of us."

Mr. Phillips smiled at Kiara.

"And like we said, this isn't an interrogation and none of your children are suspected of any kind of wrongdoing. We're just having a brief conversation to get a clearer picture of what happened last night."

"Priscilla isn't talking to anyone without our lawyers and us present," a man on the line who Kiara guessed was Priscilla's father said. "I don't care what fake friendly act you have on. Priscilla, don't say a word. You have rights."

"You're just going to make things worse for your daughter," the officer said. "We aren't claiming they did anything. We're just gathering facts."

"If their daughter doesn't have to speak, then why should ours?" Kiara's dad said.

"Your father's right," Kiara's mom said. "Don't say anything without a lawyer. Okay, honey?" It was a sweet sentiment from Kiara's mother. But unlike Priscilla, there was no way they'd be able to afford a lawyer in this or any situation.

Kiara had to do something. She had to make this go away.

"It's fine," Kiara said. "Really. They're just trying to make sure we're all okay." Swallowing, she turned to face the officer. "Priscilla and I were in the park with the rest of the seniors last night. But like everyone else, we went back to our hotel room after. We don't know anything about what happened. Tommy was the one who organized the senior prank night. Maybe whoever helped him set up that night will know more," she said, and she looked pointedly at Ren, waiting for him to speak.

But he didn't say anything. Instead, he just stared back her, raising an eyebrow as if daring Kiara to reveal that he'd been the one to help organize the prank in Sunny World with Tommy. Kiara swallowed and slunk back into her seat.

"You heard them," Priscilla's mother said on the other end of the line. "Now, if you have any further questions, you can talk to our lawyers."

Mr. Phillips nodded. "You do have their accounts now, at least. If there are any other questions for your investigation, you can conduct it through more official channels," he said, which was a nice way to say that it was clear Priscilla's parents would find a way to sue the officers and their school for all they were worth if they mishandled the investigation.

With no other choice, the officer let the two girls go.

"Get some breakfast and then head back to your rooms," Mr. Phillips said when the group disbanded. "You all deserve it after this morning."

Kiara smiled appreciatively. Despite the situation, Mr. Phillips was trying his best to take care of them all. Having him here and their parents supporting them from home meant everything. Especially with the vitriol spewing on the internet.

The officers called another group of students in for interviewing while Ren's father remained behind to listen in. Jason went off to his room to call his parents, but Priscilla said she'd stay in their room and order room service instead of joining their other classmates in the hotel restaurant.

But as Mr. Phillips began escorting Kiara downstairs, Ren stopped them.

"Do you mind if I talk to Kiara for a moment?" Ren said, giving Mr. Phillips a warm smile. "My father and I wanted to specifically give her our condolences as well, since, like Jason and his family, she's probably the most impacted by what happened."

"Of course, of course," Mr. Phillips said. "Kiara, I'll wait for you at the elevator bank."

Without giving Kiara much of a choice in the matter, Mr. Phillips left, leaving her and Ren in the empty hallway.

"I really appreciated that," Ren said.

"What?" Kiara asked.

"You not mentioning the arrangement Tommy and I had to help him and your classmates sneak into the park. It would have put my family and the park in a tricky situation."

Kiara looked away. "I'm not a snitch," she mumbled. Though that hadn't been the reason she'd kept her mouth shut.

Ren laughed. "No, you're not. You're an honors student with the perfect grades and GPA who's going to Kingstown University at the end of the summer."

Kiara startled at his words.

"What are you talking about?" Kiara said, unable to believe the words she was hearing.

"Tommy didn't tell you?" Ren said. "You're pretty much guaranteed a spot at Kingstown. Tommy may have set up things on his own end, but my father's recommendation goes a long way. That's why Tommy wanted it so bad. But I wanted to meet you first to see what type of person you were. You know, make sure whoever he was vouching for didn't somehow end up spoiling our family's name." He frowned. "Though, this situation with the accident is messing things up. For both of us. Don't you agree?"

The subtext beneath his words was clear.

"I don't believe you," Kiara said.

"Check the application portal when you get a chance. If your acceptance isn't there, then you can forget I even said anything," Ren said.

"And if it is?"

Ren smiled. "Then that would mean I came through, just like I said I would. But it'd be your turn. You'd owe me. You know, since Tommy isn't exactly here to hold up his end of the deal."

Kiara stared at him in disbelief.

"This is ridiculous." She pushed past him, making her way to the elevator bank.

"I'm not asking for anything illegal," Ren said. "That's Tommy, not me."

Kiara spun back to face him.

"Then what are you asking? I already kept your secret."

"But if Tommy's video guy and Priscilla let it slip that I helped Tommy and your class with the prank, it won't matter," Ren said.

"Priscilla doesn't even know you were working with Tommy. And Alex—" Well, Kiara couldn't speak on Alex. "I don't even know if he's talked to the police yet."

"Then you talk to him," Ren said. "Sunny World is already taking hits from the public about what happened. I'm going to need your help to make it clear that this whole accident was all

Tommy. No one else. Don't you want to move on with your life? Don't you want to start college as a freshmen with a clean slate and no senior trip freak-accident baggage?"

Kiara swallowed, meeting his gaze with her own. The desperation and expression in his voice mirrored Priscilla's when she'd realized just how far the internet was taking their speculations about Tommy's death. It was the same desperation Kiara felt knowing that Tommy's death would have a ripple effect that none of them would ever be able to predict. Tommy had already ruined Kiara's chance of getting into Kingstown. If what Ren was saying was true, if Kiara really had gotten her application through and accepted this time, then what kind of fool would Kiara be to let some rumors and speculation ruin her chances of having an actual future? That night in the park, Kiara had promised herself that she wouldn't let Tommy make her miserable. Not anymore.

"Tommy's death was an accident, a terrible accident," Ren said. "The park had nothing to do with it, and neither did you."

Kiara nodded. But her conscience couldn't bring her to agree. Not fully.

"So let's control the narrative," Ren said.

"How?" Kiara asked. And he smiled as if those were the exact words he'd been waiting to hear.

chapter eighteen

Priscilla

PRISCILLA PRETENDED SHE was returning to her room when Kiara and Mr. Phillips left. But earlier, when they'd been heading to the interview with the police, she'd spotted Alex among another group of their classmates. He'd been assigned to another chaperone and his group was returning upstairs. As Alex's group members went to their shared hotel rooms, Priscilla had realized that the one Alex entered was different from the room he and Tommy had been assigned to at the beginning of their trip.

So when the coast was clear and Priscilla was alone, she switched course. Thankfully, Alex's new room was in a corner, which made it perfect for slipping away unseen. She only had to knock once before Alex answered the door. When he did, she pushed him inside the room and locked it behind them.

"What are you doing?" Alex said in his usual gruff, irritated voice.

Priscilla's chest tightened. It was strange how the most mundane, familiar things—even the stuff that at one point had seemed annoying—could sometimes be a source of comfort. But Alex had changed from the boy she had known. In the dim light of the hotel room, there was a stiffness to him that hadn't been there before. His locs were pulled into a ponytail, his rich brown skin was as dark and enchanting as ever, but Alex himself seemed intent on cutting the interaction short. He stood at the door, practically blocking the view of inside his room.

Curious, Priscilla pushed past him. Inside the room, a half-filled suitcase and duffel bag lay atop his bed. The room itself looked barely used. It looked like Alex was visiting it for the first time or, more likely, unpacking his things.

"Did you change rooms?" she asked, wanting him to confirm what she already knew.

Alex stared at her in disbelief. "Tommy's dead. You know that, right?"

"Duh, I know that. It's trending online."

"You're incredible," he said, his voice laced with sarcasm.

Heat burned in the back of Priscilla's throat. "What? I'm not trying to be insensitive. I just thought they said it was an accident."

He glanced down to Priscilla's hand, which was still resting on Alex's chest from when she'd pushed him inside the room. On her wrist, the bracelet he'd given her on the gondola ride shimmered.

Priscilla yanked her hand away, hiding it behind her back.

"I'm not giving it back if that's what you're thinking."

But instead, Alex traced the line of Priscilla's neck.

"What's this makeup for?" he asked.

She hadn't expected the question. Aside from Kiara, no one had noticed the marks Priscilla had covered up that morning.

"I—" Priscilla shook her head. "It's just a new look I'm filming for a video. Stop trying to change the subject. Why are you in here?"

Alex didn't seem convinced, but he relented, running a hand across his forehead with exasperation.

"I got moved," he said. "The police closed off Tommy's room and, since we were roommates, they had me take my stuff somewhere else while they look through his things. I'm going to be staying here."

"So they already interviewed you?"

Alex nodded. "Just briefly."

"What did they want to know?"

"When I last saw Tommy. What the hacker had posted. What I think happened. You know."

"And what did you say?" Priscilla bit her lip. "Did they ask you for an alibi? Where did you say you were when the night ended?"

He sighed. "I just got out of one interrogation, Prissy. Please. Not another one."

"You owe me. At the very least, you can tell me what to expect."

"There's nothing to expect. Tommy's death will be ruled an accident, people on the internet can pretend he wasn't the biggest asshole in the planet, and the world will keep on spinning." Alex shrugged. "I'm sure you'll get plenty of sponsors and sympathy for the emotional turmoil this situation put you through. How's your follower count? Have you hit one hundred thousand yet?"

There was an icy tinge to his words that tore at Priscilla's heart. Her cheeks burned and her throat felt dry all of a sudden—the beginning of tears, Priscilla realized. She'd cried more in these last two days than she probably had in her whole life.

"Screw you," she said.

Priscilla turned to leave, but Alex was there, stopping her from exiting.

Suddenly, she wasn't in the hotel room anymore. Suddenly,

Priscilla was in the fun house, and Tommy was leering over her, slurring his words, touching, groping, refusing to relent, the pressure of his body on hers.

The tears fell then, staining Priscilla's cheeks and raining down on the ground. She didn't realize she was shaking until gentle hands cupped her own.

"Don't cry, Priscilla. I'm sorry. I didn't mean to scare you."

But the tears kept falling.

Priscilla didn't want Alex to see her like this. She hated being so pathetic and vulnerable, especially now, after her own condescending admonishments of Nevaeh and Kiara.

Alex held her close and together they knelt on the ground. Priscilla wiped furiously at her tears and Alex kept the rest of her together with his gentle, warm embrace.

"Where were you last night?" he asked. "After we left the gondola ride. Did you go see him?"

"Why?" Priscilla asked, panic churning through her insides. "Is that what you told the police?"

"What? No," Alex said quickly. "I just said I went on some rides and was filming."

Relief washed over Priscilla. She closed her eyes and tried to focus on her breathing, afraid that if she continued speaking, everything would come blurting out.

Her memory of that night was broken. What she could recall, though, was vivid, so vivid that Priscilla wished she could take gasoline to her thoughts and burn them all the way down: the floor of the fun house covered in glass, and Tommy there in a fit of rage. Priscilla had thought she'd be able to calm Tommy down. But the concoction of alcohol and substances churning through his blood had made him aggressive and agitated. Priscilla had screamed and screamed, calling for help. Crying for it. No one answered. And in his rage, Tommy turned the storm of rejection, and the humiliation he felt about his account being hacked, and Priscilla tricking him into thinking she was Nevaeh, directly at her.

And now he was gone and the police were investigating his death.

Priscilla wiped away the remaining tears from her face.

"I'm sorry," Alex said. "I know you loved him."

And for once since this whole nightmare began, Priscilla laughed. He really thought her tears were to mourn Tommy.

If only he knew the truth.

Alex moved to brush a tear from Priscilla's cheek, but as he did, the light in his eyes dimmed. She realized then that in that gesture, some of the makeup she'd put on had wiped off.

"Don't tell me he did that," Alex whispered. "Priscilla, if he did that to you—"

"It's fine. I'm fine," Priscilla said.

But Alex was already making his way to the medicine cabinet behind the toilet. He grabbed a first-aid kit from its shelf and returned to Priscilla's side on the floor. Then he began to tend to her bruises. Priscilla winced as the chemical solution grazed her skin.

"I'm sorry. Does it hurt?"

"No."

"Liar," he said.

Priscilla smiled meekly. "That makes two of us."

He returned her smile with a weak one of his own. Priscilla's heart knotted in her chest, a twisted sensation of panic and wings fluttering. How she could still be feeling butterflies and getting tongue-tied when they were in the middle of this nightmare, she didn't know. But in truth, the answer was simple. It was the gentle light in Alex's brown eyes. It was his hand against her back, holding her steady, and that ever-mischievous smirk, always on the brink of his lips. Even as Alex cleaned and bandaged her wounds, Priscilla's gaze kept returning to his mouth.

He still hadn't answered her question about where he'd been in the park. Though Priscilla guessed by now that he had a clue she'd been with Tommy.

"You can tell the police we were together," Alex blurted.

Priscilla's eyes widened. "What?"

"If they interview you again, just tell them we were together. They already know we were on the gondola ride. Half of our classmates saw us together on it. Everyone assumed that I was looking for you after you left the restroom. You can just say I found you. I already told the police I spent the rest of the night filming. Just say we were together. The park was pretty much dead after that anyway. None of our classmates would be able to prove otherwise, since most of them left by then."

"You—you'd let me do that?"

"What other choice do you have?" Alex said. "You saw Tommy. If that comes out—"

"Then people will find a way to connect me to his death, whether or not it was an accident," Priscilla said, finishing the statement.

More tears threatened to fall. But so too did the guilt Priscilla felt for manipulating Alex this way.

"I don't want to get you in trouble."

"You won't. Trust me. My alibi is solid. I even have footage that I filmed of me just wandering around the park. Obviously when you're behind the camera you're never in frame, but the time stamps from the footage are concrete evidence. We were together," he added, as if saying it aloud would make the alternate reality they were fabricating any truer.

"We were together," Priscilla said, repeating the words in barely a whisper.

With just those words, the weight clawing at Priscilla lifted. She had an alibi. She was safe. No one would ask her where she'd been and if she'd seen Tommy. And if they did, Alex would be her answer. He always had been.

"I don't know what to do with your lips," he whispered. Quickly, Alex added, "I mean, the split in the bottom one. I could try a circle Band-Aid on it if you want."

Priscilla swallowed. "Do whatever you want."

Alex hesitated. He leaned closer. Priscilla leaned closer too. The distance between them fell apart as their lips found each other. Longing, pain, wanting, all of it they kissed away. And for a moment, Priscilla felt as close to happy as its definition. But then the guilt came crashing down. And then came the fear and the panic.

If only he knew. If only he knew.

Priscilla knew what it was like to be forgotten. She'd always been the second choice, always been the other person. It's what had drawn her to Tommy in the first place. She'd watched Kiara yearn for Jason while Tommy fought for his own girlfriend's attention. And here she was, kissing his best friend even though twenty-four hours before, she'd sworn her undying love to Tommy, even as a part of Priscilla had yearned for revenge.

"He didn't deserve to die," she said, almost as if she was trying to convince herself as much as Alex. "Tommy didn't deserve any of this."

"No," Alex agreed. "But he got what was coming to him."

"Then maybe the same applies to us. We'll get our own reckoning," she whispered, looking away now. "Everyone online seems to think so."

"They only know half the story," Alex said. "You have your platform. Go live. Tell them what really happened."

Priscilla swallowed. As much as Alex worked behind the scenes with Tommy and her, he knew nothing about being a brand or running a social media account. On the internet, it wasn't just about the truth versus lies. It was about image, perception, and numbers. You had to get people on your side. You had to change the public narrative. It was so much easier for the internet to love someone who looked like Tommy than for it to try to understand someone who had Priscilla's background—especially when they were caught in a situation like this.

"I can help. Tell me what to do and we'll figure something out," Alex said.

Hope fluttered in Priscilla's chest. She hated using Alex to hide her own secrets. But she had no other choice. If she told the truth, the full truth, they wouldn't be investigating Tommy's death. The police would investigate her.

"You don't need to do anything, Alex. Look, let's keep our heads down until this investigation wraps up. I'll just need to do a better job of hiding my injuries and you need to make sure it's not so obvious how much you hated Tommy. Or that you'd decided not to film the prank with him last night." Time and time again, Priscilla had seen how public perception of people involved in investigations could change the outcome. They needed to get ahead of things. They needed to make their stories ironclad.

"Easy," Alex said. "I was his friend for years."

Priscilla bit her lip. "With friends like these, who needs enemies?"

"Tell that to Tommy," Alex said. And they both knew it was true. When his charm switch wasn't flipped, Tommy had never been exactly good at treating the people around him like, well, people.

"He *was* still alive when you saw him," Alex said. "Right, Priscilla?"

She looked away.

"Why would you think otherwise?"

"I'm just making sure."

Priscilla forced herself to meet Alex's gaze.

"After the gondola ride, I went to meet up with Tommy, but when I found him, he was high out of his mind and pissed off," Priscilla said finally. She pointed to the purple mark on her lower jaw. "He attacked me," she said, "and I fought back. I escaped. I hid while he was chasing me and lost him. I don't know what happened after that. He probably hurt himself somehow."

Alex looked pained to hear her recount the events. He squeezed her hand gently. Priscilla squeezed back. "We should be good. After the police asked me where I was—"

"Which was filming with me," Priscilla said.

He nodded, and they shared a smile as the lie came easily to them both now. "Well, after their questioning, I overheard the police say that the only other people still in the park around the time when they think Tommy had the accident were a few other seniors and Jason and Kiara. But they were together too."

Priscilla froze.

"But that's the thing," she said. "Kiara wasn't with Jason. Alex, when I left the fun house this morning after hiding from Tommy, Kiara was leaving too."

"So you think she might have been the last person to see Tommy?" he said. "Maybe she knows more about the accident?"

"Maybe," Priscilla said, remembering the terrified look on Kiara's face as they both exited the fun house that morning. "Or maybe she's like us, and is just caught up in this whole thing." Priscilla sighed. "And what about the burner phone?" She'd hidden it in Tommy's room. Had the police found it, or had someone else? Someone who'd hacked Tommy's account in the first place and exposed the girls' relationships with him? When she asked the question to Alex, he seemed just as perturbed as she was.

"I don't think the police found anything like that in the room," Alex said. "And last night, Tommy was accusing you of having the burner phone. I doubt the phone they found on his body is it, unless the person he was convinced hacked it decided to return it to him. They were even asking Jason if he recognized the phone they found on Tommy's body and if he and his family knew if it belonged to Tommy. He said they didn't. Neither did I when they showed it to me. It was some pretty old phone model, you know. White, in some dollar-store transparent phone case. It wasn't any of the equipment Tommy and I bought to run his account. It wasn't his burner phone."

Which meant that the hacker was still at large. But surely they wouldn't post again. Tommy was gone, and the internet's attention had switched from exposing him for being a toxic wannabe frat boy to mourning the loss of the notorious prank star. Whatever the case, Priscilla knew two things to be true: they needed to find the burner phone, and they needed to stop whatever online narrative that was beginning to form in the wake of Tommy's accident—at least, enough that Priscilla wouldn't be implicated in his death in any way.

The first would likely be trickier to achieve. But as long as every single loose end was tied up, Priscilla was sure she could shape the narrative how she wanted.

"Let's go over our stories again," she said.

chapter nineteen

Nevaeh

NEVAEH WAS PACKING when the call came. By now, every time
she saw Kiara's or Priscilla's number on her caller ID, her blood
went cold and a sense of dread overtook her.

"Do you need help?" Nevaeh's mother asked from across the
room. Along with Nevaeh's father and Laurence, she was folding
her own clothes into the suitcases they'd brought for the stay. Her
parents had made Nevaeh switch rooms from the one she'd been
sharing with Christina, Heather, and the other girls. Now Nevaeh
was staying with her family for the rest of the day until it was time
for their flight home. Hoping her parents hadn't noticed the call,
Nevaeh hung up quickly and slipped her phone into the pocket
of her dress.

"What? No. It's okay," she said. "I just, I need to use the bathroom for a second."

At least she'd have some privacy there. With a quiet apology,
Nevaeh slipped into the tiny bathroom connected to the room.
She turned on the sink and then crouched down in the shower to
call Kiara back.

"I thought we agreed to never contact each other again," Nevaeh hissed. "What part of 'I just want this to be over' don't you understand?"

"This is an emergency," Priscilla said on the other side of the line.

Nevaeh's heart jumped in fear.

"Did they find out what happened to Tommy?" she asked. Nevaeh had been monitoring the posts online. So far, there had only been speculation. But she, Kiara, and Priscilla were trending when you searched for Tommy since his cheating scandal was the last thing to go viral while he was alive. Seeing her parents scrolling through news about their "not so innocent" daughter had made Nevaeh sick with shame. She'd never had much of a presence online and that seemed to have made things worse. Everyone seemed to be guessing what type of person she was and whether or not she'd wanted her fifteen minutes of fame. And then there were the threats. The angry messages to her phone and the attacks against her hadn't stopped. They'd only gotten worse.

"A reporter reached out to Kiara," Priscilla said, "They're doing a story about Sunny World and Tommy's accident. They want us to share our side of what happened."

"No," Nevaeh said. "I already told you no."

"This isn't going away."

"I don't care."

"Do you want this to follow you for the rest of your life?" Priscilla continued. "Are you just going to let people talk crap about you and degrade you and do nothing?"

Nevaeh bit her lip. She thought of her parents, who still seemed unable to fully meet Nevaeh's gaze ever since they'd found out about the locker room livestream. She thought about

Laurence, who'd been quieter than she'd ever seen him before. And she thought about Christina and Heather, who had looked at Nevaeh as if she were a liar when she'd told them why she'd come back from Sunny World so late. "I know my character," she said, forcing herself to say the words even though she didn't quite believe them. "Silence speaks louder than words."

Priscilla huffed.

"Yeah. It really does, doesn't it?"

The line was silent. And then Kiara spoke, clearly having taken her phone back from Priscilla.

"I think going to the interview is a good idea," Kiara said, "but I won't pressure you to do it with us. I think we all got enough of that from Tommy."

With a soft goodbye, they ended the call. Inside the bathroom, the sound of the running faucet was a torrent beating over and over against the marble sink. Nevaeh moved to turn it off, but a soft murmur from the other room stopped her. She went to the door and pushed it open ever so slowly.

Someone was knocking on the door. The knocks were tentative at first, but as they remained unanswered, they grew more and more persistent.

"Police," a voice said. "Open up."

Nevaeh's parents had been packing still. They froze. Laurence, who had been reading a book in an armchair across the room, looked up. Everything seemed to stop in that moment. Everything except the knocking.

Then, finally, Nevaeh's father rose to answer it. The officers stood on the other side of the threshold, their figures looming and imposing, as if they were using their bodies as a barrier, caging them all in.

"Mr. Simon," the officer said. "We're looking for your daughter, Nevaeh Simon."

For Nevaeh's whole life, she'd always seen her father as a strong and stable force guiding their family with his patience and presence, leading them with his sermons. He never shrunk or wavered for anything, not even the wind. But even as her father's back straightened and his muscles tensed, for the first time in Nevaeh's life, she could see the slight tremble in his hands.

"What do you want with my daughter?" he asked.

Across the room, Nevaeh's mother stood too. "We don't have to talk to them or invite them in."

"We already opened the door," Laurence whispered.

"We're just here to talk to Nevaeh," the officer said. "We want to ask a few questions about where she was last night and this morning."

"This is about that dead boy," Nevaeh's father said. "It's a tragedy. But Nevaeh doesn't know anything about that."

"That's why we'd like to talk to her, sir." The officer glanced across the room, his gaze landing almost exactly on where Nevaeh was watching the ordeal from behind the bathroom door. "We just want to talk."

"You heard the man," Nevaeh's mother said. "You made your bed, Nevaeh. Come lie in it."

"Angelica," Nevaeh's father hissed. He turned to the officers with a light smile. "She doesn't mean that. She's upset for another thing. We found out that our daughter has been sending inappropriate photos to strangers online. She made a mistake. And she'll grow from it. But it's been very painful seeing what people are saying about her and our family. On the internet and even in our parish."

Nevaeh knew that. The internet was making memes and degrading her even more than she could have even imagined was possible. But so too were the people in her church. The community Nevaeh had grown up with, the ones who were supposed to know and care for her more than anyone in the world, were throwing her and her family out like they were nothing. And somehow that hurt even worse.

"Do you mind coming with us for a few minutes?" the officer said, ignoring Nevaeh's parents and speaking to her directly.

"Anything you want to ask her, you do it with us here," Nevaeh's mother said sharply.

Nevaeh's father gave her a small nod of encouragement. Laurence even smiled to make her feel better. Nevaeh walked to the door, and on all sides of her, her family stood, making a wall of their own against the officers.

"How did you know Thomas Harding?"

Hearing Tommy's name, his real name that he had given Nevaeh, was like a punch in the gut. Of course it would end up like this. Of course she'd only learn of the real him when he was dead.

"We were internet friends."

"Just friends?"

"I thought we were more," Nevaeh said. "But clearly he didn't."

The questioning went on like that. The officers had seen the posts by Tommy's account and the locker room livestream. But they said they were just doing their due diligence. They were just dotting their i's and crossing their t's. Tommy's death would likely be ruled an accident, and the only one who would probably have to pay for it was Sunny World Park, for their negligence.

When it was over, the police dismissed Nevaeh so they could

talk to her parents more. She went to the bathroom again, but this time, she listened with her ear against the door.

"Is there anything you can do about the people harassing our daughter online?" Nevaeh's mother said. "They're sending death threats to her phone. We're worried about her safety."

"Just have her change her number."

"Changing a number doesn't stop people from finding and hurting a person. And these are hundreds of people. Hundreds," Nevaeh's father said, anger radiating from his voice.

"They're just trolls. They're not going to do anything."

The door closed. The officers were gone. Silence returned once again. But beneath its fragile membrane, the muffled sound of sobs was suffocating.

"This is all my fault," Nevaeh's mother whispered. "I've failed her."

"We both did," Nevaeh's father said. "But we'll regroup. We'll find another parish and start over if we have to. We'll get through this."

Nevaeh pressed her eyes shut. Slowly, she leaned her head against the back of the door and slumped to the ground, her eyes filling with tears, her heart breaking.

Priscilla's words echoed through Nevaeh's mind again.

Do you want this to follow you for your rest of your life?

Priscilla and Kiara were right. This wasn't going away. It was going to ruin more lives. Nevaeh's. Her family's. Priscilla's and Kiara's.

She grabbed her phone and texted Kiara. She'd changed her mind. She'd do the interview. She was in.

chapter twenty

Kiara

IT TOOK A moment for Kiara to adjust to how bright the spot-lights were now that they were beaming directly down at her. She'd been the first to arrive for the interview after Ren had sent them the full details. The interview was with Florida local news and would take place in the same Sunny World hotel complex that they were all staying in, courtesy of the owners themselves. In this case, a conference room had been booked and closed off for the occasion. On the stage, four chairs had been positioned in the very center: one for Kiara, one for Nevaeh, one for Priscilla, and one for the reporter who would be interviewing them.

The camera crew rushed to set everything up while Ren stood on the fringes, watching everything with a probing eye for detail that was even more unblinking than the gaze of the camera that would be filming them live to local news.

One of the production managers instructed Kiara to put on a mic while someone from the makeup crew quickly powdered her face with foundation that was definitely the wrong shade. A few minutes later, Priscilla and Nevaeh joined them. Nevaeh's brother was her escort on her parents' behalf. He hugged her and wished her good luck, and then took one of the chairs in the audience that a few members of the production crew and some Sunny World workers sat in, lingering to watch after having helped to set up the conference room for the interview.

"You ready?" Priscilla asked.

"Yeah," Nevaeh said.

Kiara nodded too, but she was distracted as a notification appeared on her phone. Usually, she had it on Do Not Disturb, but she'd set a few notices to stay caught up with the reporting on Tommy's accident.

"Good," Priscilla continued. "If we can control the narrative, the internet won't have anything else to run with. Once the investigation runs its course, someone else will be the next main character online and we can go back to living our best lives."

"You mean, once we clear things up," Nevaeh said. "*Control* doesn't feel right."

"That's because there is no 'right' or 'wrong' with these kinds of things. There's just public opinion and making sure you're not the person everyone online hates."

Nevaeh frowned. "But there is a 'right' and a 'wrong.' Always."

Priscilla shrugged. "Not to the internet."

Kiara tuned them both out. The notification was an email. Her application status at Kingstown had been updated. She glanced up across the room to where Ren sat at the farthest seat in the conference room.

When Kiara logged into the Kingstown application portal, her hands were shaking.

"Are you okay, Kiara?" Nevaeh whispered. "You look like you're going to be sick."

Across the room, the production manager made an announcement.

"Five minutes until we're on-air. Girls, I'm going to need to you take your seats in front of the cameras."

Nevaeh took a seat on the far end of the row, and Kiara sat between her and Priscilla.

"My appeal was reviewed," Kiara whispered. "I got in."

Nevaeh turned to Priscilla for some sort of explanation, but the other girl rolled her eyes. It wasn't until Kiara showed Nevaeh the message on her phone that everything seemed to click for the other girl. On the portal for Kiara's application, the decision was written in bright green letters. *Accepted.* And beneath it, there was a brief letter of congratulations.

Kiara couldn't hide the joy radiating off of her.

She had grown up in a cramped apartment with her family. Despite working summer jobs of her own, she'd been forced to watch as her parents struggled to pay rent and bills, just because a high school diploma had been the highest education either of them had been able to secure. For so long, life had handed them only lemons. But here was something sweet.

Kiara had done it. She'd really done it. Four years of tireless work had paid off. Four years of extracurricular activities, volunteering, tests, quizzes, and studying—all that studying . . . Just hours before, Kiara's life had been in shambles. And now she was going to be living her wildest dreams. Kiara had achieved the near impossible.

She was going to one of the top schools in the country.

"Congratulations," Nevaeh said.

"Yeah, congrats," Priscilla said too, though there was a chilliness in her voice. Normally that would have bothered Kiara. Now it just made her smile even more.

On the right side of the stage, the reporter finally made his entrance.

He was an older man in his early fifties. At least, Kiara guessed that from the streaks of gray that peppered his precisely trimmed hair. He wore a blue suit and took a seat in the chair across from the three girls with his legs spread out informally, almost as if this were a classroom and all the girls had to do was answer a few simple questions in front of half of Florida.

The interview was about to begin and Kiara couldn't stop smiling. She knew she should stop. But she'd been holding back any sense of joy for so long that this one, momentous thing was just so inexplicable, and her muscles couldn't help it. Kiara was grinning, beaming like a bright, radiant star that had just emerged from a solar eclipse. When the reporter introduced her, Priscilla, and Nevaeh to all of Florida's local news stations, Kiara had smiled even still.

And that, she would come to learn, had been her one, fatal mistake.

"Today we're talking about the social media prank star Tommy Harding," the reporter said. "This story comes right from the Garden State into the Sunshine one. Four New Jersey teens in Sunny World for a senior trip. Three whirlwind affairs, a hacking, and a death. And just moments ago we've learned that the autopsy report for the young, notorious, and beloved prank star has left police with more questions than answers."

A trickle of apprehension ran down Kiara's spine. The news team hadn't told them that the autopsy was in—hadn't mentioned it at all, in fact. She shot a look at Ren from across the room, demanding to know what he was playing at. But he shrugged as if he wasn't quite sure where things were headed either.

"A deal's a deal," he mouthed.

Kiara clenched her fist. But he was right. Kiara had gotten her acceptance. And now she'd have to keep up her end of the agreement. Tommy still owed Ren for the recommendation letter, even though he was dead. This interview would clear Tommy's debts, and by extension Kiara's. All she'd have to do was smile and convince the world that a wealthy institution like Sunny World shouldn't be blamed for Tommy's accident.

Kiara hated how things had come to.

The cameraman drew closer to the reporter as he revealed the case's breaking news.

"Our sources have confirmed that abrasions were found on the now-deceased eighteen-year-old Harding, an indication that a physical altercation might have taken place prior to his passing. While it's unclear if these abrasions are related to his ultimate death, the official police report states he died from trauma to the head. Harding was found in an underground location beneath the park itself, near its fun house attraction, where new construction was beginning to take place."

A quiet gasp seemed to fill the room. Beside Kiara, Priscilla shifted her expression from disbelief to one of worry. But Nevaeh couldn't hide her shock from the cameras. Neither could Kiara.

A physical altercation might have taken place. Kiara chewed on her bottom lip. Heat burned against her lashes. She hadn't imagined things would turn out like this. But she wouldn't cry. Couldn't.

Tommy's death might not have been an accident. Something

more sinister could be at play. And she might have been the last person to see him.

"Mr. Harding's parents are planning to sue Sunny World Park, believing that their son's death is directly related to his presence in the park that night, despite the fact that all the gates should have been locked and none of the seniors in his class should have been able to have access to the premises after hours."

Immediately, the reporter turned to the three girls. There was a glint in his eye, one that said that this was his moment. Here was his own chance to get his fifteen minutes of fame as a cutting-edge interviewer. Kiara straightened in her seat.

"You three must be devastated to hear this news. Especially you, Kiara, since you were Tommy's girlfriend."

Kiara swallowed. "Yeah, this is . . . pretty tough stuff to learn in the middle of everything else." Tentatively, she glanced at Ren again. And then Kiara steeled herself. "I just think it's all so sad. Sunny World was Tommy's favorite place in the whole world. He wouldn't blame them for what happened. Not when he'd planned to make this senior trip, and the prank, the most epic one in our school's history. In internet history."

Beside her, Priscilla and Nevaeh shot Kiara curious looks.

"Are you saying that Sunny World isn't to blame for what happened to Tommy?" the reporter asked.

"I'm saying I don't think Tommy would think so. He's snuck into graveyards, malls, and even private suites in football games for his videos. Sneaking into Sunny World for the senior prank and letting the rest of our class in is the kind of thing Tommy would be able to do with his eyes closed."

"What about operating the rides? Only Sunny World workers would have access and the ability to do that."

"Isn't that just, like, getting the key to the ride and then turning it on?" Kiara pushed back, careful to keep her tone light, as if she was only asking an innocent question. "I don't know if Tommy paid off some employees to help him, but if he did, that's not Sunny World's fault. That's the individuals who helped Tommy, and even they were probably just trying to have some fun with our senior class. The night was just never supposed to turn out how it did."

Kiara looked up, glancing once again across the room for Ren's reaction. His expression was neutral, but he gave Kiara an ever-so-slight nod.

She was doing fine. They'd all get through this.

"Well, we're sure you know Tommy better than anyone. When we talked to Tommy's mother earlier today, that's almost word for word what she said."

"That's very sweet of her to say," Kiara said, trying to ignore the guilt gnawing at her. "I don't think anyone can know someone as well as their parents can. And Tommy's mom knows—knew him better than anyone. But I guess I just knew a different side of Tommy."

The reporter nodded, as if agreeing with Kiara, even though he was probably the most removed from Tommy and his world than anyone in the conference room.

"His mother also shared that one of the last things Tommy spoke to her about was a necklace he was buying for his girl-friend," he continued. "Tommy had told his parents that he was going to give it to you during this trip. Did he ever end up doing that, Kiara?"

At the question, Kiara froze.

"I—um—" She shook her head. Even as she tried to speak, no words would leave her lips.

She had lost the necklace—presumably in the fun house. But how could she explain that without mentioning that she'd seen Tommy that night, after their argument? It wasn't as if she could deny it either. Tommy had told his mother he'd planned to give Kiara the necklace. The reporter had confirmed that. But that didn't mean the whole world still needed to know if Kiara still had it.

"He did," Kiara said finally. "It was really beautiful."

"Do you have it with you now?"

Kiara swallowed, running through potential answers that could explain why she didn't have it. In her mind, she told herself not to blink and to make eye contact. Lying without eye contact was a dead giveaway.

"I have it, but not with me," she said. "It's in a box with my things. It's just—it's too hard to wear it right now. But I think, with time, I'll be able to. It's just so hard to really believe this is all happening. That he's really gone."

chapter twenty-one

Priscilla

PRISCILLA HAD PREPARED herself for this moment. At least, that's what she'd told herself. After years of being linked to Tommy's controversies, she was used to the harsh gaze of the spotlight.

The rules were simple: make eye contact, be humble, and never, ever smile or come off as glib on camera.

Instead of waiting for the reporter to ask another question, Priscilla chimed in.

"I think we all feel that way," she said.

For good measure, she rested her hand on Kiara's shoulder.

"Before, it almost felt like—" Priscilla shook her head. "It's as if this whole thing was just one big prank and Tommy will come out of hiding any minute and be like, 'Sike!' Honestly, we wish it were the case."

"That would be a pretty heartless prank," the reporter said.

"Not for Tommy," Kiara said softly. "That's just how he was. He'd go to any lengths to get good content for his channel."

Priscilla nodded in agreement. "That's why we were all in the park so late that night at all," she explained. "We were filming content for the vlog. Pranks were what Tommy was known for. They're why the world loved him."

"And did you all love him?" the reporter asked.

Even though the question was to all of them, the reporter's attention remained on Priscilla now that she had spoken. "Is that why you kissed Tommy in your hotel room earlier that day, as the posts on his social media account showed? How long had the two of you been involved?"

Priscilla stiffened. To be honest, she would hardly have called what she and Tommy had done a kiss—it was more like tongue wrestling. But it wasn't like she could say that now.

"Tommy and I were good friends," she said finally. "That kiss was a mistake. It never should have happened."

She turned to Kiara and took her hand. "I'm sorry for disrespecting your relationship with Tommy the way I did. I'm sorry that Tommy isn't here to apologize for himself, because I know he would have wanted to if he were still here."

Reluctantly, Kiara squeezed Priscilla's hand back. The crowd in the chairs below clapped softly.

Priscilla pursed her lips, fighting back her own smile now.

chapter twenty-two

Nevaeh

UNLIKE PRISCILLA AND Kiara, Nevaeh needed her parents' consent to do the TV interview since she was still a minor. But it hadn't taken long for Nevaeh to convince her parents to let her go through with it. They were worried about the messages and threats she was still receiving from Tommy's fans. And after the encounter with the officer, they'd been rattled enough to let Nevaeh tell her side of the story.

Nevaeh had even memorized a statement to say on camera when the time came.

I'm sorry for disappointing my parish. I'm sorry for disappointing my parents, who didn't raise me this way. I thought I was in love. But I never should have sent those photos or been in the park that night. I wish I could explain to Tommy how hurtful it was for him to leak our private conversations. But he's gone. And all that I ask now is for the world to join me to pray for his family and all the loved ones he left behind.

Maybe Tommy's fans and strangers on the internet would stop hating Nevaeh. Maybe even members from their parish would stop icing out Nevaeh and her family.

Every inch of Nevaeh was desperate to get the interview right.

Yet of the three girls, Nevaeh couldn't believe how well Priscilla was pulling this off.

She parroted the perfect amount of nervousness and hurt, while maintaining a grace and humbleness that felt genuine. And to apologize to Kiara on TV . . . Nevaeh was sure in a few hours, the world would be falling head-over-heels for Priscilla, the side chick who took the side of the girlfriend.

This was exactly what Nevaeh needed to do. She needed to rebrand. She needed to get people to understand how she'd gone from having zero social presence to becoming a main character in an internet drama. She needed to be loved.

"I'm sorry too, Kiara," Nevaeh said, placing her hand over Kiara's and Priscilla's now. "I didn't know you and Tommy were together. And you don't know how much I regret ever sending him those photos."

At Nevaeh's words, a light of curiosity gleamed in the reporter's eyes.

"Are you sorry for sending them, or do you regret that Tommy went on to share them with the internet?" he asked pointedly.

Now this, Nevaeh realized, could be her make-or-break moment. If she criticized Tommy, people would think she was tearing down a dead boy, even though their last encounter had been one where he'd filmed her without her consent. And even outside of the photos Nevaeh had sent Tommy, how many other students and workers at Sunny World had Tommy filmed changing? What other videos did his account have that could be released?

This interview was supposed to vindicate Nevaeh, even if it meant going along with a public narrative that favored Tommy in his death.

But what if this was Nevaeh's only chance to point out the negative impact of how Tommy had treated people while he was alive? The secret videos he'd filmed, the lies, his manipulations—all of these things had wrought damage. And now, even in his death, its ripple effect was still hurting Nevaeh, Kiara, Priscilla, and who knows how many other girls?

But before she could find her words, Priscilla answered for her.

"Tommy didn't share those photos of Nevaeh to the internet. His account was hacked."

In that moment, the very voice Nevaeh had been searching for, the fighting spirit that had been blooming in her soul, was smothered out.

The reporter nodded along to Priscilla's words and then turned back to Nevaeh with a follow-up question.

"And do you believe that?"

Nevaeh took a deep breath, pretending to ponder the question for a beat before she spoke.

"I—I mean, that's what happened. A hacker got into his account and made posts."

"So has he ever publicly shared photos you've sent to him before?"

"Um, not that I know of. I hope not." Embarrassment filled Nevaeh as the realization hit her. "I mean, I've never actually sent him anything like those photos before, in terms of content. We've been dating online and I wanted to do something special because, yes, I loved him, and that's what I thought you did when you love someone. You make them happy. We were about to see each other for the first time in person and Tommy said photos like that would make him happy, so . . . I sent them to him," Nevaeh said. "But I regret it. It's not me. It's not how I was raised." Nevaeh frowned, trying to remember the words her parents had drilled into her. "I'm sorry for disappointing my parish. I'm sorry for disappointing and hurting my family. And, I mean, it was hurtful that he leaked it—his account, I mean. Tommy even told me the whole thing was a mistake."

"Was that after the locker room video leaked, or later on, when the account posted about your relationships? Did you see Tommy after that to hash things out?"

Nevaeh's heart jolted. He was asking if Nevaeh and Tommy had met in the park that night. If Nevaeh answered, she wouldn't be able to explain the fallout of that night. Not without looking guilty. Without even knowing where the words had come from, though, a lie escaped her lips.

"No—my friends went back to the hotel. I was there shortly after them. Our church group had to be up early the next morning, and I was upset," she explained, hoping the deflection from exactly revealing her whereabouts would be enough to appease speculations. "I found out about what happened to Tommy the next morning when I went back to the park but I couldn't get in because the police were escorting people out after a body was discovered. I didn't even know it was Tommy's until I saw the news on my phone. Just like the rest of the world." Anxiously, Nevaeh yanked on the collar of her dress. "It's been such a huge blow knowing that Tommy's gone forever. Yes, I was humiliated, embarrassed at myself, and ashamed after the locker room incident. But I just wish things hadn't ended up so messed up like they did."

The reporter tilted his head, seeming to scrutinize every word Nevaeh chose.

"And what do you think went wrong?" he asked.

Nevaeh frowned. "What do you mean?"

"Do you think Tommy's death was truly an accident?"

To Nevaeh's relief, Kiara interrupted.

"And why wouldn't it be an accident? The police reports are saying it was."

When he spoke this time, the reporter was clearly directing his words to an invisible audience. "I think I speak for all our viewers when I ask this, but—well, you three girls are being very kind and tactful about this whole situation. Clearly you lost someone you all loved deeply, but the fact that all three of you were in love with this boy, well, it doesn't seem like you knew about each other or the fact that he was cheating." He turned to face the camera directly. "Right now, I'm going to play a clip from a recording one of Tommy's classmates posted."

Nevaeh tensed, and she could almost feel the panic radiating from both Kiara and Priscilla.

There was a small screen across the room for them to watch. In the footage, Tommy and Kiara were at the center of a crowd. While the lighting was dim, it was clear that the footage was just a few hours before Tommy's death. Rage glimmered from Kiara's eyes as she shouted at Tommy that it was over between them. She spun away, only for Tommy to continue the confrontation. He brought up Priscilla's name and the camera shifted to where she stood in the crowd before she pushed through it and disappeared into the night. The camera shifted back to Tommy and Kiara yelling at each other in the crowd. Suddenly, there was a harsh crack. Kiara had slapped Tommy, and he stood there, clutching his cheek, stunned.

"Had you ever hit Tommy before?" the reporter asked.

"What?" Kiara said. "No. That was—that was the first time. I shouldn't have."

"And has Tommy ever hit you? Were the two of you known to fight?"

Kiara suddenly looked cornered. Her eyes were wide, her lips parted. She rubbed her palm with the rhythmic back-and-forth of a habit that must have been formed as a coping method. On the other side of her, Priscilla brushed her neck absentmindedly. She'd practically caked her neck in makeup for the interview.

Something was wrong. Nevaeh didn't know what, but the air felt too dense all of a sudden.

"Tommy's not here to answer if he's done any of that," Nevaeh said, "but Kiara's here and she can explain the situation that led to her actions. But just because there aren't any videos of Tommy being violent doesn't mean he's innocent either."

Kiara eyes widened. Slowly, a grateful smile formed on her face. She squeezed Nevaeh's hand.

"Thank you," she mouthed.

Nevaeh's cheeks burned. Instead of using that moment to say the speech she'd prepared, Nevaeh had gone off script. She hadn't meant to put a magnifying glass to Tommy as a person. But how could this man sit here and interrogate Kiara as if she were a villain when Tommy had been theirs?

"What she means is that it was a stressful night, for all of us," Priscilla said, speaking in Nevaeh's place. "I'm sure Kiara regrets reacting the way she did."

"Of course. That's very understandable," the reporter said. "What I'm trying to lead up to is the fact that there was alcohol, as well as other substances, on the premises during this senior prank night. The coroner's report even shows that Tommy had a concoction of those things in his system." Once again, the reporter turned his fiery stare toward the three girls. "Kiara, you were Tommy's girlfriend. Priscilla, you were his cohost. And Nevaeh, you were the church girl he corrupted. Clearly emotions were high. The question some viewers have is simple: were emotions high and inhibitions lowered enough to spark a situation that could have led to Tommy's death?"

Priscilla shook her head.

"No, of course not," she said.

Nevaeh nodded. "It wasn't like that at all."

"We had our ups and downs," Kiara said. "And obviously that fight in the park was an ugly moment, and I one hundred percent wish it never happened. But Tommy was—at his best, he was really supportive and funny. I think whatever happened after we all left the park was clearly an accident, just like the reports say."

"Yeah, he was," Nevaeh said. "I wish I could explain to Tommy how hurtful what he did was—I mean in, you know, leaking our private conversations. But I'm sorry for disappointing, you know, everyone. Especially my family and our parish. And, um—" She scrambled to finish up the speech and fit everything in that she wanted to get across. But her sentences were like molasses against her tongue. She searched for them, yet found herself grasping at empty words.

Thankfully, Priscilla once again cut in, shifting the conversation to how everyone was still shocked from what happened. The reporter walked them through a few more questions. And then, as the interview came to an end, Priscilla had the final soundbite.

"We all cared about Tommy in different ways," she said. "But Nevaeh and I both know that Kiara was Tommy's true love, not us. There's no animosity between us, or with Tommy. We are praying for Tommy's family. And as we all grieve during this time, at least we have each other."

The camera crew gave the girls a thumbs-up and the reporter finished his final monologue to the audience.

"As you can see, there's nothing but heartbreak here in Sunny World Park. Tommy will be missed, but the love he left in the world will forever endure. Just ask the three girls who loved him the most."

chapter twenty-three

Kiara

BEFORE THE CAMERAS stopped filming, Kiara was forced to "hug it out" on TV with Nevaeh and Priscilla. Truly, the whole sister-wives bit Priscilla had them performing was Oscar-worthy.

Yet as the girls stayed in each other's embrace, Kiara couldn't help feeling a sense of gratitude toward them. Nevaeh had defended Kiara during the interview. And Priscilla had somehow managed to keep the conversation from unraveling. As different as the three of them were, they were here, together. And that, Kiara realized, made a world of a difference.

"Let's hope we never have to do that again," Priscilla said.

Kiara almost laughed at how quickly that optimism had shattered. So much for sisterhood.

"You said this was supposed to let us 'control' the narrative," Nevaeh said. "Why didn't you screen the type of questions the reporter was allowed to ask?"

The two girls spoke in animated whispers. From the corner of her eye, Kiara watched as the reporter himself spoke to a member of the camera crew about an angle he hadn't wanted to be filmed in.

As they argued, the production team began to disassemble the set, picking up chairs and moving lighting equipment back into vans outside the conference room. A few Sunny World hotel workers who had come with Ren seemed to have been enlisted to help with the disassembly efforts too. Some of them were their age; others were managers and senior park staff who clearly had come just to get a glimpse of the drama. Ren gave a curt nod to Kiara, seemingly satisfied by how she'd defended the park in the interview. But he didn't approach her. He just exited the conference room with little more than a second glance. Their deal was even. Never again would Kiara have to think about underhanded bargains Tommy had made on her behalf.

"Relax," Priscilla whispered to the two girls. "People are bound to ask those questions. It's good that we're getting them early. This way our responses won't feel reactionary."

"It felt pretty reactionary to me," Nevaeh whispered. "They made us look like side pieces."

"We are side pieces," Priscilla said. "At least, you and I are."

"I don't like how it came off as if the only thing of value we've done in our lives was date Tommy," Kiara said. "As if him dying is something I should add to my résumé."

Priscilla shrugged. "I mean, tragic dead boyfriend would make for a pretty good vlog."

Kiara glared at Priscilla.

"What? You don't think Tommy wouldn't be filming a 'My girlfriend died on our senior trip' vlog if he were still alive?"

"Shut up," Kiara said. But the thing was, Priscilla was right. Of course Tommy would have jumped on the tragedy to build his brand.

In the middle of their conversation, Priscilla thanked one of the workers as they grabbed her chair and Kiara folded her own to help speed up the process.

"And what was up with that Sunny World thing?" Nevaeh said, poking Kiara gently to get her attention again. "It was kind of like you were one of their sponsors or something. I don't think you had to defend them so much."

"I was just being honest," Kiara said, the lie slipping out easily. "Our class is the one who snuck into the park against Sunny World's policy and our school's. It's not fair to Sunny World to get the blame for the accident."

"I'm just worried we won't look good once it comes out," Nevaeh said.

Priscilla laughed.

"Why? Because you were blatantly lying?" Then, in a voice that was clearly meant to imitate Nevaeh, Priscilla said, "I left the park with my church friends. We had curfew, so we went back to the hotel."

"I didn't say that."

"You didn't say where you really were either," Priscilla said. "So, were you in the park or had you really gone back to the hotel?"

The question was something Kiara had peeped too during the interview. All three girls had known Nevaeh was supposed to meet up with Kiara and Priscilla after the account's post went live. But when she'd bailed, she'd never explained fully what happened. All Nevaeh had said was that she'd gone back to Sunny World in the morning to retrieve the phone she'd left there and that, when she'd been passing by the fun house, she'd overheard the police identifying the spot where Tommy's body had been found. So why had Nevaeh lied about not being let into the park the next morning? And what about her phone? If it really had been dead and Nevaeh had left it overnight in Sunny World Park like she'd told Kiara and Priscilla, then how could she possibly have found out that the body in the park was Tommy's by checking it? Why had she suddenly changed her story on camera?

With a soft voice, Kiara placed a hand on Nevaeh's shoulder. "You don't know more about Tommy's accident than you're claiming. Do you, Nevaeh?"

Nevaeh shook her head, but she wouldn't meet their gazes either.

"I was just—trying not to overcomplicate things. Plus, well, my family saw the locker room video and I—I don't want people to think anything more happened that night, you know?"

"Did anything more happen?" Priscilla asked.

"Of course not!" Nevaeh snapped. "And if it had, do you really think I'd trust either of you two to say otherwise?"

Neither Kiara nor Priscilla could argue against that fact.

"Look," Nevaeh continued, "I don't want anything to do with this drama anymore. I said my piece. I'm moving on. And I don't ever want to deal with Tommy or you again. Okay?"

Priscilla laughed.

"Finally, something we can all agree on," she said.

"Fine," Kiara said, following suit.

She yanked out the earpiece the film crew had given them earlier and handed the mic and its pack back to the crew. Priscilla and Nevaeh followed suit.

"If we don't like or trust each other," Kiara continued, "then I say let's put this whole thing behind us. From here on out, we never speak of what happened that night."

"And let's never contact each other again," Nevaeh added. "For real this time."

Priscilla smiled. "Cross my heart and hope to die."

Kiara rolled her eyes. Nevaeh shook her head. Priscilla was beyond extra.

As if aware of that fact, Priscilla shrugged.

"Pretend however much you want," she said, wincing ever so slightly as she brushed her hand against her neck. "I'm glad that asshole can't hurt us, or anyone else, again."

Nevaeh hushed Priscilla. Kiara too couldn't help but look around to see if anyone had overhead too. While one of the Sunny World workers glanced in their direction, everyone else was in a frenzy of activity clearing up the set. No one seemed to have heard Priscilla's cutting words. Because if they had, they would have caught a glimpse of the light of agreement in Kiara's eyes or Nevaeh's nervous nod.

WHEN KIARA AND Priscilla had spoken to the crew, they'd been told the interview would air on the news later that day. Hours passed. Yet despite the nonstop coverage of Tommy's death, the interview still hadn't aired.

Later that evening, though, Kiara was packing her suitcase. Everyone's parents wanted their children back, so their school had folded. The flights back to Jersey would start later that night for students who wanted to leave immediately. Kiara herself hadn't exactly called her parents to warn them about the interview, but she hinted that she'd be sharing her story with the public. Had she framed the whole situation as a broadcast honoring Tommy's legacy rather than one to remove any association Kiara might have with his death? Possibly. But unlike Priscilla's parents, who were planning a family vacation to make up for the trauma Priscilla experienced on this trip, Kiara's parents wanted her to get back to her regular life. Starting at Kingstown in the fall would be the next chapter they all needed to put this one behind them.

As Kiara folded and unfolded clothes in endless monotony, the familiar voice of a male reporter on the evening news yanked her from her reprieve.

In the bathroom, Priscilla ended the makeup vlog she was filming to raise the volume on the TV.

The image on the screen showed all three girls. Kiara's photo was from when she and Tommy had been crowned junior prom king and queen, Nevaeh's was from some church event, and Priscilla's was from talent show day at school.

Priscilla groaned.

"Of course they used that photo of me from freshman year. We literally have all our photos on our social media pages. Why would they dig through those old school pictures? I didn't even know how to draw a wing with my eyeliner back then."

Kiara rolled her eyes.

"Wow, how tragic."

Priscilla was as shallow as it came.

But it was kind of refreshing to be around her chaotic energy. It was almost as if the other girl's absurd behavior was meant to help them deal with the turmoil of emotions they were both coping with. In that way, Kiara was kind of relieved to have Priscilla as a reluctant support buddy. She wondered how Nevaeh was doing and if she had anyone else to be there for her through all of this. Since leaving the conference room earlier, they hadn't spoken.

"I loved Tommy," the Kiara on the TV said.

"We all did," TV Priscilla added. "This whole situation is a tragedy."

Watching the interview back was like viewing a parallel-universe version of herself. The editors had managed to chop off all the awkward and tense moments of the interview to make it cohesive and not as terrible as Kiara had feared it would be. Sure, she came off a little conniving and self-absorbed when she mentioned being the class president and getting into her dream school—a moment Kiara barely recalled even now. But at least the segment of the interview Kiara had feared most—her fight with Tommy and the necklace bit—had barely gotten any screen time.

The reporter asked the girls if their relationships with Tommy had been in any way rocky that night, and they all answered as truthfully as they could.

"Tommy was Tommy. For the good and the bad," Kiara said. "If I had known that fight would be the last time I would see him, I wouldn't have let things end the way they did."

"And I'm sorry for my mistake," Priscilla said. "I regret what me and Tommy did to you, Kiara."

"I do too," Nevaeh said. "I didn't know he had a girlfriend, let alone someone as kind and amazing as you, Kiara. Not that it would change anything if you weren't so wonderful. I just don't think Tommy realized what he had either. But now I think we're all connected. We're sisters now. And we can grieve him being gone together."

There was no mention of the altercation in the crowd or whether or not anyone deserved the outcome of the current situation.

"We send our prayers and love to his family," Priscilla said.

"They lost a son, a brother. The pain we feel could never amount to what they're going through. So we just ask everyone, online and at home, to give them and us all time and space to get through this tragedy."

The camera panned in on the girls hugging before the segment ended. Then, the scene shifted to where the reporter stood live in front of Sunny World Park. Crowds of tourists continued to stream in and out of the theme park even as the reporter ended the segment.

"Heartbreaking. Just heartbreaking. A life gone too soon, and so many families impacted. As the police finish up the investigation surrounding Tommy Harding's death, we know the community at Fort Grover High School will be leaving their senior trip forever changed from this moment."

The segment ended, and almost immediately, both Kiara's and Priscilla's phones lit up. Messages from classmates and strangers on the internet ballooned in their notifications. Some people were even reaching out to them in DMs and commenting on old Tommy posts where the girls had been tagged.

"People are already taking sides," Priscilla said. "Team Kiara versus Team Priscilla and Team Nevaeh."

Kiara scrolled through her phone. Just as Priscilla had said, the messages and posts on Kiara's public pages were from strangers online defending her for whatever stiffness and awkwardness she'd displayed in the interview.

User287544: The fact that Tommy managed to score Kiara is the real crime here. He cheated on her and lied to her. Trash human. He had it coming. #TeamKiara

Silly82: Priscilla has been nothing but gracious through this whole situation and interview. She was one of Tommy's best friends. Yes, she made a mistake, but she's owning up to it. Love the sisterhood she exudes in the interview. She needs all the support she can get now.

Honey65: I feel bad for Nevaeh. It was wrong of Tommy to film her in the locker room and it's so messed up that his account—hacked or not—leaked photos of her. I hope she sues to get them removed. Makes me wonder if Tommy is as great as a guy as everyone says he is.

Mandy58_: I need more people talking about the fact that Tommy is a serial cheater and a creep, plz? Filming girls in locker rooms. Cheating on his girlfriend? Kiara did nothing but support him their whole relationship, even when he posted that prank video about messing up her college applications. She deserves better. So glad she got into her dream school. #TeamKiara

Seagurlheartsharding: No one's talking about the necklace Tommy gave his girlfriend? Funny how she suddenly doesn't have it. #They'relyinginourfaces

After hours of scrolling, Kiara and Priscilla put their phones down.

"See," Priscilla said. "I told you things would be fine."

But despite Priscilla's reassurances, Kiara couldn't help but worry. One of the comments had mentioned the necklace Tommy had given her. If some stranger on the internet could pick up on such a tiny detail, then surely others would start wondering about it too.

Part of Kiara had hoped she'd find it as she'd begun packing her things. Yet even as she put away her wax-print headscarves and jewelry, even as she rifled through everything possible of hers that she'd brought on the trip, still Kiara couldn't find it.

Which only meant one thing.

It must still be in the fun house. Kiara remembered the sound of it clattering against glass when she'd torn it off her neck.

If Tommy's parents asked to see it, Kiara wouldn't be able to make up another excuse now that she had publicly admitted to still having the necklace. And then there were the police. No doubt, authorities would be searching the area near where the body had been found even harder now that the autopsy had come out. If they found the necklace in the park, they'd make the connection that Kiara had been in the fun house when Tommy had died. That maybe the person he'd gotten into an altercation with was her.

She had to find it. Kiara had to make sure no more rumors could crop up about her and Tommy's accident.

Kiara was almost to the hotel door when Priscilla stopped her.

The smug smile had fallen from Priscilla's expression. What was left was an echo of terror that made Kiara's blood curdle.

"What's wrong?"

But Priscilla wouldn't speak. She had one hand on Kiara's arm and the other still holding her own phone. The screen was open to Tommy's account page and a video was playing on loop. The audio was muted. But the images on the screen showed moments from their senior trip.

In it Kiara, Tommy, Alex, and Jason were drinking in Tommy's hotel room.

Tommy was staring directly at the camera with a wild panicked look in his eyes. It took Kiara a moment to realize that Priscilla had filmed this footage right before the group would head into Sunny World, back when they were partying in his room and searching for the burner phone.

Without asking Priscilla, Kiara raised the volume on the clip.

"If anything in that burner gets out, we're all screwed. Some secrets are better left with the dead."

The footage changed to screenshots between Nevaeh and Tommy.

Thomas: I was hacked.

Nevaeh: I don't care. Delete them. Please. If you care about me at all, if you really love me like you say you did, just delete them forever before the hacker can post them.

Thomas: Just meet me at the fun house in half an hour. You can take my phone and delete the messages directly from there so you know they're really gone. I just want us to talk first. You're my saint. You're the only thing that keeps me away from the dark.

Nevaeh: Okay. I'll meet you there. But if you're lying again I'll never forgive you.

Again, the footage changed, this time to just after the interview. It was an obscured clip recorded amid the chaos of the production team and Sunny World workers running up and down the conference room. Kiara recognized the scene—it was when Kiara, Nevaeh, and Priscilla had taken a moment to speak among themselves. Someone had filmed them. The view was nestled between two seats, but the shot was too far to actually record the conversation the girls were having. In fact, the footage and the audio didn't match, yet somehow the sound was as crisp and clear as if the camera had been standing right next to them with a microphone in hand.

"Him dying is something I should add to my résumé."

"Tragic dead boyfriend would make for a pretty good vlog."

"I don't want people to think anything more happened that night."

The realization hit Kiara then.

Their mics had been on.

The whole time the girls had been speaking, the crew had been recording their conversation. And they hadn't even noticed. Whoever made this video must have gotten access to the tapes and cut the audio clips together with their video.

Priscilla came to the same conclusion too.

"This is bad," she whispered. "This is so bad."

The audio in the video jumped, switching instead to Priscilla interrogating Nevaeh with suspicion in her own voice.

"You were blatantly lying."

"Let's put this whole thing behind us," Kiara's voice echoed on the clip. *"From here on out, we never speak of what happened that night."*

Then, another recording of Priscilla's voice followed Kiara's.

"Pretend however much you want. I'm glad that asshole . . . is . . . dead."

The last part of Priscilla's voice sounded strange, the intonation different from how her sentence had begun. It was almost as if the words had been stitched together.

"I never said that," Priscilla said. "I never said I was glad he was dead."

Kiara knew that. Or, at least, she couldn't remember Priscilla saying that exactly. But confronted with the recording, even Kiara wasn't quite sure what she herself had said in that moment.

But it didn't matter. The post wasn't finished. After the audio recording and the distant scenes in the conference room, the video changed. The image was grainy, so much so that Kiara wasn't sure if a phone had filmed it or an old security camera. Faintly, she could make out the background of a room. A locker room. Just like the one where they'd spent last night changing into costumes for the prank. A sign reading *Employees Only* was taped to the wall and above it was a digital clock. For a moment, Kiara thought the video had frozen, but then suddenly, text appeared on the screen on top of the image.

The saint.
The sinner.
The girlfriend.
Each of them had a reason to want him dead.
Don't believe the lies in their interviews.

The final clip was from in the park. It showed a replay of the argument Kiara and Tommy had been having with Priscilla as the rest of their classmates looked on.

Tommy was clutching his cheek. Kiara glared at him as if the simple burn of her gaze might incinerate him.

"*We're over,*" Kiara in the video said. "*And don't you ever, ever, ever, try me again.*"

chapter twenty-four

Priscilla

IN THE SPAN of a three-minute, terribly edited video, Priscilla had gone from the vindicated boyfriend stealer to Tommy's killer.

This was it. Her life was over.

One by one, her sponsors left concerned messages and distressed phone calls notifying Priscilla that until everything was cleared up with Tommy, they didn't feel comfortable having Priscilla represent their brands. This was hilarious, considering that most of the products themselves were toxic and didn't actually work at all. The fact that Priscilla had managed to convince her dedicated followers to buy the products was a miracle in itself.

But just as the brand deals kept falling through, so did comments from Priscilla's followers. There were DMs and messages from avid fans begging Priscilla to go on live and deny the posts from Tommy's account. At least for now, they were still on her side. But if they found out about the shoddy deals and products Priscilla had been pushing, it would be one more example of her being the liar Tommy's account was claiming her to be.

"What are we going to do?" Kiara whispered.

Priscilla shook her head. "I'll talk to my lawyers." Which in reality meant she'd talk to her parents, who would hopefully talk to lawyers for Priscilla.

"You didn't talk to your lawyers before you pushed us to do the interview?" Kiara said, practically screaming.

"Um, if I remember correctly, *you're* the one who pushed us into doing the interview in the first place. And I called them. They just didn't call back and we didn't have time to go back and forth on a decision, so I made an executive one."

Kiara was pacing now, which was really not helping the situation.

"My parents are the ones who pay for them. And my parents aren't exactly aware that things are going so bad right now. I have all their phones set to block my name on search engines. The only reason they found out about this situation is because the school called them," Priscilla admitted. "I'm also incredibly good at spinning things."

"You mean manipulating people."

"Says the girl who still won't explain how she got in contact with this clearly shady reporter," Priscilla snapped back.

Tears began to form in Kiara's eyes. "We're going to jail."

"We're not going to jail. Tommy's death was an accident."

"That's not what everyone else thinks," Kiara said. "Do you see how many times that video has been reposted? There are even major accounts talking about it now. Some people are even saying Tommy's the one posting. That he's trying to get justice for his death from beyond the grave."

Kiara's parents had even called her, demanding answers to the rumors. Priscilla listened to her lie and tell them she didn't know what was going on, but the school was handling it and she'd be home soon. It wasn't like they'd be able to do much. Buying last-minute plane tickets and leaving work early wasn't something Kiara's parents could afford, she'd said. The thought of never seeing her family again, of being stuck here, was devastating to both of them.

"Well, some people are imbeciles," Priscilla snapped. "And everyone knows all the accounts just do gossip, not actual journalism. They're completely focusing on the wrong thing. What they should be worried about is the hacker. Clearly, they're the ones pulling all the strings here, and for some reason, they've decided to target us."

Kiara gasped.

"What?" Priscilla said, frowning. "Go ahead, spill."

The other girl shook her head, clearly running an idea in her head.

"Hello?" Priscilla snapped impatiently.

"Remember when Tommy was looking for his burner phone?"

Priscilla rolled her eyes. "Yes, how could I forget? He was so freakin' annoying about it."

"Well, back there, in the park, he said he thought the hacker had his burner phone. Tommy was literally convinced that the hacker was you and you were trying to get revenge on him or something."

"I'm not the hacker," Priscilla said. "I can't believe he would even say that." But a part of her could believe it. Because Tommy would do anything to play the victim. Even if it meant villainizing the real victims.

"But what if he's right? Not about you being the hacker, but about the hacker having his burner phone?" Kiara said. "It would explain the posts, how his private footage and texts are leaking. It could explain why they could have all this information on Tommy and us."

The plausibility of the idea struck a chord for both of them.

"That could make sense," Priscilla said. "Plus, did you see the footage from the interview? Someone was filming from the conference room. They might be the same person. That's how they could have gotten the audio from our mics." In her head, Priscilla ran through the stream of faces she'd seen sitting in the mostly empty seats during the interview. "They could be one of our classmates who came to watch the taping. Maybe someone who was in the hotel room with us right before we headed to the park? Daniel and Leah had been at the party, right—maybe it's one of them?"

For a moment, Priscilla thought to mention how she'd hidden the burner under Tommy's mattress. But Tommy had already suggested to Kiara that Priscilla was the hacker. She didn't want to look even guiltier by admitting to having hid the burner phone from Tommy at some point.

"Maybe they stole it when we were all partying in the room together," she said instead. Maybe they were in it together?

"I don't think Danny and Leah would do something like that," Kiara said.

Priscilla laughed. "You don't know Tommy's friends."

"They're my friends too," Kiara said.

"Whatever you say," Priscilla said. "Look, I just need to go back to Tommy's room and confirm something."

"Something like?"

"If the phone's still there," Priscilla said, skirting around the fact that she'd purposely hidden it. Kiara refused to come clean about how she'd landed the interview for them, so Priscilla was just keeping her own cards close to her chest too. They could work together. But that didn't mean they needed to completely trust each other. They were in the same boat and, for now, that was enough to keep them together.

"If it's not, then we can narrow down the culprits and I can have names for my lawyers to go after in our slowly forming libel suit. Trust me, once the hacker gets a good cease-and-desist letter, the account won't dare make another post again."

They just had to figure out how to get past the chaperones monitoring the halls. Part of Priscilla didn't expect Kiara to agree to her idea. But with the fallout of Tommy's recent posts, it was clear that they were backed into a corner.

"Fine," Kiara said after Priscilla had explained her plan. "But if this goes wrong—"

"Then we're both screwed," Priscilla said, cutting Kiara off. "We're in this together."

So much for the senior trip of their dreams. No, this was a senior trip of nightmares.

As they ran through possibilities, they were interrupted by a sudden knock on the door.

Priscilla and Kiara froze.

"What if it's the police?" Kiara whispered urgently.

Priscilla swallowed. At the rate things were going, that could be a possibility. With everything happening, it was only a matter of time until the investigation intensified from courtesy conversations in hotel suites to downright interrogations in precincts.

"Just be cool," Priscilla said. "Stay calm. We'll figure this out." She gave Kiara a harsh look before opening the door.

There, standing right outside their door, were Mr. Phillips and two police officers.

"So much for staying calm," Kiara whispered.

Despite the wave of nausea beginning to overtake Priscilla she managed to force a smile.

"Is it our turn for dinner yet?" Priscilla asked.

Mr. Phillips looked solemn.

"No. Actually, the school just sent out an announcement that we'll be delaying the return back to New Jersey until the investigation subsides."

"That's great," Priscilla said. "I hope they find out what happened soon."

But Mr. Phillips didn't return her smile with one of his own.

"Now, I don't want you girls to be alarmed," Mr. Phillips said, which was, like, a terrible way to not alarm them. "But the officers specifically requested to speak to you girls along with a few other of your classmates who they'd like to interview again."

"I need to call my parents," Kiara said.

"The school is in contact with all of them already. Once we're finished here, you can go ahead and call them yourselves. Now," Mr. Phillips said, "come with us."

AS MR. PHILLIPS AND the police escorted Priscilla and Kiara to their makeshift interrogation room, Priscilla caught a glimpse of Tommy's hotel room.

Yellow tape guarded the door and the area itself was being

monitored by two officers. There was no way Priscilla would be able to slip in and search for the burner phone without getting caught, at least not until the officers changed shifts.

The hallways were otherwise empty during the rest of the walk. Most of their classmates had been restricted to their rooms. A few of them peeked out from behind doors to get a look at the girls retreating, only for Mr. Phillips to snap at them to go back to their rooms—and after they'd taken a few photos.

This time, their interview was being conducted by detectives.

The first of the two was a tall white man with red hair, freckles, and somber green eyes. The other detective, a Latina with dark brown hair and a nose piercing, stood a few inches shorter than him. They introduced themselves. They must have. But the moment they flashed their badges, Priscilla's mind got stuck on only those numbers: 1807 and 1817.

Together, the two led the group into a lounge where Alex, Jason, Daniel, and Leah were sitting along with Mrs. Hall. On the table in front of Alex was a box filled with camera equipment, which Priscilla recognized as his own. From the looks of it, he'd been able to reclaim the rest of his things from his and Tommy's old room.

Priscilla took the seat beside Alex while Kiara sat on her other side next to Jason.

"Hi," Priscilla whispered to Alex. He looked away. But beneath the table, his hand found hers. Their fingers twined. The warmth of his touch anchored Priscilla. It was as if in that moment, everything would be okay.

"I was just explaining to Mrs. Hall that after the first round of questioning, you guys kept getting asked by people online about what was going on," Alex said. "You thought it would be better to talk directly to Tommy's fans through the interview since they were harassing you guys in your DMs."

It took all the restraint Priscilla had to not kiss Alex then and there. How was he always there, defending her, trying to protect her in his own way? She squeezed his hand, hoping he understood the gesture of thanks and, well, more.

"Yes. That's exactly why we decided to do that very public interview," Priscilla said. "We wanted to clear things up as much as we could. But we should have talked to the school and our chaperones first. We're sorry."

Detective 1807, the redhead, closed the door behind them.

"Well," he said, "how about you talk to us? Where were you both last night before Tommy Harding died?"

It was the interview all over again, but this time, the officers standing in front of them were writing down notes and making recordings of their own. Priscilla tried to keep her voice measured as she spoke, but all she could think about was the fact that someone among them may be the hacker, and whatever they said in this moment might wind up on Tommy's account, or worse, indict the two girls further in the eyes of the justice system.

"Leah and I went to the park with everyone else," Daniel said. "But we had way too much to drink. We wound up crashing in the teacup ride, where one of the Sunny World workers found us the next morning."

"Alex and I were filming in the park," Priscilla lied again. She shot a quiet glance at Alex, hoping that he hadn't rescinded his offer to be her alibi now that foul play in Tommy's death was a possibility. He looked uneasy, close to being sick, honestly. Licking his lips, he spoke softly.

"I showed your officer friends the videos we filmed in the

park. They all had time stamps. I was teaching Priscilla how to get a good night shot."

"But she wasn't in any of the shots," Detective 1807 said.

"Neither was I," Alex said, speaking more firmly this time. "Directors are always behind the cameras. Not in front of them."

With a curt nod, Detective 1817 wrote something down.

All eyes turned to Kiara who, even during the interview, had yet to answer where she was when Tommy died.

"Ms. Stephens?" Detective 1817 prompted. "Where were you when the incident took place?"

Kiara's lips parted. "I—I was with Jason. After Tommy and I had that very embarrassing public fight, I—I met up with Jason. He was trying to make me feel better about the situation. We stayed together for the rest of the night and went right back to the hotel."

Leah gasped in shock. "No freaking way. You two really were seeing each other behind Tommy's back."

Priscilla winced. With the hacker on the loose, this was definitely information Kiara wouldn't want at least one person in this room to know about.

"We're just friends," Kiara said. But even she didn't sound convinced by her own words.

"Mr. Chen?" Detective 1807 said. "Is this true?"

It was almost like everyone was holding their breaths now, waiting for Jason to either confirm or deny Kiara's statement. But Priscilla already knew the truth. Kiara and she had seen each other that morning. They'd staggered back into the hotel together. And from the look on Jason's face, clearly he knew that too. Yet, he didn't answer immediately. Instead, he gave Kiara a long, searching look. Silence stretched between them. The moment felt like an eternity. Then, finally, Jason spoke.

"Kiara doesn't want to tell the truth because it doesn't look good," he said. "But it's true. We were together that night. As a couple. Not just as friends."

Priscilla was stunned. He'd lied. He'd really lied and said he was with Kiara the whole time. But why? Why, unless at least some of what the account had been posting was true?

Did Kiara really have something to do with Tommy's accident? Did Jason? Is that why he was willing to lie for her and be her alibi even if it meant revealing the fact that they'd had a secret relationship? Had Tommy known about them before the accident? Or was this all somehow connected?

"Wait till the account finds this out," Leah said.

"There will be no account involved in this matter," Redhead Detective said. "All of these accusations are just that until we can create a timeline of how Tommy Harding ended up dead during his senior trip."

Priscilla raised her hand. "If none of us was with Tommy when he died, can we leave now?"

The detective glared at her, but since they clearly had alibis, there wasn't much they could do about keeping them for questioning any longer. But if they did try to keep interrogating them, Priscilla knew she'd have to invoke the fifth. Not because she was guilty or anything, but more to keep her words from being misconstrued by the hacker or the police.

"Hotel footage will be reviewed to corroborate all of your statements," Detective 1817 said. "That will decide if you were all telling the truth, or if a deeper investigation needs to be done."

"There was a power outage that night," Alex said. "Tommy orchestrated it so we could sneak out of the hotel without our chaperones finding out. I don't think there will be footage, but fingers crossed right?"

The detectives exchanged looks.

"He's right," Detective 1807 said. "No hotel footage from that night."

Detective 1817 sighed. "That makes things harder," she said, "but we'll speak to more witnesses and see what the hotel staff has to say for as long as it takes."

Alex stood.

"Great. So can I take the rest of my equipment now that you're finished looking through it?"

"And can we leave?" Leah asked. "I have to call my parents." She clutched her phone tightly. But clearly she was dying to spread the news that Kiara and Jason had been secretly seeing each other even though Kiara was supposed to be with Tommy.

Reluctantly, the detectives nodded.

"Bring the next group," Detective 1807 said, reluctantly passing the box of recording equipment back to Alex. Priscilla spotted a camera sticking out over the top edge, along with a tangle of cords. "And Mrs. Hall or Mr. Phillips, would one of you mind staying behind for a moment? There are a few follow-up questions we'd like to ask about what kind of access the kids might have had to the park during the trip."

While Mrs. Hall stayed to talk to the detectives as they waited for the next group, Alex grabbed the box and Mr. Phillips escorted their group out of the lounge. As they left, though, Priscilla heard the trail of a whispered exchange between Mrs. Hall and the detectives. Their voices were low, but she could clearly hear the words.

"This case will likely be escalated to the homicide department."

Priscilla turned to look at Kiara, who had clearly heard the words as well. They were screwed. Totally and utterly screwed.

"Girl?" Priscilla whispered.

Kiara shook her head. "I know. Just, not now," she whispered.

They were still within earshot of the group. Jason walked in the center of the pack next to Alex, while Kiara and Priscilla trailed behind. When Mr. Phillips, Daniel, and Leah turned the corner, Jason stopped midstep. Priscilla, Alex, and Kiara practically ran into him.

Priscilla stifled a gasp as Jason yanked the group aside into a small alcove.

"What the hell?" Alex said, barely managing to keep his box of equipment from tumbling to the ground.

"You stole the words from my mouth," Jason said. "What just happened back there?"

Heat burned against Priscilla's cheeks. Alex refused to meet Jason's gaze, while Kiara suddenly seemed to be very interested in her nails.

"Kiara?" Jason said. "Are you going to explain why you had me lie for you or should I go back to the others and tell them how we weren't actually together when my brother died?"

"Jason," Kiara began.

"Don't 'Jason' me," he snapped. "Do you know what my family's going through right now? My stepdad has barely been able to eat since the news came out, and here I am, lying about being with the one person who might actually know anything about what happened to Tommy. You left me to go see him, Kiara. You said you were giving him the necklace back. And the next morning, his body is found in the park and the police are saying his cause of death was linked to injuries he suffered that night. And now there's all these rumors from his account. The only reason I'm not marching you back there myself is I want to hear you say what happened yourself. Not some sanitized crap for some interview. The truth. The real truth."

Kiara shot a look at Priscilla and then at Jason, as if a battle was raging in her head. But the fact that Kiara and Priscilla had left Sunny World together that morning didn't answer where Kiara had been alone before.

"It's going to sound bad if I say it," Kiara said.

"I don't think anything can sound as bad as what I'm possibly thinking right now," Jason said. "Just tell me. Please."

Kiara looked away, biting her lip as she searched for words. When she spoke, her voice trembled. It was the first time Priscilla had ever seen the girl look so . . . vulnerable.

"I was going to give the necklace back," Kiara began. "Just like I said. And that's the only reason I went to see him. I swear. But I was drunk. Like, really drunk. And I thought if I just returned it and everything he'd ever given me, then we'd be even. Mostly even. Even enough. I remember hearing Tommy in the fun house but not really seeing him, and then getting lost and confused and scared. Instead of trying to find a way out, I just sort of gave up and went to sleep in the fun house overnight. When I woke up, I was still there. Obviously. I walked outside and Priscilla was coming out of the fun house too. We ended up going back to our hotel together."

Priscilla struggled to keep her expression blank during Kiara's revelation. So the other girl had seen Tommy that night. It hadn't just been Priscilla. And the account. It had posted that Nevaeh had met with Tommy too. All of the revelations left one question: which of the girls had seen Tommy before he died?

The thought was suffocating. Priscilla was only able to bury it when Alex stepped between the two, the box of equipment he carried working almost like a barrier shielding Kiara.

"Don't bring Priscilla into this. The police already know the two of us were filming together the whole time."

"So does that mean you were in the fun house too? Is that why you have Tommy's stuff?"

"What are you even talking about?" Alex said.

But Kiara was already reaching into his box of things. She pulled out a smartwatch and dangled it in front of Alex.

"This is Tommy's, isn't it?"

Now it was Alex who looked defensive. He grabbed the watch from Kiara's hands and shoved it back into the box of equipment. As he did, his shirtsleeve rode up so that his own smartwatch was clearly visible on his wrist.

"Tommy's watch was one of the things the police recovered in the investigation in the park. He left it in the locker room when we were changing into our costumes," he said. "They already looked through it and didn't find anything."

Priscilla shot Alex a questioning look.

In the park, Alex had said he'd accidentally swapped his smartwatch with Tommy's. If the police had recovered Alex's watch in the park, then of course they wouldn't have found anything. Because that night, Alex had Tommy's watch. So why hadn't Alex given it to them for their investigation?

"And in case you hadn't realized," Alex continued, doing his best to avoid meeting Priscilla's gaze, "Tommy and I ran a whole company together. I was Tommy's brand manager and videographer. Of course I would have some equipment we shared. I'm the one who paid for it, so they gave it back to me."

Kiara laughed. "Oh, yes. I'm sure."

Priscilla wanted answers too. But she wasn't about to let Kiara and Jason be the ones to interrogate Alex. Not when Alex had already done Priscilla such a huge favor.

"He's right, though," Priscilla said. "We shared tons of equipment. That doesn't mean Alex had anything to do with what happened to Tommy." Kiara was just grasping at straws. She couldn't prove anything.

Jason turned to Alex. "Then what about Tommy's phone?"

Alex frowned. "You know he was looking for the burner the whole time we were at the park."

"No," Jason said, "I mean his real phone. The one the police found with his body wasn't his. When the police were talking to my stepdad earlier, they let it slip that the phone was one of the employee ones Sunny World workers use. None of the Sunny World workers know who it belongs to because the phones rotate depending on the shift. But the person who'd originally been assigned to use that particular phone hadn't stayed in the park after hours during our senior prank. Whoever was helping Tommy get access to the park might know why Tommy had the phone instead."

Alex glared at Jason, defiant.

"Unless Tommy stole it himself," Alex said. "Like I said to the police, I was with Priscilla. If Tommy was planning a prank or filming extra vlog content for his account with one of the Sunny World workers, I wouldn't know."

"He's lying," Kiara said. "They're both lying. You can't trust either of them."

"And I don't know who to trust," Jason said. "You need to go to the police. You need to tell them everything you know."

"Jason, the police are using a hacked vlog account that clearly has a grudge against us for answers to this case. Do you seriously think they'll believe what any of us are saying?"

"And you guys can't even keep your freakin' stories straight. Why the hell should I trust you?"

"Because we want the truth just as much as you," Priscilla said. "These lies and half-truths the hacker is going around spreading— it's to target us."

"But why?" Jason said.

"If we knew that, this wouldn't be happening," Priscilla shot back.

Priscilla pulled out her phone. Since the video had gone out she hadn't gotten a chance to watch it again. To be honest, she didn't want to. But there had to be a reason. There had to be something in the account's posts that exposed the hacker for who they really were. Swallowing, Priscilla played the video back. Jason, Kiara, and Alex watched over her shoulder as the footage played again. It showed the behind-the-scenes from the interview, the fight, and then the final clip with the text over the background in the locker room. Priscilla was just about to play the video again when Kiara stopped her on the clip with the text.

"Yes, we all saw the labels the hacker gave us," Priscilla said, rolling her eyes.

"It's not that. Can you zoom in? To the background right before the text comes on-screen?"

Priscilla rewound the footage and paused just before the text appeared.

"That's just a clip from the locker room video," Priscilla said.

"I thought so too. But do you see the clock above the employee locker room sign?" Kiara said. "Shouldn't it say, like, midnight or something if it was from the livestream where Tommy was filming Nevaeh? Or even from last night at all? But the clock says *PM*. And the date and time on it. It's from today. It wasn't even two hours ago."

Priscilla frowned.

"As in?"

"The person who took that photo shot it in the park," Alex said, finishing the thought. "Right before they posted it onto Tommy's account today." He pointed to the time stamp of the post, which showed that just five minutes after the photo had been taken, the account had posted the video onto Tommy's page.

The realization hit Priscilla. It was so visceral it almost knocked the wind out of her.

"The hacker could still be in the park," she whispered. "If they took this photo for the post, then they might still be in Sunny World now, preparing for the next one."

A rush of questions churned in Priscilla's mind. "Who were the people in the conference room with us when we were filming the interview?" she said, directing the question to Kiara. "Did you pay attention to any of them? Did you see anyone filming during it?"

At the time of the filming, Priscilla had been too focused on answering the interviewer's questions to notice any commotion in the audience. But clearly, someone—the hacker—had been among the crowd watching in the conference room. That's how they'd managed to film the behind-the-scenes video and it's probably how they'd gotten the sound bites from the girls' mics from the sound crew. When the girls had returned to their rooms, the person had gone back to Sunny World Park, where they'd then posted on Tommy's account.

"Nevaeh's brother was in the audience," Kiara said. "And so was Ren. But I was watching him. He didn't have his phone out once."

"Ren?" Priscilla repeated. Jason seemed just as clueless as Priscilla. But Alex's reaction caught Priscilla off guard. It was subtle. His eyes widened just a little, and his lips parted as if he was going to say something. But in a rare, very unlike Alex move, he stayed quiet.

Silent alarm bells went off in Priscilla's head. She didn't know why she was feeling like this. Alex had been her alibi. She'd been the one to trick him into agreeing to cover for her. But Priscilla couldn't shake the simple fact that, as their video-man and producer, the only other person who might have access to Tommy's account was Alex.

"Renton Davis," Kiara said, cutting off the trail of thoughts in Priscilla's mind. "His father owns Sunny World. He's also the one who helped set up the interview for us."

"And somehow the audio leaks and the interview is botched?" Priscilla said.

Kiara shook her head. "It wasn't Ren. Tommy cut a deal with him to let the seniors into Sunny World for the prank. But he's been just as screwed as we've been since this whole situation blew up. The park's reputation has taken a hit, and it's not exactly going well for them since they've kept it open while the investigation is happening."

"Is that why you did the interview?" Jason said. "So you could help Mr. Sunny World with his park's rebrand?"

Priscilla stared at Kiara, waiting for an answer too. But her silence was answer enough.

"You used us," Priscilla said. "Not to make this about me," she said sheepishly at the exhausted look Jason shot her way.

"My parents were planning on suing Sunny World," he said. "The Davis family has done nothing to help with the investigation. But instead of helping us find out what happened to Tommy, you were working with them."

"I'm sorry," Kiara said. "I was wrong."

"I just want to know what you got out of it," Priscilla said. "Like, did he, like, pay you or something?"

"What? No," Kiara said. "I just—I just thought it would be a good idea to stop all the rumors and everything the internet was saying about all of us. I truly thought Tommy's death was an accident and we were clearing the air," Kiara said. "But I was wrong. So I'm fixing it now, okay?"

Kiara placed a hand on Jason's arm. Even though he flinched, Jason didn't pull away completely.

"Give us twenty-four hours," she said. "In twenty-four hours, if we don't find the hacker and the truth of what happened, then we'll walk everything we know over to the police. You have our word."

Jason looked hesitant. In the distance, they could hear the approach of footsteps as Mr. Phillips must have realized the group had ventured off.

"How can I trust you?"

Kiara looked pained at his words. "You don't have any reason to," she admitted. "But I want to prove that I didn't kill Tommy. The police don't care about the real truth. Neither does the account. But we do. So we need to work together. All of us," Kiara said.

"And you think Nevaeh will help?" Priscilla asked. "Isn't she halfway out of the state?"

"She'll help," Kiara said. "I'll convince her. She trusts me."

"Yeah. Just like when it came to the interview, right?"

At the very least, Kiara had the sense to look ashamed of herself.

The three turned to Jason, waiting to see if he would agree. His phone chimed, and from the caller ID, Priscilla could see it was his stepfather calling.

"Fine," Jason said. "Twenty-four hours. And no more lies. Because if you don't expose the truth of what happened to Tommy, then that hacker will—and they sure as hell aren't on your side. Based on what the cops told my parents, they can't take the account's accusations seriously without evidence to back them up, but the footage they've posted, and the texts? Those are fair game."

His words were both a warning and a threat. Priscilla had been worried that the hacker's posts were gaining traction with the public. But they'd just heard the officers whispering about escalating the case to the homicide department. And if Jason was telling the truth, that meant the girls were one wrong accusation away from being charged in connection with Tommy's death.

They'd be screwed if that happened. Because just like Kiara, Priscilla had fought with Tommy. But it had been in the fun house, likely moments before his death. If the account twisted that night's events like they had with the audio footage after the interview, then no one would believe Priscilla's story about what really happened.

Priscilla would be charged. She was sure of that.

"Let's see if Nevaeh's seen the post," Priscilla said. "We'll probably have to catch her up with everything we know."

In that moment, Priscilla made a choice: whatever it took, whatever levels she had to stoop to, she would make sure that the person who took the fall for Tommy's death wasn't her.

chapter twenty-five

Nevaeh

"DID YOU FORGET anything?"

Nevaeh didn't move from her seat. In fact, she barely remembered sliding into the back seat of her parents' car. She hadn't even listened to her mother's lectures or her father explain how their flight would be leaving in a few hours.

The account had manipulated the footage.

Just a few hours before, she'd been relieved knowing that the interview had gone well. But now, the harassing messages were still trickling in. Strangers on the internet were demanding that Nevaeh turn herself in for the role she might have played in killing Tommy Harding. And it was all because of Tommy's account.

Whoever hacked it had a vendetta against the three girls.

She was going to throw up. Nevaeh didn't know how she managed to sit in the back of her parents' car and act like everything was all right when her insides felt like someone had taken a shredder to them. But everything wasn't fine. That's why they were leaving. Nevaeh's parents didn't think it was safe for her to stay in the state. And since there was no real warrant keeping her in Florida, now was their safest chance of returning home before anything else escalated. If the police needed her to continue the investigation, then her parents said they'd cooperate from across state lines.

Laurence nudged Nevaeh from the next seat.

"You good?"

Nevaeh nodded.

"Yeah, just feeling a little sick. I have everything, though."

Her parents continued to talk from the front seat.

"We're almost at the airport," their father said. "Your mother and I will head back to the hotel after we drop you off and finish off the last two days of the conference. You and Laurence will be picked up by your aunt at the airport back home."

Laurence nodded.

"Nice. It'll be cool to have the house to ourselves when we get back. Wasn't there a movie you said you were dying to see? Maybe it's on streaming by now?"

"Yeah. Maybe," Nevaeh said.

And they didn't know how desperately she wanted to leave Sunny World.

Even as the thought crossed Nevaeh's mind, her phone dinged. In her inbox, there was a message from Kiara. Nevaeh's heart jolted in horror.

Kiara: Meet us at Sunny World. It's an emergency. We need to go to the fun house and figure out what really happened.

Had Kiara lost her mind? Sunny World? The fun house? They had to be working with the hacker. Why else would they want Nevaeh to show her face in the park where the crime—no, accident, Nevaeh reminded herself—had taken place.

No. No. No. Nevaeh wasn't going to do this. She wasn't going to be roped back into this mess. Not again.

Her father pulled into the airport and they navigated through ramps up to departures leaving the state.

Nevaeh's mother unbuckled her seat belt, then reached over to Nevaeh to do the same, like Nevaeh was some sort of toddler in the back of the car.

"I can do it myself," Nevaeh whispered.

"If you could do anything yourself then you wouldn't have wound up in this situation," her mother said. "I still can't believe you. Sending dirty pictures to boys. Sneaking from your hotel room at night to go do who-knows-what."

"That was only once," Nevaeh said, but even as she'd said it, she knew she'd cornered herself.

She couldn't hide it from her parents and Laurence.

"So you're not denying it. You saw him that night."

"I—"

Her mother held her hand up, her stare scorching Nevaeh. "No. Don't answer that. In fact, don't speak at all."

In the front seat, her father bowed his head, whispering softly in prayer. Unlike with his sermons, he spoke in Twi, his voice rising and twisting with emotion. Nevaeh's mother joined him, bowing her head, whispering, though in English.

Laurence held out his hand for Nevaeh to join them. She shook her head.

Despite his voice calling after her, Nevaeh slipped out of the car and slammed the door behind her.

Everything was unraveling and it was all because she'd let Kiara and Priscilla manipulate her into doing that interview.

Forget the dead body found in the park. Forget the rumors

swirling on the internet. The truth of Nevaeh and Tommy's encounter that night would be an indictment.

Nevaeh had wanted to delete the photos from Tommy's phone and she'd done so at lengths even she knew had been too far. If the account could twist a simple interview, than what would the hacker do once they found out what Nevaeh had done?

Nevaeh walked quickly into the airport. Inside, palm trees craned their heads back against the sunny room. The crisscrossing metal beams cast octagonal shadows across the crowds that filled the building. She moved without direction, pushing past travelers and baggage carts filled with luggage.

When her phone rang, Nevaeh looked down to see her mother's name on the caller ID.

Instead of answering, though, she dialed Kiara's number.

Knots of trepidation wove through Nevaeh's chest. She couldn't breathe, couldn't speak.

"Hello?" Kiara said.

"We promised to put this behind us," Nevaeh whispered, trying to stifle her rage the best she could. "So why is the account making more posts and you're messaging me about going back to Sunny World and the fun house when you know the hacker is literally stalking our digital footprints?"

"Because the police are going to escalate the case to the homicide department," Kiara said.

"What does that have to do with me?" Nevaeh said, practically screaming. "I'm leaving Florida. I'm going back home. I want nothing to do with this."

"It's too late. We need to clear our names before the hacker frames us. Meet us at Sunny World. The park's still open. They've only closed off the fun house and the area where his body was found."

"As in that underground section of the park?" Nevaeh said, remembering what she'd overheard the police say from before.

"The hacker posted a photo from the locker room. So we think they might do the tunnels next. When the police were talking to Jason's family, they said those tunnels are connected to the fun house and the gondola ride. Sunny World employees apparently use them to get through the park quickly. Maybe if we split up, we can catch the hacker before they post again."

"So find the hacker yourself. I'm not going back. The more mixed up you all get into this, the worse things will be."

"Give me the phone," a voice on Kiara's side of the line said.

"I'm talking to her."

"Just give it," the voice said. There was a pause, and then Priscilla's voice came on the line. "Nevaeh?" Priscilla said, ever so sickly sweet.

"I'm hanging up," Nevaeh said.

"And what will the hacker say when it's revealed that you left the state in the middle of a murder investigation?"

"There's no murder investigation," Nevaeh said. "And there's no warrant from the police saying we have to stay."

"Not yet," Priscilla said. "But you suddenly finding the first flight out of here when things are going wrong might have the public asking why the case isn't being treated that way. Just listen to us. Jason is going to buy us some time with his family. If we can find out who the hacker is, we can buy some time with the public while we figure out what really happened."

"And how are you going to do that?"

"By beating the hacker at their own game. They don't realize they left clues in the posts they made, or that we know they're still in Sunny World. How else do you think they got that footage and audio from the hotel interview? The photo they took from the park locker room right before posting on Tommy's account makes it clear they could still be in the park. And the screenshots they posted of your messages with Tommy last night. Was it true that you were going to meet him and delete the photos he took, even though you told us you weren't planning on meeting him at all that night?"

Everything inside Nevaeh didn't want to answer that question. But the world already knew. Because of the hacker. Because they had somehow found the messages Nevaeh had sent Tommy right before she'd bailed on meeting up with Kiara and Priscilla in the park. Right now, the two girls were the only other people in the world who probably understood what Nevaeh was going through. Nevaeh didn't trust them. Not quite. But at least they'd be able to understand her enough to see beyond the accusations of the account. Swallowing, Nevaeh answered.

"Yes," she admitted. "I met him. Just like you two did. But that's what I don't understand. There shouldn't be any evidence of our texts left—I deleted everything. I literally wiped all of his image files just to make sure the stuff was gone."

"What are you talking about?" Priscilla said. "Nevaeh, you have to tell us what happened with you that night."

If she could scream, Nevaeh would. But so many people were around her. She walked farther, and as she did, Nevaeh realized that instead of the departures section of the airport, she had stumbled all the way across the building to the arrivals section.

Crowds of families and tourists exited the airport with laughter in their eyes and smiles on their lips. In the distance, a group of men and women in Sunny World uniforms held up signs for a high school class. Nevaeh wondered if they too would be visiting the park on a school trip.

"What happened when you wiped all the images off his phone?" Priscilla asked. "Any information could make a difference at this point."

Nevaeh sighed, rubbing her forehead. She didn't want to think of that night again if she could help it. But she forced herself to recall the memories.

"He was drunk. And also on something, I think. He kept talking about someone targeting him. I got his phone and I was only supposed to delete some photos, but like I said, I wiped all of his albums and removed our message history." She closed her eyes, and underneath her eyelids the image of him emerged: Tommy leaning over her shoulder, his eyes widening with the realization of what she'd done. "He tried to take his phone back, but I ran away with it. I ended up going through the tunnels that connected the fun house to another ride. I think it was the gondola ride. Two of the Sunny World workers who were there that night found me. I asked them if they could give the phone back to the person it belonged to. I—I figured since they helped your class set up the prank, they'd know someone in Tommy's grade who could get him his phone back. But like I said, that was on the gondola ride. I'd lost Tommy by then."

"The police and our school chaperones interviewed everyone," another voice said this time, this one a guy. "None of them found or were given Tommy's phone by a Sunny World worker."

"Which means the worker might still have it," Priscilla said. "Tommy's phone was linked to the burner. He was trying to use the Find My Phone app on it. If we can find the real phone, we can trace the burner."

"But I deleted everything," Nevaeh repeated. "I made sure all his photos were gone."

"His main phone and burner are linked to the cloud," another voice explained, this one deeper than the first boy who had spoken. "You deleted the photos locally, but the ones on the cloud are backed up on the burner. It's where he keeps all the unusable footage from the pranks we film, things that cross too many lines to go out publicly without him getting canceled. I'm guessing the burner's what he used to talk with you when he was trying to keep you a secret from Kiara and Priscilla."

Nevaeh's heart deflated. So it was all for nothing. Everything she had done, everything she had risked to delete the photos, and none of it mattered.

"Why are the police focusing on us instead of the hacker?" Nevaeh said helplessly. "They're the one who started this whole thing by exposing him and his relationships. Clearly they have a vendetta against him, at the very least."

"And clearly the hacker has a motive to want to target us three. Because the only thing we all have in common is Tommy," Priscilla said. "So we need to find out what he was doing in the park that night and why the hacker wanted him gone."

There was a pause, and then Kiara's voice returned on the line.

"I think our answer is those Sunny World workers. Whoever found Tommy's real phone, whoever you met when you were running from Tommy, must be our clue. Do you remember what they looked like? The hacker would have been in the audience during the interview too. Was there anyone who looked familiar?"

Nevaeh shook her head, but obviously they couldn't see that.

"It was dark. I don't remember. Some girl and some guy? She was white and, um, wearing the Sunny World uniform. He was Black but wasn't in uniform. And I wasn't really paying attention during the interview. I was just trying to memorize what I had to say."

"Wow, so helpful," Priscilla said.

"Shut up, she's trying her best," Kiara snapped. "Why don't you ask Alex? Isn't he the one who literally helps Tommy put together all his messed-up pranks?"

"Not all of them," the deep-voiced guy said. "And not this one."

"Think harder," Priscilla said. "Is there anything about them that stood out?"

Nevaeh pressed her eyes shut. "Why am I being interrogated? Shouldn't you guys save this for the hacker?"

"Yeah, because we have them on speed dial. Again, not helping," Priscilla said.

But Nevaeh wasn't listening anymore. An idea had come to her. Quickly, she opened up the page to Tommy's account. Kiara, Priscilla, and the two boys were still arguing. But Nevaeh couldn't think of anything else that might fix this. She had to do something, something to stop this.

What do you want from us? Why are we your targets? Nevaeh wrote. Then she sent the DM to Tommy's account.

Part of her didn't expect an answer. Yet one appeared. Except it was in another private message thread, this one completely different from Nevaeh's DM. The hacker had created a group message with Nevaeh, Kiara, Priscilla, and Tommy's account. It included a screenshot of Nevaeh's initial private message. Three dots appeared as the hacker began to draft a response. When the message was delivered, it was just one sentence, yet Nevaeh's blood still curdled.

Confess your sins. Or the murderer among you will be revealed.

Nevaeh dropped her phone and it clattered to the ground. A terrible crack cut through the screen, fracturing the words from the hacker.

All around, heads turned in Nevaeh's direction. Heat crept up Nevaeh's cheeks and her head was swirling, spinning. The oxygen flow from her lips to her throat tightened painfully. And her eyes—Nevaeh could barely see through the glassy veil that suddenly blurred them.

"Sorry," she whispered.

She picked up her phone and hurried away.

From the corner of her gaze, Nevaeh spotted that same group of high schoolers. There were more of them now, most of whom wore matching T-shirts that read *Arlington High Senior Trip*.

Nevaeh zipped her hoodie. She lumbered to the edge of the group, close enough that she looked like she was one of them while still far enough away that they didn't quite notice her.

"Are you still there?" Priscilla asked.

Nevaeh grabbed her phone, holding it at a distance from her ear, lest the glass cut into her skin.

"I am. Sorry. I'm here."

This time, it was Kiara who spoke.

"The account just made another post."

Nevaeh didn't want to know what this new terror would

be. And yet, she found herself returning to the account's main page. Glass grazed her finger as the cracked screen tore into her skin. When Nevaeh pressed the new post, a trickle of blood oozed against the screen. The smear of red felt like an omen.

The latest post began with that very same screenshot of the group conversation between the three girls and the account.

What do you want from us? Why are we your targets? Nevaeh had written.

Confess your sins. Or the murderer among you will be revealed.

The account had been waiting for them to contact it. And now, Nevaeh realized, its next trap was in motion.

The next image in the carousel was a video: a scene from a hotel room. Nevaeh recognized Tommy and Kiara in the video, but it was harder to catch the faces of the others around them.

It was footage from the same live the account had played earlier—the pregame in Tommy's room. Then the camera zoomed in on the screen, showing Priscilla slipping something under the mattress while the party raged on.

"Oh my gosh, is this live?" a familiar voice said off-screen. For a second, and only a second, the camera swung to catch a glimpse of two white girls with Solo cups in their hands, chugging away at their drinks. Nevaeh's heart tightened as recognition took hold. Christina and Heather. They'd been partying with Tommy that night. And like everyone else, they'd seen as Priscilla hid something that looked like a phone under the mattress.

Confess your sins. Or the murderer among you will be revealed. And here Christina and Heather were, partying with Tommy, watching along with whoever else had been viewing the livestream as the key to Tommy's account, his burner phone, was buried between sheets by his so-called side chick.

If Christina and Heather had taken the burner phone, if they had found the photos between Nevaeh and Tommy before they'd met her in the park, they would have known about all of the lies she'd been hiding. No wonder the account had called Nevaeh the saint.

No wonder they seemed so desperate to destroy her perfect image.

The video continued, but this time the clip changed to another scene. It had been taken outside, in Sunny World Park. It was dark, with only a few streetlights illuminating the path ahead. In the distance, the waning sounds of laughter and music could be heard. Nevaeh recognized the poppy song that was playing; it was from the party with Tommy's classmates. The heavy bass reverberated through the video as the person filming trekked through the park toward the entrance of the fun house.

As they watched the scene unfold, the high schoolers Nevaeh had joined had gone quiet. A moment before they'd all been laughing and making jokes; now all of them were looking at their phones, whispering loudly to one another. They were watching Tommy's posts on their phones too. The collective volume on their phones was raised so high that Nevaeh didn't have to bother holding her phone to her ear in order to hear the audio from the footage as the person filming ventured deeper and deeper into Sunny World Park.

Ahead of them, the figure of a girl loomed. She was so shrouded in darkness and far enough away that it was hard to tell exactly who she was, except for the fact that she was dressed in a miniskirt and a crop top. A silver wig gleamed on her head and, behind her, a set of white angel wings hung at her back.

Nevaeh's heart pounded in her ears. This couldn't be happening. Not after the interview. Not after she'd already publicly lied about her alibi on the news.

In the video, the girl entered the fun house and the person recording followed at a distance. The video cut. In the next scene, the person filming had finally entered the fun house too, sweeping their camera over the walls and floor. The scene inside looked like the remnants of a violent altercation. The mirrored walls of the fun house were shattered. Glass covered the ground and blood splatters trickled across the floor. Against the fractured images, Nevaeh could make out two reflections: the person filming the video and another person walking beside them. Their images were more fragments than forms, but a hint of a tutu and feathered hat was there in a moment and then gone as they ventured deeper into the fun house. Nevaeh's heart hammered in her chest.

They continued walking until they stopped suddenly. Up ahead, a figure loomed in the fun house: the girl again. But she wasn't alone. There was another person with her and the sound of his cries sent a cool shiver down Nevaeh's back.

That voice had whispered sweet nothings to her. That voice had stirred Nevaeh's dreams.

Tommy.

In what must have been mere hours before his death, someone had stumbled upon their meeting and recorded it.

In the dark of the fun house, the footage was grainy, almost impossible to fully make out. Their shadows reflected on the broken fun house mirror walls like twisted phantoms and the sounds of their confrontation bled through; Tommy screamed, cursing at the girl. Something crashed against the wall. Then came the sound of footsteps, not one person's but two pairs of them, Tommy's and the girl's.

Nevaeh recognized the figure of the girl in the distance. Because last night, that had been her.

Nevaeh pressed her eyes shut, terror clawing against her throat. She wanted to grab the phones from the crowd, tear them away and destroy them so they could never see what would take place in the moments after the chase. But to her relief, the video went black and the clip from the fun house ended. Instead, there was a simple caption at the end of the post.

At midnight. Join the livestream. Make your confession. Or the murderer among you will be revealed.

The video ended with a countdown to midnight.

In a few hours, one of the girls would confess their part in Tommy's death. The revelations from the videos were all too much for Nevaeh to take in. Already she could feel the beginnings of a panic attack seeping through; her palms were sweaty, her breath caught in her chest. She counted backward, hoping it would subside, only for the sound of her phone to startle her again. Kiara had called back.

"Did you watch it?" Kiara said the moment Nevaeh answered.

"Yes. But it wasn't me," Nevaeh said.

There was silence on the other end of the line. The lie had spilled from Nevaeh's lips before she could stop herself. She'd already told Kiara and Priscilla that she'd met with Tommy and taken his phone. But with Tommy's death being investigated as a murder, desperation consumed Nevaeh. She couldn't admit to being the girl in the video. She wouldn't. Not when it would mean taking the fall for what happened to Tommy. Yes, she'd lied and tricked Tommy that night. Yes, they'd argued and things had spiraled out of control. But Nevaeh hadn't killed Tommy. She wasn't a murderer.

Even if the footage of the girl in the angel costume made it seem otherwise, the only other person who could have disproved this fact was dead.

"I think it's Priscilla," Kiara whispered.

Nevaeh froze, disbelief anchoring her back in reality. Before she could ask why or how the other girl had come to that conclusion, Kiara continued.

"When I woke up in the park after the party I—I saw Priscilla leaving the fun house. She was wearing the same angel costume as you. She got rid of it before we went to our hotel."

Hope stirred in Nevaeh's chest.

"You mean—you think she was impersonating me to trick Tommy?"

"Why else would she have been wearing the costume?" Kiara said. "She must have met him last night and pretended she was you. She could have been the last person to see him alive."

"Do you think she killed him?" Nevaeh asked.

Kiara was silent for a moment.

"I don't know," she said. "But something happened last night. Something terrible that ended up with Tommy dead."

It made sense. Nevaeh had told the two girls that Tommy had wanted to meet her. If Kiara was right, that meant that Priscilla had gone to see Tommy too. But the question was, when?

Had Priscilla met Tommy before Nevaeh had been able to? Or had Nevaeh been the last to see him alive?

"We need to create a timeline of when everything happened last night," Nevaeh said. "We need to go to the police."

If they could place Priscilla at the scene of the crime, no one would suspect Nevaeh as being the girl with Tommy in the video.

"She literally has the whole internet on her side," Kiara said. "Even with the interview, she was so obsessed with making us do it even after you said it was a bad idea."

Nevaeh's eyes widened as realization took.

"The hackers," she whispered. "She's working with them."

"Hackers?" Kiara repeated, letting the question in her words hang in the air.

"I think I know who they are," Nevaeh said. She closed her eyes, as the image of Christina and Heather in Tommy's hotel room replayed in her vision. "The party you guys were at, my friends Christina and Heather were there too. They saw Priscilla hide the burner phone." Nevaeh didn't add that she'd seen the girls at the end of the night after she'd left the fun house herself. They'd looked grim and kept their eyes trained on their phones. Nevaeh had hidden and watched them leave. If they had followed Nevaeh into the fun house before then, they would have been there to film the footage of the fight between Nevaeh and Tommy.

"I think they're working with Priscilla to take me down."

It all made sense now, why the hacker was obsessed with bringing down Nevaeh and Kiara. Priscilla was jealous Tommy had chosen them over her. And Heather and Christina. This whole time, she had thought the two girls had been encouraging Nevaeh to break out of her shell because they cared about her. They'd been the ones to urge her to go to the party in the park. They'd been the ones to dress her up for Tommy. All of it, they'd claimed, had been for Nevaeh's sake, when really they'd wanted to watch their church's so-called saint fall from her pedestal. They didn't care about Nevaeh at all.

Outside, the bus pulled up for the students.

"So you're coming?" Kiara asked.

Nevaeh swallowed. If she left with her family, the account would have full rein to connect Nevaeh to Tommy's death. Priscilla, Heather, and Christina were already working with one another. Which meant that Kiara was the only other person who Nevaeh could rely on. She didn't have a choice. Not anymore.

"I'm coming," Nevaeh said. "But you have to pretend you don't suspect Priscilla. Just keep her distracted and we'll play along with the hackers until we can find proof."

"I will," Kiara said.

"Then I'll meet you at the fun house," Nevaeh said. "We'll beat them at their own twisted game."

When the call ended, it was like all the air had left Nevaeh's lungs. The guilt of lying to Kiara, of manipulating the situation, was suffocating. But Heather and Christina's betrayal stung even more. Nevaeh wasn't going to let them ruin her life.

Not anymore.

She joined the line of students getting onto the school bus that was headed to Sunny World. As they all climbed on, Nevaeh kept her face hidden to keep from being called out.

The school bus filled up. Nevaeh took a seat next to the window, turning her face away as one of the students sat beside her.

If they noticed she didn't belong among the group, the student didn't say anything.

Nevaeh pressed her eyes and leaned her head against the window. And then the bus pulled away from the airport and headed back to Sunny World Park.

chapter twenty-six

Kiara

WHEN KIARA REJOINED the group, Priscilla met her first.

It was hard for her to look at Priscilla the same way. After Kiara's conversation with Nevaeh, Kiara had no doubt that Tommy's death wasn't just an accident. It was murder. And Priscilla was looking more and more like the missing link to solving it.

"Is Nevaeh going to turn herself in to the police?" Priscilla asked.

Kiara swallowed, forcing herself to meet Priscilla's gaze with her own.

"And why would she do that?" Kiara asked, attempting to stay somewhat neutral while still displaying her doubts about Priscilla. The best lies came from the truth. So that's what she'd do. Tell as much of the truth as she could while pulling out real answers from Priscilla.

"Um, did we just watch the same video? Nevaeh was with Tommy at the fun house."

"But so were you and I," Kiara said.

"The girl in the video was wearing an angel costume," Priscilla countered.

293

"And so were you by the end of the night. Remember?"

Behind the two girls, Jason and Alex stirred. They'd been huddled together, watching and rewinding the clip from the footage, but the confrontation had pulled both of their attention.

"Is that true?" Jason said. "You were wearing the same costume as the girl in the video?"

Priscilla swallowed. A light of panic flashed in her eyes. It was there and gone in a moment.

"It was a costume party," Priscilla contended. "There were plenty of people dressed up the same." She turned to Kiara and flashed her ever-plastic smile. "Isn't that right, Kiara?"

Part of Kiara wanted to completely throw Priscilla under the bus. There was enough doubt about her involvement in Tommy's death already. If Kiara used the situation to cast more speculation about Priscilla to Jason then surely his word would be enough to get his family to investigate the girl. Priscilla had cheated with Tommy. She'd lied to Kiara and used them both to get what she wanted. Everything inside of Kiara told her she should hate Priscilla and want her to take the fall for Tommy's death. But that wasn't why Kiara had come this far. She wanted the truth. The real truth. She didn't trust Priscilla. But that didn't mean she could just accuse her fully of the crime without real, concrete evidence.

"Both Nevaeh and Priscilla were wearing the angel costume," Kiara admitted. "But that video doesn't prove they killed Tommy. The girl in the video and Tommy had fought, yes. But you could hear them chasing after each other by the end of it. He was still alive."

"So then what's the timeline?" Jason snapped. "You say one thing, she says another. The lies keep getting tangled up in half-truths covering up what happened to my stepbrother."

"We need to find the hacker," Alex said. "The video footage they have is probably time stamped. We can't go off just he-said, she-said accounts anymore. If we can get access to Tommy's account, we should be able to piece everything together."

Relieved that the conversation had switched back to their common enemy, Kiara pulled open the group chat between Priscilla, Nevaeh, and Tommy's account, showing it to Jason and Alex.

"Nevaeh thinks there are multiple hackers," she said. "Those two girls at the party, she knew them. They're her church friends or something. Nevaeh thinks they're the ones with the burner phone. She thinks they're trying to take her down."

The group was silent for a moment, and then Alex spoke.

"I mean, if they were those two drunk girls in the room, they definitely saw you hide it in Tommy's mattress," Alex said, turning to Priscilla. "And so did however many people from our school who were watching the livestream."

"Unless she was just pretending to hide the burner phone the whole time and still has it," Jason said.

Priscilla laughed. "You seriously still think I'm the hacker? I would have just gone out and said you and Nevaeh were to blame if that was the case. And why would I implicate myself?"

"I don't know. For the likes? What else motivates you clickbait junkies?" Jason shot back. Kiara tugged on Jason's sleeve.

"No accusations. We need to work together," she said.

"Yeah, listen to the girl who you chose over your own step-brother," Priscilla said, glaring at him.

"Priscilla," Kiara warned. "I'm trying to help you. Can you not make things worse?"

Priscilla pouted but relented.

"I don't like Nevaeh confronting her friends on her own,"

Kiara continued. "If it really is them, then I don't think her facing off with them in the park will end well. They would have known Tommy was dead before anyone else and still done this anyway. And that's just twisted."

"Well, I couldn't care less," Priscilla said. "The Sunny World worker with Tommy's real phone is our only key at this point. We can piece together the timeline of when Tommy died, and if the hacker tries to post again, we could log the burner phone out of Tommy's account and stop the hacker."

"Unless the hacker already thought to log Tommy out and change the password," Alex said.

"Well, we won't know until we get it," Jason said.

"Let's split up," Priscilla said. "Since you two are so worried about Saint Nevaeh, you catch up with her in the park. We'll find the Sunny World worker."

"Or," Kiara said, stepping in front of Priscilla, "Jason and I meet Nevaeh in the park and you and Alex stay here and confirm the phone really is missing from his old room. It'll also give you plenty of time to prepare for the live if we aren't able to find the phone before the hacker's deadline."

"Um, I am not going on that live. A, I'm not taking the fall for this. B, and I repeat, the girl in the video is Nevaeh, not me. And C, have I not spoken enough about how this whole mess is killing my brand deals? If you believe her so much, why don't you go on? Take the fall for the team."

"Why were you even dressed in that costume?" Alex asked.

Priscilla bit her lip. If there was one person who she'd be honest to, it was him.

"You know how Tommy texted me that he broke up with Kiara?"

Kiara's eyes widened. She hadn't known Tommy had done that. The fact that he'd moved on so quickly to his roster of girls was sickening.

"Yeah," Alex said, "I remember."

"Well, he texted Nevaeh to meet him too. Even though Ne-vaeh told us she wasn't going to see him, after I found that I"—Priscilla looked away—"I went as her instead of myself. I was angry and jealous and just wanted to get back at him and maybe even her."

"Did it work?" Jason asked. "Did Tommy believe you were Nevaeh?"

Priscilla laughed. "Yeah. For a second. And then he found out." She pointed to the bruises on her body. "That's how I got these."

Jason cursed under his breath. Alex squeezed Priscilla's hand.

Kiara's heart ached. She'd wondered but hadn't dared speculate.

"I'm sorry," Kiara whispered.

Priscilla continued. "He forced a kiss on me, saying since I wanted him so bad that I'd gone as far as pretending to be Nevaeh, then why stop the act now. I tried to push him off me but he just got more and more aggressive. So I used his weight against him. But when he fell back, he crashed into the fun house mirrors. I think he hit his head. There was blood. Mine and his from the fight. He was still breathing. I know because even after I crawled away, he chased after me. I found a hiding spot and I stayed there all night before heading back to the hotel in the morning."

Moments ago, Kiara had been sure Priscilla was the girl in the video. Now a cloud of doubt hung over her. But if Priscilla hadn't been the one in the video, then that meant Nevaeh was lying. Which meant that they could be walking into a trap that Nevaeh and her hacker friends were orchestrating.

Priscilla seemed to have the same train of thought. She gave Kiara a knowing look but didn't articulate her suspicions either. It was as if, even though each girl doubted the other, they had a quiet agreement: they wouldn't let others tear each other down. They would face the world as a united front, even if beneath the seams their tangled sisterhood was unraveling.

"We don't have much time left," Alex said. "The day's almost over, and we won't get anywhere if we search the park in the dark."

"Which is why we should split up," Priscilla said again. "People online are already voting which one of us the video clip belonged to. If we can't find either the burner phone or Tommy's real one by then, and if the hacker or hackers really end up having the live, then whoever gets the highest votes should go on."

Kiara sighed. There was no going around this.

"All right," she said finally. "When Mr. Phillips escorts us back to our rooms, Jason and I will meet up and head to the park to see if we can track down the Sunny World worker or Tommy's phone. Alex and Priscilla, you sneak back into Tommy's hotel room and look for the burner or any clues about where it could be."

"Great," Jason said. "Just one question, though. The park police and the authorities have restricted the fun house so no one can enter. How exactly are we going to get past them?"

And this was the part Kiara was dreading. Because it would mean once again relying on her relationship with Tommy to get what she wanted. But these were desperate times, after all.

"I think I know someone who can help," Kiara said.

Suddenly, a loud cough sounded behind the group.

Mr. Phillips had finally backtracked to where they'd been hiding.

Immediately, Priscilla jumped into character.

"Sorry, Mr. P. Alex dropped his equipment and we were help-ing him."

Mr. Phillips frowned. "Next time, let me know that before you have me walking down half the hall by myself. You're supposed to be with a chaperone at all times." Annoyed, he gestured for them to join him. "Come on. Let's get you all back to your rooms."

chapter twenty-seven

Priscilla

THE FIRST THING they did when they were escorted back to their hotel room by Mr. Phillips was order room service. Kiara made two calls in the bathroom and Priscilla changed into black leggings and a black top from when they'd snuck into Sunny World.

They didn't talk. They just paced in their rooms as the countdown until the livestream ticked by. When room service arrived, Kiara made a show of sticking her head out of their hotel room and waving at Mr. Phillips as he monitored the halls. Mr. Phillips gave her a curt nod, but he didn't question as the bellhop entered their room wheeling a draped cart filled with the trays of food they'd ordered.

"Finally," Priscilla said, reaching for the food. "I'm starving."

Kiara hissed at her. "Girl, focus, please," she said, locking the door behind them before turning to the bellhop.

"Thanks again for agreeing to this," she said. "We really owe you, Ren."

The boy, Ren, smiled.

"I always wondered how I'd look in these uniforms," he said, grinning, adjusting the bright orange bow tie. Priscilla raised an eyebrow.

"Ren? As in the owner of Sunny World's kid?"

"That's my middle name, actually," Ren teased.

He was flirting with her. Priscilla didn't blame him, of course. But nepo babies weren't her vibe.

"You're the one who helped Kiara set up that fake interview," Priscilla said. "If you were so interested in the bellhop uniform, you could have just gotten a job to work at your dad's hotel," she said.

"And you're the one who Tommy's account claims is his side chick. I guess he had a type," Ren said. He shook his head. "Never thought I'd be jealous of Tommy. Yet, here I am."

"Tommy's literally dead."

"And Icarus flew too close to the sun," Ren said, smirking. "Guess he should have used more sunscreen."

"I thought this guy was supposed to be Tommy's friend?" Priscilla said, which only made Ren laugh again.

"Oh, Tommy didn't have friends. He had fans, and everyone else who had to deal with him."

Ren wheeled the cart of food next to the hotel fridge. "And then there were the people he used, and the ones who owed him."

"Guess we all know which category you fall into," Kiara said.

Ren smiled. "I was the one he never should have tried." His words were light but they sent chills through Priscilla. Even Kiara seemed unnerved.

"Let's just get on with this," Kiara said.

They began clearing the empty plates off the cart so they could make space under the tablecloth. When the cart was finally empty, Priscilla slid in beneath it and Kiara joined her. Then Ren readjusted the cart's tablecloth, curtaining them behind it.

"Hang tight," he said, returning to his playful disposition from earlier.

Priscilla wrapped her arms around her legs, placing her head against her knees to keep from hitting the top of the cart. The world shifted beneath them as Ren rolled the cart from the room, clicking the door shut behind him.

They had less than twenty-four hours to track down Tommy's phone and the burner and stop the livestream. Every minute counted. They had to get this right for the plan to work.

Ren rolled them farther and farther down the hallways. He stopped in front of one of the hotel rooms and there was a click as his key card unlocked the door.

"Guess that's my stop," Priscilla said. The door opened and she slipped inside Tommy's hotel room quickly.

She locked the bolt on the top of the door and booked it to Tommy's bed. Alex would already be there waiting for her, and together, they would search Tommy's old hotel room for the burner.

But when Priscilla entered the room, Alex was nowhere to be found. Part of her wanted to search the rooms for him, wondering if he was hiding or just hadn't been able to arrive yet. But she had a mission. Priscilla needed to find the burner phone.

She hurried to Tommy's old room, which had been taped off too. Then, Priscilla dug through the mattress, riffled through sheets, stuck her head under the bed, and still no burner phone. Defeated, Priscilla turned her search elsewhere. Most of the room had numbered yellow cones where officers had marked evidence in the case. Tommy's suitcase was still spilling with items that had fallen out of it—just as it had been the night of the party. But his laptop had been left on his desk. Priscilla hadn't remembered it being there the day before.

So she inched toward the laptop. When she tapped the space bar using the sleeve of her shirt, the lock screen emerged. Priscilla didn't know Tommy's password, but even if she did, she wouldn't have risked typing on the keys and leaving behind her fingerprints. That had been the only reason she'd been bold enough to search through the mattress: the bedsheets wouldn't likely leave behind any traceable fingerprints. At least, Priscilla hoped they wouldn't. But time was running out and Priscilla was *not* going on that livestream. She just wouldn't. And Alex, he was supposed to be here with her, searching through Tommy's things. So where was he?

Priscilla sent him a text. When he didn't answer, she called.

Alex picked up on the second ring.

"Hello?" he said.

"Um, hello to you. Where are you? We were supposed to be meeting in Tommy's room, like, half an hour ago."

"Sorry. I—uh, something came up. And then the chaperones caught me when I tried to sneak out. I had to sit through this lecture from Mr. Phillips. Could you search on your own for a bit? I just want to check something."

"Well, Tommy's computer is here but it's not like I know the password or can log in without leaving fingerprints."

"Yeah, I know. The cops singled it out when I was packing, so I couldn't mess with it either."

"Did you find anything when you were moving out that could help us? Anything?"

Alex was silent for a long moment.

"No. I didn't. Listen. I don't think I'll be able to meet you in Tommy's room or in the park. Mr. Phillips and the chaperones are basically doing a stakeout in front of my room at this point."

Priscilla frowned.

"So he's, like, basically just standing in front of your door right now."

"Yeah, I'm stuck. Sorry, Prissy."

But Priscilla was looking out through the peephole in the door. Mr. Phillips and the other chaperones were gathered down the hall. They spoke somberly with one another and made their way to their respective hotel rooms while the chaperones on the clock prepared to take their shifts monitoring the halls.

Alex was lying to her. He was straight-up lying to her face. Unless he really was in his room at this moment and had just made a mistake about the chaperones lurking in front of his door. But there was only one way to be sure. Priscilla had to check Alex's room.

Just as she was about to exit Tommy's room, the Google Alert Priscilla had created for Tommy's account sent her a notification. Priscilla's breath caught. The account had posted again. It took all the courage inside of her to open the accounts page and click on the video posted just two minutes ago.

It's almost midnight. The truth will be revealed soon. Confess. Or the murderer will be exposed.

The text disappeared from the screen, shifting suddenly to blurry video in Sunny World Park. Two figures stood in the distance and, as the camera drew closer, Priscilla could make out her own figure standing across from Alex's.

"Let's get drunk."

"You're already drunk."

"Let's get drunker. And go—on rides. All of the rides. Screw it all. Screw Tommy and my followers and those corny sponsors with their weak-ass, cheap-ass, bootleg snake oil they have me selling. I want to literally party until I black out."

Priscilla's heart dropped. A text notification appeared on her screen. It was from Leah.

Leah: Found that footage in my camera roll from last night. Sent it to the account and the authorities. May Tommy rest in peace.

Attached to the text was the same footage that the account had just played of Priscilla and Alex in the park.

Another notification went off on Priscilla's phone. Then another, and another. These ones were direct messages from fans.

Liar.

So you were selling us crap?

Sinner and a scam artist for real.

You killed him. This video is proof that you wanted him gone.

Confess on live while you still can.

Priscilla couldn't breathe. Even as she gasped for air, she couldn't seem to find it. Her trembling fingers led her back to the video that had paused when she'd tapped out to Leah's message. Priscilla hit Play again and the video continued.

The screen was black again this time, just like it had been when footage of Nevaeh in Sunny World had leaked. This time, though, three voices could be heard.

"You think I wouldn't know who you were?" Tommy screamed. *"You think you could lie to me?"*

The sound of Priscilla's own voice in the video sent chills through her.

"I'm sorry. Tommy, I'm sorry."

There was a crash, the same terrible crash that had echoed in Priscilla's mind ever since last night in the fun house. Even without images from the video, the scene played out in Priscilla's vision like a shattered memory stuck on loop, the mirrors of the fun house crashing to the floor.

In the audio, Priscilla was sobbing. But it didn't show the pain she'd felt, how her face and her arms ached as if fire had been set to her nerves and the shards of glass from where she'd crashed into the mirror tore at her skin. Priscilla squeezed her eyes shut, the clip meshing with her memory, then pulling her under completely. . . .

"Tommy——" she began as he approached her. But his lips crashed against hers. Priscilla drew back against the harsh metallic taste of his blood, but he pulled her closer and closer, his arms like steel cages trapping her. His tongue shoved its way to the back of her throat while his other hand fondled her violently. She tried to scream but his grip only grew tighter, angrier, and her cries went unanswered in the dark. He pushed her against the mirrored wall, not releasing his hold on her. Pain jolted through Priscilla as her head hit the hard glass. Something warm and wet spilled against her head. Blood. Priscilla's blood this time.

Tommy cursed under his breath and in that brief moment of confusion, Priscilla found all the remaining strength she had to use the force of his weight against him.

They crashed into the glass mirror, but this time, the sharp crack that ricocheted through the walls was of Tommy's body hitting the glass. Priscilla stumbled to the ground, gasping for breath. When she looked back, Tommy was on the ground. He wasn't moving. She called his name, but he didn't answer. So Priscilla crawled to where he lay beneath shattered glass. He was still breathing. She remembered that vividly. Her fingers found the pulse behind his ear, and when she'd hovered her hand over his nose, faint warm air brushed against her palms. And then there were the last words she'd remembered him saying, a curse directed toward her and a promise that she'd regret this.

Priscilla knew she should have called for help after she'd stumbled away. But she'd been afraid Tommy would come after her, so afraid that she'd lost her way in the fun house. Hours passed. Somehow, she'd fallen asleep. And when she'd woken up, Priscilla had used the trail of light flittering into the fun house to find an exit. Outside, Tommy hadn't been there. Instead, she'd met Kiara.

But the audio from the account didn't show any of that. No. It kept replaying a warped version of Priscilla's screams.

Kill him.

Kill him.

Kill him.

Still, the accusations from her fans and strangers wouldn't stop.

Murderer

Liar

Scam artist

Killer

Sinner

How could the account have gone from playing footage of Nevaeh and Tommy to this? How had someone even been able to get that recording of Priscilla? But then, Priscilla remembered how Nevaeh had spoken of taking Tommy's phone from the fun house. That must have been before Priscilla had confronted him. Had Nevaeh witnessed the whole fight? And instead of helping Priscilla, had she just watched and recorded the altercation?

Before, Priscilla had fought back her tears. Now she let them consume her. The bitter sting of betrayal was suffocating. Had they all been working together, against Priscilla? Maybe Leah had sent that video to Tommy's account on Kiara's behalf? Or had it been Nevaeh and her friends, the ones who the girl swore had been in Tommy's hotel room during the whole party. Whatever the case, someone was lying. One of the girls was working with the account, feeding information to it as a means of self-survival. So why was Priscilla here, searching through Tommy's things in his room, risking her own future from two girls who had just thrown Priscilla to the wolves anyway? No. She wasn't going down without a fight. Screw the livestream. Priscilla was going to burn everything down.

With shaking hands, Priscilla tapped on the icon of a profile she used to post content anonymously. She found the second video Tommy's account had posted, the one with the footage between Tommy and Nevaeh where the livestream had first been announced. There were already a few trending comments underneath the video.

KMHeartsTommy22: Priscilla aka the sinner is totally the killer. She's put on this fake personality long enough. Finally the truth is being revealed and she can sell her makeup in jail.

Girlsnotgrey: Yeah Priscilla was so jealous the whole time Tommy and Kiara were dating. It's obvious she broke them up and killed him when he chose the prettier girl.

Priscilla laughed, perhaps a little manically, at the last comment. That was like comparing the sun to a star, or an ocean wave to the tide. It was redundant, futile, and completely oblivious to the fact that beauty couldn't be deconstructed through comparison. To think someone had the audacity to pit Priscilla and Kiara against each other in this way—well, Priscilla honestly felt secondhand embarrassment for the person. Priscilla shook her head. And then she started typing.

Priscilla and Kiara are both beautiful, hot baddies in their own right. Respectfully. But what about the saint? Does anyone really know about her? Like who is she? She literally has no info about her online and somehow she's implicated in a murder? Pretty shady if you ask me.

Even after she posted her comment, a dozen likes appeared next to it on the screen. With a deep breath, Priscilla logged out of her second profile and logged into the third one she used for fandom purposes.

> **Boyinluv2788:** I go to the same church as this so called saint everyone is talking about. Yeah. Not actually a saint. At least I didn't know any saints like that.

Priscilla cringed as she clicked the water emoji and the tongue-out emoji. Then she added:

> Her dad's a pastor and she claims she went back to a church conference that night. But just listen to the audio and the crashes in the video. This so called saint was in a house that night, all right. But it wasn't one of worship.

More notifications filled her screen as a slew of accounts liked the two comments she'd posted. Then, Priscilla logged back into the final account she'd created on the vlogger app years ago. This one was different from her personal vlog (one hundred thousand followers) or the sock-puppet accounts she'd made (zero followers each). Priscilla's OfficialFansofHarding&Frimpong account had over five hundred thousand dedicated followers. It'd been a fan page dedicated to following Tommy and Priscilla's content, one she'd managed for years in secret, even without Tommy or Alex knowing. It'd been weeks, though, since the account had posted any status updates and the thousands of DMs from fans clearly showed that they were eager to hear the account's take on the investigation.

Priscilla typed the post quickly, not caring how many spelling errors she was probably making or the fact that once she posted it, things would never be the same.

When she hit Send, it was like clarity had finally washed over her. Priscilla wiped her tears, and then she slipped out from Tommy's room, making her way to Alex's. She'd already been lied to by Nevaeh and maybe even Kiara. But now, she was going to find the truth, even if it meant being on her own.

chapter twenty-eight

Nevaeh

IT WAS STRANGE to be back in Sunny World after everything. All around her, the visitors and park guests seemed oblivious to the idea that anything had changed. But a boy had died here, and with his death, the lives of three girls had come crumbling down.

Priscilla and Kiara still weren't answering her. Nevaeh wondered if they'd bailed on her after all. It would make sense, wouldn't it? Right now, the official Tommy Harding and Priscilla page was even pointing the public in her direction and anonymous posts were making Nevaeh out to be the one connected with Tommy's death in the fun house.

OfficialFansofHarding&Frimpong: Rest in peace Tommy. You will be missed. Priscilla's account also posted a touching goodbye to her cohost. Like and share her post to celebrate Tommy's memory.

Boyinluv2788: What memory. Tommy was a creep and a terrible person. We see the truth now. It's all being exposed. And it all started with that disgusting locker room livestream. He got what he deserved. I'm glad the girl in the angel costume got her revenge.

OfficialFansofHarding&Frimpong: @Boyinluv2788 Tommy posting the livestream from the locker room was wrong. There's no doubt about that. We send our deepest well wishes to everyone involved in this tragedy, including the girl wearing the angel costume during the locker room livestream.

The posts had seemed innocent enough. And yet, with the locker room livestream back to the public's attention again, people were making new connections: Nevaeh had been wearing the same costume in the livestream as the girl who had confronted Tommy in the fun house before he'd died.

The internet was going wild with the missing link that the Official Fans of Harding & Frimpong account had pointed out when responding to an anonymous commenter.

Revenge. That was the motive they'd ascribed to Nevaeh. Revenge, even though all she'd wanted was to move on.

She'd gone to meet Tommy to delete the photos he still had of her, not to get back at him or hurt him like he had Nevaeh. But now, the very people cheering on a rumor were linking her to a motive, one that could make her take the fall for Tommy's death.

Nevaeh really was on her own now.

"You wanted to talk?" a voice said.

Nevaeh looked up to find herself staring back at Christina and Heather. She'd sent them a text that she'd wanted to meet them at

Sunny World before returning home early. Both girls had agreed to meet with Nevaeh. But seeing them now, after knowing everything, was harder than Nevaeh could have ever imagined.

It didn't help that, even though Sunny World was still up and running, with Tommy's murder and the police presence everywhere, it was hard not to feel the sinister tension radiating throughout the park. Most of the areas near the fun house and the gondola ride were sectioned off, and park visitors traveled in large groups, plastering fake smiles on their faces as they tried to get their money's worth. After all, Sunny World hadn't offered them refunds.

Nevaeh's heart hammered in her chest as she set her plan in motion. Secretly, she began a voice recording on her phone; then she switched the screen to the group chat DM between Nevaeh, Kiara, Priscilla, and Tommy's account.

"Recognize this?" Nevaeh said, holding the phone for Christina and Heather to see.

Christina took the phone from Nevaeh's hands. Her eyes scanned the message before she passed the phone to Heather.

"You can't be serious," Heather said. "You actually reached out to the hacker?"

Nevaeh ignored her words. "Give me your phones. I want to see for myself."

"What are you talking about?" Christina said. "Nevaeh, you should be going to the police, not doing—whatever it is you're doing."

"Stop. Just stop. I'm sick of the games. I'm sick of pretending. Just tell me the truth," Nevaeh said. "Tell me you weren't at the party in Tommy's hotel room last night. Tell me you didn't plan everything that happened at the park."

Christina and Heather just stared back at Nevaeh as if she'd lost her mind.

"Romans fourteen, verse thirteen," Nevaeh whispered. "You wanted me hungover. You wanted me to make all of those terrible drunken choices that night because you wanted me to stumble. You wanted me to crash and burn. Well, congratulations. I fell for it. I fell for everything. I ruined my life. So can we just stop now? Can we just end this? I'm not a saint. I never was. I don't deserve to live or be happy or make mistakes."

"What are you talking about?" Christina said. She turned to Heather. "What is she talking about?"

But Heather didn't move. She was still staring at Nevaeh's phone, staring at it as if a spotlight had caught her by surprise. Christina seemed to realize this. She grabbed Nevaeh's phone back from Heather and clicked on the video that Nevaeh had used to begin the DM with the hacker. It was the video recording with Tommy, the one that had started the countdown to midnight. Christina played it, and then a look of horror emerged on her face. It was all the answer Nevaeh needed.

Nevaeh spun then, not caring that Christina still had Nevaeh's phone or that she had no way of confirming the full truth from them. The look in Christina's eyes had been clear. She'd recognized that recording, which meant that Christina had probably taken it herself.

Nevaeh ran and ran. She could hear Christina and Heather calling after her. The gondola ride was up ahead. Nevaeh charged forward, skipping the line of people making their way through the entrance of the ride. Instead of following the crowd to the ride itself, Nevaeh made a right, to the employee entrance she so faintly remembered from the last time she'd seen Tommy. It led into a locker room that had two other doors on either side. None of the workers were inside, but Nevaeh could have sworn she'd heard one of them calling after her when she cut through the line.

Footsteps pursued her. Nevaeh yanked on the doors of each locker, one after another after another until one opened. She locked herself inside just as Christina and Heather emerged in the locker room.

"Nevaeh," Christina said. "Nevaeh, we know you're in here."

The girls started yanking on lockers too.

Nevaeh needed to think. Maybe she'd be able to find a way to stop them from posting by midnight?

"Nevaeh," Christina said. "We're not the hacker. We swear we're not. I'm sorry, Nevaeh. You were right. I didn't tell Heather to send the account the recording I had of you and Tommy, but she did it for me. Because I was angry and hurting. We followed you that night in the park. I was the one filming the two of you fighting. I was going to delete it. I swear I was. But I sent a copy to Heather, and we watched it over and over, trying to figure out what happened between you and Tommy because the account was saying all these things claiming one of you three killed him, and I didn't know what to believe. And then there were all those lies you told. All this time you were acting like your relationship with Tommy was just some innocent long-distance thing. You never told me how deep things had gotten between you and Tommy or what was really going on. Even when I tried to ask you what really happened, you lied to our faces."

"But that doesn't mean I killed him," Nevaeh said. "I stole the phone when we met because he was going to keep blackmailing me." Tears filled Nevaeh's eyes. "I just wanted to delete the videos and messages we sent. I didn't want him to be able to control me. That's what that video showed. He was still alive when I left him.'"

Christina and Heather stopped trying to open the locker doors. Nevaeh could see that even through the slats in the locker. They stood in the center of the locker room, speaking to thin air as if Nevaeh were a spirit whose presence they were desperately trying to reach in another realm.

"I'm sorry, Nevaeh," Heather said. "I thought the account was trying to expose the truth."

"That's not why you sent the video," Nevaeh said. "And it's not why you brought me to the park last night. Aren't we all being honest here now? Aren't we telling the truth?"

Both girls remained silent.

"You're right," Christina finally admitted. "Maybe we thought you were guilty, but that's not why we sent it." Christina sighed. "You're my best friend, the perfect church girl. I never meant to pressure you into doing anything you didn't want to. And I know you felt pressured to be a 'saint' because of your family. But sometimes you would say things, and even if I knew you didn't mean them the way they came off, it just made me feel like I would never be good enough no matter what I did. And all the while, you were hiding a whole secret relationship with a bad-boy prank star."

Nevaeh wanted to scream. She wanted to burst out of the locker room so Christina and Heather could see the hurt pouring through her and the rage burning through her. She closed her eyes, balling her hands into fists as she spoke through the locker.

"So you just wanted to put me in my place? You wanted to tear off my so-called saint halo and humble me? That's why you sent the recording to the account? That's why you let it black-mail me?"

"No, never," Christina said.

"She had nothing to do with the account getting that footage," Heather said. "I sent it. After the interview. I don't know why I did. I just—you were literally lying to the whole world about what happened. It just felt so hypocritical. And seeing you ped-dling all these lies and crap—like saying you went back to Sunny World the next morning but couldn't get in the park even though you told us both you'd been stuck inside it overnight—I just lost it. I'm sorry."

"I asked the account not to post the footage after Heather sent it," Christina said, "but it blocked us both. But we've been doing our best to get it taken down. We've been trying to find the hacker too. Nevaeh, we think it's one of the Sunny World work-ers. They're the only people who would have easy access to the footage Tommy took in the park that night."

"What footage?" Nevaeh said. "What are you talking about?"

"Remember the hidden camera in the locker room?" Heather said. "Tommy was filming something, probably one of his pranks. He had to have had gotten help from one of the workers in the park to hide the camera in the locker room at all. When we talked to the workers in the park, they said that the park's main cameras were also disabled that night, which is why the police have no footage of when Tommy died. But Tommy's own cameras might still be up. And the hacker knows it. We think this whole count-down to midnight is just them buying time to get rid of the real footage of Tommy's death."

Christina stepped in front of the locker that Nevaeh was hid-ing in.

"You have to believe us, Nevaeh. We messed up. I know. But we're going to make this right. I promise we will."

Nevaeh looked away, as if Christina could actually see her through the locker door. A rush of feelings churned through her: betrayal, hurt, and, somehow even more than that, hope.

"You're really not the hackers?" Nevaeh said.

From the other side of the locker, Christina shook her head.

"My video-editing skills are choppy at best," she said with a weak smile.

Nevaeh laughed. "Yeah, but now Heather's a sound-mixing wizard, apparently."

Christina grimaced at the jab.

"I'm sorry."

Nevaeh looked away. "Just don't," she said. She didn't know if she'd be able to forgive them. Not yet. But still. Still, she could at least admit her part in this messed-up situation.

"I never should have lied in the interview. I shouldn't have tried to hide what was going on with Tommy."

Once again, warmth burned at the back of Nevaeh's throat as tears began to form.

"We met last summer. The first time we did a video call, I was going door-to-door with Laurence, and Tommy's mom answered it. She was talking to him on FaceTime, since he lives in Jersey with his father and stepmom, and she put him on the phone with us while we were there. We kept in touch after that. And things just kept moving really fast between us. I couldn't tell you or anyone about him because I—I was ashamed. The things that I was doing, how each time I thought if I just gave in a little more, I'd be proving that I really did love him and we were meant to be. I had to change myself to be with him. I had to twist and bend and tear away all of the pieces of myself that made me whole. Our friendship was never like that. Never."

"You must have felt so guilty this whole time," Christina said. "But making mistakes doesn't make you a bad person. Maybe it won't make you a saint. It just means you're human."

"Did you at least have fun?" Heather asked.

Christina laughed, which made Nevaeh chuckle too, even if the sound was tinged with bitterness.

"I thought I was. But it was miserable trying to be someone I'm not for him," Nevaeh admitted. "I didn't know what I was getting into, and he used that against me to get me to go further and further." Nevaeh laughed, wiping away the last traces of tears on her lashes. "That's the funny thing. I thought being a saint was pressure. But doing all those things with him, trying to keep up with the other seniors in the park by taking shots and making him think I was sexy or something, was so much pressure too. And to be honest, I think trying to be 'the saint' was the only thing that helped ground me. At least then, I wasn't trying to keep up with what Tommy or you guys were doing. I was just trying to figure out how to be a version of myself that people could look up to. That I could look up to. But it also felt suffocating too. So I'd go back to Tommy and it was like the cycle kept continuing."

"I'm sorry," Christina said.

"Yeah, it did seem like a lot of pressure."

"Truly," Heather said, agreeing.

Nevaeh smiled. "John one, one, verse eight, right?"

"Right," Christina said, smiling now too.

Tentatively, Nevaeh placed her hand against the locker door.

"You and Laurence used to say I always tried to do the right thing, the good thing," she said. "That's me. That's always been me."

But the last few months, Nevaeh had been trying to be what she wasn't. She realized now that's how things had gotten this far. So if she confessed to everything about Tommy live on the account, then maybe that could be a way of returning to being the person she had always been. Not perfect. But authentic. Herself.

The realization was freeing. Nevaeh moved to open the locker, only to lose her balance when the door swung wide more quickly than she anticipated.

She screamed, covering her face with her arms as she landed on the ground. Christina and Heather hurried to Nevaeh's side.

"Are you okay?" Christina asked.

But Nevaeh was looking at the floor, where the items from the locker had fallen too. All around her, notebooks and folders and photos lay. She picked one up only to find herself staring back at a picture of Tommy.

chapter twenty-nine

Kiara

AFTER THEY'D DROPPED off Priscilla, Ren pushed the trolley on-
ward through the hotel. Which meant that Kiara's part in the
plan was about to begin. They ventured down the hallways, one
after another after another, and from beneath the gap between
the tablecloths, Kiara could see that they were getting farther away
from the elevator bank.

"Ren?" she whispered.

This was not part of the plan. He was supposed to drop her off
at the elevators and Jason and she would head down to the park
together and meet Chelsea, who Ren had suggested could help
them with Kiara's plan. But instead, Ren was driving the cart to the
sectioned-off rooms where the police interviews had taken place.
Two officers sat huddled over chairs, and when Ren arrived with
the cart, they greeted him excitedly. Kiara's heart hammered in her
ears. She didn't move, didn't breathe, afraid that even the slightest
movement would alert them to her presence beneath the tablecloth.

"Room service?" Ren asked.

One of the officers thanked him as he handed Ren dishes
while another was speaking into a walkie-talkie.

"Can you describe it? Okay. Okay. What you're going to need to do is bring the item to forensics for testing. No, no, don't deal with the Sunny World people. They've been a nightmare throughout this whole thing. Just have it sent to forensics. We've been in contact with the owner. The assholes won't shut it down until that order comes through from the state. How can twenty-four hours of park video footage be deleted just like that? Just like that. You're telling me no one at Sunny World knew that the Harding kid died under their watch? Not even the owners or the workers helping those kids with the prank?"

"Anything else I can do for you?" Ren asked. His voice was stiff, and between the slits in the tablecloth, Kiara could see the blue veins against his knuckles from how tightly he was holding on to the cart.

"No thanks. Appreciate it. Here's a tip."

The officer handed Ren a five-dollar bill, which Ren slipped into the pocket of his uniform before wheeling the cart away. The world beneath Kiara shifted again, but this time it wasn't because the cart was rolling down the hallway.

All of the missing pieces were finally clicking into place. The Sunny World employee phone that had been found at the scene where Tommy had died. How Ren had believed Kiara and Tommy had broken up when Kiara had met Chelsea and him at the hotel restaurant, even before news of Tommy's cheating had gone public. Why he'd been so desperate for Kiara to do the interview to clean up Sunny World's image and stop the suit Tommy's parents had filed against him and his father. And then there were Ren's words back then, and even now.

Make sure you tell Tommy we're even now, though. No more favors. No more asks. After tonight, I'm done with his crap.

The less you worry about what he's up to, the better off you'll be.

I was the one he never should have tried.

The hacker would need to have unlimited access to Sunny World and its resort hotels, enough to be able to delete the footage from the night Tommy died and the aftermath of a cover-up. And more than anything, they'd need to have a reason to hate Tommy, a reason to get even. Hadn't Tommy even said it then?

"That's just the difference between you and him. One of you pretends to like me to get what they want, the other knows I could make their life a living hell and bury them with the dirt I have on them. Take a guess at which one is you."

·That was it. That was why Tommy had been so desperate to find the burner phone. It wasn't just the photos, messages, and videos he had on the girls on it. It was blackmail. Tommy's death hadn't been an accident. And if the police really were narrowing in on the real suspect, what better way to get them off the scent than to blame three innocent girls who all had relationships with Tommy and all had reasons for wanting him gone too. That's what this whole thing was. A cover-up. The hacker's posts were slowly incriminating the girls, and now there was the livestream, designed to push them to come forward and admit their guilt over a murder they'd had no part in. They'd even gotten Nevaeh, Priscilla, and Kiara to turn on one another, when really they should have protected each other.

Confess your sins. Or the murderer among you will be revealed.

There was no good option. Eventually, the truth would be exposed. But now, it was a question of which of the girls would confess to their role in Tommy's death and which would take the fall for it. And somehow, Kiara had walked right into danger.

She had to be calm. She had to act like nothing was wrong.

"Are you taking me to the elevators?" Kiara called up through the tablecloth.

Ren didn't answer her, but the cart kept moving. Then they stopped in front of a door. Before Kiara could peek out of the cart to get a closer look, Ren pushed through the door and a burst of freezing air enveloped Kiara.

"Sorry about this," he said, "but I'm going to need you to stay here for the time being."

Kiara screamed, reaching for Ren from the cart, but he pushed her back and then the door to the room slammed shut behind him. There was a loud click as the door locked. Kiara crawled out from the cart, her head throbbing from where the metal shaft of the cart hit her.

"Ren. Ren, wait!" She slammed her palms against the door, shivering against the cold as she screamed.

It was locked. No one could hear her from inside the freezer room. There was no service on her phone either. Kiara collapsed in defeat. Midnight was approaching. And in just a few hours, Ren would make one of the girls take the fall for Tommy's murder.

The cold bit into Kiara, making it hard for her to breathe. She didn't know how much time had passed, but when she felt two warm hands against her shoulders and a voice calling her name, Kiara was jolted back into reality. Slowly, Kiara's eyes opened. She smiled softly as she peered up into Jason's warm brown eyes.

"Kiara," he said. "Are you okay? It's freezing here."

Everything felt faint and distant. Kiara pressed her eyes shut then opened them, her hands still shaking as she brought them to her lips. She hadn't eaten all day, and the cold wasn't helping.

"We need to get you medical attention," Jason said. "I'll call Mr. Phillips."

Kiara shook her head.

"No. We need to meet Chelsea at the gondola ride. We need to warn her and Priscilla and Nevaeh and everyone. You guys were right. Ren's behind it. He's behind everything. Tommy's murder, the cover-up from Tommy's hacked account. All of it."

Jason's shock at Kiara's claims was matched only by the worry in his expression. So she explained everything quickly: how Ren had locked her in the hotel's freezer after they'd overheard the police talk about his father and the park's role in obstructing the investigation of Tommy's body in the park and how this whole time, he had everything to lose if the truth behind Tommy's death really came out.

"We need to go to the park. Now," Kiara said, gasping through the cold.

"Kiara, the last place you want to be at is in Sunny World," Jason said. His voice was firm but there was a harshness to it that jolted Kiara to her senses. Jason's nails burrowed into Kiara's arms, almost as if to stop her from standing rather than to hold her up.

"It's almost midnight, Jason. We don't have any more time."

"Kiara, it's enough. No more lies. Please, that's the least you owe me after everything I've done for you."

Nothing was making sense. Not the way Jason was looking at her, not the cold that seemed to have burrowed in Kiara's body, nothing. Kiara closed her eyes, and in the distance, when she focused clearly, she could hear the sound of voices shouting and doors being slammed shut.

"What's going on?" Kiara said slowly.

Kiara realized now that it wasn't just her hands that were shaking, but Jason also couldn't seem to stay still.

"They found your necklace, Kiara. Tommy's blood was on it

too." Again, his grip on her arms tightened and suddenly Kiara realized that he was holding her there. "Kiara, there's a warrant out for your arrest."

And there they were: the words Kiara had been dreading, the ones that had played over and over again in her nightmares.

"I didn't kill him. Jason, please. This is a setup. You have to believe me."

"Blood was on the necklace, Kiara. You can't be serious."

"It's a setup," Kiara repeated. "The hacker, Ren, killed Tommy and is trying to frame me. Why do you think all the video footage is missing from the park or why all the leaks about the case keep coming out?" Kiara tried to yank herself out of Jason's grip, but he was too strong. "I'm not lying. Jason, I swear this is real. I didn't kill him."

The voices were getting closer. Time was running out.

"Why are you doing this to me?" Jason groaned, and there was heartbreak in his voice, pure pain that made Kiara's heart ache too. "Kiara, he's my family."

"Just take me to the gondola ride. If what I'm saying isn't real, then I'll go on the livestream and confess to everything. I'll let you walk me to police custody."

The footsteps drew closer. Kiara closed her eyes fighting back the bitter tears that had begun to burn against her lashes. When she opened her eyes again, her gaze met his. His irises were bright with conflict, and then they steeled as he made his decision.

"Fine," he said. "Midnight it is." He yanked his jacket off and pulled it over Kiara. The cold was still biting but the warmth of his clothes eased some of the pain.

Jason stood and Kiara followed suit, gently holding on to him as her own strength failed her. He put his arms around her shoulders and hurried her down the hallway to the employee elevator bank just as two officers went in the other direction.

"Don't you dare leave my side this time," he said.

"I won't," Kiara whispered.

She knew he wasn't trying to be some knight. His words were just a reminder that if Kiara made one wrong move, he'd turn her in himself.

How could she blame Jason? Now even he knew that Kiara was with Tommy during what might have been Tommy's last moments alive. Yet still, Jason was there, helping her. Even if it was just a small, hopeful part of him that still saw her as "Kiara Stephens" and not "the girlfriend." And that was enough. In the face of all the lies and the rumors and the half-truths, even Kiara had begun to doubt if the reality she'd lived through was the same one everyone could see beyond their screens. But this was real. Every step Kiara took, every turn she faced, was leading her closer and closer to the truth about what really happened to Tommy.

As they waited for the elevator, Kiara texted Chelsea so the other girl knew they were still meeting as planned. There was a *ding*. The elevator doors opened, and then Kiara and Jason stepped inside.

WHEN THEY ARRIVED at Sunny World, all of the tourists were leaving. Police cars were stationed near the front gates. The red and white lights from the cruisers were nearly blinding.

Kiara and Jason wove through the exodus toward a discreet employee entrance. Chelsea had told them to wait for her there while she let them in the park.

They stood in silence. Kiara took to rubbing her hands as the warm Florida air slowly melted the cold that had encased her.

"This doesn't make any sense," Jason said. "Why would Ren want to kill Tommy? He's literally the heir to Sunny World. What the hell could Tommy have on him that would make him resort to murder?"

Jason was still reeling from everything Kiara had told him about her suspicions about Ren being the hacker and Tommy's murderer. She was still piecing through the theory herself. But no matter how Kiara looked at it, only Ren would have had the resources to destroy the Sunny World footage, plant evidence, and have access to the burner phone.

"Every other year that the senior prank has happened in Sunny World, they've never had anyone operating rides," Kiara said. "All of the seniors from last year saved up from summer jobs to buy out the park for the night. They must have gone through Ren back then to have done that. But this year Tommy gets it booked out for free and there are rides being operated by workers too? Jason, how else did your brother get Ren to agree to all of this if not with some serious sort of blackmail? Why else would Ren literally lock me inside of a freezer?"

"I know. I know. I just— Murder. I can't wrap my mind around it."

"But you believe I would kill Tommy?" Kiara said.

Shame washed over Jason, but he couldn't deny the fact that he still had not let go of her arm since they'd been reunited, even if his grip had loosened slightly. "I believe it could have been you, or Priscilla, or Nevaeh. And yeah, everything you're saying makes it seem like Ren might have the motive."

"I guess murder sounds more likely when a bitter girlfriend, a jealous side chick, or a fallen saint could be the culprit?"

Jason grimaced. "I guess that's what Ren thought too."

Before Kiara could speak again, the door to the employee entrance flew open. Chelsea peeked her head out, confirming that it was Kiara and Jason before ushering them in.

"Thanks so much again for meeting us," Kiara said.

"Sure. Things are a bit nuts right now with the police being everywhere. They're not saying what they found in the park, but it isn't looking good."

"That's just the thing," Kiara said. "We think the hacker killed Tommy."

Chelsea's eyes widened.

"Aren't they the one trying to prove what really happened?" she said, her voice taking on a false impartiality that Kiara knew Chelsea didn't mean. The two girls had never been on amazing terms and Kiara was pretty sure that, like the rest of the world, Chelsea thought one of the girls was the killer. But at least she was giving Kiara a chance to prove her innocence. That was more than Kiara could say about most people.

"Here's the thing," Jason said. Chelsea led them through the rear employee corridors and, together, Kiara and Jason explained her theory about Ren.

"When Nevaeh was here the night Tommy died, she had Tommy's phone," Kiara said. "His real phone. We think if we can track that down in the park we'll be able to find the full truth that the hacker is trying to bury by framing us three."

"But if you find Tommy's real phone, isn't that evidence that should go to the police?"

"Exactly. Except we need to find it first before Ren or his family get rid of it," Kiara said. "Do you know if any of your co-workers mentioned finding a phone or being given one last night? You were there, Ren was there, and there must have been a few others to help operate the rides we were on."

"Jacob, Taylor, and Gigi," Chelsea said. "And yeah, there were a bunch of things your class left behind. We had to be the cleanup crew. You guys were, like, beyond drunk. If they found anything, they probably would have left it in the cave."

Kiara and Jason exchanged looks.

"The cave?" Jason asked.

"It's where we keep the lost items visitors in the park leave behind. Like, yeah, there is a legit lost and found, but if you pick up a phone or a tablet in the park, you'd want to keep it for yourself instead of, like, letting some random park visitor pretend it's theirs. At the end of the summer, we all go through it and pick what we want from it. Ren's the one who came up with the idea a few years ago after he first started letting senior classes pay him to stay in the park after hours."

Jason cursed under his breath. Kiara smiled.

"See. I told you he was doing shady things."

"Just how much does Ren make from charging senior classes money to visit the park when it's closed?" Jason asks.

"I mean, we all get a cut," Chelsea said. "And it's not just senior classes. Any schools who visit, he hooks them up. That's how we met Tommy. He was trying to film something deranged in the park and got in touch with Ren for how to do it. It was during a family trip a few years ago, not for school. I honestly don't know all the details."

"I don't know," Kiara said. "It sort of sounds like you do."

Before Kiara could finish the thought, they arrived at the gondola ride. Now that all the park guests were leaving, the ride itself was practically empty. The lines were thinning and only a few employees lumbered about, pointing visitors to the exit.

Chelsea led them through the emptying corners of the ride where the line would normally be. Then, she made a sharp right past the employee locker room to a door marked *Security*. Two park security guards greeted Chelsea, but they didn't question the group as they ventured in.

Inside the room, a slew of monitors showed camera footage of rides and various rooms inside the gondola ride attraction. Another guard, alone this time, sat in front of the main computer, operating the cameras.

"Hey, Nathan," Chelsea said. "Have you seen Ren?"

Nathan pointed to one of the monitors. Ren stood in the employee locker room. But he wasn't alone. Nevaeh, Alex, and two other girls were with him. Kiara recognized the two girls from the party in Tommy's room. Christina and Heather. But where was Priscilla? And why was Nevaeh looking so friendly with Ren and Alex?

Nevaeh sat on the ground surrounded by an assortment of items that had clearly fallen out of the locker while Alex and Ren had an animated conversation.

"What's going on?" Jason said.

Kiara shook her head. "I don't know."

But everything inside Kiara was telling her that something was very, very wrong.

"If Ren's the killer," Chelsea said, "then it looks like he didn't work alone."

Jason squeezed Kiara's hand and the gesture centered her, if only for the moment.

"Should we confront them?" Jason asked. "Maybe we could find a way to get the audio from their conversation."

Kiara shook her head.

"We need to get Tommy's real phone," she said. "Without it, we can't prove anything."

"Then to the cave we go," Chelsea said, and she gestured to the other side of the room, where a small ladder with the label *Maintenance Only* descended into the dark depths of the gondola ride's belly.

Chelsea climbed down first and Kiara and Jason followed.

There was no turning back, Kiara realized. Not anymore.

chapter thirty

Priscilla

PRISCILLA'S SUSPICIONS WERE confirmed the moment she entered Alex's room.

He wasn't there, waiting for her like he'd promised. Instead, the door was locked. She knocked on it discreetly, to no avail. If she wasn't afraid of alerting him to the fact that she knew he was lying, Priscilla would have called him too. So Priscilla broke in.

It wasn't hard to steal a key card from one of the chaperones. Throughout the day, Priscilla had watched them make changes as they switched shifts. Inevitably, one of them went to the restroom and left their key card with their phone out on the counter. Priscilla grabbed the key card before making her way to Alex's room.

Alex's suitcase was still unpacked on the bed. But on the desk beside it, Alex had begun to tinker with a film setup. His camera was on a tripod, and a smartwatch and tablet lay on his desk.

The only thing missing was his laptop.

Instinctively, Priscilla was drawn to the smartwatch. It was the same one Kiara had noticed among the things he'd taken from Tommy's room. Just as she'd told Kiara, both boys had used their smartwatches to schedule and plan the pranks they filmed. But

while Alex was perpetually glued to his, Tommy was forever forget-
ful and seemed to leave it anywhere, unlike his burner phone. The
watch would be synced to each of their phones. But Alex had
mixed up his watch with Tommy's when they'd changed into their
costumes. The police had cleared Alex to take the watch back
after they'd accessed it and identified it as belonging to him. Had
Alex switched them back after Kiara had called him out and Priscilla had covered for him?

Priscilla knew there was only one way to find out. If the watch
was Alex's, Priscilla would be able to see proof of that in their
recent text conversation. But if it was Tommy's, then his text and
call history would be reflected on the screen.

Priscilla picked up the watch and immediately it lit up. The
request asked for a passcode. Priscilla groaned. There was no way
she'd ever figure out what Alex had set up. He was literally the
password king who refused to save his passwords on any app and
changed it monthly. But Tommy, on the other hand . . .

Priscilla typed in the first digits that came to her head.

Three-three-one-two, the exact number of Tommy's three
point three million followers the last time he'd checked.

The moment Priscilla typed the two, the watch screen faded
to the home page. She dropped the watch in shock. Kiara was
right. Alex had Tommy's smartwatch. Had he found it in their
room when he'd been grabbing his stuff? Or had he taken it from
Tommy elsewhere? Like maybe in the fun house, off of Tommy's
cold, dead body.

Priscilla shook her head. She wasn't going to let herself jump
to conclusions. Ever since senior prank night, her life had been
filled with other people jumping to conclusions about who she
was and wasn't. Alex had lied to her. But that didn't mean he had

any more to do with Tommy's death than she did. Besides, she was still convinced that Nevaeh and her friends had were the ones connected to Tommy's hacked account. Hopefully Priscilla's posts would shed light on the case.

Priscilla didn't know how much time she had until Mr. Phillips or another chaperone figured out they were down one master key card. The first thing she did was check to see if the watch was still logged into Tommy's online account. Her heart dropped when she saw that whoever had the burner phone had changed the password already. That was a dead end. Priscilla tried his messaging app next. When she pressed it, there was a chain already opened, which meant that Alex probably hadn't had much trouble figuring out Tommy's passcode either.

But upon opening the message thread, Priscilla froze. The message thread was between Tommy and someone he'd listed as "Puppet." She'd seen that name before. When she'd first hidden the burner phone between the sheets, Tommy had received a message from the person then. *This was a pretty big favor this time. I held up my end. Your turn. You owe me,* the message had read. Priscilla had assumed the message had come from the person helping Tommy with the senior prank. But scrolling through the chain that Alex had been reading, she realized she'd been wrong. Puppet wasn't the one coordinating getting the seniors into Sunny World that night; Puppet was a Tommy superfan.

Their messages dated back to eighth grade, down to the month Tommy had first started filming content for his channel. Puppet was one of Tommy's first followers and apparently the manager of his fan club. Priscilla didn't even know Tommy had a fan club, let alone one that was monitored by his very first fan. Puppet set up follow chains and competitions among Tommy's fans to see who could share his content the most. The most recent competition they'd set up was a meet and greet. The location?

Sunny World Park.

To be considered for the competition, fans had to boost Tommy's posts and make their own content about him. Whoever's post went the most viral would secure the meeting with Tommy during his senior trip. In the messages between Tommy and Puppet, they were going back and forth about when exactly Tommy would meet the winning fan. But within the chain, something caught Priscilla's eye.

Puppet: I have a few of your fans willing to send some photos.

Tommy: Cool. Send me their social media accounts. I'll DM them myself.

Puppet: Sent.

Puppet: To confirm, you want to meet the winner during your senior prank night?

Tommy: Sure

Puppet: speaking of. . . . so like, when are we gonna meet? I live here and you're here. This long distance thing is really hard.

Tommy: Idk. I'm kind of busy

Puppet: You said you'd do a girlfriend reveal.

Tommy: I will

Puppet: So you dumped Kiara then?

Tommy: Yeah. It's over with us. I told you I was going to end it with her during the trip.

Puppet: So why can't you do the reveal then? Why can't we meet to celebrate? Like, you should be planning an amazing date. Why am I the one who always has to ask for things?

Tommy: I've been asking you to send photos or even do a video call for years and you always bail. I don't even know what your face looks like. What if you're catfishing me?

Puppet: I would never lie to you like that. Why are you being so mean?

Tommy: I'm just frustrated. Okay? I've got a lot going on and you're being pissy when we've never even met and your avatar is literally fan art of what it would be like if we did meet. At least use a real picture of yourself and photoshop us together.

Puppet: I just want our reveal to be special. Is that so wrong?

Tommy: Babe. I'm sorry. I have 3.3 million followers. Do you know how hard it is managing a brand?

When Puppet didn't answer, Tommy sent another message. It was a photo of a necklace. Priscilla frowned. Then it hit her. That necklace was the exact same one Tommy had given Kiara. She'd seen the girl wearing it only once during their trip. It'd been the night of the party, before the account revealed Tommy had been cheating. Kiara hadn't been wearing it the morning after, though. And the messages between Tommy and Puppet were dated the evening of the prank, which meant the same time Tommy had gotten a necklace for Kiara, he'd gotten another for this so-called Puppet.

There was another girl.

Priscilla didn't know whether to laugh or cry at this point. How many other girls were there? How many had known about

Kiara like Priscilla had, and still entertained the idea that it was okay to keep flirting with and pursuing Tommy? And even worse was the fact that Tommy had played them all, using the promise of his attention and their feelings to benefit himself.

This girl was literally running his fandom empire for free, solely on the promise that he'd break up with Kiara and date her. Priscilla had let Tommy borrow her lawyers when his controversies had gotten him in trouble. She'd helped him film and given him so much of her time and ideas, all because she thought maybe someday he would see the lengths she'd gone to on his behalf as a sign of her love. Nevaeh had done the same. She'd compromised her values in the hopes that Tommy might commit to her. But he would never pick Puppet, or Nevaeh, or Priscilla. He'd never pick any of the girls, not even Kiara. Because the only thing Tommy loved more than himself was the fame he got online.

At the image of the necklace, Puppet sent a row of heart emojis with tear eyes, which was overdoing it, to say the least.

> **Puppet:** Soooo when are you going to put that around my neck?
> **Tommy:** When we meet. I'm busy until later tonight. Meet me at the fun house?
> **Puppet:** Yessss. I'll bring your favorite treats too. Hehe saving on shipping finally.

After she wrote *treats,* Puppet added pill emojis. Priscilla laughed in disbelief. Puppet was also Tommy's dealer. Not only was this girl breaking labor laws for Tommy, but she was risking federal ones too. The secondhand embarrassment Priscilla felt for this girl was only measured by the firsthand embarrassment Priscilla felt for herself knowing that she too had once simped for Tommy Harding.

As much as she could, Priscilla took photos of the messages using her own phone. She would have taken screenshots and sent them to herself, but she didn't want to risk tampering with evidence.

As she continued to scroll, Priscilla landed on a conversation between Puppet and Tommy that had occurred just an hour after he'd sent the necklace photo. In it, Tommy had sent his final message to Puppet.

> **Tommy:** Actually, and I'm real sorry babe, but something came up. Sorry. We can meet another time when I'm in Sunny World. You know I would have wanted to see you if I could.

Puppet never responded. Once again, Tommy did what he did best: disappoint, use, and gaslight.

Priscilla exited out of the exchange and then opened another recent conversation. This one was between Tommy, Alex, and Ren. It was about a prank Tommy was planning on filming that night in the midst of the party the senior class would be having in Sunny World. Ren and Alex were coordinating the details, which involved Tommy traversing the park unseen and hiding cameras on the rides.

> **Tommy:** What about the locker rooms?
> **Alex:** Why would you hide cameras in the locker rooms?

Tommy: Everyone's going to be changing into costumes. It'll be funny.

Ren: Your sense of humor sucks. Sicko.

Alex: Ignore him. He's trolling.

Tommy: Yeah. It was a joke man.

Priscilla's blood went cold. This whole time, Alex had lied about knowing Ren. He'd acted like Tommy had set up the prank in the park by himself, but he hadn't. Both boys had helped him in some way or another. They'd both overlooked the possibility that Tommy hadn't been joking about his locker room prank at all.

The betrayal stung deep. It took everything in Priscilla to keep reading. But she scrolled down. In the messages, the group decided the prank would take place a little after midnight for the remaining seniors partying in the park. Then, Ren suggested that Tommy reach out to a Sunny World worker who knew the park even better than him. Ren offered to introduce Tommy to the worker in order to finalize logistics and made a point of mentioning that the worker was a huge Tommy fan themself. He asked Tommy if he'd be able to provide an autograph for the worker and, of course, Tommy agreed.

Alex: So how much will this whole thing cost?

Priscilla expected Ren to quote a huge number like seniors before had paid in order to buy out the park. Instead, Ren answered: *Tommy and I already have an arrangement. Right Tommy.*

Tommy: Yuuup

The emoji Tommy added at the end of the message was a sly smile. Priscilla's heart clenched. Just what kind of deal had they worked out?

The last message between Tommy and Ren shared the number of the Sunny World employee Ren had suggested Tommy reach out to. Priscilla exited out of the conversation and opened the chain between Tommy and a number Tommy had labeled "Sunny World Chick."

Tommy: Hey. Ren gave me your number. Said you were a big fan? I'm Tommy Harding. Nice to meet you.
Sunny World Chick: I know who you are. I guess I'll be helping the King of Pranks with his senior prank at Sunny World
Tommy: Lol of course you know. And yeah, feeling honored yet?
Sunny World Chick: Yeah. Such an honor.

The conversation shifted to Tommy explaining what he needed from the worker.

Sunny World Chick: there are tunnels throughout the park. That should help you get around.
Tommy: Sweet. Looking forward to the private tour;)

Priscilla rolled her eyes. She expected more messages between them, but that was the last one Tommy had sent to the worker. His final text message was, to Priscilla's shock, sent to himself. Late around midnight, Tommy had texted a message from his actual phone to the burner phone.

Tommy: Hey, whoever has my phone, can you return it to me? Seriously I'll pay you whatever you want. Just give me back my phone.

The response was from Tommy again, but clearly it was the person with the burner phone talking.

Tommy: Screw you.

Priscilla's heart raced as she kept reading. This was it. This was the chain between Tommy and the hacker. This was the answer she'd been searching for. The real Tommy had sent another message asking for the identity of the hacker. The response had come back seconds later.

Tommy: Who the hell are you?
Hacker: Who do you think?
Tommy: Kiara?

When the hacker didn't answer, Tommy sent three more guesses.

Tommy: Priscilla?
Tommy: Nevaeh?
Tommy: Leah?

Again, Priscilla almost dropped the watch in shock. He'd been seeing Leah too? Was he literally just cheating with everyone in their school and on the internet?

She scrolled down in the chain to the hacker's response.

Tommy: Did you already forget our little tour? It's your so called Puppet, you asshole.

The messages ended there.

Here the truth was, yet still it felt out of reach.

Fact 1: Puppet was the Sunny World worker who had given Tommy the tour.

Fact 2: Puppet was Tommy's superfan and his hacker.

Puppet was the one targeting the girls. They were the one who had plotted revenge on Tommy.

Priscilla had been wrong. It wasn't Nevaeh or her friends. This whole thing was just another one of Tommy's botched relationships.

Priscilla clicked on Tommy's contacts, scrolling through the information Tommy had saved about Puppet in search of a more concrete identity.

In his notes, he'd included a link to Puppet and an online account page: Seagurlheartsharding.

It was the same account that had commented on Tommy's livestream just the day before. In fact, Priscilla had remembered reading aloud the comment from the account to Tommy and the rest of the group during the pregame livestream.

You deserve to be with someone who cares about you, for you. Not someone who uses you for clout.

Puppet had been watching the livestream. That meant they'd witnessed Priscilla hiding the burner phone just as clearly as anyone else partying in the room had that day. As a Sunny World worker, they'd also be able to sneak into Tommy's room and steal the burner phone right when the group had left for the park. They'd also set up cameras throughout the park for Tommy's prank. The footage would have shown Tommy's fights with the girls. All of this would make it easy for Puppet to plant evidence and cover up Tommy's death.

Had Alex known about Puppet? Had Ren? Were there more clues that Priscilla was missing? Priscilla's mind was racing. She recalled the moment when Kiara had admitted to working with Ren to orchestrate the interview. Alex had been on the brink of saying something. But he'd stayed quiet.

She texted Alex and then called him. When he didn't answer, she texted him again.

Priscilla: You know Ren.

This time, Alex didn't leave her on Read. His response was quick, but the words were rushed.

Alex: I'm sorry. I didn't want to jump to conclusions in case I was wrong. We were so messed up by what Tommy did in the locker room. I wanted to investigate on my own so things didn't spiral like how they did with you, Kiara, and Nevaeh.

Priscilla's heart leaped. She called him, her fingers trembling as she hit Call. But the line went dead immediately.

Alex: Can't talk. With them now. But the answers are in Tommy's watch. I left it there for you. It explains everything.

Priscilla had already checked the smartwatch. But had she missed something more? Her mind trailed to the box of equipment that Kiara had first noticed the smartwatch in, which Alex had been carrying after their interview with the police. Maybe there were more clues inside it? More evidence to unravel the truth behind Tommy's death?

Immediately, Priscilla began searching for the box. She spotted it easily. It sat at the corner of the room behind the door. She hadn't noticed it when she'd first walked in.

Alex had returned most of the items to his suitcase or had placed them on his desk. But inside the box was something else: a sticky pad. It was the same one Priscilla had written on with her lipstick for the brand video she'd been filming. She'd been coming up with lipstick names and had asked Tommy and Alex for ideas. Priscilla must have left the pad and the sticky notes in Tommy's room and Alex had taken it. But as Priscilla flipped through the pad and the sticky notes attached to it, she realized that one of the phrases she'd written was missing.

It struck Priscilla then what it might mean if anyone found it. And in Tommy's room, of all places.

Before she could stop herself, Priscilla sprinted from Alex's room. She ran past Mr. Phillips on his way back from the restroom. But Priscilla didn't stop for him or any of the chaperones calling after her.

When she arrived at Tommy's room, she used the master key card and yanked the door open. Once again, Priscilla dug through Tommy's mattress. In her first search, she hadn't noticed it crumpled beneath his sheets. Priscilla unfolded the sticky note. There, written in bold red letters, were two words along with the impression of Priscilla's lips: *Sweet Revenge.*

She'd written it as a joke. But in the context of Tommy's murder, the note was damning.

Behind Priscilla, the door burst open. But her gaze had risen to the ceiling, where the white light of a camera blinked at her.

"What do you have in your hand?" an officer said. "Hands up now!"

Kiara had warned Priscilla that the hacker was setting them up, and here Priscilla was, walking right into Puppet's trap.

Instead of just targeting Tommy, the person who had hurt them, Puppet was targeting the girls he had hurt too. It was a sick, twisted turn of events. A victim hurting other victims. Priscilla knew the cycle because she realized now, she had played into it too. Instead of letting herself be hurt and angry at Tommy for the wrong he had done to her, Priscilla had lashed out at Kiara and Nevaeh. She'd let herself play into Tommy's mind games instead of holding Tommy accountable.

Violently, viciously, the officers once again shouted the command for her to put her hands up.

She dropped the note and raised her hands high above her.

"She's just a kid," Mr. Phillips shouted. "Would you just stop already?"

He rushed to Priscilla's side and unfolded the note. But when he read it, horror shone in his eyes.

The officer flicked a glance at the note too.

"Stand up," the officer said. "You're coming with us."

chapter thirty-one

Nevaeh

NEVAEH HAD STILL been coming to her senses when the two boys entered the locker room. Tension clung to the room as the boy with locs approached with his hands tentatively raised, as if Nevaeh, Christina, or Heather might break into a run and bolt from the scene if he got any closer.

"You're Nevaeh, right? I'm Alex. This is Ren."

She knew that voice. Nevaeh recognized it from the conversation she'd been having with Priscilla and Kiara back at the airport. Alex had been there, speaking in the background with the girls as they'd warned Nevaeh about the hacking situation.

And Ren . . . something about him was familiar. Something Nevaeh couldn't quite piece together.

"You're not supposed to be in here," the other boy, Ren, said. "You should leave. Now."

But Nevaeh wouldn't let go of the photo she'd found of Tommy. It looked like a screenshot that had been printed. The photo itself had fallen out of a red journal. It was one of the many items that had scattered on the floor when Nevaeh fell out of the locker.

When Nevaeh turned the notebook over, a *TH* logo was embossed on the front and meme stickers of Tommy were plastered along the cover too. Nevaeh opened the notebook. There were even more photos of Tommy taped inside.

Some of the images included text chains and messages Tommy had sent, clearly screenshots the person had taken and printed. Nevaeh flipped through. The writing in the notebooks was little more than chicken scratch, but Nevaeh managed to make out some of it. It was dated back years, all the way to when Tommy was in eighth grade and had just started his vlogging channel. The writer had been an early fan of Tommy's, and along the margins of screenshots they'd printed out, they'd clearly written a fan-fiction–like love story of meeting Tommy and the two falling in love. As the years passed, though, the gushing journal entries and bullet-journal lists of everything perfect about Tommy grew less and less. Instead, the images in the journal shifted from centering on only Tommy, to photos of other girls. Each photo was followed with a journal entry with a name scratched in Sharpie on top of the photo and a profile description. There was a girl named Leah. The notes the person had written detailed her age and school, her social media account pages, and life events.

Tommy and Leah go to a concert together. Cheating? Leah had mono a week before Tommy. Connected somehow?

Nevaeh's heart sank. She didn't know why she'd been naive enough to think that there wouldn't be more girls. And when Nevaeh kept flipping through, she came across profiles the writer had made of her, Priscilla, and Kiara. Kiara's entry was nearly half the worn pages of the journal. It listed everything from when she and Tommy had gone online-official with their relationship status, to angry notes about Model UN and a spelling bee. There were even dedicated segments that deconstructed Kiara and Tommy's viral couple posts and whether or not their relationship was just a publicity stunt.

The last few entries, though, spanned up through Tommy's death. The words *hypocrite* and *liar* were scribbled over and over in the notebook, all of which had been dated just a few hours ago, after the interview aired.

Nevaeh looked up at the locker, where more Polaroids were taped inside. In most of the pictures, Tommy was alone. In one of the photos, though, Tommy was standing with a person who was clearly Kiara. But her face had been cut out and replaced with a pale girl with brown hair, green eyes, and freckles. The girl was the same one who'd escorted Nevaeh into the park. And now, seeing her face so clearly in the image, Nevaeh realized that the girl had been there operating the gondola ride when Nevaeh had left Tommy's real phone with one of the other workers.

Nevaeh stood and grabbed the Polaroid. On the top of the shelf were unlabeled containers, and behind them all was a flash drive.

"Is this some sick shrine to Tommy Harding?" Christina asked.

Heather and Ren joined Nevaeh in front of the locker.

"I told you it was her," Alex said, turning to Ren.

Nevaeh picked up the flash drive and turned it in her hand. It had a little key chain with a college logo on it.

"Does anyone have a computer?" she said.

Alex nodded, setting down his book bag and pulling it open. He took out a laptop and Nevaeh handed him the flash drive. His

350

computer booted it up, and then he opened the folder. When he did, the screen was filled with dozens upon dozens of files.

"That's security footage from the park," Ren said. "And from the cameras we set up from the prank."

"Click the one from the fun house," Nevaeh said, and Alex acquiesced.

The security footage popped up on a video player. Even with the grainy lighting, there was a visible time stamp dating the footage to the night before. Nevaeh recognized the fun house. Tommy and Priscilla were inside. Priscilla said something, and suddenly, Tommy was ripping the mask off her face and pulling off the silver wig. The force of his rage was all-consuming. Priscilla crashed against the mirrored walls and glass shattered over her like crystal rainfall.

Alex grimaced, a pained expression clouding his eyes.

"I'm going to speed this up," he said. Nevaeh nodded.

Alex skipped the video forward to a scene of Tommy on the ground and Priscilla stumbling away. Blood trickled along his forehead. For a long time, he lay there immobile. But then Tommy rose. Ever so slowly, he stumbled his way deeper into the fun house. It was there where Tommy came across Nevaeh.

She remembered that moment, how hurt he had been, how she'd used it to her advantage.

Nevaeh had pretended to help him, but instead, she'd taken his phone off him. As he chased her, she'd made a turn and stumbled into the tunnels that led to the gondola ride. Two workers had been there. Nevaeh had already deleted the photos off Tommy's phone by then. She'd alerted the worker that someone in the tunnel needed help and then had given the other worker Tommy's phone. One of the workers had raced into the tunnels, while the worker who

Nevaeh had given Tommy's phone to had promised her he'd have it returned to the student it belonged to when the night ended.

It hit Nevaeh then. That's where she recognized Ren from.

He'd been the worker she'd given Tommy's phone to.

"Keep going," Nevaeh urged. "Skip a little further."

Alex did. In the footage, Tommy was still stumbling after Nevaeh. But he must have gotten lost in the tunnels because he backtracked, only to wind up where Kiara was.

Unlike Nevaeh, Kiara actually tried to help him. She hurried to Tommy's side, but he pushed her away.

Shame washed over Nevaeh as she watched the scenes and realized how, over and over, she'd made choices that led them into this nightmare. Yet as Kiara reached for Tommy, he slapped her hand away. The two stared at each other for a long time, then Kiara unclasped the necklace around her neck. She threw it at Tommy and turned away, leaving him behind. Alex fastforwarded the footage.

The time log skipped to hours later. Still Tommy ventured on, until he reached a part of the fun house that still looked under construction. Scaffolding loomed high above him, and there was an unfinished ledge that was clearly being constructed to be an extension of some sort of attraction. Tommy finally stopped there to rest. At first, Nevaeh had believed that Tommy was simply stumbling aimlessly through the fun house and the tunnels. But then she realized he was meeting someone.

Their shadow emerged in the dim lighting, pointed and sharp and ominous. The person was dressed in a Sunny World uniform, and from their profile, Nevaeh realized it was the girl whose locker she'd desecrated. When the girl arrived, she fussed over

Tommy's injuries. Tommy pulled her into a kiss. When they separated, he held up a necklace and began to put it on her. Smiling, the girl examined it, but then her smile faltered and she tore it off her neck, yelling at Tommy while pointing to the necklace.

From the glint in the camera, it was clear that the necklace was engraved. But the initials on the necklace weren't the girl's. The initials were Kiara's. *KS.*

Tommy seemed to realize his mistake. He shuffled through his pockets and pulled out another necklace. This one was almost identical to the first, but, Nevaeh was sure, with the correct initials this time. But it was too late.

In that moment, it seemed as if the girl had reached her breaking point. She was already walking away from Tommy, and when he reached for her to come back, she spun away. They argued for a moment before the girl pulled out a phone and hurled it at the scaffolding. Rage seized Tommy. He shoved the girl to the ground and began to climb the scaffolding, desperately trying to reach the phone. Somehow, he managed to get to the top of it. But when he retrieved the phone, his expression fell. It wasn't horror but disbelief. Way down below, the girl shook with laughter. Again, she reached into her pocket, and this time, Nevaeh got a good look at the phone she was holding. It was almost identical to the one Nevaeh had taken from him, but this one was a lighter shade in the security footage.

"She switched them," Ren said. "The one she threw up there was one of the employee phones we have workers use during shifts, and the one she kept was—"

"Tommy's burner," Alex said, finishing the sentence.

That explained why his body had been found with a Sunny

World phone and why Tommy's burner had never been located. The girl had kept it the whole time. She'd been using it to wreak havoc on them all.

As Tommy yelled at the girl from the top of the ledge, the girl began filming and taunting him. Still screaming at the girl, Tommy began his descent. But as he did, his foot missed one of the poles he had used to climb the scaffolding. It happened in an instant. Tommy was clawing to maintain his grip. And then his body hit the ground, his head snapping back violently against the impact. Blood oozed beneath him. A nail or some sort of instrument on the ground must have torn into his flesh when he'd fallen. But Tommy was still alive. He reached for the girl, pleading for her to help him. She stood there, frozen in shock for a moment.

Tommy clasped the ankle of her jeans. She stared down at him. And then she kicked his hand away. The violence of the act seemed to shock the girl herself. But then she did it again. Again and again, her blows struck his stomach and his chest, leaving Tommy breathless and gasping, a shell of himself as the girl screamed at him, tears of betrayal falling down her cheeks. Then, without looking back, the Sunny World worker wiped away her tears and left Tommy Harding to his fate.

"We need to get this to the police," Heather said. "This is murder. She killed him."

"It wasn't—" Ren said. "Chelsea wouldn't—I mean, you all saw him fall by himself. She just—"

"She could have helped him. He could have survived."

"No, you're both right," Nevaeh said. "She didn't kill him. But she let him die."

And that was the most twisted part of this whole thing. Nevaeh, Kiara, and Priscilla had all seen Tommy right before his death. Even Priscilla and Kiara had tried to help him. But Nevaeh hadn't. If she'd been in this worker's place, watching him fall from the scaffolding, would she have called for help or left him to die, taking in those last moments to enact her own revenge? The fact that Nevaeh wasn't sure of her answer made her feel sick to her stomach.

"We need to talk to her," Nevaeh continued. "Maybe she can explain what happened? Maybe Ren's right. Maybe she just lost it. We don't know if she came back later to get him help."

"Nevaeh, she's trying to frame you for something that she did," Christina said. "I understand not wanting to make accusations and giving her the benefit of the doubt, but this isn't that kind of situation."

In her heart of hearts, Nevaeh knew Christina was right. All the girls had made the same mistake when it came to Tommy. Instead of holding each other, comforting each other, and commiserating over how they'd been hurt, they'd tried to claw their way into his heart by using each other as stepping stools. Nevaeh had thought Priscilla was just a shallow influencer, and she'd been jealous of Kiara for being unflinchingly bold and smart. Chelsea had used that against all three of them.

No more.

Nevaeh refused to let all the scars of what Tommy had seared into her determine her future.

"Give me your laptop," Nevaeh said, holding out her hand to Alex. Tentatively he pushed it to Nevaeh from where they both sat on the ground.

They had less than a half hour left before the livestream. That would give Nevaeh just enough time to do what she needed to do.

chapter thirty-two

Kiara

IT WAS HARD for Kiara not to feel a sense of déjà vu as they wandered through the tunnels of Sunny World Park. She'd never been here before, but the deeper they ventured in, the more eerily familiar the area became.

"This connects to the fun house and the gondola ride," Chelsea said. "The park is building a new attraction that combines the two."

"Creepy," Jason said.

Kiara couldn't help but agree. It was one thing to be stuck in line for an attraction and a whole other thing to be underground, crammed in with other visitors, while doing it. In the ceiling, electric wires wove along support beams. It was almost suffocating the way lights gleamed from them in the dark and how the ground beneath their feet was still being excavated.

They walked in silence as Chelsea led the way. Kiara kept her eyes on her phone, as if sheer willpower could keep the seconds from ticking away. But the time for the livestream was approaching. Underground, her service was spotty and barely reliable. She just hoped Priscilla and Nevaeh would think of some way to buy them time.

"I saw that interview you did," Chelsea said, using the flashlight on her phone to light their way. Up ahead, there was a fork in the path. Chelsea took a sharp right and Kiara and Jason followed. Kiara made a mental note of where they were going and how many turns it had taken in case she needed to remember the directions to the cave later on.

"So why did you do it?" Chelsea continued.

Kiara frowned. "Do what?"

"Lie about him. In your interview, you made it seem like you had such an amazing relationship with Tommy and like he was this wonderful person. I mean, clearly with his account active again and this whole situation, he wasn't."

Jason and Kiara exchanged looks. But Kiara answered the question anyway.

"I mean, isn't it a faux pas to speak ill of the dead?"

To that, Chelsea actually laughed.

"You're lying again," she said. "The account is proving to the world that Tommy had dirt on you and the other girls. That's why you're so desperate to prove it wrong, even if it means going on this wild-goose chase."

"Look, if you don't want to help us, you don't have to," Jason said. "Just show us where to go and we can look for the phone ourselves."

They arrived at a section of the tunnels that was in worse shape than the others. The ceiling here arched high above a steep incline still under construction. Yellow police tape circled the area. It wasn't until Chelsea flashed the light over the scene that

Kiara caught a glimpse of the remnants of white chalk outlining a form. Kiara's heart jolted.

This was it. This was where Tommy's body had been found.

Chelsea's gaze followed Kiara's to where the outline of Tommy's body was.

"He was an idiot for picking you," she said. "He deserved what he got."

Maybe it was the knowledge that Tommy's body had been a few feet away only twenty-four hours earlier, or maybe it was being in this tunnel, surrounded by flickering lights where their voices echoed in the dark and knowing that time was running out, but a restless gale stormed through Kiara. "What's your problem?"

"You're my problem," Chelsea spat. "You and Nevaeh and that Priscilla. Everyone is acting like you didn't want Tommy dead in the first place. But you did. Everyone hated Tommy. But now they're pretending he's some kind of martyr, like he's this great person, and they're just erasing all the damage he caused. You basically gave him a whole rebrand with that interview."

In the dim light, Kiara could make out the silver glint of something around Chelsea's neck. She took a step closer, and in that moment, Kiara realized that the necklace the girl wore was the same one Tommy had gifted her only a day earlier. Chelsea had tucked it into her shirt earlier, but it must have fallen out while they'd been walking, revealing it. It was a silver heart-shaped pendant with a small, possibly real, diamond in its center. Chelsea was still ranting, but Kiara wasn't listening to her anymore.

"Why do you have that necklace?" Kiara whispered.

"What?"

"Why do you have that necklace?" Kiara said again, raising her voice. "Where did you get it?"

"Please," Chelsea said. "They sell these in every gift shop in Sunny World. Did you really think you were special? He got me one too."

"Who is 'he'?" Kiara asked, but Chelsea didn't answer. Instead, she moved to cover the necklace, but Kiara was too quick. She grabbed it from Chelsea's neck and turned it over. Initials had been carved in it: *KS*. Kiara Stephens.

"Kiara," Jason whispered. But the thought was racing through Kiara's mind too. The police had found a necklace at the scene. And if Chelsea was telling the truth, Tommy must have gotten her another version of the heart-shaped necklace with different initials on it. But the jewelry found at the scene of the crime must have belonged to the girl who'd really been there when Tommy had died.

"You killed him," Kiara said. Even as she spoke the words, her breath caught on the severity of the accusations.

"What are you talking about?" Chelsea laughed. "Are you seriously trying to pin this on me now?"

"You're not answering the question," Jason said. "Did you kill my brother?"

"He died on his own," Chelsea said, still not answering.

"But you were there," Kiara said. "You're the hacker. You're the one trying to cover everything up."

Kiara knew it was the truth even without the look of admission on Chelsea's face. All this time, the hacker had been right under their nose. Watching them. Taunting them, luring them into this sinister trap of their own making. But if Chelsea was the hacker, then that meant the burner phone—she must still have it on her.

"Empty your pockets," Kiara said. "Now."

Jason stepped forward, looming over Chelsea. "You heard her. My family is going to press charges for what you've done. Don't make this any harder."

"Don't forget Priscilla. She'll sue the crap out of you for defamation and this whole cover-up," Kiara said. "And if you don't give us the burner, then we'll have the police looking up and down these tunnels and through your so-called cave until they track down Tommy's real phone."

It was a lose-lose situation. Either Chelsea gave them the burner phone or she'd have to work with the police to track down Tommy's main phone.

Chelsea laughed. Like, the girl literally had the audacity to laugh in that moment. She reached into her pocket and pulled out an old phone.

"You mean this?"

In an instant, Kiara's heart dropped. She'd seen that phone before, just once. Back on the bus, when Tommy had pulled the phone out from his pocket after Kiara had accidentally dumped her iced coffee on him.

The burner phone.

On the screen a post on Tommy's account had been queued in the drafts. The video showed photos of Kiara, Ren, and a cropped-out Chelsea from when they'd gotten lunch together at the hotel. Narration from the video echoed through the tunnels, but the voice was staticky and robotic.

"Now just how did the deceased Tommy Harding get an admissions officer to let his ex-girlfriend into her dream school?"

The screen changed to a series of messages between Ren and Tommy.

Ren: My dad already wrote the recommendation letter.

Tommy: That's not enough. I need a real contact Ren. Or do you want daddy to know how you've been scamming high schoolers into renting Sunny World after hours?

The time stamp showed that a few hours had passed between Tommy's threat and Ren's answer.

Ren: Here's the guy. He's head of admissions. that's his cell.

Tommy: K

Ren: We good now?

Tommy: Yeah. We're good.

The screen changed again, this time to messages between Tommy and the admissions officer. But instead of asking the admissions officer to reconsider Kiara's application, Tommy was posing as a young girl. At first normal messages were exchanged. Then came the other photos, photos that were sick and twisted.

The text on the screen changed.

Not Tommy sending pics he got from his fans to blackmail admissions.

"That was what he was doing," Chelsea said. "Blackmail. Extortion. That's how he got everything done. He blackmailed Ren for secretly charging seniors to use the park after it closed. He got girls like Nevaeh and even his own fans to send him intimate photos." There was rage in Chelsea's eyes, rage and guilt. "And I helped him. I ran his fan club. I got dirt that he could use on others. I was just making his dream come true. And we were doing it together. We were building up his fandom and getting sponsorships and climbing that sick, toxic world of influencers. But when I saw the livestream of Priscilla hiding his phone, after he lied again about breaking up with you, I wanted to find out the truth myself. And that's what I found. He's a liar and an abuser, and it's so much deeper than I even thought. I hacked his account to warn you and everyone. But instead of helping me expose him, you, Nevaeh, and Priscilla went on TV and claimed he was innocent and a good person."

"I didn't know," Kiara said. Chelsea laughed. Kiara closed her eyes and tried again. "He used me, just like he used everyone else. He said he built his following organically. That all his brand deals and connections were legit. I didn't even know about you or his fan club. Do you seriously think I'd be okay with him using photos of his fans to blackmail an admissions officer? All he told me was that I should meet with Ren and give a good impression. I never would have accepted his help if I'd known the truth."

"That's what makes it even worse," Chelsea snapped. "You benefited from my hard work in your relationship and in your academic career. Tommy deserved to die. But I'm not going to take the weight of what he's done anymore. I'm not going to take the fall for this."

"So we're just supposed to?" Kiara said.

Chelsea smiled.

"Exactly. So you can go on that livestream and say either Nevaeh or Priscilla killed him. Or you can confess to the murder yourself. Otherwise I'll pick one of you girls to take the fall."

"Oh, how benevolent of you."

Chelsea held up the phone threateningly.

"There's another option too. I can just upload this post and let the internet decide."

Before Chelsea could move, Kiara launched herself at the other girl. She tried to snatch the phone, and Jason got between the two girls, attempting to grab it as well. But they were too late.

Even with the shoddy cell phone service underground, Chelsea managed to post the preloaded video. In seconds, the view count soared to triple digits.

Jason snatched the phone from Chelsea. In one quick motion, he deleted the video from the account.

"That's enough!" he shouted. "Changing the narrative won't erase the truth. We have the evidence we need. Let's leave, Kiara. She can tell her side of the story when she's on trial."

But Chelsea grabbed Kiara. With a flick of her wrist, she pulled a switchblade from her pocket and brought it to Kiara's throat.

"Give it back or I'll hurt her. I swear I'll cut her throat."

"Let her go. You're just making this worse for yourself," Jason said.

Pain jolted through Kiara as the metal sliced into her skin and blood trickled down.

"No. You're making it worse for her," Chelsea said. "I won't ask again. Give me the phone."

Kiara pressed her eyes shut, her lashes fluttering wildly against the pain.

"Just give it to her. It's okay."

Without another word, Jason knelt down and slid the phone over to Chelsea. The plastic thumped against her Sunny World–branded sneakers.

"Pick it up," Chelsea said, pressing the knife deeper against Kiara's throat. "Then hand it to me."

"Okay, okay," Kiara whispered. "Just relax. We don't have to fight. We can figure this thing out together."

"Shut up!" Chelsea snapped.

Her pupils were dilated, more than was surely normal for someone fully in tune with their senses. Chelsea was jittery too. She couldn't seem to keep her hand from shaking while holding the blade. Tommy had been like that too, last night.

Slowly, Kiara knelt down. The phone screen on the burner was still on Tommy's account and his notifications were going haywire. There was one that kept rising to the top. A request to go live from an account called The Saint. Kiara didn't know if the service underground could handle a full livestream. But she didn't care. Kiara picked up the phone, just as Chelsea demanded. But in that same motion, Kiara accepted the live request.

Suddenly, the faces of the two girls appeared on camera. One, then two, then twenty, then a hundred, and more and more viewers tuned in to the livestream. On the other end of the live, Nevaeh, Alex, Ren, and two other girls were on the screen.

"Kiara!" Nevaeh screamed. She cupped her face in horror as the pixelated image emerged of Chelsea pressing her switchblade against Kiara's throat.

It took that moment for Chelsea to realize what Kiara had done.

She screamed and pushed Kiara to the ground in an attempt to grab Tommy's burner and stop the livestream. But Kiara was too quick. She threw the phone as far as she could, up into the ledge of the incline. Hopefully someone had taken a screen recording of Chelsea with the knife. But if not, they'd had thousands of witnesses online, including Nevaeh, Alex, and the two other girls.

Chelsea raced to meet Tommy's burner, dropping the switchblade as she rushed up the scaffolding.

Kiara shut the knife, pressing the back of her hand against her throat as her blood continued to trickle from the cut. In mere seconds, Jason was beside her, holding her, comforting her.

"Keep your hand pressed to your neck," he said. "Don't let go."

Kiara wanted to tell him she was fine. But she was afraid that if she spoke, the cut would somehow deepen. And Chelsea was still in hysterics. The girl had begun to climb the scaffolding, desperately clawing in the air for Tommy's burner phone. Up and up she went at a speed that was dizzying. But when she made it halfway to the burner phone, she lost her balance.

Her body was like a weight, all matter and mass hurtling down, down, down. And then all that mass and matter fell to the earth.

The sound of Chelsea's body hitting the ground was deafening. It was the last sound Kiara heard before everything went dark.

three months later

chapter thirty-three

THERE WAS SOMETHING haunting about returning to Sunny World Park. In the wake of everything that had happened, it seemed as if nothing had changed.

The air was still filled with that familiar tinge of buttery popcorn and funnel cake. Screams drifted off into the distance as a rush of roller coasters and attractions carried tourists and students through the park. They climbed upward to the sky and then sunk toward the depths of the earth. And even beneath that, farther down below, a maze of interwoven tunnels was hidden. But at the foot of the park's gates, an anchor and TV crew began a news broadcast.

Kiara, Priscilla, and Nevaeh sat perched on a bench not far from where the filming was taking place. Kiara was dressed in jeans and a pink blouse, and had styled her hair in box braids. Nevaeh wore shorts and a plain T-shirt, with her curly, natural hair combed into a bun. On the other side of the bench, Priscilla twirled a stray lock from her Afro as the orange sundress she wore fluttered in the wind.

In the silence, all three girls waited for their names to be called.

Had it really been just months ago that they were here, watching as police and EMTs rolled Chelsea from the tunnels in handcuffs? After the investigation, Ren had been forced to pay state fines for the clandestine visits he'd operated at his father's park. He'd admitted to locking Kiara in the freezer because he'd been suspicious that she had been working for Tommy—only to learn that it had been Chelsea all along. Alex had helped piece together the case in a series of highly researched documentaries that he'd filmed and released. And amid calls from Jason and Tommy's family requesting that Chelsea be charged for attempting to cover up his death, voices from across the internet and all over the country were speaking up. Some of them were Tommy's victims. Others had been like Chelsea and had found themselves perpetuating the very same pain that they had suffered at his hands.

But even louder than naysayers and Tommy apologists were the stories, posts, and vlogs offering comfort and support to the victims.

And now, the three girls were finally telling their full side of the story. Not as The Girlfriend and The Saint and The Sinner, but as Kiara and Nevaeh and Priscilla. Witnesses. Survivors. Friends. Sort of.

"Do you think we did the right thing?" Nevaeh asked, squeezing Kiara's hand.

Instead of answering, Kiara turned to Priscilla. The other girl was busy painting on a new coat of lip gloss. Unlike Kiara and Nevaeh, she'd done her own sort of tell-all just a month earlier. And though her sponsorships had dried up, Kiara had watched in awe as Priscilla had used her signature sharp wit and humor to carve out an audience that was as organic (and cruelty-free) as the products she now sported from her homemade makeup line.

"Why?" Priscilla asked. "Having regrets already?"

It was such a simple question, yet the swirl of shared emotions that encompassed them was dizzying. Kiara's life was at a crossroads. In a few weeks, she'd be starting university. Not at an Ivy League or a top school like Kingstown, but one where Kiara knew she could make her dreams come true, even if that dream had evolved. Nevaeh had begun a youth program at her church focusing on mental health, peer pressure, and building healthy relationships. And even though Priscilla continued to build her social media empire and studied to be an aesthetician, it'd been hard for any of them not to have regrets over what had taken place the night Tommy died. But regrets now, at this moment? Kiara searched and searched but only found the warmth of relief.

She shook her head. Nevaeh smiled. So did Priscilla.

"We're doing what we should have done before," Kiara said. "And this time, it's not about him. Not anymore."

And when the production team ushered them to take their places in front of Sunny World's gates, that truth crystalized. This was just the first of many steps in shedding the guilt and shame of their mistakes and building a future without the weight of Tommy's lies hanging over them. But no soundbite, post, article, or vlog could capture the tender, complicated fragments of their voices or the depth of their stories. Because in the aftermath of loss and life, truth and lies, Kiara, Nevaeh, and Priscilla had discovered each other. And through that, they'd found themselves.

acknowledgments

I never thought I'd write a thriller. I've always enjoyed the genre as a reader, but speculative contemporary stories, historical fiction, and fantasy have always been the genres of my heart as a writer. Writing *Heart-Shaped Lies* was a new challenge for me, but oh so rewarding. There's just something about the thriller genre that is a different kind of a sandbox for crafting and playing with characters—the morally gray ones, the ones who can't be trusted, the ones who are learning to trust themselves. In writing Kiara, Priscilla, and Nevaeh's characters I was able to dive into these themes and figure out the voices of three very different girls trapped in a terrible situation.

Thank you to my editors, Lydia Gregovic and Krista Marino. Thank you, Krista, for first sparking this idea, for the calls, notes, and feedback, and for sharing a taste of your thriller expertise to help bring the threads of the story together. Thank you, Lydia, for taking the reins and getting deep in the trenches with me to bring the final story to life. Many thanks to my agent, Suzie Townsend, for all your support, for reading so many drafts and being the incredible advocate you always are. Thank you, Kate Sullivan, for your astute editorial notes and for helping to shape the story, and to Sophia Ramos for always helping move things along and cheering me on every step of the way.

Thank you to the team at Penguin Random House for everything you do and for helping bring this story to readers. Thanks to Marla Garfield and Colleen Fellingham for your copyediting expertise. Thank you to Casey Moses and Aarushi Menon for designing the cover and to Michelle Crowe for designing the interior of the book. Thank you to Tamar Schwartz in managing editorial and Shameiza Ally in production. Thank you to the entire RHCB marketing and publicity teams, including Shannon Pender, Jasmine Ferrufino, Michael Caiati, and my publicist, Joey Ho. Thank you to Delacorte Press Publisher Beverly Horowitz, Random House Children's Book Publisher and President Barbara Marcus, and Executive Vice President and Deputy Publisher of Random House Children's Books Judith Haut.

So much love and many thanks to Stephanie T. for being the first reader of *Heart-Shaped Lies* and so many of my other of my stories. You've always been so honest with your feedback while being encouraging and kind. I'm so grateful for our friendship and for the role you've played being a part of my writing journey.

Thank you to my sisters for reading early chapters and helping me guide the type of story I wanted to tell. Thank you to my brother for always being willing to listen to my wild scenarios for the story and brainstorming. Many thanks to my parents, always. Being a teenager is hard enough as it is; I'm so grateful to have had you and our family as a guiding force throughout my life.

And of course, thank *you,* reader, for your patience with Kiara, Priscilla, and Nevaeh—in hearing them out, listening to their story, and giving this book a chance. There are so many people in our society who don't get a chance to be seen, who aren't listened to and feel that their voices aren't heard. We all have a story to tell, and I hope we can find it in our hearts to hear one another.

about the author

ELIZABETH AGYEMANG is an illustrator, printmaker, and storyteller. She writes about magic, history, folklore, love, and fairy tales and draws from elements of her Ghanaian heritage and faith. *Heart-Shaped Lies* is her debut young adult novel.